Also by John Linssen
TABITHA fffOULKES

Yellow

Pages

A novel by
John Linssen

ARBOR HOUSE
NEW YORK

Copyright © 1980 by John Linssen

All rights reserved, including the right of reproduction in whole or in part in any form. Published in the United States of America by Arbor House Publishing Company and in Canada by Clarke, Irwin & Company, Ltd.

Library of Congress Catalog Card Number: 78-73873

ISBN: 0-87795-226-4

Manufactured in the United States of America

TO MY PARENTS.
IN SPITE

Genius . . . might be more fitly described as a supreme capacity for getting its possessors into trouble of all kinds and keeping them therein so long as the genius remains.

SAMUEL BUTLER
1835–1902

From the tape recorder of Rameses P. Tillevant, Ph.D., LL.D. (Hon.), M.B.A., M.S.S.

1

I SHALL tell all. All. No matter how it further frays my self-esteem. Dr. Ampiofratello, the head psychiatrist here, has encouraged me to speak out in this way. He says that recording the facts in the privacy of my room at the Vellutomano Center for the Nervously Exhausted, at any time of the day or night that the mood takes me, will be every bit as efficacious—indeed, more so, perhaps—as my couch sessions with him. Dr. Ampiofratello tells me that he is a pioneer of this method, and that his patients, once they have overcome any allergy they may have to the sound of their own reproduced voices, find that they can speak even more freely, with far less desire to hold anything back, than when their doctor is in the room with them, creating by his very presence a certain restraint, a sense of shame, a fear of criticism.

Not that I have ever had any such reactions in any session with Dr. Ampiofratello. He is such a dear man. Does that sound gay? I assure you that I am not a latent homosexual. I have always been content to slake my, uh, sexual appetites in the most unimaginative manner when such action became unavoidable. In the matter of sublimated masturbation, perhaps Paul Darrell was right, curse him. There is also the matter of the Weird O Ranch, but that is something else. Perhaps the most convincing proof of my, uh, normalcy is that when, last year, some temporary disturbance of my excretory functions rendered it necessary for me to undergo a rectal examination, I found the experience thoroughly distasteful. When, therefore, I say that Dr. Ampiofratello is a dear man, I mean it in the most platonic sense. I suppose it is just part of the transference. As for listening to my recorded voice, I am an old hand at this sort of thing.

In our very first session Dr. Ampiofratello understood at once what I meant about Paul Darrell. Paul Darrell is one of my noirest bêtes. It is entirely because of Paul Darrell that I am here, with eggs Benedict all over my face. Until I was afflicted with Paul Darrell I had traced my smiling path through life, unraveling each snarl with quiet persistence, using the most approved psychological and material methods and systems. Every time I even think of Paul Darrell I have trouble with my hackles. My other vexations are simply part of the Paul Darrell complex. They hang upon him like strips of phosphorescent cloth tied to the arms of some grisly scarecrow.

The pygmies. That shocking cinematograph film. The shameful history of Ms. Kalman. The Catastrophe. Oh God.

It seems to me that in my anxiety to tell all I am starting off by trying to tell everything at the same time. I have always prided myself on my tidy thinking. It is only the name of Paul Darrell, and of course far more his physical presence, that sends the convolutions of my cerebellum into spasm. But I will be strong. Strong and brave. I will control myself. Shunning the temptation to indulge in selective amnesia, I will relate in chronological order the whole sorry tale of my war with Paul Darrell. The many minor skirmishes as well as the several pitched battles.

After all, as we are historically reminded, there is always the erase button.

2

TAKE, FOR example, the episode of the window curtains in my office. There were several windows in my office. Large windows, running from floor to ceiling. Well, it was a large office, befitting my status as Administrator of The Dickstachel Research Institute. I believe that in other parts of the building, where the, uh, technical people worked, there was a good deal of loose talk about my office. I would be the first to admit that the areas of the building where these good people performed their, uh, technical duties were less than adequate; but there was a failure on the part of the, uh, scientific staff to appreciate the superhuman efforts which I was making to raise the funds for a major extension, or even, in course of time when the general economic situation improved and the Government also was able to allot adequate Federal Funds, a whole new building which would have been worthier both of the prestige—I will not say glamor —surrounding the name of Dickstachel, and of the varied and important work which was carried on there for the good of humanity at large.

When one is, if I may use the expression, wooing persons who in spite of the deplorable tax situation are still able and willing— willing, mark you—to donate considerable sums towards such a worthy end—and please do not let me hear any depreciatory remarks regarding the fact that such donations are tax-deductible—when one is wooing, I say, it is desirable to do so in surroundings as nearly as possible akin to those in which these admirable, though frequently pejorated, individuals pass the greater part of their lives. If they are solicited in a large-scale ambience they will the more readily accept the idea that the new construction should be on a similarly large scale, and that includes the problem of site costs.

My office naturally acquired additional charm when the sunlight, smiling through these windows, played upon the petals of the domestic and exotic flowers which our horticultural contractor so tastefully arranged in pleasant variety throughout the year. But there are many days upon which the sun does not shine. I expect we have all noticed that. Often it rains, or snows, or simply sulks. At such times I find it less easy to maintain the placid cheerfulness with which I strive to lighten the toil of those around me. Indeed, I have actually found myself thinking nostalgically of certain smaller, windowless offices which I have occupied in the earlier stages of my upwardly mobile, thank heaven, career. If it were ever possible to set status on one side, there is a good deal to be said for the insulated sensation one derives from solid pastel walls with shadowless lighting. Out there in the real world folks are getting wet, or run over, or investigated, or stabbed, or they are dying of coronaries. Naturally I always sympathize with such unfortunate people, but I find it easier to feel sympathetic in controlled temperature and humidity with no hint of Old Mother Nature's more somber moods. It is as if one were a computer in its shrine. A most reassuring sensation. Unless, of course, there is an arsonist in the building.

Therefore my windows had wide, heavy curtains which could be drawn across them until the meteorological situation improved. It would of course have been possible to draw them by hand, hauling on a cord, or rope, in a somewhat nautical manner; but in view of the weight of fabric to be moved this would have involved more muscular effort than I felt I could well expect my secretary to exert, although she was a big, powerful girl such as I prefer, and certainly the profile view of her torso when thus engaged . . . but I wander. In fact these curtains were operated by an electric motor, or possibly two electric motors, I am not *au fait* with these, uh, technical details. This motor, or motors, was or were controlled by two buttons set into a panel on my desk. There were other buttons, whose function I will describe in due course—in fact later on I will take you on a little guided tour of my whole office, which I flatter myself was not uningeniously arranged—but for the moment I will confine myself to these two buttons. One button closed the curtains, you understand, and the other opened them again.

At least, that is what was supposed to happen; but on that particular morning, when a high wind from New Jersey was positively hurling damp snowflakes against the glass, the device evinced a serious malfunction. When I activated the CLOSE button the curtains closed, to be sure, but they immediately opened again, and thereafter they continued to close and open, close and open in a kind of drunken dance, accompanied by an eerie swirl of bright-colored fabric and a most infernal clicking of runners. I must apologize for this expletive, but this unprecedented, uh, technological phenomenon was seriously affecting my nerves, and even now I find it hard to recall the incident with anything like my normal philosophical smile. I activated both buttons several times without bringing the curtains to a halt, and at last in desperation I telephoned the head electrician, who, good fellow, presented himself in person only moments later.

Here let me interpolate that I was never able to understand the complaints about the electrical maintenance department that were so frequently raised at staff meetings. The most absurd allegations were made, such as that it could take as long as two hours to get a fuse mended or several days to replace a fluorescent lighting tube. I always pointed out that I had never had any cause for complaint myself, and I reminded those raising the issue that a smile, a smile in the voice as well as on the face, worked wonders. I am a great believer in smiling at anyone who is in the least likely to be of use. It is not for nothing that I am known inside The Dickstachel Research Institute by the affectionate—I am sure—sobriquet of Smiling Jack. Until recently I even tried to smile at my wife.

However, promptly as the head electrician appeared, and highly qualified as he was, as must be all those who are in any way connected with The Dickstachel Research Institute, he had difficulty in finding the cause of the clashing and swirling. After a few minutes, a distinct odor of burning insulation became apparent, accompanied by wisps of black smoke which drifted through cracks in the window casing. At this he hastily departed, muttering something about finding the fuse box. I suppose he was successful in this, as shortly afterwards the curtains ceased to move and the smoke lessened and stopped. The curtains, however, were neither open nor shut, an indeterminate state of affairs such as St. John the Divine has strongly, though somewhat vulgarly, deprecated.

I had just, albeit with some trepidation, endeavored to switch on the lights, only to discover that they too had ceased to function, when Paul Darrell galloped into my office and, querulously as a garbage truck, screamed:

"My semen. You've ruined my semen."

3

I HAD many times been tempted to kick Paul Darrell in the, uh, testicles, or balls, but I had never actually done so. There were several reasons for this, one of the principal being that he was a karate expert and would probably kick first. Thus, on one side, I could only rationalize his extraordinary accusation by assuming that on this particular morning he was actively, rather than putatively insane. In order to obtain confirmation of this I said to him:

"Mr. Darrell, have you taken leave of your senses?"

He did not attempt to answer this question, but treated me to the following outburst, measuring at least seven on the Richter scale:

"Six months work down the pan. Six months blood, sweat and insomnia. I was almost there, Tillevant. I swear to God this would have been a perfect batch. And *you*, you have to fuck everything up by cutting the juice to my lab. You and your goddamned curtains."

Tears rolled down his cheeks. He wiped his eyes with a filter paper and added brokenly:

"They're dead, Tillevant. Dead. Every last one of them."

I really could not pretend to remember on the spur of the moment all the extraordinary activities on which the, uh, technical people were engaged at any given time. I had far more important matters to absorb my attention. For example, there was the latest re-design of the form for requisitioning stationery. When I first took up my duties at The Dickstachel Research Institute this was a paltry affair of barely half a letter-size sheet. In very short order I had two of my assistants at work on it, and in no time at all they had expanded it to three pages. As a result of their current efforts I had every hope that the document would extend to five, or even six, legal-size pages printed on both sides, with at least one carbon. It will readily be understood that when an administrative project attains this height of virtuosity, a great deal of nervous strain is involved for everyone concerned, and not least myself.

Nevertheless, by dint of hard and rapid thinking—and I flatter myself that in an emergency no one thinks faster—I managed to recall the broad outline of the project upon which Darrell, as Scientific Director of The Dickstachel Research Institute, was engaged. It had something to do with increasing the fertility of cattle sperm and ova—disgusting terms—by passing an electric current through them at a very low temperature. Or a very high temperature, I really cannot recollect which. The purpose was to increase the supplies of beef, and reduce its cost, by causing cows to have two or more calves at a, so to speak, sitting. The project was of course an easy mark for lavish Federal Funds.

I fear that last statement carries with it an implication of flippancy which is quite unintentional. I have the utmost respect for Federal Funds. They provide a major portion of the lifeblood of our great country, and certainly of The Dickstachel Research Institute. So pronounced is my reverence for Federal Funds that I feel the phrase, wherever printed, should be in black letters. Like this: **FEDERAL FUNDS** My goodness, if you cut off a man's Federal Funds you might as well cut off his—excuse me.

But it occurred to me that if in fact the disaster was of the magnitude which Darrell was so emotionally ascribing to it, I might be faced with a somewhat embarrassing situation, since that year's budget was drawing peacefully to its close. I was already engaged in preliminary negotiations for a further grant, and up to that point I had felt justified in painting for the gentlemen from Washington a picture roseate with the prospects of success. To put it crudely, there is not nearly so much money about as there used to be say twenty years ago, or as much official naiveté either, although thank heaven the supplies of both are by no means exhausted.

It was not so much the, uh, technical snafu which gave me a queasy feeling. For reasons which I can well guess, but feel it would be foolhardy to enumerate, such things have become part of The American Way. Our railroad trains fall off the track like children's toys, or remain motionless in the midst of trackless wastes because of what is shruggingly explained as "equipment trouble." Telecommunications gear behaves as if the cat had got its tongue at moments when it should be faithfully carrying the vital pronouncements of our greatest national figures to the breathlessly waiting multitudes. Visiting European orchestras are left sitting high in the air, exposed to the coarse jibes of a jeering populace, because hydraulic lifts malfunction. Oil tankers equipped with all manner of ingenious but nonoperative aids to navigation crash into bridges, lose their way on the high seas and vomit their cargoes hither and thither in a manner which would have reduced any old-time whaling captain to blasphemous apoplexy. One can, as the saying goes, scarcely pick up a newspaper.

No. What I found particularly distressing was the thought that my personal office, which is, or should be, sacrosanct, and certainly as little to be suspected as Caesar's wife—although from what I have read about her husband's personal conduct I really do feel that he was applying the double standard in a very extreme manner—should be, might be . . . let me start again. I did not want any part of the responsibility for the wrecking of Darrell's experiment. There. I hope that is a sufficiently definite statement.

We faced each other, Darrell and I, there in the semitwilight brought about by the half-drawn curtains and the wholly nonfunctioning fluorescents. Since he was facing the window I could see, in what light there was, the expression on his face. I always fancied that there was a special expression on his face when he looked at me. Not so much as if I was something the cat had brought in, but as if I was something the cat would not even bring in. As if he was about to say:

"Why don't you stop doing a deserving mortician out of a job?"

I was glad that my own face was almost totally in shadow. I was scared. I will confess it, I was scared. And I was scared of showing that I was scared. I thought it best to temporize until I could regain at least partial control of the situation. I said:

"Please sit down, Mr. Darrell, and let us discuss this like reasonable beings."

"Sit down? In this whorehouse? Tillevant, have you no respect for my mother's memory?"

I flatter myself that my reply to that was really rather neat:

"Mr. Darrell, I have indeed the greatest respect for the memory of your mother, who I believe was a most unfortunate lady."

It was not often that I managed to score off Darrell, but this time he twitched all over and remained silent for some seconds. This gave me an opportunity of saying:

"As you know, Mr. Darrell, I am always ready to make allowances for the high-strung nature of you, uh, scientific people. I am therefore prepared to overlook this little episode. No one regrets more than I do the unforeseeable interruption to your most important work, but I assure you that, provided they are properly requisitioned, fresh supplies of, uh, semen will be promptly forthcoming, and I am certain that the experience you have gained during the past few months will enable you speedily to bring the new series to a successful and repeatable conclusion. I say speedily, Mr. Darrell, because as you know, the time is fast approaching when Washington will be expecting our report in order that they may consider whether or not to renew the grant of funds. It would of course be most regrettable if there were anything in that report which would lead to a negative financial recommendation."

I tapped my fingertips on my desk and gazed at the wall in what I hoped was a significant and foreboding manner. I was happy to note that I had at least stemmed the flood of Darrell's insulting remarks. He merely replied, in tones of awe and wonder:

"I don't know about you, Tillevant, I really don't know about you."

This, for him, was moderation itself.

He began to leave, looking about him and muttering disconnectedly:

"I dreamt that I dwelt in marble halls . . . those goddamned six-by-eight cells of ours downstairs . . ."

I was not slow to seize the opening which this gave me.

"One moment, Mr. Darrell. I am well aware that you, and I believe many of your colleagues, are under the delusion—and it is a delusion, Mr. Darrell, I assure you—that Administration has no sympathy with the admittedly overcrowded conditions which you are presently enduring. So far from this being the case I am in a position to tell you—for your ears alone, Mr. Darrell, for your ears alone—that the Trustees and I are in the very earliest stages—I must emphasize, the very earliest—of a plan for expansion which would most materially, *most* materially, increase The Dickstachel Research Institute's physical resources. It will take time, Mr. Darrell, it will take time. I need not remind you of the familiar saying about Rome, Italy, nor that we are in the position of having to pay our construction workers and of somehow raising the necessary funds—an ever-present problem with which you scientific gentlemen may give thanks that you do not have to concern yourselves. But if you had even an inkling of the magnitude of what is passing through my mind at this moment, I believe it would have a powerful effect on your way of thinking."

At this moment a fleeting shaft of sunlight shone through the opening in the curtains onto Darrell's face like a spotlight. It was indeed an interesting study. Hope, disbelief, and something which I could not identify except that I imagine a juvenile delinquent looks like that when he has just remembered where he left his switchblade. He said:

"Tillevant, you wouldn't by any chance be trying to bribe me?"

The tension had very noticeably relaxed. I am sensitive to these things. I felt that I could unbend even more:

"My dear Paul, what an extraordinary thing to say. Bribe you? To what end? For what possible purpose? Now, why don't you go and get that requisition in the works? The sooner it gets into channels, the sooner you'll have your new, uh, semen to play with, or rather, of course, to work with."

He turned away. Not graciously, but he turned away. I felt like a circus trainer who has just subdued a recalcitrant animal by firmness and guile. I could not resist adding a crack of the whip:

"And by the way, Paul, while I'm only too well aware of your distaste for paperwork, how about catching up on your reports at the same time? You must be at least sixty days in arrears."

"Fifty-nine," he said, and he went away by no means as exuberantly as he had come in; in fact his shoulders sagged. He was probably hoping to escape before I mentioned one or two other matters, such as the weekly Non-Progress Report, showing percentage of success and estimated date of complete success of the various assignments being carried out by the other members of The Dickstachel Research Institute's staff, together with a breakdown of type of work done, economies effected, anticipated cost-effectiveness of research results, and so on.

Frankly, Darrell set his own staff a disgraceful example in this respect. It is at all times difficult enough to get this type of person to submit administrative reports on their due dates, although they will fill whole notebooks with data for their own private information. They simply will not get into their thick heads that reports, reports, reports, completely filled out and handsomely filed, are an essential item in the armory of any administrator in his constant battle with Trustees, donors, endowment devisers and, of course, the serried and puissant ranks of Federal Funds bestowers. I can hardly conceive a more hideous sight than that of a half-empty filing cabinet, or a thing of greater beauty than the same cabinet as it approaches repletion and raises the exhilarating question of how to find room for its contents in the already congested back-storage space, and the equally exhilarating conclusion that additional space will have to be built. It was a fact, although I saw no good purpose to be served in publicizing it, that the proportion of such space to the total facilities of The Dickstachel Research Institute was already twenty-five percent. I could conceive no reason why, allowing for the geometrical progression of such things—or do I mean arithmetical or perhaps algebraical—this figure should not increase to fifty percent or even more before I reached retirement age.

However, to expect Darrell to share my feelings on the subject was hopeless. At the mere mention of the word "report" he accelerated his departure from my office—remember, it took quite a while to travel from my desk to the door on foot—ejaculating:

"Oh God, there has to be a better way of earning a living. O.K., I'll let you have your reports, Dr. Tillevant, *sir.*"

I knew quite well what would happen. He would sit up all night —or for a couple of nights—filling out report after report with the most illusory figures and statements stemming from his own all too fertile imagination and bearing not the remotest semblance to the facts. When he had fulfilled his quota and brought himself, however temporarily, up to date, he would devise some puckish way to get them to me. Once it had been two Brink's armed guards bearing them in a sealed chest marked in huge letters, "Only for the eyes of Dr. Rameses P. Tillevant, Ph.D., LL.D. (Hon.), M.B.A., M.S.S." The men had bullheadedly insisted on delivering their load inside my office and obtaining my personal signature.

On another occasion he interleaved the reports with centerfolds from some of the less reputable girlie magazines, which he also used for the outer wrapping of the package that he dumped on my table in the executive dining room, favoring me with an obscene wink and saying loudly:

"Here's the stuff you've been badgering me for, Tilly boy."

Some of the centerfolds were unfamiliar to me, and provided interesting viewing, but really. . . .

Once he sent me at my home a batch of ninety-two reports, one at a time, by ninety-two separate employees of various messenger services, at half-hourly intervals starting at midnight on Friday and ending late on Sunday evening. I was recuperating from influenza at the time, and each report was accompanied by an extremely vulgar get-well card.

I was never able to trace the cost of these pranks on his expense sheets, although I am reasonably adept at unmasking other people's deceits. I can only assume that he paid for them himself. I know that he had private means in addition to his salary. I wondered what fresh eccentricity I should be exposed to this time. But for now he had, thank heaven, completely left my office. At the same moment my curtains closed and stayed closed, and the room was filled with the soothing rays of the eighteen Nature-Tone fluorescent tubes which I had had specially installed for the better health of my exotics.

4

I SHOULD not like it to be thought that the antagonistic relationship which existed between Darrell and myself had been allowed to grow up without efforts on both sides to develop a better mutual understanding. Indeed, Darrell made the first move in this direction at an early stage of our professional association when he asked me to his place for drinks. Frankly, I felt that he was proceeding a little too fast. Although as heads of our respective fields of activity we were theoretically equal, I was senior to him in length of service, even if by only a few months. I felt that protocol would have been better served if the first gesture of extramural sociability had come from me. Indeed, I was planning something of the sort to mark the end of his first year of service to The Dickstachel Research Institute. However, as I did not wish to appear unduly standoffish, I accepted his invitation.

Darrell lived in an elderly but still, from outward appearance, solid and respectable apartment block quite near The Dickstachel Research Institute. I did not feel that it accorded particularly well with his position as Scientific Director, but I was prepared to reserve judgment, although the proximity of the two locales removed one possible excuse for the persistent unpunctuality which he was already evincing.

I did, however, receive a notable shock when I entered his living room, the sparse furnishings of which seemed to consist about equally of old packing cases painted in gaudy colors which failed to disguise their real nature, and of period pieces, such as an enormous Edwardian sideboard, which were still in the dowdy period of their existence, needing another decade or so before they attained the status of valuable though unwieldy antiques. Only one item stood out among this heterogeneous decor. It was a full-size Steinway concert grand, the case of which gleamed with flawless luster.

Darrell's feet were shod with sandals, and he was attired in several yards of white cloth arranged in graceful but complex style. It may have been merely a sheet, but to my startled eyes it seemed at first that he had joined the ranks of those who haunt our public places in the interests of the Buddhist faith. However, the elaborate folds of this garment across his chest, the fact that his head was not shaven, and the presence of a wreath of what I presumed to be laurel as a crown to his shining fair hair, led me to the conclusion that he was, for reasons known only to himself, impersonating a citizen of ancient Rome. I was at that time a comparative stranger to his varied sartorial eccentricities, and the door had hardly closed behind me before I was seeking to invent a good reason for hasty departure. But Darrell, an inexorably welcoming arm across my shoulders, had set me down on an extremely uncomfortable four-legged backless stool before I could put my panic reaction into practice.

"We shall drink," he said, and without offering me any choice seized in both hands a large, vaselike receptacle from which he poured a dark red liquid into two silver cups. He handed me one and raised his own in a toast:

"*Ad majorem scientiae gloriam.*"

I was unable to figure out the meaning of this somewhat blasphemous remark until next day; this was partly because I did not even recognize the language and partly because, having mechanically taken a hearty swallow of what I assumed to be fruit punch I found that I had actually imbibed an extremely powerful wine of singularly nauseating flavor. When I had finished coughing I found Darrell examining me with an expression analytical rather than welcoming.

"The immortal Falernum. How strikes it your palate?"

"Unusual flavor," I said with some difficulty.

"Myrrh and marble dust. Perhaps you would prefer to follow tradition and have some water with it."

Water did nothing for the taste, but it prevented him from giving me more wine for the time being. By taking only an occasional token sip I managed to spin out my cupful for a while. Darrell refilled his own cup and said:

"I have a feeling, Dr. Tillevant, that your own interest in my side of the Institute's work is merely incidental."

Although the wine was already affecting my senses, it seemed to me that this was a potentially dangerous question. I remember making some confused reference to the cobbler sticking to his last, and adding:

"Of course I am interested in anything that leads to the solution of everyday problems."

"Such as?"

For some extraordinary reason I replied:

"Well, I wish I could find somebody to do something about the noise inside my head when I brush my teeth."

He seemed to take this quite seriously.

"A silent toothbrush? I'll think about it. How about a silent electric razor?"

"I never use one. The old-fashioned two-piece safety razor is good enough for me. The fact is, I always use those English blades from a manufacturer of ceremonial swords. Very romantic. The Crusades. The Charge of the Light Brigade. I dub thee knight."

I can only ascribe my thus revealing two of my most private fantasies to his having refilled my cup when I was not looking. Darrell's reaction continued to be ostensibly friendly.

"I must try that. It might be an interesting way of relieving early-morning trauma. Very good value at five for a dollar-twenty."

"Plus tax."

"Plus tax, of course."

He picked up a small tube from one of his brightly lacquered packing-case tables, put it to his lips and blew into it. To my ears the resultant sound was dolorous but oddly sensual, like a farewell to a once-beloved mistress. Not that I had ever had such a thing.

"The lascivious flute," he commented, and put the instrument down. "Dr. Tillevant, have you ever wondered what agonies an ameba suffers when it divides?"

"No, I can't say I—"

"Callous, callous, like the mass of humanity. Will you have a chocolate eclair?"

I have a decided weakness for cream cakes, so I accepted eagerly. When I bit into the confection, however, my mouth felt as if it was full of needles, a fact which my best efforts to behave as a well-conducted guest evidently failed to hide.

"Perhaps I should have warned you. The cream is laced with horseradish. I find it provides an interesting sweet-and-sour effect."

"Very," I managed to reply, but he was busy extracting from the corner of the room a peculiar object which I identified as a Turkish hubble-bubble. He set this infernal contrivance going, offered me one of its several mouthpieces, which I had the wit to refuse, threw himself to the floor in the lotus position and emitted clouds of sensuously perfumed smoke while regarding me gravely. Finally he spoke:

"Dr. Tillevant, in what way would you like to die?"

"Good God—"

"Oh, don't be alarmed. You are perfectly safe here. Now *I* think it would be very pleasant to die while fucking and eating a sandwich."

"What kind of a sandwich?"

"Liverwurst on white, hold the lettuce and mayo. But perhaps you're not fond of sex?"

"What makes you think that?"

"Some people take the view that after God made Eve, Adam made Eve, and it would have saved a lot of trouble if his name had been Onan. But that's the way the elephant farts. You're interested in music, Dr. Tillevant?"

"Up to a point, yes."

"Your favorite composer is Richard Strauss?"

"Why yes, but how did you—?"

He only chuckled. I was quite concerned at this display of apparent clairvoyance. How could he possibly have known the inner strengthening which I derive from the loud side of *Also sprach Zarathustra,* or from the scarlet-and-gold rodomontade of that divinely gifted composer's *Fanfare?*

"Do you do any technical reading?"

"Well, as you may imagine, Mr. Darrell, I have little spare time for matters outside my official purview. And I must confess that in my earlier days I found so much in, say, biology that gave me pause—"

"For example?"

"Well, uh, there is one statement I remember which even now

causes me to raise a quizzical eyebrow. It is this: The heart of mammals is an asymmetrical screw. Now really—"

"Quite so, Dr. Tillevant. Anything else?"

"Yes, there is something I came across quite by accident when I was checking another word in the dictionary. It's called Johnston's organ. Actually it seems to have something to do with the way flying insects find their way around, but I do think it could have been less suggestively named."

"Indeed yes, Dr. Tillevant. We scientists are a foul-minded lot. And what else?"

"Well, you know, I have always been troubled by the stages of development which the human fetus undergoes. It has quite put me off eating fish."

"You have an original mind, Dr. Tillevant. I should be interested to hear your views on art."

"Why, uh—"

"There are in the Metropolitan Museum two ceramic statuettes of the Kiang h'si period. They respectively represent the God of Wealth in his Military Aspect and in his Civil Aspect. The first manifestation of the military-industrial complex, wouldn't you say?"

"Why, uh—"

"Oh, please don't lose your cool. I'm well aware of the important relations between the Pentagon and the Institute. I'm sure they will remain harmonious so long as you are in charge of apple-polishing the brass. Dr. Tillevant, I've been wondering. What would you consider a really worthwhile project for the Institute to undertake?"

"It's a funny thing you should ask me that, Mr. Darrell. You know, of course, that these days the number of people who live on desert islands far exceeds the number of available desert islands?"

"Certainly. Please proceed."

"Surely it would be possible to produce inflatable islands, like furniture and life rafts, only of course much larger. They could be transported to any desired spot, dropped overboard and anchored, and—and *voilà!*"

Darrell considered this, letting a soft note or two escape from the flute which he had taken up again. At length he said:

"Swordfish." He went on:

"I was considering the technical problems. A very interesting suggestion, Dr. Tillevant. The main difficulty would seem to be that they would become so popular that the level of the temperate oceans would be raised sufficiently to cause inland flooding, besides defeating the original purpose of the exercise. Well now, Dr. Tillevant, it's been a real pleasure listening to your stream of unconsciousness, but I see it's getting dark outside, and I'm sure you wouldn't want to be so antisocial as to put temptation in the way of any passing mugger. *Good*bye, *good*bye, see you in the morning."

As I waited for the elevator I heard the sound of Darrell's piano. He was playing Debussy's *Minstrels*. I could not make out why it sounded so appropriate.

5

I COULD not exactly explain why, but on my way home from Darrell's apartment I had a confused idea that while I was undergoing his peculiar, to say the least of it, hospitality he had continued to insult me both subtly and blatantly, and not once but several times. The confusion was of course due to that peculiar drink, far too much of which he had contrived to pump into me. When it wore off I had no doubt at all.

However, I was still at the stage when I was confident that in the long run I could bring him to, so to speak, heel. The return match would of course be played on my home ground; but first I had to make reasonably sure of the cooperation of my wife by a promise that she would either behave with at least superficial courtesy or go out for the evening.

I had to wait nearly a week before embarking on this scheme, since my wife's mood at the beginning of the day is a fairly reliable indicator of what it will be at the end of it. Five times in a row I awoke to the sound of her powerful contralto in the bathroom:
"Oh, what a horrible morning,
Oh, what a godawful day . . ."

This misquotation from that classic American musical, *Oklahoma*, apprised me that any request for collaboration had a minimal chance of success. The prospect was even gloomier on the second and third mornings, when she deliberately left bathroom and kitchen faucets dripping at an excruciatingly slow pace. I say deliberately, because in each case she had placed a small metal bowl where it would catch and amplify the sound of each drop. My wife is apparently impervious to such noises. It is useless to turn off the faucets, as she merely turns them on again.

Moreover, on each of those five evenings, when I entered my bedroom on returning home the wrinkled face of an unmade bed scowled at me. I am always willing to bear my part in the household chores, but bedmaking is something I particularly abominate. It was distinctly understood that if I did the vacuuming she would make the beds. To console myself I entered my study and took from a locked drawer in my desk a slab of milk chocolate of the size which, once weighing eight ounces, has by some contrary operation of the economic inflationary process now shrunk to six and a half. Even so there still remains enough for a minor sensual orgy, and I ate it in large, guilty chunks, not always managing to keep my chin clean. There are times, dear Dr. Ampiofratello, when I wish I could buy all the candy in the world and eat it in great gobs. It would be a wonderful way of passing the time on a portable desert island.

The reason for my wife's display of temperament was that clock-changing time had come around again. In the interests of precision I insist on attending to this myself, arising a few minutes before 2 A.M. in order that the first adjustment may be made exactly at the officially appointed time. My own watch, and our various electric clocks, present no problem, and I am even adept at stealing in and out of my wife's room to deal with her bedside timepiece without awakening her. I have given up as a bad job her own watch, which she insists on wearing in bed.

I admit that a certain problem does arise with the chiming granddaughter clock which stands in the entrance hall, since the hands cannot be rotated to the necessary extent without pausing at each quarter and on the hour itself to allow the various gongs to sound. In the course of this necessarily protracted process my wife invariably awakens and indulges in personal abuse of an increasingly vulgar nature.

On the sixth morning, however, my wife accompanied her ablutions by a somewhat disjointed rendition of the Hallelujah Chorus from the *Messiah* and, using a candy thermometer, personally heated my low-fat breakfast milk to the exact 120° Fahrenheit, which, allowing a minute or so for cooling while I ingest a tablet of kelp or alfalfa, as the mood takes me, enables me to drink it at the most comfortable temperature. I was emboldened by these signs to wish my wife goodbye on leaving for The Dickstachel Research Institute, and from behind the newspaper she made a distinctly audible, and not unfriendly, response. These were the first words we had exchanged during the week. I debated further marking the cessation of hostilities by kissing her on the forehead, but in view of the size of the newspaper resolved not to press my luck by what might have proved to be a somewhat clumsy gesture involving the marmalade.

When I returned home that evening I was even more careful than usual to remove my shoes before entering the apartment. My wife always does this, and insists on my doing so, for the protection of the wall-to-wall. The idea, which I presume is of Oriental origin, is an excellent one, although since it is impossible to leave one's footwear outside for fear of theft I am reduced to entering my home carrying my shoes in one hand, thereby presenting to any passing neighbor, telephone installer or burglar a somewhat laughably guilty aspect.

On encountering my wife I was at once conscious of a pleasing aroma which I assumed to emanate from her.

"How nice you smell," I said.

"It's my new laundry detergent," she replied; but she seemed pleased. It may be that therein lies the germ of a TV commercial, but at the time I was morosely reflecting that when I first met or even thought of my wife I used to get an erection, whereas at that moment all I was experiencing was tight stomach muscles. However, the superficial amicability of the moment persisted through dinner, and when eventually, though still with some hesitation, I explained my desire to return Darrell's hospitality, to my surprise she assented quite enthusiastically and declared her entire willingness to act as hostess. Frankly, I should have preferred her to spend the evening at her sister's, but once again I decided not to press my luck.

When Darrell presented himself at our humble abode she greeted him in the most friendly manner possible. So much so indeed that I was forcibly reminded of his good looks. My word, you should have seen her posing her hips at him when he proffered a bouquet of sweetheart roses. She behaved beautifully all the time he was there, except of course to me. I had determined to revenge myself for that filthy wine and those trick eclairs. But when I said:

"Mr. Darrell, I hope you're fond of yogurt. I can give you a choice of strawberry, orange or natural flavors—" she simply struck in:

"Oh, don't let him work that ghastly stuff off on you. What will you have—scotch, sherry or white wine?"

I countered by saying:

"Do have a kelp tablet. And one of these delicious polyunsaturated cookies. So good for the arteries—"

She came back with:

"For heaven's sake, Mr. Darrell isn't like you. He won't have to worry about his arteries for years and years."

Everything considered, he behaved very well, although in no time at all she was calling him Paul and he was calling her Tina, while he and I were still addressing each other by our professional titles. He drank sherry and orange yogurt alternately, and ate largely both of my health cookies and of triangles of toast thickly spread with caviar—caviar, mind you, at today's prices. And beluga at that, as I ascertained from the only canapé I managed to intercept before my wife whisked them away with the admonition:

"No more, *darling*. You know what caviar does to your poor old liver."

I was stung into replying:

"My liver is not so old as all that, and in any case caviar has a most beneficial effect on it."

My remonstrance was useless, as my wife merely continued to hold the plate where I could not reach it without resorting to undignified acrobatics, which in the circumstances I felt it better to abjure.

"Paul, do you find the Institute tremendously exciting, or would you rather have a steady job in a bomb factory?"

"It depends on whether they would let me design my own bombs. Sometimes I'm all agog, quite often I'm only half agog. Would you —let me tell you about an idea I should really like to work on. May I have some more sherry? That sofa looks comfortable."

And there they sat side by side while he explained his wretched idea and I stood around like a fool—well, anyway I stood around. I could not sit with them because of course Darrell had ignored the big sofa and was squatting on the loveseat, confound his impudence. I could not understand a word he said, and I am sure she could not either, but to see her looking into his eyes while he babbled about energy sources, and antimatter, and shifting atoms—if I had only known what was to come of it I would have put ground glass in his drink. I believe that is a very slow poison, but I had nothing quicker on hand just then.

6

DEAR DR. Ampiofratello, you now have a fairly adequate action picture of the adversary with whom I spent so much of my valuable time coping, or, as it seemed to me in moments of dejection, not coping. In appearance he was tall and elegantly slender. To me he always gave the appearance of quivering—not that he actually did quiver; his dissections, for example, were unfailingly exquisite—but he seemed to have a reservoir of energy which was constantly on the point of overflowing. I greatly envied him this, particularly since any contact with him left my own inner reserves greatly depleted.

Why did I stand for Paul Darrell? Why did I bear with his insults, verbal and visual, his retarded intelligence in the matter of practical jokes, his contempt for the most elementary administrative detail, his—his total Darrellishness? Why did I not, well, not exactly denounce him, but make it clear to the Trustees that he, uh, that they, uh—in fact that they should never have picked him, that he was a disruptive influence and that, in a word, I wanted him fired?

In the first place, he was a genius. He had only one post-graduate degree, whereas I—but modesty forbids; but he was unquestionably a genius. Not in the limited sense in which the word is used as applied to the top percentile of an I.Q. test, but in the earlier, unbounded meaning with which the word was applied to such world-spirits as Leonardo or Francis Bacon. I confess I should have found them very trying to deal with too. While I believe I am not totally lacking in moral courage, it would have taken all my fortitude to upbraid Ludwig van Beethoven for being behind with his daily output reports. But these people's patrons were private individuals, and their administrative setup was probably of a very low order.

Of course Darrell himself was born out of his time. There is really no room in today's world for people of his genre. I do not mean that he was necessarily on a par with da Vinci, and it is questionable whether he will ever achieve a landmark discovery on a par with Einstein, although his latest effort, while in a very different category —but I anticipate. When I dub Darrell a genius I mean that he had the type of mind which, though apparently spending much of its time on two wheels, could by itself and unassisted by a team or a committee intuitively reach the core of an unprecedented problem and arrive at a solution not only unorthodox and divorced from the thinking of other people working on the same assignment but, as it seemed to me and to many eminent, uh, scientists, bordering on the fringe of ignoring the well-established laws of physics.

Whether other, more commonplace solutions were possible I am not competent to say. I can only admit—reluctantly but incontrovertibly—that there have been several occasions on which commonplace solutions have not been forthcoming from the other staff of The Dickstachel Research Institute, or indeed of any other institute —and Darrell's peculiar way of thinking has saved both the day and the budget.

In speaking thus of Darrell I think I clear myself of any charge of unreasonable prejudice against him. I freely admit his professional capacity—God help me, I can do no other. On the grounds of his achievements alone it was obvious that no words of mine were likely to carry weight with the Trustees. Indeed, after he had been with

The Dickstachel Research Institute only a few months I dropped some pretty broad hints, but the sole response was some unwanted advice on the best way to humor a lone wolf. I know that the mere fact of his name as Scientific Director appearing on our letterhead, the masthead of our monthly newsletter—annual subscription fifteen dollars—and our various public relations brochures added considerably to our prestige and eased my task so far as the raising of money was concerned. It was typical of him that he referred to some of these publications as having been written with a molasses-dipped typewriter, and to others as masturbatory masterpieces.

Yes, Darrell was not only a genius, but almost a universal genius. In these specialist days people like that—people on whom no particular tag can be pinned—are generally regarded, and rightly so in my opinion, with suspicion. Da Vinci, to whom I have previously referred, would certainly be difficult to fit into the organization chart of, say, General Motors or IBM. On the other hand, after our regular and potential clients had overcome their justifiable hesitation, new assignments came along in, I am bound to admit, a most gratifying manner.

I am of course reluctant to reveal too much detail of the assignments with which The Dickstachel Research Institute is entrusted, but last year a certain eminent aircraft manufacturer came to us with the problem of a new Army plane which was giving unmistakable signs of disintegrating in midair whenever it approached its design speed. News of this had leaked out, and not only Congress but even the Air Corps was raising a considerable amount of, uh, hell, since this was the third time in a row that the products of this particular manufacturer had evinced this undesirable trait.

At the very first meeting, when some most distinguished service and civilian personnel were present, Darrell wandered in, late as usual and carrying a ukulele. Striking dissonant chords on this quasi-musical instrument, he listened cursorily to the reasoned though choleric explanation which was being delivered at length by an Air Force general and contradicted, or at least watered down, by the head of the manufacturer's design department. While the general was actually speaking, Darrell leaned over his shoulder, glanced at the drawing spread out on the table and pointed with the neck of his ukulele at a small protuberance on the nose of the aircraft.

"Bend that the other way," he said, and began to lope out of the room.

The general turned a very opulent color at being interrupted, but such was the authority inherent in Darrell's strident voice that he contained his protest. Neither did the designer—and aircraft design chiefs are by no means the most cooperative of people—neither did the designer query the essential rightness of the proposed solution. He only asked, in a somewhat bleating manner:

"How far?"

"About twenty-five degrees," Darrell said from the door, and departed in a diminuendo of ukulele chords.

His suggestion was tried out, and proved to be so much on target that the modification was incorporated not only in future production but in such of the earlier machines as still remained intact.

Spectacular as were these results, they were only a further proof of Darrell's complete detachment from the practical aspects of life. The Dickstachel Research Institute had negotiated a very satisfactory cost-plus fee for this assignment. In view of the brief time which had actually been spent on it, and the laconic manner in which the remedy had been propounded, we had the utmost difficulty in collecting more than a derisory amount.

Naturally, as soon as the meeting ended a number of our less senior, uh, technical personnel were put to work compiling a detailed statement of the problem as it had been posed to us, and an equally detailed recitation not only of the remedy but of the, uh, technical phenomena therewith associated. Since the modified prototype was flying satisfactorily before the report and appendices had much exceeded seven hundred pages, the entire document, reasonably impressive as it appeared, was, I confess, rather a dead letter, although it did prove of some use in our final showdown with the General Accounting Office.

If this had been the only discipline in which Darrell revealed a superhuman grasp of his subject, he would at least have been classifiable. I had almost said certifiable, but that would have been a

Freudian slip. No, indeed. He appeared to be equally in tune with the Infinite Intelligence on questions ranging from weather control to the synthetic duplication of Clos Vougeot '49, a supersecret project which I really should not have mentioned.

It may seem strange that he had not been enlisted in the fight against certain major diseases which have not so far proved to be amenable to the application of Federal Funds. In fact he had several times been invited to turn his unique faculties in that direction, and the Trustees on more than one occasion had raised enough courage to exert noticeable pressure; but here they came across an undeniable kink in the otherwise perfect circle of his universality. He had not the slightest interest in matters medical. On one occasion, when it had been represented to him that he owed it to suffering humanity to use his apparently mediumistic gifts along those lines, he hesitantly agreed to tackle a particular assignment; but his boredom was such that he approached the problem in the most bumbling manner, and soon relinquished it.

This was the only time that he was ever known to apologize for anything. He pleaded—well, no. One could never imagine Darrell pleading. He *stated* that there were many other subjects which occasioned in him an acute sense of ennui: all kinds of sports, pop music, TV programs, instant gourmet foods. It seemed rather an odd list, but of course it was Darrell speaking. For none of these allergies, he pointed out, could he be reproached, and he was as little blameworthy for his revulsion to medicine as to any other subject.

Another factor which made it difficult to start a Dump Darrell movement was his friendship with people who wanted or at any rate could be persuaded to give money to The Dickstachel Research Institute, and when I say money I mean Money. No one with that sort of social contact need fear ostracism so long as their friends' assets and philanthropic instincts remain unimpaired.

It seemed to me that only Darrell's or my own death, natural or enforced, or an exceptionally tempting offer from some other institute or a university, could rid me of this troublesome priest, as Henry II put it in another connection. I knew of several other laboratories and campuses—properly speaking, campi—which would have been delighted to welcome Darrell, but his contract with The Dickstachel Research Institute was a long-term one.

So far as the Grim Reaper was concerned, I really felt it was too much to expect me to regard my own death as a happy release, although at the present moment my views have changed. The reports on my annual checkup had always been exceptionally favorable, and I continued to have no difficulty in increasing my life insurance. I come of long-lived stock, and provided I could continue to survive the daily hazards of urban life I had every hope of proving worthy of my forefathers. Suicide I have always regarded as a last resort.

Darrell's health appeared to be disappointingly first-rate. It would be a very foolish mugger who would tackle anyone with Darrell's reflexes and training in unarmed combat, and apart from a lucky revolver shot or some natural disaster such as the perfectly timed fall from a height of a lump of coping, there seemed little hope.

Personally I think Darrell has lived so long because the devil knows what a disruptive influence he would be in hell.

I willingly confess that I evolved many schemes for eliminating Darrell without anyone but our two selves being aware of it. Some of these ideas were, I flatter myself, not without ingenuity. For example, a candlelight dinner—myself of course being absent—at which the candles were filled with dynamite. Booby-trapping the refrigerator in which he kept certain specimens and chemicals. A curare-tipped thumbtack on the seat of his chair, or a pailful of acid balanced on the top of his office door—practical jokes for a practical joker. If I had ever been able to solve to my own satisfaction the problems of logistics and concealment I verily believe I should have taken some drastic action along these lines.

Heaven knows what reciprocal ideas seethed in Darrell's brain. Once he sent me an elaborate funeral wreath with a card saying "Jolly Good Show."

However, fortune put in my way an idea which, while by no means guaranteeing the desired result, would at least absolve me of complicity in any untoward denouement, while providing, as I calculated, a pleasing variety of potential mischances.

7

It is a little hobby of mine to collect unusual old books. No, no, nothing of that kind—at least—well, anyway, my other specialty is writings by travelers in times past; partly because reading about the hardships they suffered enables me more easily to endure with a philosophical smile the misadventures with which, in common with the rest of us, I am frequently faced either in my journeyings to and from work or farther afield at convention time. I find, for example, that descriptions of men with their heads in the middle of their chests, or creatures with the outward appearance of a woman down to the waist, but thereafter of a dragon or manatee, lessen the impact of the other mythical creatures who invariably sit next to me in airplanes; and accounts of thirst-maddened mariners straining their eyes for a sight of land make it easier to bear the twenty-fifth circle in the stack at JFK after the liquid refreshments have been irrevocably locked away.

A few days after my rencontre with Darrell apropos of my window curtains I was browsing in one of the secondhand bookstores on Fourth Avenue. I was delighted to find there a slim volume in my favorite category. Its leather binding was sadly scuffed, the spine cracked and the pages yellow; but sufficient of the gilt title remained for me to read the words "voyage" and "Amazon." A cursory examination of the text convinced me that I had stumbled on something after my own heart. I therefore paid the person in charge—a distrait man who was listening to classical jazz records through headphones —the exorbitant sum of five dollars plus tax, and went home.

When I was able to examine my purchase at more leisure, I found that the full title of the work, which had been published in the early Victorian period, was *Letters from a Son to His Mother, Describing His Missionary Travels in the Unexplored Regions of the Upper Amazon. With Eight Steel Engravings.* I suppose the Victorians had more time to recite such mouthfuls when visiting their booksellers.

The writer's name was given as the Reverend Bertram Francis Nugent-Nugent. There was, oddly enough, no publisher's imprint, suggesting that the book might originally have been issued for private circulation. A further lengthy inscription on the title page stated that the volume had been edited by His Sorrowing Mother, and was intended to serve as a Memorial to a Saintly, Dutiful and Traduced Son. The editress, Lady Athanasia Nugent-Nugent, continued this eulogy in an introduction filling nineteen and a half pages of extremely small print, very little of which I attempted to read at that time.

The letters themselves, however, were in a more kindly typeface. There were fewer than two dozen altogether, and I confess that I found the earlier ones, as records of travel, disappointing. They merely referred unflatteringly to the depravity of the Reverend Nugent-Nugent's fellow-passengers and crew, the incivility accorded to his attempts to administer the comforts of the Gospel to those prostrated by sea-sickness, the poor quality of the shipboard food, and some trite observations on the majesty of the open sea.

What did, however, immediately strike me was the warmth, indeed ardor, with which he expressed his sorrow at being thus parted from his mother. Such phrases as "far from the beams of your dear bright eyes" and "the healing comforts of your bosom" and "fond remembrance of the exultant ecstasy which transfused my whole being in our closeted hours" seemed to me more than filial. There were also many references to an Uncle Augustus, who was described as prurient-minded, meddling and overbearing; together with conjectures as to the train of reasoning which could have led Nugent-Nugent's papa, taken so untimely from their midst, to appoint such a person as executor of his estate and guardian of his son. It seemed that it was at the urgent prompting of Uncle Augustus that the Reverend Nugent-Nugent had been dispatched on his missionary travels. I decided that later on I would again tackle the small print of the Introduction in case it shed further light on what seemed to have been something of a family imbroglio.

I leafed through the Eight Steel Engravings, which must perforce have been made far from the scenes they described and were of an extremely stereotyped nature. Then I returned to the Letters.

After his arrival in Ventrivia, as that part of the largely uncharted

Upper Amazon was apparently called, the Reverend Nugent-Nugent seemed to have been little impressed by the novelties which surrounded him. He merely complained, with a petulance increasingly shrill and rising at times to a note of terror, of the glutinous quality of the heat and the enormous size and repulsive appearance of the insect and animal life which, instead of fleeing the awe-inspiring sight of white men, pressed in on him with lively and at times ferocious curiosity.

He sought to damp down these complaints by pious references to the infinite variety of the Creator's handiwork, but these did not in the least hide his evident wish that the divine versatility had been demonstrated in ways closer to the mores of the village of Melbury Bubb, somewhere in southwest England, whence he was exiled.

Nugent-Nugent also made lively reference to a warlike tribe known as the Bellaki. These violent savages had saluted the missionary expedition with poisoned darts which, ill-aimed though they were, had by chance inflicted some mortality on the native bearers; though, "Heaven be praised," Nugent-Nugent and the leader of the expedition, a belligerent-sounding person named Canon Smurge, had escaped injury. Apart from poor marksmanship, the Bellaki apparently suffered from poor supply services, as they were unable to discharge a second flight of darts until they had retrieved the first one. Before they could do this Canon Smurge cowed them into acquiescence by advancing on them, "his face scarlet with rage, his mutton-chop white whiskers bristling," and not only shaking a brawny fist in the air but delivering a straight right to the chin of an obstreperous native who had sought to bar the Canon's progress.

Such militant Christianity had won all Bellaki hearts, and the tribal chief had immediately opted for conversion. After the necessary formalities the party had pressed on, leaving an anonymous junior member to represent the occupying troops. Canon Smurge, thrusting aside lianas and tarantulas alike, had led for most of the way, but he had also insisted on Nugent-Nugent's taking his turn at this chore and thus first encountering any vivacious unpleasantness, whether dropping from a tree branch, rising from under his very feet or making a flank attack from some malodorous body of water. On several occasions Nugent-Nugent evidently tried to escape by night, taking with him more than his share of the provisions; but so unskilled was he in the woodsy arts that he twice landed back in camp just as day was breaking, and in three or four other instances Canon Smurge recaptured him with contemptuous ease, headed in the desired direction but leaving a trail which almost the youngest Amazonian child could have traced.

With Letter XII, however, there is something of a change of tone. So important is this Letter, so directly was it the cause of many of the unhappy events which later befell me, that I shall give it in its entirety.

8

My dearest mama,

At last, at last my sufferings are eased, though for how long this state of bliss will last only He can tell. Two days ago I was staggering through this accursed jungle, streaming with sweat and reeling with fatigue. I was leading the party, with my arms stretched in front of me and my eyes closed so that I could not see the horrors which pressed upon me from all quarters. I was relying on Canon Smurge's frequent irascible shouts to correct any deviation from the proper compass bearing which this admittedly unorthodox method of progression might occasion. Suddenly there was a cessation of the whipping of nameless tropical vegetation against my face, the hissing of mighty serpents, the snarling and whooping of I know not what ferocious wild animals, and the discordant cries of the huge, brightly-colored, *un-English* birds whose wings had been blowing the torrid air against my very cheeks without, alas, bringing any cooling relief.

So mesmerized was I, however, that methought 'twas only a waking dream, brought upon me perhaps by one of the evil spirits which in spite of my belief in the Almighty I am sure haunt this jungle, in order that my tortures might be all the keener when I awoke. I therefore continued to press forward until I was brought up short by Canon Smurge vociferating:

"Stop, stop. Nugent-Nugent, I say. God bless my soul, has the fool gone deaf. Nugent-Nugent. Hoy-hoy. STOP."

As it appeared that Canon Smurge, as usual, meant what he said, I did stop, with what degree of thankfulness I need not tell you, and ventured to open my eyes. The jungle was behind us. Ahead was a great open plain covered with lush grass. Far, far away in the distance was a huge range of mountains, all but their tops enveloped in a purple mist; but close at hand was the evidence of human habitation—for I insist on calling the inhabitants of these regions human. I saw a cluster of rude huts with walls of vertically arranged logs and roofs of grass. Naked children were playing outside them, naked women were working at their simple domestic tasks, and naked men were squatted against the huts watching them. The air was full of their happy laughter. It was indeed a peaceful scene, and what made it even more idyllic was that, at the moment at least, none of the men were armed.

Canon Smurge's shouts, no less than our emergence from the jungle, had attracted the attention of the natives. The men now rose, formed themselves into a body, and led by one who was evidently their chief, advanced towards us. This is always a ticklish moment. Canon Smurge and I, as harbingers of divine serenity, of course carried no arms. The Canon had not yet made his way forward when the natives reached us. Taking me to be the most important man of our party, the chief, who like the other adults was not more than three feet high, stretched up and offered me a wooden bowl full of some liquid. I knew the importance of readily accepting this friendly gesture and was in any case extremely thirsty. I therefore took the bowl, bowed courteously to the chief and drained the liquid.

Canon Smurge now came up, exhibiting signs of ill-temper most unbecoming to a man of the cloth, and endeavored by signs to establish his rightful position as leader. These signs included pointing to himself, smiling, throwing out his chest and raising his hand as high as he could, then pointing to me, frowning and putting his hand as near to the ground as he could manage without falling over. The effect was quite ridiculous, and I was unable to restrain my merriment. However, the chief, who appeared to be a man of quick intelligence, seemed to understand what Canon Smurge was endeavoring to convey and despatched one of his attendants for a further supply.

When the refilled bowl arrived, however, Canon Smurge, who had been eyeing me with a severity unusual even for him, took only a token sip and handed the remainder back. The fact is, dearest mama, that the liquid which I had imbibed with such incautious freedom was a most potent intoxicant. To it, far more than the absurd gestures which the Canon had been making, was to be ascribed my uncontrollable merriment, which had now overcome me to such a degree that I was compelled to resort to slapping my knees, blowing out my cheeks and eventually rolling on the ground and kicking my heels in the air. Even when my laughter temporarily died down, one look at the expression on Canon Smurge's face, as he endeavored simultaneously to establish working relations with the chief and to quell me into something resembling my normal demeanor, was enough to set me off into another paroxysm of mirth.

Such an advanced degree of exhilaration could not last, however. I found myself briefly experiencing extreme contrition for my conduct to such an extent that copious tears fell down my cheeks. I would have entreated the good Canon's pardon and blessing, were it not that my legs folded under me, I sank again to the ground, and fell into a deep slumber.

When I regained consciousness my head ached more excruciatingly than after any wine party which I had attended during my abbreviated stay at Oxford. The light was dim, but I could just make out that I was lying on a rough palliasse inside one of the native huts. At my first movement I was unable to repress a groan of agony. This brought to my side a native maiden—I supposed—who had been patiently waiting in another corner of the hut for the first signs of my recovery. She tendered to me another bowl, much smaller than the one whose contents had been my undoing. I was not unnaturally reluctant to sample another unknown liquid, but she was so insistent, and so charming were her smiles, that I did as she wished.

The flavor of the draught reminded me of the mixture of raw egg and Worcestershire sauce with which I had been accustomed to soothe myself on similar occasions at home in dear, but ah so far, England. The improbability of real Worcestershire sauce being available in these wild regions led me to conclude that by some coincidence the natives had hit on a very similar solatium using such ingredients as they had at hand.

In a few minutes I was so much restored that I thought it would be prudent to go in search of Canon Smurge. Resisting, though with difficulty, the importunities of the native maiden, I left the hut and found that with the aid of one of the interpreters who formed part of our baggage column, the Canon had already entered upon the purpose of his visit. It seemed that his preliminary exordium on the benefits to be expected from immediate baptism was meeting with a favorable reception, as the chief's face was wreathed in smiles, interspersed with bursts of laughter, which were of course reflected and echoed by the other members of the tribe. Joyful as such an occasion always is, I fear that I found myself wishing for a little more restraint, since the quality of these peals of merriment struck somewhat harshly on my ear.

However, Canon Smurge's face bore evidence of his lively inward satisfaction, and his reception of me was almost forgiving. In a few words he confirmed the impression I had formed, and told me that the chief had already given orders for the first converts to be lined up at dawn on the following morning.

A great feast was prepared, to which we were bidden as soon as it became dusk. Vast quantities of the same intoxicating liquid were consumed—its name, so far as I am able to literalize the native pronunciation, is Whammo—but I deemed it wise to keep my consumption of it to a minimum. Canon Smurge, as a rigid teetotaller, merely put the bowls to his lips and passed them on. He confided to me afterwards that he was suffering severe pangs of conscience over the small amount of Whammo which he had imbibed earlier in the day. He also complained bitterly of the pangs of thirst which were a concomitant of the richly seasoned food we had eaten. This appeared to be entirely composed of various forms of pig, an animal which, though running wild in the jungle, the natives seem to have partly domesticated. I was suffering similar discomfort, and between us we emptied several canteens of boiled water before retiring —a singularly uninspiring ending to our jollification.

Shortly after midnight we were shown to our huts, from which the regular occupants had been evicted. In view of the darkness and the strange locale, it was some little while before I made out that the Canon and I had been given a hut apiece. In the ordinary way we made it a rule to occupy the same shelter, however primitive, sleeping in two-hour watches and standing guard in turns. This departure from custom gave me little anxiety in view of the unparalleled friendliness with which the Cosamo, as they are called, had received us. Indeed, our hosts' concern for our comfort did not end there. In my own hut I found not one but two native maidens, as I still supposed, ready to help me undress and in other ways administer to my creature comforts. Being mindful of my duty to the cloth which, however reluctantly, I wore, I made some attempt to repel their more intimate attentions; but first they barred my escape from the hut and when I attempted to thrust them forth they resisted me with their combined strength—for such slight creatures they were amazingly muscular—and forced me on to the palliasse, where they immediately joined me, evincing a versatility which I should never have deemed possible.

Dearest mama, pray do not be jealous. Consider my situation —thousands of miles from Melbury Bubb, in a gigantic sparsely populated area peopled only by heathens who, for all their amicability so far might well turn on me at any moment for violating one or more of their tabus, which might include refusing to cohabit with their freely proffered beauties. On the morrow, or within a day or two at latest, we should have the authority to impose our own tabus; but this time had not yet come. It was, therefore, with a clear view to my own safety that I sank back on the sweet-smelling palm fronds and allowed the first caresses of my fair companions. As I did so I heard as from afar a series of full-throated roars in what could only have been the voice of Canon Smurge, who I assumed was dealing with a similar situation in his own way. I was, however, too busy to pay much attention to them, and after a while they died away.

But here, dearest mama, comes the most curious part of my whole story. At our first encounter with the Cosamo we had naturally not been able to take in all the details of their being. Now, however, it seemed that while my female companions had long dark hair on their heads, exceedingly fine in texture, they had *none anywhere else.* Their torsos were innocent of even the most gossamer down. Even their private parts were completely denuded, a fact of which I convinced myself both by the sense of touch and, when daylight came, by visual observation of other members of the tribe. Discreet inquiry confirmed that this was their natural state, in no way due to razors or depilatories. Dearest mama, again I beg you not to be offended when I say that this arrangement seems to me *so much nicer.* It is after all only another instance of the infinite variety of the Creator's invention, and we should in all reverence express our wonder. . . .

9

I FELT a certain sympathy with the reactions of Nugent-Nugent—I beg his pardon, the Reverend Nugent-Nugent—to his great discovery. John Ruskin, that other eminent Victorian, I believe felt the same way. *So much nicer.* Nevertheless, at this point I stopped reading for a while. It seemed to me that I might have made, or perhaps it would be more accurate to say remade, a discovery of the utmost importance not only, uh, scientifically but in relation to the expansion of The Dickstachel Research Institute. And, just as important, with any luck a final solution of my relations with Paul Darrell.

Taking the, uh, scientific aspects first, a number of questions occurred to me. Although I trust I have made it clear that such base mechanic matters are foreign to my nature, self-interest speaks all sorts of tongues, as La Rochefoucauld neatly put it. Could, I asked myself, the unique deficiency in the local fauna which Nugent-Nugent described be pinpointed as the physical cause of their exceptional friendliness? What was their average lifespan? Cholesterol level? Relative susceptibility to venereal disease? How would it affect their performance at lacrosse? How would they react to implants?

The ingenuity of these questions, and the total uselessness of any answers which might be found would, I was convinced, elicit several millions in Federal Funds with far less effort than is required to induce the average insurance company to settle a forty-five-dollar claim. Moreover, their solution would require a great deal of floor space. I envisaged a new tower of at least twenty stories. At last The Dickstachel Research Institute could begin to move up from being a mere couple of adapted buildings to what could justifiably be termed a Complex. As Administrator of a complex I should after many weary disappointments attain the status level which I felt to be my due.

And if I could contrive to pack Paul Darrell off to the Upper Amazon, he might never come back. Canoes might capsize in flooded, crocodile-infested rivers, or he might fall a victim to the warlike Bellaki, or hitherto unknown tropical fevers might strike. For any of these reasons, he would never again bring sweetheart roses to my wife.

I hastily skimmed the remaining Letters. It appeared that the entire Cosamo tribe had lined up for the initiatory rites, and by good organization and hard work by both Canon Smurge and the Reverend Nugent-Nugent they had all been baptized by sundown. The procedure must have closely resembled the inoculation parade which I involuntarily attended on my induction into the Army quite a number of years ago, except that to the scandal of Canon Smurge it was marked by unceasing laughter, especially at the most impressive parts of the ritual. The Canon seemed to have been under the weather throughout. He was described as unable to meet his co-worker's eyes when they first rejoined each other, and as having replied to a polite inquiry "whether he had slept well" in a manner almost unclerical.

Thus far, fairly good; but from then on, distinctly not so good.

The Cosamo, still in the most affable way, had refused to make the slightest change in their way of life. They had been overcome with uncontrollable mirth at the heavy, somber garments which had been taken from the bearers' packs and freely offered them to clothe their nakedness; and they had absolutely refused to wear them.

Canon Smurge had experienced no more success in attempting to introduce the subjects of monogamy, chastity, sobriety, the Ten Commandments, the Thirty-nine Articles or the Victorian Sunday. When he finally demanded of the chief, through the interpreter, in as good round terms as he dared, "Why in the name of all that was holy the Cosamo had allowed themselves to be baptized at all?" the answer astounded him. The Cosamo, it seemed, had previously been received into, in alphabetical order, the Baptist, Catholic, Congregational, Lutheran, Methodist, Presbyterian, Seventh Day Adventist, Unitarian and Wesleyan churches. This left the Church of England in a very poor competitive position, launching its own product late in the day in a much overcrowded market.

The good Canon had then demanded why the Cosamo had agreed to undergo this extraordinary range of serial conversion. To this the chief had replied that it had appeared to him and to his predecessor that the ceremonies proffered by succeeding visitors had been merely the usual, though quaint, social customs of the white man on first meeting. The Canon, who was by then in a pitiable state of bewildered rage, had further asked why there were no visible signs of any of this sacred cavalcade—no church, not even an open-air altar, and above all no clergy. The chief's laughter had redoubled, and his answer, as interpreted, was brief:

"They go mountains."

Further details on this important subject were not forthcoming, perseveringly though the Canon probed; but he had been told, still with unfailing courtesy but with unshakable resolution, that the Cosamo did not consider themselves any more bound by the terms of this latest installment of salvation than by its predecessors. Their merriment on being told emphatically that they were all bound for eternal damnation became hysterical, and the chief's reply was:

"Yes, we know. All say that. Very funny joke. We tell Alorra. He laugh too."

Alorra, it appeared, was the Cosamo god. (They were at least monotheistic.) The Canon was unable to obtain a sight of this deity, as although the Cosamo were willing to admit him into the temple, they insisted that he would first have to remove all his clothes. This he refused to do, and had to content himself with a verbal description of the god—a gaily painted image of a laughing man which was, so to speak, rededicated once a year. If it had been a bad year with much disease and hunger, Alorra was broken to pieces and a fresh image substituted. If on the other hand all had gone well, the old Alorra was repainted and allowed to survive another twelve months, after which he was considered to be worn out. A striking foreshadowing, it occurred to me, of some modern democratic practices.

At this point Canon Smurge gave up, having exhausted even his great reserves of obstinacy, and decided that next day he would push on to the mountains as his predecessors had done, hoping to find a more favorable business climate. Nugent-Nugent, however, managed to obtain more information about the mountains from his current team of maidens—they were changed every night, like sheets in a motel. The area between Cosamo territory and the mountains was, so far as was known, uninhabited; but ancient legend had it that the mountains themselves were the domain of a powerful devil in which the territorial imperative was so strong that anyone who invaded its sanctuary disappeared without trace. Beyond this horrid summary, further details were naturally not available.

Nugent-Nugent formed his own theories, which ranged from giant poisonous snakes to a cannibal tribe even more aggressive than the Bellaki. He set out again with his party, noting that the happy laughter of the Cosamo now fell harshly on his ear; but this time, his tracking abilities perhaps improved by terror, he managed not only to escape from the first night's camp but to elude the inevitable search party and return to the Cosamo, who received him as hospitably as ever. This may have been in part due to the fact that he had what they lacked, and mutual novelty fostered mutual, so to speak, relations. In the end homesickness overcame him—or perhaps he had exhausted the supply of maidens—and he set out for the coast, intending to return to England no matter what reception awaited him from Uncle Augustus.

This was the gist of Letter XXIV, but Lady Nugent-Nugent made it clear that no more was ever heard of her dutiful—too dutiful?—son, or Canon Smurge for that matter. This point determined me. If I could obtain even shadowy confirmation of the continued existence of the Cosamo I would move heaven, earth and the Board of Trustees to send Paul Darrell to Ventrivia.

I will freely admit that later that night I awoke with certain doubts. For example, there was a risk—and I should have to make it a calculated risk—that before plunging into the mysterious depths of the Ventrivian jungle Darrell might encounter Boanerges. On the other hand Boanerges had always been a pretty close-mouthed fellow. Unless he had taken to drink he was probably safe enough.

But the word "murder" circled in my mind. What could it be called when one sent a man—several men—into the shadowy unknown without revealing my private information as to the odds against their survival? Toh, I said to myself as I mixed a dose of Burpine. Murder is not so much these days. We are living in an advanced civilization that extends proper sympathy to the problems of the killer and recognizes that the so-called victim probably deserved his fate. To amend the old quotation, I was convinced that Darrell should have died not hereafter but long before. His demise would provide the occasion for some elegant elegiacs, in which I flatter myself I am fairly proficient, and at such a time I should not stint.

As the antacid circulated through my gastric system, my qualms faded. I awoke next morning with a calm mind and stomach.

10

FOR THE next week or ten days, though to the detriment of an important new system for receiving incoming supplies at The Dickstachel Research Institute, involving some thirty-five percent increase in personnel, with a concomitant growth in computer usage —where was I? Oh yes. I spent most of my spare time and some of my office hours poring over atlases and such publications as *National Geographic*, *Scientific American* and *The Golden Bough*. While I acquired a good deal of interesting and even titillating information in this way, most of it was irrelevant.

Ventrivia is not one of the most advanced South American countries, as is perhaps evidenced by the fact that for the last hundred and fifty years it has been a hereditary dictatorship, although the legitimacy of some of the generations may be doubtful. While it has at last formed rather uncertain ties with some of the better-known organizations for promoting universal brotherhood, enough xenophobia remains. Almost only the new data I gathered was that what Nugent-Nugent had referred to as jungle was more likely to be rain forest, which was probably even worse—or, from my point of view, better. I also learned that the warlike Bellaki were still fighting fit; but so far as the Cosamo went I was, to put it colloquially, buffaloed.

I could of course have made inquiries on a reciprocal scholarly basis from various scientific organizations; but until I had more closely formulated my plans I had an instinctive feeling that I might be well advised to remain as private as possible. Happily I bethought me of a fellow I used to know at college and for some time after, until he found it advisable to take up employment outside the United States—by fortunate coincidence, in this very country of Ventrivia.

I had no idea whether my old, uh, buddy was still in Ventrivia, or out of jail, or even alive; but if he were all these things I hoped that the memory of certain past incidents would induce him to be helpful. I therefore sent the following cable to the address which, after a good deal of rummaging, I found in an old notebook over the yellowed pages of which I shook my head in wistful remembrance:

REMEMBER THE MAINE AND THE ALAMO STOP HAVE YOU EVER HEARD OF THE COSAMO STOP ARE THEY STILL AROUND STOP RAM.

Several days later I received the following reply, which, owing to the fact that a burst water main had put my home telephone out of action for forty-eight hours, Western Union was reduced to mailing to me:

```
BBF13)1056)(1-109214G352)PD6/24/78/1055
ICS IPMIIHA IISS
PMS BSN MA
AWQ 569 VIA ITT CTB514 BSE517 F238
USNX XO GBBS 010
SAN P VNTRV
TILLAVON NEW YOR
YES UNFORTUNATELY BOANERGES
SA TR61736 785 39 02114
NNN
NNNN
```

For some time I assumed this to be a lengthy dispatch in code. It was not until I had made various unsuccessful efforts to solve it —hindered rather than helped by vague memories of Edgar Allan Poe, James Thurber and Sir Arthur Conan Doyle—that by chance I discovered the brief message so overshadowed by the mass of electronic narcissism.

    YES UNFORTUNATELY BOANERGES

While this gave me the basic information I needed, I wished that my old college chum had been either a little more or a little less explicit, in view of the ominous implications of the word "unfortunately," which rendered the cable hardly suitable for inclusion in a presentation to the Trustees. However, with a philosophical smile I decided to make the best of what I had.

My next step therefore was to remove from the book all the Letters from XV to the end and put them in my wall safe at home. The remaining portion of Nugent-Nugent's narrative-narrative—oh dear. At all events, Letter XIV, where the book now ended, left him on the crest of the wave, enjoying to the full the primitive hospitality which was being lavished on him and as yet with no inkling of a less toward outcome.

I was somewhat doubtful about the Introduction by His Sorrowing Mother. By then I had, though with considerable eyestrain, read all the twenty-nine and a half foxed pages of unrelieved lamentation in which Lady Nugent-Nugent blamed everything and everybody from Fate to the steamship company, not forgetting Uncle Augustus and Canon Smurge, for the final disappearance of a son whom she termed, I am sure without justification, unique in the annals of filial relationship. Finally I decided that this too must come out, although as a literary curiosity I would keep it also in my wall safe.

With so many pages removed, the book now presented a forlorn appearance, but in a curious way this added to its authenticity. I had little doubt of the effect it would have on the Trustees, men and women of remarkable financial and commercial ability and attainment—except for Mrs. Stahl—but whose private interests, as outlined in *Questionmark,* the house organ of The Dickstachel Research Institute, ran exclusively to such matters as football and, more recently, championship tennis. I did not expect them to show any interest in or knowledge of foreign travel except as represented by the better class of package tour or as the claims of export sales or raw materials exploitation might dictate. I hoped these side issues would not come up, as I could imagine delicate situations arising. However, there was no point in burning my bridges before I came to them, if that is what I mean.

In addition to what was left of the book, I was also armed with a long and detailed letter from my friend in Ventrivia. It confirmed the continued existence of the Cosamo as reported from time to time by wandering hunters and traders, described them as continuing to live an idyllic existence and, most importantly, confirmed that all accounts agreed on their total lack of pubic hair. In conclusion it stated the writer's conviction that the Cosamo represented not only an untapped but a potentially fruitful field for anthropological, medical and sociological research. I could not have wished for a more persuasive and convincing document to reinforce my presentation. This is not surprising, as I had written it myself, obtaining the signature of one of the doormen at my apartment, who was under the impression that he was witnessing a will.

11

I THINK it might not be amiss at this point to provide brief sketches of the ladies and gentlemen of the Board of Trustees of The Dickstachel Research Institute whom I should within the next few days have the task of selling, or perhaps a more appealing word would be enthusing, on the Cosamo project.

As is only due to his rank, I begin with the Chairman. His name was Lothair X. Haversham. He was a portly gentleman of sixty-eight, who at the proper time had retired from the Presidency of the Fourth National Polk-Fillmore Bank and Trust Company. This institution, although by no means the largest in the country, had been very highly regarded ever since it had been set up by one of the founding fathers. Even in these egalitarian and expansionist times it had maintained a certain aloofness by subtly discouraging the account of any individual whose net worth was less than half a million dollars.

Mr. Haversham was so well-shaven as to be a convincing testimonial to the razor he used—a replica, as he once very democratically confided to me, of the first Gillette safety razor. At all Trustee meetings he adhered to the black vicuna jacket and striped pants which had been his unvarying style throughout his business career.

One of his favorite remarks was:

"No one's going to do me, even in a foreign language."

In this great country of ours everyone is entitled to his own opinion.

Mr. Haversham was a widower, his late wife, the former Eleanor Hargreaves, having succumbed to partly concealed alcoholism. He had two sons and a daughter. One son had succeeded him as President of the Fourth National Polk-Fillmore Bank and Trust Company, with a large staff of highly qualified specialists to prevent him from breaking it. The other son was the senior senator for one of the Western states, which position he had filled for the past fifteen years to the advantage of everyone concerned.

The daughter married one of the Liebowitzes who have of course been known and respected on Wall Street since 1832, although following the events of the late nineteen-sixties this branch of the family is now living rather quietly in the Bahamas. There are various grandsons and granddaughters, one of whom recently served six months of a twenty-year sentence for selling heroin to the members of her mother's country club.

Next in seniority was Mr. V. Walter Krebs, also retired, in this instance from the Presidency of the once-famous Krebs Brewery. In its heyday Krebs Beer was almost the only brand available throughout the Midwest; but unaccountable outbreaks of fire in the taverns and other outlets where it was sold rendered its competitive position untenable, and after a while Mr. Krebs quietly sold the business, for a considerable sum, to a consortium of doubtful provenance which, with poetic justice, found its investment equally doubtful, since the name of Krebs was now associated in the public mind with violent death or painful injury. Only drinkers with a pronounced masochistic streak could be induced to enter bars displaying the once-popular sign of the crayfish.

As a matter of policy the Krebs family had always been noted for publicized good works. Mr. Krebs's current benevolences ranged from disadvantaged ghetto children to the Crayfish Stakes, run annually at Pimlico, Maryland, in the vain hope that in course of time it would outshine the Preakness. It was perhaps because of some form of guilt feeling arising from his previous occupation that he had contributed generously to The Dickstachel Research Institute in the hope of finding some sure preventive for kidney disease.

In distinct contrast to these gentlemen was Franklin Webster Morwitz. I quote from an issue of *Questionmark*, the house organ of The Dickstachel Research Institute, at the time of his appointment:

"Mr. Morwitz, who was born in 1932, was graduated from the University of Wyoming in 1955 and obtained his law degree from New York Law School in 1958. He began his career as an assistant to the District Attorney in Trenton, New Jersey, and is now a partner in the legal firm of Scarfe, Valentine, Stock, Monk and

Beige. Mr. Morwitz, who was General Counsel for the Congressional Joint Committee on the Pursuit of Happiness, was a consultant in the setting up of the Office of Short Views in 1967. He is a founder-member of the Friends of Everybody and a Director of the Parabolic Microphone Union Against Privacy. His publications include *Why America, But Would They Want It* and an autobiography entitled *I Was Never Lovelier.*"

I am not sure that Mr. Morwitz had ever completely recovered from his birth trauma. His face always seemed to me to bear the self-satisfied look of one who at that moment is worth several million dollars, modified by the equivocal expression of one who within the next twenty-four hours may, starting at penthouse level, put the theory of gravity to a new proof.

12

I MUST, I suppose, also describe Ms. Kalman.

Yes. Well.

I should dislike Ms. Kalman even if she was not a protégée of Paul Darrell.

He introduced her in this wise:

He knocked softly at the door of my office, though it was already open, and coughed in a timid but penetrating manner. When I looked up I saw that he was clad in pinstripe black pants and a black vicuna jacket and waistcoat, of the style affected by Mr. Haversham. His shirt collar was of the archaic pattern known as butterfly, around which was arranged a broad necktie of the obsolete fashion known as ascot. He held in front of him a derby hat, which he rotated by a ceaseless movement of his fingers on the brim, thereby creating a nervous and supplicatory impression.

The effect of all this was somewhat impaired by the fact that his garments were crumpled and shabby, that the uppers of his six-eyelet laced shoes were cracked, that he could not have shaved for two days, and that by some means he had imparted to his countenance an appearance of extreme pallor and, indeed, famine.

I was pretty sure what these shenanigans portended. He was about to make another attempt at an increased allocation. I said:

"Yes, Mr. Darrell, what is it?"

My tone was anything but welcoming. I was having an extremely trying morning. At least half of those who should have been present had not been present at the weekly Recapitulatory Survey Meeting, whose nature and importance I will explain later. On top of that, a staff secretary suffering from deuteranopia, one of the more common forms of color-blindness, had hopelessly confused the distribution of my new seventeen-copy Non-Progress Report, printed on specially dyed paper in shades chosen by the Chromatic Resonance Subcommittee of the Aesthetic Review Committee, so that although every department concerned had received a copy, it had been the wrong color. This had led to endless delay and confusion among the more conscientious department heads—I intended to deal very severely with the others—and absolute chaos not only in Central Records but in Branch and Sub-Branch Filing. Persian Coral copies were getting filed in Moonglow cabinets, and so on throughout the astronomical number of permutations and combinations possible with the base number seventeen.

This appalling state of affairs had actually obtained for three weeks before it had been brought to my attention. I had no idea how we were going to disentangle these arrears. At that moment I was manfully wrestling with the problem of the future. The obvious thing would have been to transfer the secretary in question to less demanding tasks, replacing her by a girl carrying an oculist's certificate in her purse; but the President of Local 387 of the Chroniclers and Archivists Association had pointed out to me in her usual hectoring manner that the girl was extremely sensitive about her affliction and would inevitably develop an occupational psychosis leading to a general work stoppage.

The only solution which occurred to me, crude though it might be, was to have the forms reprinted on white paper throughout with the name of each department prominently displayed in the top lefthand corner, or possibly the bottom righthand corner, depending on the result of recognition tests which would have to be carried out by a sub-subcommittee of the Subcommittee of the Synergistic Functions Committee. Apart from the additional tardiness which this would cause, there was the unpleasant fact that the existing forms, of which, with a view to economy in printing runs, five years' supply had been prepared, would have to be, putting it bluntly, scrapped at, putting it equally bluntly, a dead loss of a tidy chunk of moolah. Not to mention the cost of having the file cabinets resprayed.

You will recognize, dear Dr. Ampiofratello, that my lapse into such unwonted informality indicates the tension of which I was the victim at the moment of Darrell's hoked-up entrance into my office. You will also recognize that I was in no mood to listen to any pleas, however dramatically framed, for increased appropriations for the, uh, technical people. When I said:

"Yes, Mr. Darrell, what is it?" he could not have been unaware that his reception was going to be frankly antagonistic. He ignored the hostile inflection of my voice, however, and said:

"I ask your pardon for interrupting your labors, sir, but might I make so bold as to ask you to grant an audience to a friend of mine?"

It is a constant source of surprise to me that Darrell has any friends. In fact, he has a great many of both sexes and from all walks of life. He seems to have a peculiarly magnetic effect on females. At an official reception I once found myself hemmed in a corner by an extremely attractive young person—I had meant to hem her in, but it worked out the other way around—who spent five solid minutes describing to me in the most syrupy colloquialisms the charm which she alleged vibrated from him. In spite of what must have been my obvious lack of enthusiasm she was still in full flow when Darrell himself vibrated into view and she left me, as the saying goes, flat.

I even dislike people who like Darrell. This very natural reaction puts a great strain on my ceaseless attempts to follow the injunction which is laid upon us to love our neighbors. Nearly all of my neighbors at work and elsewhere are already sufficiently hard to accept, let alone to love, without their making my task more difficult by being friends of Darrell. Since I suspected that the friend, or alleged friend, would turn out to be some mountebank whose aid he had enlisted in his quest for funds, I replied with increased frigidity:

"Mr. Darrell, I am exceptionally busy just now. I regret that I cannot interrupt my work for any, uh, social interlude."

Darrell's shoulders drooped and he turned towards the door, murmuring:

"No, sir. I quite understand, sir. I apologize for wasting your time, sir."

He shuffled a few steps further, turned around and added:

"It was simply, sir, that my friend wishes to make a trifling donation to the Institute. Only a hundred thousand dollars or so, but as you yourself have so often said, every little helps, and I did think—"

I was again shocked into a departure from my wonted dignity of exposition. I snapped:

"Oh, for godsake bring your friend in and quit assing about."

Darrell then ushered into my presence, continuing his servile masquerade, a woman. A huge woman, with an enormous and to me totally unattractive bust which one would imagine to be encased in some substance such as sheet plastic of exceptional thickness. Her torso was incomparably solid, and the massy columns of her legs and thighs, outlined by closely fitting jeans, supported it nobly, although I do not like the adjective in connection with Ms. Kalman. Her ill-groomed nylon wig, slightly askew, was the color of limed oak. She could have filed her nails on the carborundum-textured epidermis of her cheeks, and her face would have looked better if it had been concealed by a beard. Her first words to me, in a quelling voice, were:

" 'Ow are yer, ducky?"

Even after, a few minutes later, she had laid before me a check for a hundred thousand dollars I was still convinced that the episode was a hoax. However, after my secretary had discreetly telephoned the bank I was reassured that the check was genuine, and by the time the lady departed—her farewell words were: "Bye-bye, ducks. I'm sure you an' me's goin' ter be gryte friends"— I had, I flatter myself, managed to establish some kind of rapport, although up to that time persons remotely resembling Ms. Bettina Kalman had been, thank God, outside my, as it were, ken. Since Paul Darrell had been instrumental in bringing in this money I could think of no way of preventing him, or rather his department, from laying hands on at least some of it. In fact his commission, as I thought of it, amounted to as much as twenty-five thousand dollars.

I had by no means heard the last of Ms. Kalman. Not only was she possessed of major assets herself, but she evidently had a considerable circle of wealthy acquaintances. Through her agency, checks of very imposing dimensions, with equally imposing signatures, reached my desk from time to time. In due course it became apparent, to my horror, that she had a strong claim to be nominated to the Board of Trustees. Indeed, the suggestion was made by none other than the Senior Trustee, Mr. Lothair X. Haversham. I had no option but to send her an invitation, although I couched my letter in such terms as suggested that she had doubtless many other calls on her time and that it would be fully understood if she felt unable to add to her engagements. It was in vain. Not only did she accept, she accepted in person, crying:

"I fink it's eversernice of yer ter arsk me, I do reelly."

She followed this up by kissing me on both cheeks. I must confess to a certain weakness for dominant women, but I do ask that they have a certain *je ne sais quoi*. What the *quoi* was that Ms. Kalman had, *je ne sais*.

Such a forthright person would not perhaps be suspected of undue reticence or modesty as to provenance, but I found it extremely difficult to obtain from her the biographical details needed for the customary announcement in *Questionmark*. All I could establish was that she had been born in London—a fact self-evident as soon as she opened her mouth—and that she had married an American during World War II.

It was naturally with considerable misgivings that I ushered her into the Trustees' Conference Room on the occasion of the first meeting which she attended. Her outward appearance, even in these days when everyone seems to be outbidding everyone else in oddity, caused a noticeable hush. In fact Mr. Haversham, on whose initiative she was there at all, turned almost purple in the face and sat down with an ungallant abruptness which she could not fail to observe. For a moment I feared that she was about to come out with some characteristic remark, but in the flurry of introductions the incident passed off, and for some months her Trusteeship proved uneventful. Indeed I am bound to admit that on several occasions her native shrewdness proved invaluable and even elicited praise from other members of the Board.

Between her and Mr. Haversham, however, there remained a distinct constraint.

13

THE LAST character sketch which I shall attempt is of Mrs. Clarence Stahl. Now I would not articulate a single syllable in her disfavor. She was a very lovely person. That is to say, *inwardly* she was a very lovely person. That is to say, her gifts to The Dickstachel Research Institute totaled many hundreds of thousands of dollars. Many hundreds of thousands of dollars. What a beautiful phrase that is. But as a result of these donations she seemed to imagine that it was her right to be met at the revolving doors by myself and preferably at least two of her fellow Trustees, to be presented on each occasion with a bouquet of flowers, however unseasonable, and to have her photograph taken for inclusion in *Questionmark*, the house organ of The Dickstachel Research Institute every time.

She arrived in a small cane-sided Rolls-Royce which she had inherited from her grandmother. It was driven by a venerable Negro chauffeur beside whom sat an equally venerable Negro footman. As soon as the car stopped, the footman would leap rheumatically to the door, open it and without apparent enthusiasm receive into his care a small falsetto-voiced dog of a no longer fashionable breed. Holding this under one arm, and being lightly scolded if it yapped, with the other arm he would assist Mrs. Stahl to leave the car. Chauffeur and footman would then accompany her through the revolving door, transfer the dog to her care and the lady to ours, and retire to the sidewalk. In some ways I could not help admiring this semifeudal ritual; but it did seem to me that in view of the developments of recent years her faithful servitors might be wishing that the walls of their rut were lower.

These, then, were the people whom I had to convince of the

righteousness of my cause, the vital necessity of finding out what the Cosamo were really like, the even more vital necessity of prestigious new accommodation to house this double-meaningful project, and —perhaps the most sensitive area of all—that it merited sending the Scientific Director in person on an expedition which could take him away for perhaps a year or more from the mainstream of The Dickstachel Research Institute's activities.

I will confess that on the morning of what I might term the fateful meeting I breakfasted on only a cup of coffee and a tranquilizer instead of my usual ginseng, alfalfa or such, a slice of health bread and a glass of non-fat milk heated, with the aid of a candy thermometer, to exactly 120° Fahrenheit. As a general thing I disapprove of coffee. I am surprised that the harmful effects of its stimulant qualities are so generally ignored by an increasingly health-conscious public. However, I do keep a little by for medicinal use.

As the hour of eleven approached I approvingly checked my outward image in the full-length Louis Quinze mirror in its gilded frame which was affixed to the wall opposite my desk and took the elevator to the reception area, noting that for the third time someone had stolen the solid brass indicator plates from inside the car. I made a mental note to have these replaced with plastic and took up my position of welcome for Mrs. Stahl, whose arrival put the meeting off to a bad start before she even entered the Board Room. She was so eager to give me the bad news that she even omitted her usual high-level handshake.

"Oh, Dr. Tillevant, I'm so nervous, I nearly begged off the meeting. Poor little Donzel must be sickening for something. He wouldn't eat his brekkums, and when Cicero took him for walkies, *nothing happened.* But *nothing.*"

"Oh dear," I replied. It is a serviceable observation which has stood me in good stead on many occasions. I averted my eyes from little Donzel and gazed through the door with what I hoped was the right amount of sympathetic suffering. I happen to be an expert lipreader, and I noticed that at that moment Cicero, gray and dignified, was saying to his companion-in-arms:

"Fucking little bastard."

It was of course possible that they were discussing the shortcomings of some mutual acquaintance, but from the intensity with which they were gazing in little Donzel's direction it seemed much more probable that he was the subject of this comment, with which I heartily agreed. I was grateful to Cicero for saving me from thinking it, as I do not approve of words of this nature, but I made a note of them in case at any time I should require Cicero to do me a favor. Meanwhile Mrs. Stahl horrified me by saying:

"*Do* you think Mr. Darrell could have a look at him? He's so clever, I'm sure he could suggest something."

Quite apart from the fact that Mrs. Stahl was now trying to add free veterinary care to her list of fringe benefits, I could not imagine anything less apropos, on that morning of all mornings, than any meeting between Darrell and Mrs. Stahl. I knew that Darrell disliked Mrs. Stahl more than he disliked all the other Trustees put together, although Mrs. Stahl seemed to be drawn to him as a cat to its nip. I knew also that Darrell had again reached a crucial stage in his seminal experiments, and to suggest that he should drop what he was doing in order to treat a constipated Yorkshire terrier—I needed all my strength, wits and luck for my presentation. Because of this wretched woman I should have to dissipate them in either fending her off with someone lower in the hierarchy or risking a most unfortunate scene.

Up to a point, however, God appeared to be on my side, inasmuch as that very moment Darrell himself came in, apparently for the first time that morning and thus disgracefully late. However, to put it colloquially, that let me out for the time being. Mrs. Stahl swooped on him with a cry of delight, and in practically the same terms as before told him about little Donzel's excretory problems. She was in no wise deterred by the fact that Darrell was in the second day of imitating Charles Chaplin, complete with one-inch mustache, bowler hat, baggy pants, and all. She finished, in a coy undertone:

"I believe his voice is changing. Do you think that could have anything to do with it?"

To my amazement, Darrell listened with grave attention only marred by the twitching of his eyebrows and the flexing of his whangee as he leaned on it. In a moment he had taken little Donzel from his owner's arms and put him on the floor.

"Didn't eat any breakfast? Good God, I should think not. Poor little brute's disgracefully overweight. Exercise, that's what he needs. Come on Yorkshire, let's see you jump over that."

He held his cane a couple of inches from the ground in front of the animal. Mrs. Stahl's protest was shrill and instant.

"Oh *no*. His *heart*. His poor *heart*."

But little Donzel, overweight and all, had already joyfully leaped over the cane, turned around and jumped back, yapping like a roomful of New Year's noisemakers. Then he picked a fight with the end of the cane, chewing at it as if it was candy.

"See what I mean?" Darrell said. "Cut his rations in half and keep him jumping, not just parading on a lead."

"Oh, do you think so, Mr. Darrell? Do you really think so?"

"I don't think, I know. Worst thing you can do for any dog is keep it mooning around like a statue of Buddha. Hey, gimme back my stick, you little devil."

I felt it was time to reassert myself.

"Why, that's perfectly splendid. Thank you very much indeed, Darrell. I'm sure Mrs. Stahl is most grateful. Now, shall we—?"

My intention of course was that Darrell should, however belatedly, get on with his work while we proceeded to the Board Room, although I could not imagine how we could transact any business, let alone the important matter which I wished to broach, while little Donzel was in his present excited state. Feeding him my usual doped biscuit was obviously out of the question.

But Mrs. Stahl was not willing to let it go at that.

"Well, Mr. Darrell, I have great faith in you. If you say the poor little fellow must go on a diet, so it must be. But you must recommend, you know. Will you let me have your thoughts about his meals, with a calorie chart and everything?"

While all this had been going on the other Trustees had been arriving, catching sight of us and making smartly for the elevator to avoid becoming embroiled. It was now ten minutes past the advertised time of starting, and I could imagine them sitting around the table, doodling testily on their scrap pads and perhaps even speaking to each other under the influence of a common grievance. I said again, with increased heartiness:

"Why, Mrs. Stahl, I'm sure Mr. Darrell will be glad to do that. I'll have it sent to your apartment by messenger. Now we really mustn't keep everybody waiting any longer, must we? Come along now."

But Mrs. Stahl was not willing to let it go at that either.

"Mr. Darrell, *could* you spare the time to come up to the meeting and keep little Donzel amused? I would ask you to take him to your laboratory or whatever it is so that you could *observe* him, but he gets so dreadfully unhappy away from his mumsie, don't you, darling?"

Little Donzel was too busy inventing his own diet—the Kiwi off Darrell's clown boots—to reply, but Darrell, eyes glinting evilly, answered:

"Why, Mrs. Stahl, I'll be glad to do that. I'll have the diet sheet sent to your apartment by messenger. Now we really mustn't keep everybody waiting any longer, must we? Come along now."

I had an odd impression that I had recently heard almost those exact words. It was not until we had reached the third floor that I realized they were my own, and what was more, to all intents and purposes in my own voice.

It was of course strictly irregular, as Darrell well knew, for him to attend a Trustee meeting unless he was unanimously summoned, but Mrs. Stahl explained his presence at some length. The meeting then started, in an atmosphere of stupefaction, half an hour late.

Thus it was that I was forced to expound my cherished plan to the accompaniment of an almost ceaseless yapping and growling as little Donzel jumped repeatedly over the cane held by Darrell, retrieved a ball of paper thrown by Darrell and performed a thousand merry, mischievous tricks invented and instigated by Darrell. In desperation I proffered a doped biscuit. It was sternly forbidden by Darrell. Never was a proposition put forward in less favorable circumstances. By the time I had concluded my presentation I was hoarse, sweating and, I was sure, defeated. By Darrell.

What therefore was my amazement when a vote was taken and the Trustees declared themselves unanimously in favor. Five to nothing. Not even the Investigation into the Sexual Orientation of the Wild Etruscan Goat had done better than four to one.

It came to light in due course that two of the three male Trustees had been able to hear distinctly less than twenty-five percent of my remarks, and of that they understood only half but would have voted for anything in order to get out of the room. Mrs. Stahl was in such a euphoric mood that her agreement was automatic; Ms. Kalman seemed to be following some private and personal line of thought; and Mr. Haversham was subject to the John Ruskin syndrome, a marked recoiling from the sight and feel of pubic hair. He gave some hint of this by making it clear that his favorable vote was conditional upon the expedition bringing back with it several female Cosamo. Later on this proviso was to cause considerable trouble, but it may well be imagined that in my moment of triumph I was in no mood to quibble.

There was something of a stampede, as of elderly buffalo fleeing a Metroliner, after the vote had been taken. In no time I was alone with my aforesaid moment of triumph, Darrell, Mrs. Stahl and little Donzel. While I regarded this animal with no less revulsion than before, I was dimly beginning to understand the part it had played in my victory. I am a fair-minded man, and I could almost have found it in my heart to offer it an unspiked cookie. All thoughts of this nature quickly vanished when little Donzel copiously defecated on the recently installed wall-to-wall carpeting, which bore the insignia of The Dickstachel Research Institute specially woven into every square yard.

14

I HAVE mentioned in passing the Wild Etruscan Goat project. Since it affords another excellent example of Darrell's intuitive genius, and the repulsive way in which he manifested it, I will go into further detail.

Oddly enough, the Wild Etruscan Goat cannot be found in any standard reference work, but I have the most practical evidence of its existence. The project was stated by its sponsors to be of the highest ecological importance because these animals, perhaps through some contemporary change in air, water or soil, or by reason of the hostility with which they were regarded by the indigenous peasants, were in danger of extinction through the spread of homosexuality among both males and females. They now survived only in a single and diminishing herd of twenty-five.

The favorite food of the Wild Etruscan Goat was commercially grown flowers. It descended on the market gardens only at night, when the darkness, combined with its speed, agility and cunning, made it extremely difficult to shoot. The spreading of nets was equally unavailing, since the animals chewed their way out of such snares with contemptuous ease. Poison sprayed on the blooms they seemed to regard as a delicate sauce.

The Wild Etruscan Goat extended its malign activities to the only other important industry of the area, the tourist trade. As visitors approached their lair, which commanded a superb view all the way out to Corsica, a massed charge was made which not only dispersed the tourists but resulted in at least one major injury and resultant lawsuit. Even the most rascally package tour operator now declared the region off limits.

The only exception to the inexorable xenophobia which these animals displayed was the advent of students, individually or in parties. The tousled and tattered appearance which these wandering troubadours usually presented seemed to resonate in the bosom on the Wild Etruscan Goat, which ambled shyly up, bleating softly and rubbing itself against the nearest student with all the insinuating charm of a pampered kitten. The only damage known to result from these encounters was the loss of a mouthful or two of prefaded denim, hardly noticeable among the already prevailing dilapidation.

These coy demonstrations of affection led to many misunderstandings between the students and the older generation of peasantry. Already prone to regard this type of visitor with surly suspicion —why did a rich country like America export its tramps, from whom only a few thousand lire could be extorted—the more superstitious accounted for the empathy between students and goats to demonology and witchcraft. Recriminations in halting Italian and staggering English often reached the carabiniere-on-a-bicycle point.

Disagreement also arose between opposing bodies of students, some of whom defended the animals' title to self-extermination while others picketed the area with hastily adapted Right to Life signs.

The matter came to a head when it was proposed to build a new autostrada whose route would have driven straight through the rocky defile which the dwindling herd called home. The proposal was hailed with delight in Etruria, not only for the employment which it would provide but because it would mean the final extinction of those *dannati capri.* Here the students showed their mettle. They telephoned their parents collect. They wrote to their congressmen. They wrote to the Environmental Protection Agency. They contacted every conservation group which had ever sold inscribed T-shirts at unconscionably inflated prices. They further muddied the waters of certain multinational corporations involved with earth-moving equipment and other highway matters. They caused near-riots in the Little Italys of New York, Boston, and other gateway cities. Questions prompted under the rose (and thistle) from very high quarters indeed were asked in the British House of Commons.

In spite of the reasonable protests by the Etruscan Government about interference with its internal affairs, those students made such a nuisance of themselves that the autostrada came to a dusty halt only a few feet from the aforesaid rocky defile, into which the construction workers, protected by their armored machines, had barricaded the surviving goats, now reduced to a mere eighteen not merely by natural attrition but by sundry misguided onslaughts on the bulldozers in which naturally the attackers had come off worst and provided the workers with several tasty meals.

The barricades were removed and the autostrada rerouted, at a cost of several billion lire, in a rather tight and unexpected curve which subsequently caused the deaths of several carloads of people every week. The locals were thus deprived of the service station and restaurant from which they had expected a number of permanent jobs, and of course they were still afflicted with the goats, which the latest census showed to have increased to twenty-one thanks to the ill-timed fecundity of a couple of reactionary survivors.

The students were thus in worse odor than ever with the neighborhood residents (an unintentional pun, I assure you, dear Dr. Ampiofratello). But I say God bless them, sir, God bless them. For thanks to their efforts the Wild Etruscan Goat was now officially designated a threatened species. Its black, wet, whiskered muzzle and satanically colorless eyes appeared on postage stamps issued by two separate and distinct countries, and it was the subject of no less than forty-two learned papers in various languages. Sixty-three distinguished animal psychologists were commissioned, at fees very satisfactory to themselves, to investigate and report on ways to normalize the Wild Etruscan Goat.

The favorite theory was that the environment was at fault. The animals were removed, with considerable difficulty and danger, to a meadow of sweet grass and wild flowers, with specially built shelters against inclement weather, provided with drinking troughs filled with fresh mountain water piped in from a considerable distance. All this was supervised by a staff of attendants drawn from the more unemployable *ragazzi* of the district. The goats refused to eat, and at the first opportunity charged through an open gate, trampling several attendants, and made straight for their old home, pausing only for a hasty meal from a particularly fine crop of double chrysanthemums in their first, but as it proved by no means last, daylight raid.

Various other devices were tried, including the broadcasting of music by composers ranging from Purcell *(Dido and Aeneas)* to Handel *(Entry of the Queen of Sheba)*. This produced no result except that the locals hung around listening at a safe distance, thereby reducing their personal productivity still further. When exposed to punk rock, reggae and other forms of pop, the enraged animals charged and wrecked the loudspeakers, one particularly aggressive billy encumbering himself with a large section of Altec-Lansing which took him the best part of a week to dispose of.

Needless to say, I had been particularly distressed that none of the substantial funds involved had come the way of The Dickstachel Research Institute. I had been doing all I could to remedy this sad state of affairs; but when I was finally approached, through the medium of one of those transatlantic telephone calls where, owing to some, uh, technological malfunction, you hear your own words repeated in your ear after traveling some six thousand miles, while the remarks of the speaker at the other end are infuriatingly abbreviated, it was almost too late. The herd was down to a bare dozen, two of whom were reported to be looking distinctly unwell, although I cannot for the life of me understand how anyone could see any difference.

My caller was practically in tears, since failure in such a highly publicized project could only have the most detrimental effects on the availability of future funds. Such was her desperation that a highly gratifying fee was arranged after no more than sixty minutes' haggling at rather more than a dollar a minute, and an exchange of signed agreements was rapidly achieved, using the services of an air courier, paid for of course by the other party. From bitter experience, neither I nor my caller had any faith in the ability or even willingness of our respective dyslexia-and-lethargy-ridden post offices to effect delivery in any reasonable time, or even at all.

No sooner was this done than I sent for Paul Darrell. He came into my office dressed in elastic-sided boots, an Inverness cape of a somewhat reverberant check pattern, and a deerstalker cap of the same material, with the earflaps down. An enormous calabash pipe was clamped in his jaws, and he was making great play with a large magnifying glass through which, stooping, he examined the carpet until he reached my desk, when he stood up, looked at me through the lens, and ejaculated:

"The Giant Rat of Sumatra, I presume."

I was able to ignore this by virtue of the feeling of euphoria which pervaded me after the deep sniff of oxygen which I had had the forethought to inhale from the miniature cylinder which I always keep in my desk. I was about to speak when he held up one hand in a commanding manner, raised one of the earflaps and buttoned it on top of his cap, and ostentatiously turned the exposed ear towards me, saying:

"Pray give us the essential facts from the commencement, and I can afterward question you as to those details which seem to me to be most important."

He added in an explanatory manner:

" 'The Five Orange Pips.' "

I held on to the last of my oxygen and did as he requested as briefly and persuasively as I could. I even began, with assumed facetiousness:

"No, Paul, not a Giant Rat, but a Wild Goat. The Wild Etruscan Goat."

He stepped out of his role and ejaculated:

"There ain't no such thing as a Wild Etruscan Goat."

"I don't care what there ain't no such thing as," I replied, with more force than grammatical correctness. "Please listen."

I continued to expound. Darrell interrupted me only once, to say:

"I hear they scrapped the *Titanic,*" but when I had finished he shrieked:

"You want me to go to Italy to be pimp to a bunch of queer goats? Not bloody likely, cobber."

I put my arms akimbo and glared at him. He avoided my gaze and from a pocket in his Inverness produced a Turkish slipper filled with what I assume to have been shag tobacco, although, heh-heh, it smelt more like shag carpet. He crammed an enormous quantity of this vile substance into the calabash, used the lens and a sunbeam to light it, and blew out suffocating clouds. After a minute or two of this he grunted:

"You say they eat flowers. What's their favorite?"

"Uh—roses, I believe."

He grabbed my gold-cased felt-tip pen from my presentation set and, using the back of the uppermost document on my desk, scribbled for a few seconds. For a wonder, he restored my pen to its place. Then, tossing what he had written towards me, he turned to an imaginary companion and hissed:

"Quick, Watson, the game's afoot."

After that, thank God, he left, the noise of his loud-checked cloak dying behind him. While the air conditioning was dealing with his tobacco fumes I read what he had written:

> Spray the nannies' asses with attar of roses.

While I was recovering from the shock of this rude communication, I turned the document over and discovered that it was my card of admission to the annual meeting of the American Institute of Administrators, which would take place at the Waldorf-Astoria that very evening. It would of course be impossible for me to present it in that condition. At that moment I caught sight of my face in the Louis Quinze mirror. I must confess that my philosophical smile more nearly resembled a fiendish grin. I instructed my secretary to obtain a duplicate invitation which, as they were sent from New Hampshire, involved her in a lengthy and no doubt expensive telephone call to what sounded like a very cynical person in Concord, plus a further scurrying of air couriers.

Meanwhile I turned my attention to the rendering of this latest of Darrell's cryptic one-liners into sufficiently costly sounding English. Once again his incisive way of going to the heart—well, in this case scarcely the heart—of a problem had in all probability saved the day, but once again I had to deplore his lack of commercial sense. Nothing impressed a client so much as a display of prolonged thought, preferably by a specially assembled team or, in a matter of extreme urgency such as the present, two or even three specially assembled teams. Indeed, an even better gambit is to begin with a Feasibility Study, which is an excellent way of finding out, or not finding out, whether it is possible to do, or not to do, anything or nothing about practically everything. Our best achievement to date consisted of a series entitled Draft Report, Report, Minority Report, Revised Report, Revised Minority Report and, the minority members having been fired, Final Report. None of these was less than eight inches thick.

At one time I had hoped to beat this record, but in the present chaotic situation which that damnable man, that snake in the grass, that sneering, fleering—nurse, I am dreadfully thirsty. May I have a cup of tea? Why not? I don't want ice water. I want a cup of tea. This is ridiculous. I shall report it to Dr. Ampiofratello.

Where was I? Oh yes. With the aid of one of the more amenable, uh, technicians from the staff of The Dickstachel Research Institute I contrived to surround Darrell's crude laconic with a sufficient number of, uh, technical terms, distasteful-sounding as even some of these were, plus a number of euphemisms of my own invention, to make up a 532-word cable which was at once dispatched at full rate. So far as the detailed report was concerned, I eventually had to fall back on a device which, *in extremis,* I had occasionally employed before. This was what I had named our Standard Section. It consisted of 631 pages of facsimile typescript, consisting entirely of upper- and lower-case x's arranged in realistic-looking paragraphs.

The fact that no one had ever queried this perhaps slightly questionable device merely confirmed my somewhat melancholy suspicion that no one ever read our reports beyond the summary with which they began and the four pages of conclusions with which they finished. If any query had ever arisen, of course it could easily have been explained as a computer malfunction.

Apart from this, there is the question of the very socially oriented custom which at my instigation The Dickstachel Research Institute now follows. Every time The Dickstachel Research Institute issues a report, The Dickstachel Research Institute plants a tree in its Garden of Remembrance, located at the rear of the buildings. A plaque associating each tree with its particular report is affixed to the protective framework around the sturdy sapling. Envious detractors —and I am sure I need not specify *who* is among their number— have objected that these ornamental flowering trees cannot replace those cut down to make the paper for the reports; that in any case the number of reports is so great that in very short order the Garden of Remembrance will be a solid arboreal mass; and so on and so on. My reply to such nitpicking—there is really no other word for it— is "Toh." The idea is a very beautiful one, and has coaxed sizable donations from several of Mrs. Stahl's friends.

Darrell's recommendation was immediately put into effect, though not without considerable grumbling on the part of the underlings who were compelled to chase nanny goats hither and yon with aerosol cans of sweet-smelling liquid (the propellants were of course non-ozone-layer-degrading). The results from the conservationist viewpoint were most gratifying, notwithstanding that the local peasantry were reduced to paroxysms of impotent rage. The billies began to chase the nannies with pertinacious enthusiasm. Those nannies which continued to exhibit a preference for their own kind were soon compelled to abandon such pursuits by being rendered emphatically pregnant; and at the last census the herd numbered 632 and counting. The market gardens are up for sale as factory land; and a special appeal for funds has just been launched to provide the Wild Etruscan Goat with adequate supplies of its favorite diet, imported from great distances.

15

LATER ON, the Trustees were surprised to discover that they had voted a quarter of a million dollars towards the Cosamo project. They let it stand, however, partly because it would have been embarrassing for them to admit that they not known what they were doing and partly because by that time I had spent or committed a major part of the money.

A quarter of a million dollars was of course only seed money for a project of the magnificence which I planned for the Cosamo. The new building would run into millions, and then of course we should have to buy some kind of equipment. Already I was mentally calling it The Tillevant Building. I had always dreamed of having a building named for me. Somehow buildings are always named after the largest contributor. Why not? Why not, I ask, after the unsung individual who has begged, persuaded—I will not say lied, but certainly economized the truth—and generally demeaned himself in public and in private, before Foundation committees, before civil servants permanent and temporary, before eccentrics living in cooperative triplexes and tycoons dashing for the private 747's which will take them to their uncooperative Caribbean hideaways.

I imagined that I could see The Tillevant Building, more beautiful than an architect's drawing, soaring towards the clouds though not reaching them except on particularly low-lying days—I knew I should have to content myself with a modest twenty to thirty stories. Above all I could see the inscription over the entrance that would lead to the lavishly proportioned reception foyer, fitted with equally lavish accessories sturdily secured to the living concrete and defying all but the most skilled and determined neighborhood underprivileged. Deeply incised into the polished granite by the most skilled craftsman our great nation could provide, the gilded letters shone before my eyes, already dimmed with anticipatory pride: THE TILLEVANT BUILDING.

Ah, foolish, foolish dream.

But before I could fully concentrate on launching this, my greatest fund-raising enterprise to date, I had to make sure that Paul Darrell was not only willing to go to, but had actually left for, the Upper Amazon. It would not wreck the project if he turned down the assignment. There were at least two other quite senior people on the staff of The Dickstachel Research Institute who I was sure would leap at it, or at least could be prodded into it like reluctant tigers at a circus when the beautiful lady administers the electric shock from the rear of the cage outside which she is coyly lurking. But Darrell was so integral a part of my Master Plan that I could not bear the thought of his capricious refusal to participate.

Yet when, on the morning of the fateful vote, we turned back from restoring Mrs. Stahl to the care of her faithful servitors, I detected an all-too-familiar look in Darrell's eyes. I was sure that however vague the Trustees might have been as to the purport of the meeting, Darrell had absorbed and understood every word of my presentation, and was preparing to resist. I had already determined to use reverse English on him. I said as carelessly as possible:

"This may prove to be a great day for The Dickstachel Research Institute, Darrell."

He replied, with a vigor which drew an uninhibited giggle from a laboratory technician on her way to lunch:

"It will, in a pig's asshole."

I was sufficiently accustomed to his often unspeakably vulgar manner of expressing himself that this remark occasioned me no unusual distress. I merely continued:

"By the way, I should appreciate it if you would turn the matter over in your mind and let me know which member of your staff you consider best qualified to lead the expedition."

He stopped, removed his Chaplin mustache with a suddenness which made me wince, and looked at me with evidence of surprise.

"Oh sure," he said. "Anything like that. Any little thing at all."

He went off, tossing his mustache into an ashtray in a manner which, I felt, revealed inner uncertainty. I was not at all surprised when early next morning he marched smartly into my office wearing a solar topee, khaki shorts, an open-necked, short-sleeved shirt of the same color, long woolen stockings turned over below the knee and showing the tags of green silk garters, and chukka boots. In his right eye was a monocle. Over his shoulder was an enormous rifle, suitable, I imagine, for shooting elephant. This surprised me. So far as I am aware there are very few, if any, elephants in the Upper Amazon, or indeed anywhere in South America. It seemed that for once Darrell's enthusiasm had overridden his usually meticulous eye for detail.

He came to a military halt in front of my desk and addressed me as follows:

"Trip no further, pretty sweeting. I am the man for Operation Bareballs. Off we go into the wild rain forest yonder."

He then sang, to the tune of "Chicago":

"Cosamo, Cosamo, that wonderful tribe—"

No doubt he would have gone even further if I had not managed to check him by standing up with unprecedented abruptness and saying in an impressive baritone which I cannot always command:

"Mr. Darrell, this is absurd. I repeat, absurd."

At this he burst into a fit of laughter, bending over, stamping his feet and pointing his finger at me in really a very insulting way. I continued:

"Do you imagine for a moment that I could sanction the absence of the Scientific Director from The Dickstachel Research Institute for an unstated period? How can you possibly be spared from the Project for Determining the Role of Lefthandedness in Resistance to Botulism? Or the Inquiry into the Frequency of Agoraphobia in the Midwestern Corn Belt? Or the Effect of Foreign Yodelers on Domestic Milk Production? And for heaven's sake, *is that gun loaded?*"

Darrell replied cheerfully:

"Of course it's loaded. Would you want me to face the perils of Upper Broadway with an unloaded gun? Relax, Tilly, the safety catch is on."

But he laid it across a chair with the muzzle pointing away from me. We then spent some time in argument, during which I had great difficulty in hiding my amusement. I produced every reason I could think of why he should remain in the United States. The most cogent, of course, was the need to finalize his work on cattle semen. Here he gave me a distinct shock.

"Oh, that's all off, didn't you know?"

"*Off?*"

"Off. I was wondering how they were going to feed all those steers when they got them, so I called"—he named a very senior person at the Department of Agriculture. "He'd never even thought about it, nor hadn't nobody else up there neither. You'll be getting the stop-work order in a day or two."

I could hardly contain my indignation as this new instance of his total disregard for protocol. At any other time I should have let myself go in no uncertain manner; but I managed to control myself and keep the conversation on its original lines. Eventually I began ostensibly to yield.

"Nevertheless," I said, "if, against my better judgment, I agree to your going, I must make one condition. You will of course be perfectly free to choose anyone you like to act as your assistants, but I must insist that you include Laura Milton in the group."

"Lecherous Laura? You wouldn't do that to me?"

Here I must explain that the lady to whom he had so slightingly referred was a very highly qualified biologist and anthropologist whose work had always been on a more than competent level. However, her appearance was, as the saying goes, against her. She was short, bandy-legged—a fact which even her professional white coats did not hide—her hair was dry, her lips thin and her torso flat and straight as a Roman road. Unfortunately she possessed a sexual craving which in these circumstances must have been difficult for her to gratify. She was always seeking to arouse her male colleagues by rubbing against them—once she had even rubbed against *me*—and her visible annoyance when these advances met with no response really did not make for good working relationships. The idea of sending her on the Cosamo project was not mine, but had stemmed from an unofficial delegation of her fellow workers.

Darrell continued:

"Look at the way she moves, even. Either she's a virgin or she's been fucked so much she can hardly walk. And it's a thousand to one which is the right answer."

"Mr. Darrell, I am not making this recommendation in order to provide you with amatory solace on your travels. I am sure you are capable of attending to such details without any assistance from me. However dimly you may regard the prospect, the news of Miss Milton's accompanying you will meet with a most sympathetic reception from a large number of her co-workers. Do we understand each other?"

"Oh yes, we understand each other. Most of the time you and I resemble two partially deaf diplomats trying to communicate over a malfunctioning scrambler telephone, but right now—oh well."

But Darrell had a resilient psyche. He went away in the best of spirits, brandishing his gun in the air and calling to the imaginary leader of an imaginary train of bearers to follow him.

In the event, he was nearly prevented from going after all. Two or three minutes after he had left my office I heard a loud report, only partially muffled by distance. I rushed out of my office, evincing, I flatter myself, considerable courage, and followed the path which I assumed Darrell had taken. When I caught up with him in the lobby I found a good deal of pandemonium, only partially subdued to the discreet level which was due to the academic aura of The Dickstachel Research Institute. It appeared that Darrell had intercepted a theeing flief—I beg your pardon, a fleeing thief—who was making off with a quantity of narcotics which he had abstracted from one of the, uh, laboratories. Darrell had discharged his weapon with such dexterity that he had shot the booty from the miscreant's hand, thereby disintegrating it but doing no harm to the thief beyond a wrenched wrist. The incident had, however, broken the robber's nerve to such an extent that he had fallen to the ground, alternately weeping bitterly and cursing in the most unimaginative manner, using no word which one would not commonly hear at the cinema or other contemporary public entertainment. Darrell, leaning on his upended rifle, had one chukka-booted foot on the prostrate body in the classic manner of the big-game hunter and was beaming cheerfully around.

As it turned out, he had the necessary permit for the gun and, it was adjudged, had only minimally infringed on the thief's civil rights; but it was a near thing. It would have been a pretty kettle of shoes to have the Scientific Director of The Dickstachel Research Institute jailed in his own country.

16

I PERSONALLY saw Darrell and his motley crew off from John Fitzgerald Kennedy Airport. Thanks to the efforts of the Chief Public Relations Officer of The Dickstachel Research Institute, the departure was well attended by the media. It was an animated scene, worthily demonstrating the degree of sophistication, gracious behavior and smooth-running efficiency which this great country has attained, only two hundred years after the barbaric eighteenth century.

Flash units flared into everyone's eyes, microphones were thrust into recoiling faces. A miscellaneous horde of religious shakedown men, protected by the majestic authority of the Constitution, aggressively demanded contributions to their respective faiths and from time to time practiced the martial arts on reluctant donors in a manner worthy of Canon Smurge himself. From the sidelines, proponents of various secular causes adjured the milling throng to Stop This or That Now, to Free Him, Her or Them, to Clean Up, to Leave Be, to Ban, to Legalize, to Acknowledge, to Deny. Occasionally the public-address system burst forth all too audibly but with a very indifferent degree of intelligibility, interspersed with demonic howls when employees of two different airlines competed for its use.

By degrees those about to travel, bidding their loved ones perhaps a last farewell, seeped through Security and into the departure lounge, where they sat or sprawled on form-fitting chairs designed for people of quite a different shape, or prowled uneasily about, glancing at the blank TV screen on which confirmatory details of flight departures should have appeared, in the touching hope that it might eventually begin to function. Everyone cast sidelong glances at everyone else, suspecting terrorists who had slipped through the net.

A singularly beautiful woman stood in an attitude of graceful anxiety and scanned the check-in area. For a delayed traveling companion? A faithless lover? She had such lovely legs. Stately she was, yet wistful. I imagined myself walking up to her and saying:

"Madam, may I help you? Let me be your true knight, your Lancelot. Tell me whither you are bound, that I may purchase a ticket and accompany you. Together we will wander hand in hand—"

Of course it was sheer nonsense. I should never have the nerve even to offer to light a strange woman's cigarette. In any case at that moment a security guard came up to her and said with menacing courtesy:

"Madam, have you been processed?"

She shrugged angrily and went off to the torture chamber. Ah, what an age we live in when we can speak of such a lovely creature being processed like a packet of cheese. Because of this diversion I had not actually said goodbye to Darrell, and now he and his party had gone into limbo. In happier times I should have gone up to the observation deck to watch their takeoff. I like watching airplanes take off. Although I have not yet witnessed such an event, there is always the possibility that one will crash and burn. That morning it might have been the one in which Darrell, his seat belt no doubt sloppily fastened, was riding. But the observation deck was closed for security reasons. Ah again, what times we live in.

I walked slowly to the outer air, listening for the sound of disaster, watching for a column of black smoke. I paced up and down until half an hour, three-quarters, after the advertised hour of departure, by which time I felt that even the most congested runway would have sent Darrell en route. I listened to my car radio all the way back to The Dickstachel Research Institute, and to the radio in my office, every hour on the hour. The third bulletin contained news of a fatal crash, but it was not only the wrong plane but the wrong airline.

My eagerness for good bad news was unabated by the fact that on my desk was a lengthy and almost incomprehensible communication from Darrell. From the few words I could understand it seemed to be on the same subject that he had expounded to my wife when they were side by side on the loveseat. At the memory of that evening I ceased trying to make sense out of his jargon and gave the papers to my secretary to file. I must confess that my receptivity had not been increased by the small plastic box which had been sitting on top of them, containing a single but very fine specimen of the genus *Rubus,* or raspberry.

17

To DISPEL the effect of these irritations I closed for the nonce the door of my office, through which, thank heaven, Darrell might never again burst. Slowly surveying my domain, I prepared to enjoy the spiritual reinforcement which it was wont to bring me.

A while back, dear Dr. Ampiofratello, I promised to take you on a little tour of that pleasant place. This seems to be a good moment. Who knows if I shall ever see that majestic apartment again; and if I do, how sadly changed, but as I lie here, vainly endeavoring to reconcile the convexity of my spine with the opposed convexity of the mattress, I can still wrap its soothing influence around me like a placenta.

I begin with that most intimate matter, my desk. Its smooth and shining surfaces, its vast top inlaid with newborn calfskin dyed *eau de Nil;* its matched grains; its invisible joints; the hushed motion of its drawers; the solid, gleaming brass of its handles. This masterpiece of cabinetry was created for me by an ancient Scandinavian craftsman, last of a line which helped built the royal palaces of Europe. He died shortly after its completion. His hand retained its cunning to the end, but nature has broken the mold and in this power-saw age no one will ever be able to command a piece that could stand in the same room as this without cracking apart in very shame.

The chronographic clock on my desk displayed the day and date. It incorporated a stopwatch indicating in fifths of a second, an elapsed time recorder up to thirty minutes, and the exact time in no less than four different places on the earth's surface. Unfortunately this multiplicity of information makes it rather difficult to ascertain what time it is in my office.

I pass lightly over the more ordinary accessories: the desk pad framed in sterling silver; the Florentine dagger that serves me as a letter opener—time and again have I refrained from plunging it into Darrell's heart; the Charles I silver tankard which houses my pencils; and a few more oddments of the same nature. The plaque bearing my name, a hand-carved fragment from a seventeenth-century Connecticut barn, was a presentation from the members of my personal staff. I always felt that it struck a somewhat discordant note, but I would not for the world hurt the feelings of these excellent people.

There was the usual array of touchtone telephones, one of which was for outgoing calls only, with a special cable that was supposed to be tap-proof. And two tobacco pipes, which I felt lent a somewhat manly air, especially now that the craze for small jeweled pipes for women seems to have gone up in smoke. I had no tobacco for them, because in fact a pipe always makes me vomit; but occasionally I picked one or other of them up and blew through it.

Then of course there was an inlaid panel with some of those buttons which you do not actually push, but merely lay a fingertip to. Apart from the curtain controls, and the one which summoned my secretary, and the one which operated my remote-control weather station, showing inside and outside temperature, barometric pressure and wind speed and direction, none of these were actually connected. I was sure, however, that eventually I should think of something.

Inside my desk was the miniature oxygen outfit to which I have previously referred. It was intended for use in case of a heart attack, and was a gift from my wife. I must confess that when I received it I had some qualms lest it was charged with cyanide, but these were dispelled after I had laughingly offered a sniff to my secretary.

The mahogany chair in which I sit—alas, sat—was 180 years old, and of a solidity and amplitude unthinkable in this century. Originally built to accommodate the ample posteriors of some Dutch burgomaster, it accepted my lesser tonnage without a creak. The Metropolitan was after it, and in Boston and San Francisco the predators were alert; but I outwitted them. There was also a Chippendale armchair for special visitors plus two ordinary chairs for ordinary visitors.

The butcherblock unit behind me housed a small self-defrosting refrigerator and adequate implements and supplies for tendering hospitality to the visitor whose financial or political status merited such a tribute.

Along the wall to my right stood my Duncan Phyfe bookcase, acquired at the breakup of an old Southern estate. Its leaded-glass doors protected my working library—leatherbound texts on Administration and similarly clad copies of the most fameworthy Reports of The Dickstachel Research Institute. Next to it was an armoire of undoubted provenance which once belonged to the late J.P. Morgan. It housed—perhaps a shade incongruously—an exercise bicycle which would have been very handy if I had ever been too busy to leave my office for a workout.

You may wonder, dear Dr. Ampiofratello, how in these troubled times I managed to retain all these valuable objects for more than twenty-four hours. Quite simple. My office was cleaned under the personal supervision of our head Sanctuary Warden—a title I thought up myself to supersede the needlessly menacing Security Guard—and after that a fireproof, and, so far, burglarproof door was closed, sealing my domain from the outer world.

Let me see. Have I forgotten anything? My goodness, yes. My Mind Reader. I must say that if one must have, uh, scientists—and I suppose they are an unavoidable feature of present-day living—they could not have produced a more useful electronic device. It was only ten inches wide by seven and a half deep by four high. It had a keyboard and a screen for the display of messages. I could enter appointments, or things to do, and at the right moment it would beep at me and produce a visible reminder. It did, in many ways, what one would expect a good secretary to do, although it was not so attractive to look at either fullface or profile. It had, however, one major deficiency. It did not remind me to make the necessary entries in the first place. Consequently, when I asked it for information, as often as not it simply sat there and stared at me with a faintly contemptuous expression on its blank screen—again closely resembling a human secretary in similar conditions.

As a matter of fact there is a painful circumstance associated with this ingenious device. I was sitting at my desk one morning, establishing good relations with a senior official from the Department of Health, Education and Welfare, when my Mind Reader beeped at me. On glancing at the screen I was horrified to see the following words passing across it with maddening iteration:

TILLY IS SILLY TILLY IS SILLY TILLY IS

I was even more horrified to discover that my visitor, who I presume had not seen a Mind Reader before, was craning his neck in order to decipher the message. I was unable to discover any means of turning the wretched thing off, and was reduced to entering some nonsensical random instructions via the keyboard. This had the desired effect of causing the vile message to disappear, but it also elicited a distressing noise from the device, after which it ceased to function. I had it repaired, but frankly I was never thereafter able to raise the courage to press so much as a single key for fear of the consequences.

There is no doubt in my mind as to the originator of this fell mischance, but I could only prove it by endeavoring to obtain a personal admission through a frontal attack. Yet figure for yourself, dear Dr. Ampiofratello, the amount of nervous energy it would be necessary to raise before telling anyone—let alone Paul Darrell—that an inanimate device had delivered itself of so opprobrious a comment. I could imagine Darrell replying that the designers had builded better than they knew; and where would that have got me?

But if only my adrenals had served me better and I had tackled Darrell squarely, told him that this time he had gone too far, that as man to man I was not going to take any more of this sort of thing, that karate champion or no I would give him at least a bloody nose at the very next recurrence—might it not have prevented the far worse that was to come? Might it not forever have freed me of the persecution of that abominable, taunting, handsome—

Mind your own business, nurse. My eyes are *not* starting out of my head. Well, and if they are, wouldn't yours be? Have you no bowels, woman? No, I am not being obscene. Look up 1 John 3:17. Take that damned tranquilizer away. I won't swallow it. I'll spit it out. I'll—*ogllp.*

Oh. Oh. Oh.

18

I HAD of course impressed upon Darrell the vital necessity for prompt, regular progress reports. I had even told him that I would overlook the fact, which I ascribed to the pressure of his preparations for departure, that he was again seriously in arrears with his routine reports. I admit that all the time he was away, and right up to and even after the moment of his unfortunately safe return, his reports, if such they can be called, did arrive with some regularity. However, instead of being on official Dickstachel Research Institute paper, many of them were on extremely vulgar postcards of a type which I understand has been popular in England for the last three-quarters of a century. I do not know how Darrell managed to obtain them in Ventrivia unless, as seems likely, he had brought them with him. They are, I understand, known as seaside postcards. So far as I was concerned they could all have been buried in the depths of the ocean.

The first of these revolting documents to arrive was but a mild introduction to the excesses of the rest. It depicted a young man, stylishly dressed in the fashion of the twenties. He was standing in some kind of shop, speaking to a female clerk, whose young charms were depicted in a manner which I can best describe as exaggerated. The caption was:

HE: Do you keep stationery, Miss?
SHE: Well, sometimes I wriggle a little.

On the other side of this dubious missive Darrell had written:

REPORT #1. Oh-oh, Tilly, I saw you peeking, you dirty old man. Paul.

I think this epitomizes the whole nature of my struggle with Darrell. I had been, not unnaturally, beset by inquiries not only from the Trustees but from members of the, uh, scientific staff, among whom Darrell was for some extraordinary reason extremely popular, as to whether I had received news of the early stages of his travels. I was now able to reply that he had evidently arrived safely in South America. This was sufficient for the junior personnel, but the higher-ranking, uh, scientists and of course the Trustees were insistent in their demands to see the actual communication which I had received.

Judge of my feelings when, having come to the end of my powers of equivocation, I was compelled to produce this miserable rectangle of pasteboard. Not only did the majority of the Trustees break into laughter when they read the ribald dialog imprinted on one side of the card, they demanded an explanation of the circumstances which had led to Darrell's impertinent manuscript message on the other. Not for all the mineral wealth of the moon delivered freight paid would I have revealed the truth, that Darrell must have spied on my unproductive moment of platonic romance at the airport. I was, however, taken off the, so to speak, hook by Mrs. Stahl, who after studying the crudely drawn picture and its double-entendre caption for several minutes, looked up in a puzzled way and said:

"I don't know why everyone is laughing. I used to wriggle a little myself."

This produced an uncertain silence during which I was able to set the business of the meeting going again. At that point, however, my personal image was not such that I was playing from strength. This was doubly unfortunate because even at that early stage it was apparent that it was not the most auspicious time to launch a new building project.

Even commercial construction enterprises, as is well known, were in trouble. I need hardly mention the scores, nay hundreds, of ambitious new works which today strew every city in this fair country. They range from mere holes in the ground, into some of which the bulldozers are regurgitating their original contents, to partly finished, lopsided structures which make it seem that the construction industry has been engaged in producing instant ruins for the interest of future archaeologists.

When it was founded in the mid-twenties The Dickstachel Research Institute rejoiced in an endowment which for those times was ample. Subsequent legacies and other gifts over several decades had maintained and even improved this position; but in recent years the cormorant-greed of everyone from tenured professors down to the lowliest wastebin emptier, coupled of course with the evil demon of inflation resulting from the cormorant-greed of everyone else, had changed the situation completely.

In a laudable attempt to cope with these financial quicksands, the capital funds of The Dickstachel Research Institute, originally invested in the soundest of bonds, debentures and other debt securities, had been switched to equities in the form of the common stocks of a number of well-known and not so well-known companies. Of all these stocks it was asserted by our financial advisers, and proved by the weighty documentation of what they were pleased to term in-depth research, that their only way was up. When events again proved the truth of the old saying, "What goes up must come down," those financial advisers who were not too busy preparing their own legal defenses were as well provided as any crew of racetrack tipsters with plausible explanations and lists of unfavorable events which could not possibly have been foreseen.

My own income was affected, as there was a practical end to the commissions which I had been dividing with my cousin Susan—

Oh dear.

I really had not meant to bring that up.

Anyway, The Dickstachel Research Institute was of course not alone in its sufferings. The cold winds of failure had blown impartially, and not least strongly upon the sources whose enlightened benevolence had proved so sustaining. Private cornucopias were, if not shattered, so dented as materially to reduce their capacity. In these circumstances The Dickstachel Research Institute was not only heavily in debt but was forced to seek and depend increasingly upon Federal Funds.

I would never breathe a syllable against the seemingly inexhaustible geyser of riches—now rising higher, now for a few Republican years sinking lower—which Federal Funds represent; but it is a well-known fact that when one borrows from a relative one is liable to find one's whole lifestyle disagreeably changed by the dictates of that relative. One's friends, one's love affairs, if any, even such seemingly trivial details as the color of one's automobile, may become subject to the tastes of a person who, though linked to one by the closest family ties, differs from one at every point. Believe me, dear Dr. Ampiofratello, Uncle Sam is no exception. Almighty God must have a great deal of time on His hands now that Washington has taken over so many of His functions; and The Dickstachel Research Institute was bound to its wealthy relative by chains which, paper though they might be, even a professional tearer of telephone directories could not rend asunder.

The situation with regard to what I still fondly thought of as The Tillevant Building was by no means parlous, but it would certainly demand every ounce of ingenuity, energy and courage that I possessed. The Dickstachel Research Institute did not as yet even own the site upon which The Tillevant Building was to be erected. While one expects to do a certain amount of horsetrading in a negotiation of this kind, the price demanded by the owners of that site was wildly excessive, divorced from reality, living in a dream world. I cannot imagine what can have possessed my wife's lawyers—

Oh dear.

I really had not meant to bring that up either.

19

DEAR DR. Ampiofratello, I am so glad to see you. Perhaps you remember that at the very beginning of this oral history I mentioned the possible use of the erase button. Now I find that there is no erase button. There is a hole in the control panel where evidently an erase button once was, but that is all. I tried poking into the hole with my ballpoint, but all that happened was that I received a rather nasty electric shock. Yes, I know all about the dangers of interfering with electrical apparatus while it is plugged into the power line, but it would be a fine state of affairs if these tapes were stolen. Yes, but how do you *know* they won't be? Oh, I do wish you could stay longer.

It is not that I wish to protect my wife. It is that I see no point in providing additional ammunition which might be used against myself. I am in a bad enough state already. If the Trustees were to decide to kick me when I am down, and to denigrate the good name of The Dickstachel Research Institute, by bringing conflict-of-interest proceedings—they are not such innocents themselves, as Ms. Kalman made clear. Who are they to get holier-than-*me*? Is the Government itself that impeccable? We all know that governments classically try to exact a higher moral standard from their citizens than they are prepared to observe themselves—

Well, the, uh, the *hell* with it. I said that I tell all, and surely to God nobody would admit as evidence the ravings of a man immured for nervous exhaustion without possibility of escape until his bill is paid. Yes, yes, I shall tell all, but I am not upon my oath, am I? If I am pressed too far I shall *deny* all, or anyway such parts as come within the Fifth Amendment and *are* deniable, because of course a good deal of my story is undeniable, particularly the present condition, God help me, of The Tillevant Building and in fact of the entire Dickstachel Research Institute. A good deal of what happened cannot be denied, it happened in front of too many people, millions and millions of people all staring and gloating over the way in which I was being publicly humiliated, humiliated I tell you—

That damned nurse has just been in again, showing me her pale gums, telling me to keep my voice down, that I am upsetting other patients. I don't care about other patients. I am the only patient that matters in the entire Vellutomano Center for the Nervously Exhausted, and if she wants me to keep my voice down she should bring me a tranquilizer. Why in God's name it should be necessary for her to fill in seventeen pieces of paper before she can be issued with and administer to me a horrid little gelatine sausage filled with what look like cake decorations—and as for getting a cup of tea—and I am so thirsty, so damnably thirsty nearly the whole time. The whole trouble with this country is that there is too much paperwork and not enough practical work done.

Well, well, well. *Two* tranquilizers. This must be a feast day in the psychiatric calendar. Perhaps it is Krafft-Ebing's birthday. Happy birthday, dear Krafft-Ebing—

I was about to relate, in a calm and orderly manner, the facts pertaining to the site for The Tillevant Building. It so happens that my wife is a member of a very old family. No, they did not come over in the *Mayflower,* they came over in a ship called the *Hans van Sluyt,* which got here several years earlier; and they managed to acquire, and what is more hold on to in spite of the British, a sizable piece of Manhattan. They made themselves a good deal of money out of it before a later generation had to sell most of it to pay death duties and property taxes and gambling debts and alimony. There is only a small piece left of it now, but it produces what would be a very comfortable income if it was not divided among seventeen inheritors.

The odd thing is that about half an acre of this land had never been built on. This is hard to believe on such an overbuilt island, but it is the sort of thing that happens everywhere. The buildings come right up to each side and then for some unfathomable reason the gap is never filled. Perhaps the fact that this particular half acre had two huge pieces of rock sticking out of it, each about the size of a ranch house, had something to do with it. I suppose that in earlier times the prospect of blasting them out of the way was too daunting, and then after the area was built up it was too dangerous. Anyway, it so happened that the boundary of this precious but unwieldy half acre was next the boundary of The Dickstachel Research Institute, and it was the obvious place for any extension of The Dickstachel Research Institute. There was no other empty land contiguous, and it would have meant buying existing buildings at an enormous price and knocking them down and getting involved in accusations about the community and, oh goodness, you know how it goes.

Now this whole thing was one enormous coincidence. You could never get away with inventing such a chain of circumstances. But there was the site, and my wife, the former Hedda Huygens, owned one-seventeenth of it. I had been married to her long before I was associated with The Dickstachel Research Institute, and to suggest that I exerted all that effort, and used up so many contacts, to be made Administrator of The Dickstachel Research Institute merely to create an opportunity for, uh, unloading that wretched half acre onto The Dickstachel Research Institute is blatantly absurd. In that whole matter I was as innocent as an unborn baby. More innocent, for all I know.

I never exerted any pressure on the Trustees to buy that land. I merely pointed out to them the certain expenses and uncertain sociological consequences of trying to expand on any other side of our existing site, and when Mr. Haversham suggested moving the entire Dickstachel Research Institute to Connecticut, where there were some good golf courses, and Mrs. Stahl said she thought that was a lovely idea, it would give little Donzel better air and green grass, why, I merely reminded them that the possible battles with the Environmental Protection Agency, the Defense Department, the Nuclear Regulatory Commission, the Friends of Connecticut and heavens knows what else, might take us into the twenty-first century before the first sod could be turned.

I was thereupon duly authorized to enter into negotiations with Compass Properties, the conveniently faceless corporate title under which the Huygens estate functioned.

But alas, I had reckoned without human greed. My wife was, up to the moment of her walking out on me, sometimes quite a reasonable woman. She would have been perfectly happy to let her one-seventeenth of the half acre go for the normal figure for real estate in that area. As she put it, once she could get her hands on the cash she knew how to double or treble it, even in these hard times; and I would not doubt it. The other sixteen heritors, however, had very different ideas. Among them they conducted a kind of auction which was, if you will pardon the pun, by no means Dutch. Their final asking price, especially in view of the fact that for three hundred years that wretched little bit of land on which they had been paying taxes, mark you, had not returned anyone a single cent, red, yellow or left-out-in-the-rain, was inflated enough to float a Goodyear blimp. Moreover, they had come together for this purpose within a week of my first approach to Compass Properties—and imagine the meeting, as my wife described it. Seventeen members of a family, each with a separate lawyer, all in the same room. Well, as I said, they came together quickly enough for that, but when it became a question of negotiating they were here, there and somewhere else as well.

My philosophical smile wore thin under the stress of it all. It was a sore trial of my sense of duty—and I have a strong sense of that old-fashioned virtue, once I can see *where my duty lies*. But in this case it seemed to lie in several directions. It was my duty to The Dickstachel Research Institute to haggle the price down as much as possible. It was my duty to my wife to see that this perhaps unique chance of disposing of this unprofitable part of her inheritance was not rudely snatched from her. It was my duty to myself—and you will note that I put that last—not to lose the chance of forty-year immortality that my name on The Tillevant Building would bring me.

Was it my duty to advise the Trustees of the purely coincidental link between my wife and Compass Properties? I did not see that at all. My wife's private affairs are her private affairs, and in these days of sex equality I had no right to go blabbing them to the world at large. That at least was how I felt at the time. I have since modified my views, now that she has left me and obviously has no intention of handing over to me as hard-earned commission any part of her receipts from the sale of the land.

I need not, dear Dr. Ampiofratello, enter into the wearisome detail of how I resolved this conflict. I am not a stormer of barricades, but I think I am fairly good at wriggling underneath them. I readily admit that my wife's knowledge of the, uh, foibles of certain members of her family was of considerable assistance in bringing them to, so to speak, heel. Nevertheless, at the conclusion of this part of the enterprise my nervous and physical condition was such that I was driven to investigate the relative merits of hair implants and custom-made hairpieces, as wigs are delicately called these days. The amount of publicity attending the one, and the too-sudden transformation of appearance effected by the other, not to speak of the horrifying cost of both, gave me pause. I countered the badinage which I increasingly encountered with the old saw about no grass growing on a busy street, although to be sure this was ineffective against the harsh cries of "Baldie" with which high school students in their roving bands greeted me.

I believe the prophet Elisha had much the same trouble, although he was able to solve the problem with the help of she-bears, from which the streets of New York are, literally though not metaphorically, at the moment free.

20

WHILE I was in the midst of these distracting occupations I received another degrading postcard from Darrell. One side depicted the rear end of an undernourished donkey, above which arose, like two transatlantic balloons, the overinflated posteriors of a huge female clad in an equally huge halter-and-briefs in broad and vividly colored stripes. The caption of this loathsome composition was:

BOTTOMS UP

On the "message" side Darrell had written:

PROJECT BAREBALLS
REPORT #2
ADVANCING TOWARDS JUNGLE.   BOOMA-DIDDY-BOOM-BOOM
BOOMA-DIDDY-BOOM-BOOM

I locked this abominable epistle in my desk with the first one. Perhaps—*perhaps*—before the next meeting of the Trustees Darrell would have seen fit to transmit something more seemly. In fact, his next communication arrived the following day. It was extremely disconcerting. A cable, collect.

COSAMO TRIBE PROTECTED BY GOVERNMENT STOP MAJOR PENALTIES FOR CONTACTING THEM WITHOUT OFFICIAL PERMIT STOP OUR ENTIRE PARTY IN JAIL STOP FOOD LOUSY SO ARE WE STOP GET US OUT OF HERE REPEAT GET US OUT OF HERE STOP NO

CANCEL THAT AND AIR EXPRESS THREE THOUSAND EIGHT BY ELEVEN GLOSSIES FARRAH FAWCETT-MAJORS AND ELLEN BURSTYN STOP MY GOD TILLEVANT HOW I HATE YOU STOP DARRELL TOWN JAIL CUCLONA

Nothing could have given me greater pleasure than the thought of Darrell spending the rest of his life in the cramped confines of a primitive jail somewhere on the fringes of the Upper Amazon, eating prison stew and scratching himself. However, I could hardly ignore his request, particularly as he had several valuable members of the staff of The Dickstachel Research Institute with him. I was convinced that his request for photographs was a hoax, but in view of his peculiar methods I arranged for their dispatch, keeping one copy of each in my desk as a matter of record. The bill for air express was frightening.

I was not unduly concerned about the delay in the expedition's onward thrust. I had assumed that it would be away for about a year. This was little enough time to get The Tillevant Building sufficiently far advanced for a formal opening ceremony to be synchronized with the return of the, uh, scientific personnel. An extra breathing space would be welcome.

I confess to being surprised that no word of the expedition's incarceration had appeared in the media. Daily I expected a persecution of reporters. At one time, of course, the mere fact of one American citizen languishing in a foreign jail, let alone eleven in a group, would have been sufficient occasion for banner headlines and frequent interruption of electronic entertainment, accompanied by demands for the Marines to land and other patriotic phenomena such as in these enlightened times we are content to leave to younger nations.

However, a couple of weeks later—it was the very day that the papers were signed which transferred the site of The Tillevant Building from Compass Properties to The Dickstachel Research Institute —I received another of Darrell's reprehensible postcards. Compared with the first two, the visual aspect of this one was relatively innocuous. It merely depicted two persons of, needless to say, vulgar aspect, in the throes of verbal combat. The caption was:

To point up the personal application of this insult Darrell had signed it in full, although he had merely initialed the other side, which read:

> PROJECT BAREBALLS
> REPORT #3
> WO-HO, DEM LOCAL FAUNA
> OH, DEM LOCAL FAUNA
> LOCAL FAUNA EBERY NIGHT
> IN OUR ARMS WE HOLD DEM TIGHT—
> LAWDYLAWDYLAWDY

From this I assumed that Darrell and his party had not only been released from jail but had reached their objective. Reading between the lines—and what lines—I also assumed that the hospitable habits of the Cosamo had not changed since Nugent-Nugent's time. However, I really had not maneuvered Darrell out there merely for him to enjoy himself, and from an, uh, scientific point of view this communication was as lacking in hard facts as those which had preceded it. I blenched at the thought of having to produce it for the inspection of the Trustees, whose next meeting was beginning to loom.

However, two days before that meeting I received something approximating to a full report. In fact, it was simply a number of single-spaced pages, somewhat yellowed by damp and inaccurately typed on both sides. As every person knows if they have received more than a rudimentary education, a report should begin with a summary of a page and a half or less, proceed to the main factual account properly divided into sections or chapters, with the appropriate charts or tables, and finish with a section headed CONCLUSIONS, again certainly not more than a page and a half and preferably considerably less. Footnotes, typed on separate pages and labeled by chapter, should be placed all together at the end of the manuscript. They should be numbered consecutively. It would be impossible, in these sophisticated days, to obtain even a bachelor's degree, no matter how high a level of scholarship the work might reveal, without following these classic rules of format.

Judge for yourself, dear Dr. Ampiofratello, to what extent the following transcription meets these simple desiderata.

21

KIND FRIENDS and Gentle Hearts:

Well folks, we finally made it. Here we are in that part of the primeval rain forest, as yet unthreatened by the Trans-Amazon Highway, where dwell the happy, laughing Cosamo. Hospitable, too. I don't know if any of us can take much more of that. A big bowl of Whammo to start the day does not help to preserve the calm, detached scientific mind, especially when repeated every two hours till it's time for bedsie-byes. Min*ju*, that first bowl does help replenish the wear and tear nearly all of us feel after a spell on the palliasse, because believe you me, with the relays of charmers the Cosamo provide, just as in Reverend Nugent-Nugent's day, it's all bedsie and very little bye. Whoof.

When I say nearly all of us I do of course have reference to Laura Milton, who has been raising hell because she is not receiving reciprocal facilities. She says it is blatant discrimination, and when she gets home she is going to raise the matter with the Equal Employment Opportunity Commission. When she complained to me after the first night I did my best to help her. I told the Chief. His name is Enrico O'Toole, but mostly I call him Harry. These people still laugh at anything and everything, but he nearly bust his bellybutton over Laura's problem. He's a nice guy, though, and he did his best to help. Next night he sent along a couple of hand picked studs. They'd both seen Laura beforehand, and neither of them wanted the job, but in this tribe you do what Harry says or Harry will stop your Whammo. Next morning I heard a helluva lot of shouting, poked my nose out of my hut and there were Harry and the two studs going at it like a Congressional investigation just before the Chairman resigns. I asked our interpreter what it was all about. He said:

"Chief get mad because they no jigajig American lady."

"Whose fault was that?"

"They say her fault."

"Can't be. She was waiting for them with open legs."

"They say no can jigajig nothing less they get it up first. She got nothing to get anything up."

The tumult and the shouting rose again.

"Now what?"

"They say American lady shame their manhood. Make them feel like their balls cut off. Chief say he good mind cut them off for real, they causing international incident."

"He wouldn't really do that, would he?"

"He Chief. Chief can do anything he wants."

It didn't seem fair to the studs. I know better than to interfere with tribal politics, but I was wondering whether I couldn't show up as a kind of *amicus testiculae*. Just then, though, the two studs saluted—arms crossed on shoulders—turned around and made for a fairly important-looking hut at the end of the village. The interpreter told me:

"Chief order them spend day in temple of Alorra. Make, what you call, penance."

"No cut?"

"No cut."

That night, see this wet, see this dry, the same thing happened with a second pair of studs. And a third, night after that. So I told Harry I owed him an apology, that there were some things too far above and too far beyond, and would he please forget the whole thing. The six studs were issued with double rations of Whammo and girls (four apiece) that night. Next time I saw them they looked tired but happy.

I have gone into this episode at some length because it constitutes our first scientific findings about the Cosamo. With all this weeping and wailing about male impotence in the States, I do think it is perhaps significant that alone and unaided one American girl can reduce to total inactivity six count them six uninhibited males living in a state of nature and accustomed to a plentiful and varied menu. I believe Laura is now considering writing a minority report protesting the way the Cosamo debase their womenfolk. I must say the womenfolk don't seem to mind it very much.

We now come to the first official purpose of our no-doubt-long-to-be-famous expedition. Do the Cosamo have pubic hair? No, Tilly and ladies and gentlemen, they do not. Does that set your prurient little minds at rest? Saint-Victor, of whom you have doubtless never heard, said of the depilation of Oriental women that "it must look like a parish priest's chin." I have at the moment no opportunity of putting the two things to an A/B test, but he may well have been right, so if you want some kind of preview I suggest you hunt up the nearest parish priest.

After this little episode I have to firm up my friendship with Harry before I can start taking blood samples and all the other absurd misapplications of scientific routines which my brief instructs me to carry out. That is, if I can get any of the Cosamo to stop laughing long enough to have needles jabbed into them and so on. One of the hardest jobs is going to be getting specimens of their urine and feces, as they regard these as an extension of themselves which along with hair, nails, photographs and voice recordings, could be used as evidence against them by witches, wizards, earth spirits and anthropologists. Consequently each buries their own in what they hope are secret places. Hygienically more effective than a good deal of Western sanitation, though paranoiac.

Our *mestizo* interpreter explained all this. I was intrigued by the reference to photographs and recordings and asked him how, in their isolated and protected state, they knew about these things.

"Three, ten year behind, people come from São Paulo with all these stinks."

I remembered nothing about any party exploring this region, and there certainly had been no published findings.

"What happened to them?"

He gave me a dirty grin.

"They go mountains."

I remembered, Tilly, that this same question and answer, in these same words, occurs in one of Reverend Nugent-Nugent's letters—those wonderful letters that make you think of the kind of voice that is washing its hands the whole time. Sinister, huh? I assure you I no go mountains. Evidently there is a Secret of the Mountains. Far zime concerned it can stay that way.

You may possibly get the idea, Tilly and ladies and gemmen, that I am not according to this expedition the reverence, the hushed awe, the genuflecting tippy-toes which such a lavish expenditure of funds demands. You're damned right. I can think of at least seven things I'd rather see the money spent on. I was sent out here for bad and insufficient reasons. I regard the ostensible purpose of the exercise as just one more of those moronic ways of creating an impression of useful activity to which we as a nation seem to be peculiarly prone. I came here partly because it seemed a good way of escaping the Institute for what in effect is a year's sabbatical without counting as such, so that I am still entitled to a year's sabbatical, and don't none of you folks fergit it.

But the real reason I came was that I wanted to find out more about this habit the Cosamo have of laughing practically the whole time. It sounded pretty menacing to me. Simple, happy tribes—if they haven't all been massacred by their new overlords—they're one thing. But nonstop cachinnation is something else. I'm not going to start one of those tedious analyses of the risible aspects of the banana peel, though I'm sure it would be easy to raise half a million bucks or so for EEG's of a handpicked panel of subjects being put through a vacuum-packed series of homologized tee-hee provokers. You gotta believe, people who can't stop laughing are either retarded or they're on to something. I believe the Cosamo are on to something, and I have a rotten idea what it is.

I need to put together a lot more data; for example, I want to get into their temple and take a good look at their god Alorra. I want to get down to cases with Harry and a number of his people. I want to tell them a little—just a little—I'm not sure how much they can take, about our Advanced Civilization, to get their reactions. I don't expect any of you people are bright enough to guess what I'm getting at, but when I've filled in some of the cross-hatching I will try to explain in words simple enough not to overdistend your limited understandings.

Meanwhile I will give you one clue. Have you ever—not you, Mrs. Stahl, nor you, Bessie, but the rest of you—have you ever tried fucking a girl who's laughing so much the whole time you can hardly give her a wet kiss, let alone find your way in?

Well, Tilly, you were always moaning because I didn't send in my reports. I hope you like this one, and I give you my word there are more to come, such as I DARE you to publish.

22

I LEAVE you, dear Dr. Ampiofratello, to imagine my feelings as I perused this—this *depraved* effusion. I simply cannot describe them, although I must confess to being intrigued by what Darrell had to say about f—, uh, cohabiting with a girl who was laughing the whole time. At such moments my wife was usually seized with an uncontrollable fit of *yawning*. But how could I find the courage to submit to the Trustees a document which contained such outrageous insults, not only to me, I was too numbed by previous instances of those, but to them. I should be in the position of the classical Greek messenger bearing bad news.

Then it occurred to me in a blinding flash that Darrell—drunk, no doubt, not only on Whammo but on the illusory security afforded by a distance of several thousand miles and the, uh, womblike conditions of the rain forest—Darrell had delivered himself into my hands. Even if he ultimately returned—and it was being borne in on me that my prayers were not going to be answered, and that he would ultimately return—but even if he did surely the Trustees, after reading this quote report unquote, and presumably at least one other in the same vein—where was I? Oh yes.

Although Darrell was and is a living argument against freedom of speech, the Trustees must at last realize the sort of man they had so often adjured me to humor. Eccentric genius or no eccentric genius, watertight contract or no watertight contract, this must be the end of any association between Paul Darrell, with his solitary, puny M.A. degree, and The Dickstachel Research Institute. If any other faculty should be misguided enough to offer him a post for the sake of any remnants of aura which might still surround his name, the consequences would be on their own heads. I at least should be free of any further dealings with him.

As for his replacement, well, I believed that, to adapt the old proverb, there were as good geniuses in the files of the personnel agencies as ever came out of them. If I could sway the Trustees to that point of view, surely a brighter future lay ahead.

Sure enough, Darrell's maniacal insults to that worthy body sank deep.

"Prurient little minds?" Mr. Haversham repeated. He glared at Mr. Krebs as if holding him responsible for the epithet.

"I don't object so much to prurient," Mr. Krebs replied. "Frankly, I think everyone's mind is more or less prurient. But no one can call my mind little and get away with it."

Mrs. Stahl, however, did not seem to understand that she had been insulted.

"I'm sure I've never pretended to be clever," she said. "And I don't know what prurient means."

No one volunteered to tell her.

"Besides," Mrs. Stahl said, "I expect things look a good deal different in the jungle. I'm sure I've read about people going crazy there. It's the loneliness, and the lack of home cooking. Mr. Darrell has always been most helpful to me. Look at the way he cured little Donzel's constipation."

We all glanced at the still-visible patch on the carpet where Darrell had achieved this major, uh, scientific triumph.

Finally it was decided not to recall Darrell forthwith by an angry cable which Mr. Haversham three times started to draft and then handed to me to be shredded. Instead, Darrell was to be allowed to complete his mission and after his results had been duly evaluated he would be given the alternatives of resigning or submitting to a psychiatric examination. I was pleased at this outcome. How could I have foreseen that in the course of time it would be me, and not Darrell, whom the unconquerable tides of Fate would bring to a private room in the Vellutomano Center for the Nervously Exhausted?

We then proceeded to the main item on the agenda. This was the appointment of the architects who would be entrusted with the design and construction of The Tillevant Building—although at this stage the as yet visionary edifice was still known as Project X. I noticed that the Trustees—with the twittering exception of Mrs. Stahl and the strangely contemplative exception of Ms. Kalman—were looking on each other with a strangely bellicose aspect, and also that each had a roll of paper, or even two rolls, on the table in front of him. It soon developed that these were architects' drawings of five separate and distinct proposals for the elevation of The Tillevant Building, and that each Trustee was prepared to defend his particular proposal or proposals, and his particular architect, with a pertinacity that soon reduced the proceedings to an extremely low level of debate.

The architectural styles varied greatly, from Victorian Gothic and Beaux Arts Eclectic to what I can only describe as Junkyard Vanderbilt. One I mentally christened Desperation Contemporary, and the fifth bore a marked resemblance to the Colonial Period of the Great Atlantic and Pacific Tea Company. On not one of them would I have cared to see my name engraved.

I also noticed that when the Trustees were not occupied in glaring at each other like rival contenders for a seat on the subway, they were looking down their noses in the surreptitious manner of a person who suspects that some noxious insect may be crawling about his or her chest. The reason for this peculiar conduct became clear when Ms. Kalman boomed forth:

"This joint's bugged."

Mr. Haversham, who was at that moment eloquently holding forth in defense of his candidate (the A & P) faltered, stopped and said:

"Huh? Nonsense," in a singularly unconvincing manner. Ms.

Kalman opened her hand and disclosed a small black plastic object in the center of which a tiny red light was glowing.

"Don't siy nonsense ter me. That there's a bug detector, that is, and when that there light comes on someone in the room's wearing a transmitter."

At the same moment the other male Trustees opened their hands and disclosed similar small objects, each with its ruby telltale lit. Mr. Haversham made a hasty gesture towards his coat pocket, then stopped.

"Caught yer, 'ave I? Come ahn nah, 'Aversham, aht wiv it."

Mr. Haversham blustered somewhat, but he gave in when Ms. Kalman strode around the table and threatened to subject him to a physical search. With a vicious gesture he withdrew from his coat pocket yet another small object which even to my lay eyes was obviously some kind of recording or broadcasting device. He laid this on the table and regarded it with much the expression of a jockey whose heavily backed horse has run out and is cantering home under the disapproving gaze and loud opprobrium of the crowd.

Ms. Kalman looked from this device to Mr. Haversham, and from Mr. Haversham to the partially unrolled drawing whose virtues he had been extolling.

"'Ow much was they goin' ter kick back ter yer if yer'd put it over?"

Silence.

For the first time Ms. Kalman seemed to see the other telltales.

"Mistrustful lot of perishers, ain't we? And wiv good cause, seemin'ly."

Abstractedly she tore Mr. Haversham's plan into several pieces and dropped them to the floor.

"Nah, 'ad someone blown the gaff on 'Aversham or was you all suspicious of each uvver? I tell yer strite, I on'y brought me own little bug detector ter play wiv. When it lit up, yer could've knocked me dahn wiv a fevver."

This was scarcely true. It would be extremely difficult to knock Ms. Kalman down with anything short of a Mack truck. To my alarm, she now turned towards me.

"'Ere," she said. "'Ere. I got a proposition to lay before this flippin' meetin'. I vote we all turns aht our pockets. Mrs. Stahl an' me's the only ones what didn't bring no drorings, but we'll set a good example. You're wiv me on this, aincha, Mrs. Stahl, ducky?"

With considerable effort she unbuttoned the pockets of her denim safari jacket and pulled out the linings till they hung pendulous on her by no means pendulous bosom. They were empty. So were her pants pockets. So tightly was she appareled that there was certainly no part of her anatomy where she could have concealed even the most miniaturized bugging device without a revealing bulge. Well, there were two, but decency forbade my even suspecting them. She emptied her Gucci purse on the table.

"I'm clean. Nah then, Mrs. Stahl, all girls tergevver, eh, ducks?"

In a bemused way Mrs. Stahl emptied her own purse. It contained only a lace-edged handkerchief, a door key, a lipstick and a rather tattered dog biscuit. Ms. Kalman removed the top from the lipstick case, satisfied herself that it contained nothing but lipstick, briefly considered Mrs. Stahl's meager torso and bewildered face, gave her an encouraging nod and again looked at me. But I, conscious of my innocence, was already emptying my pockets, an inventory of which I am sure would not interest you, dear Dr. Ampiofratello. The fact is that with my usual maladroitness in matters, uh, technical, I had omitted, when testing the transmitter which Messrs. Bocks and Glasse, the well-known architects, had lent me I had omitted to turn it off. At the crucial moment, therefore, I had discovered that the batteries were completely discharged and had left what would have proved to be incriminating evidence safely concealed in my desk. While Mr. Bocks was considerably disconcerted when the expected transmission failed to come through, he agreed with me when I spoke to him that afternoon—we were in the open spaces of Van Cortlandt Park, with not a parabolic microphone in view, although one of the Shetland ponies grazing there seemed to me to have a suspicious appearance—he agreed that with people like Ms. Kalman about the mischance was all for the best.

Since there are no mirrors in the Trustees' conference room, I could not of course see the look of conscious rectitude on my face. But I knew it was there. It is something I rehearse every morning after shaving. Ms. Kalman's slight movement of revulsion led me to hope that I was not overdoing it, but fortunately she next turned her attention to Messrs. Krebs and Morwitz.

If I have compared Mr. Haversham's expression to that of a jockey about to be warned off, these gentlemen reminded me of front-row spectators at a strip joint who have been asked by one of the performers to turn around and show their faces to the rest of the audience. You may wonder, dear Dr. Ampiofratello, how I am able to draw such a parallel. I will answer your questions at some other time. Suffice it to say that after attempts to leave the room on pretexts ranging from a forgotten telephone call to an overdose of Ex-Lax—all aborted by the granitic presence of Ms. Kalman between them and the exit—the extent of their criminality was eventually laid in full view on the table.

This was indeed a pretty pair of fish, if that is what I mean. The Trustees were without doubt entitled to put forward their individual candidates for the design and erection of the new building. That nearly everyone in the room had been carrying a bug detector could have been a normal reaction to the facts of late twentieth-century life, which in many ways may be compared to that of Renaissance Italy with none of its charm and very little of its talent. But it was certainly unfortunate that in so apparently lofty an ambience as that of a Trustees' Meeting of The Dickstachel Research Institute four out of the five Trustees should have suspected each other; still more so that their mistrust should have proved to be well founded.

When I thought of what at that stage should have been classified information being scattered on the airwaves and furtively recorded by beetle-browed little men lurking in shadowy cells; when I realized, with a sinking heart, that not only Mr. Haversham but also Mr. Krebs and no less Mr. Morwitz had agreed to take backsheesh like any Middle Eastern go-between or European potentate, regardless of possible headlines and the outraged majesty of the Justice Department; when I reflected that had illness or the vagaries of the crosstown traffic prevented Ms. Kalman's attendance, the entry of Bocks and Glasse might have been ignominiously voted down . . . where was I? Oh yes. Frankly, I was happier than ever that my own transmitter had broken down.

"You rotten lot," said Ms. Kalman. "You *rotten* lot."

She sat down and lit a cigar which she had deftly removed from Mr. Haversham's waistcoat pocket.

The assorted pieces of electronic gear scattered over the table looked like sale time at Radio Shack. Mrs. Stahl raised to her eyes her lace-edged handkerchief, somewhat bestrewn with dog-biscuit crumbs.

"I don't understand any of this," she plainted. "Won't someone please tell me what's happening? Dr. Tillevant?"

Ms. Kalman patted her hand.

"Never you mind, dear. Such goings on ain't fer the likes of you. You're a lidy, you are."

Mr. Krebs now spoke.

"I deny everything."

"Don't be a fool, Krebs," Morwitz said. "There's nothing to deny."

"Oh ain't there, though," Ms. Kalman boomed.

Mr. Morwitz plucked up a little spirit.

"How you gonna prove your accusations?" he said, with a very nasty smile which had no effect on Ms. Kalman.

"Ain't myde none. All I done was arsk a question. Fired into the blue, as yer might siy. I din' 'arf bring dahn a lot of birds."

Mr. Haversham cleared his throat.

"Look here, Bessie—"

"Donchu call me Bessie."

"I shall not only call you Bessie, but I shall go on calling you Bessie until this thing's settled right. And if it isn't I swear to God I'll call you Bessie in one or two places outside this room."

Ms. Kalman's magenta complexion faded to the color of unbaked pastry.

"Yer wouldn't."

"I wouldn't?"

She failed to stare him down.

"Yus, yer would too."

I could hear her mighty lungs inhaling and exhaling.

"Orl right, if them uvver two plans is torn up I won't take it any furver."

"Shake?"

"I wouldn't shake 'ands wiv you—you know you can trust me to keep me marf shut, like I always done."

"Never mind about that," Mr. Haversham said hastily. "Tear 'em up, gentlemen. We can trust—Bessie."

Slowly, sadly, the fragments joined the other debris on the conference table. Mr. Haversham turned to me.

"Dr. Tillevant, will you please make your presentation?"

23

OH, GOOD morning, dear Dr. Ampiofratello. How well you're looking. Yes, I slept excellently. Excellently. Doctor, there was something I wanted to ask you. You may think it silly of me—what? Oh, you're so kind, but I'm afraid I've done a great many silly things or I wouldn't be here, would I? Well, anyway, do you think you could find me some nurses who are just a little easier to look at? I mean—what? Yes, I know, but after all, there are other things in life besides professional competence. You'll see what you can do? Oh thank you, thank you. Yes, I'm sure it's not easy, but just for me, you know—

And please don't think I'm grumbling, but I'm so dreadfully thirsty nearly all the time, and it seems impossible to get a simple cup of tea. All she says is "No, dear," and pours me some ice water. Is it such a big problem? Surely there's a hotplate or something—union jurisdiction? Oh dear, oh dear.

And then the other thing—you're not going, are you? I mean, you've only just come. I don't seem to see nearly enough of you. Yes, but I don't want to think of the other patients. Yes, I'll make it as short as I can, in fact I can reduce it to one word.

Security.

Doctor, will you reassure me—will you give me your word that the security arrangements here are completely watertight? I mean, one does read of people just walking into hospitals and doing the most frightful things and then walking out again. When I say watertight, you know what I mean. Darrelltight. It would be so awful if he came in here. I know he'd be easy enough to identify en route, the way he is now, but he's so cunning I believe he could slip through anywhere. And I'm sure his recent experiences haven't changed him *inside*. I couldn't bear to lie here helpless and have him mocking at me. You'll give the guards special instructions? Oh, God bless you, doctor.

I hardly like to mention it, but if you *did* want any tips on security systems, the one we have at The Dickstachel Research Institute— Use the recorder? Of course, of course. It's been running the whole time, actually.

Such a nice man. Well now. The security system we have at The Dickstachel Research Institute is really wonderful. You see, first of all there's the Sanctuary Warden at the revolving door. That has an electrical interlock and it won't go around until he pushes the button. And before he will do that you have to identify yourself in a very positive way. You have to tell him your name, and who you want to see, and he checks by telephone, and then you have to push your driving license through one of those little wicket things and he makes you spell your name. Or of course if you work there you have a laminated pass with your photograph and thumbprint, and he compares that with the records in a machine which, as a matter of fact, Paul Darrell designed. Or if you're a visitor from abroad you have to give him your passport.

Well, if you've satisfied this first Sanctuary Warden he'll release the revolving door and you can actually get inside the building. Then you go through a metal detector, and there's a dog that's been trained to sniff out drugs and another dog that's been trained to sniff out explosives. I don't mind telling you that these dogs scare the living daylights out of me, but these are the times we live in. Then there's a second Sanctuary Warden who gives you a form repeating the information you gave the first Sanctuary Warden, and the second Sanctuary Warden compares that with what the first Sanctuary Warden has written down. Of course, sometimes the first Sanctuary Warden has made some mistake or other, and that occasions a certain amount of delay, but that doesn't happen *very* often. The form is one of those neat little snapout sets. It has only three copies at the moment, but we're working on that. At least we were. Oh dear.

Of course no cameras are allowed, so if you happen to have

brought one you must leave it for safekeeping. Then the second Sanctuary Warden takes a color Polaroid shot of you and mounts it on a visitor's pass with your name, and laminates it, and you wear that all the time you are in the building.

Well, the next step is that you're assigned a guide to take you to where you want to go. Now each department is sealed off by a security door with another Sanctuary Warden behind it. Your escort gives this Sanctuary Warden the relevant information concerning you and the purpose of your visit, and the new Sanctuary Warden records it in his book and lets you through. Sometimes you have to pass through two or three departments in order to reach the department with which you have an appointment, and there is a Sanctuary Warden for each department, and each Sanctuary Warden has to be told about you and enter you in his records.

I suppose that to the layman this may sound a little complicated, but it is all very simple really, and if all goes well it cannot take more than half an hour at most.

On your way out you go through a reverse procedure, so that each Sanctuary Warden can cross you off his book; and then when you give up your visitor's badge you can reclaim your camera or your passport, or both, naturally, if you had both. And then in no time at all, or hardly any time really, you are free to go.

I have to admit that we have had one or two unfortunate incidents where a Sanctuary Warden has gone off duty while a visitor was in the building, and taken a camera or a passport, or in one case both, with him and never been seen again, but that simply points up the difficulty of hiring reliable staff these days. It has nothing to do with the system, which you can see for yourself is absolutely foolproof.

Well, when I say that, we never did find out how that fellow that Darrell shot at with his elephant gun got into the building, or for the matter of that how he managed to steal all those drugs. I suppose that was an inside job too, and again it goes to show how careful you have to be about checking on new employees, especially when you never know from day to day whether someone is going to bring an action against you for infringing their civil rights. I still say that the system, *qua* system, is probably the best in the world. We have had many favorable comments on it from high-placed Federal officials who have read the twenty-four-page descriptive pamphlet—in more formal language than I am using at the present time, naturally—which I had circulated wherever I thought, putting it bluntly, it would do most good. Of course none of these ladies and gentlemen have actually gone through the system. When a visitor is of that exalted status—and naturally that applies also to the Trustees—the first Sanctuary Warden simply releases a hinged door at the side, and whoever it is can walk right in and proceed without further molestation, although I doubt if that is quite what I mean.

As a matter of fact there are times when the system works almost too well. For example, there was the morning when I forgot my pass, or rather when owing to my wife's exasperating behavior I had omitted to put it in the zippered inside pocket which I have had built into all my jackets. I will tell you about my wife's behavior some other time, if I can bring myself to it. The point is that when I arrived at The Dickstachel Research Institute the gu— uh, Sanctuary Warden refused to admit me.

In view of my personal status I have always felt that I should be exempt from the system, but up to that point I had been happy to set a good example to the employees at large. I requested—nay, commanded—the fellow to admit me by the side door, but he would not. He was perfectly courteous about it. He replied to me in the words he had memorized from the Manual of Procedures for the Sanctuary Wardens of The Dickstachel Research Institute. I believe that in writing this Manual I have maintained a benevolent aura of fatherly authority almost throughout. It is not until page thirty-six that references to such things as blackjacks and tear gas appear.

Well, anyway, the man said:

"Sir or madam as the case may be, the procedures which are laid down for me in my Operations Manual do not permit me to accede to your request."

You will hear for yourself, dear Dr. Ampiofratello, how vastly preferable is such a form of words to the terms in which one is liable to be addressed in the course of a potentially unfriendly discussion with one of New York's, uh, finest. The fact that they were delivered in a Brooklyn accent thick enough to pickle dills hardly detracted from their emollient sonority.

However, the fellow, who had only recently completed his training, should have realized that it was not necessary to address me as "Sir or madam as the case may be," whatever may have appeared in the Manual. It only emphasizes the difficulty of writing any instruction intended to be pellucidly clear to the meanest intellect, and I must here express my profound sympathy with those whose task it is to compose the Directions for Use of any product, whatever its nature.

I said—I must admit, a trifle frostily, although I tried to maintain my philosophical smile:

"Do you know who I am?"

He replied, still strictly in the terms of the Manual:

"Sir or madam, I have great pleasure in recognizing you."

My heart sank, for I recognized this as the opening of a dialog which I had wrought only too well. From this point on an increasing acerbity crept into the conversation, if such it can be called. The man was obviously losing his nerve. He began thumbing through the Manual, evidently in search of authorized phraseology to express what was really troubling him. Doubtless this was the suspicion that he was being subjected to a test designed to entrap him into admitting me in breach of the rules, whereupon he would be summarily discharged in accordance with the terms of his contract. Since he could not find such a proviso in the Manual he explained his dilemma in his own words which, while still within the bounds of subordinate behavior, departed radically from my own distinctive style.

Meanwhile it had begun to pour with rain, a high wind sweeping across from the Palisades and, rushing under the canopy which partially sheltered me, fast saturating my clothing. My philosophical smile, or indeed any kind of a smile, had completely disappeared under the strain of these events. The man continued to leaf through his Manual and it was evident to me that he would soon arrive at page thirty-six when, being a literal-minded type, he would start shooting from the hip. I began to turn away, knowing full well that until the deluge had ceased it would be impossible to obtain a taxi so that I could go home, put on dry clothes and collect my pass. I bitterly lamented the fact that no visitor had arrived in whose wake I could enter, hoping that the Sanctuary Warden would be so flustered at having to deal with two people at once that he would omit to use his blackjack on me.

Someone in fact did arrive at that moment. In the nature of things it was Paul Darrell, disgracefully late for work as usual. To him, *faute de mieux*, I explained my problem. He seized me by the arm, hustled me to the side door, unlocked it and pushed me inside, shouting to the Sanctuary Warden:

"Hi, Charlie. Helluva day, isn't it?"

He had not even attempted to produce his pass. Shaken and sopping, I proceeded to my own office, pondering these events and realizing that I should have to insert in the Manual a section providing that in a situation such I had just endured it would be in order to summon by telephone someone already in the building who could provide the necessary identification, thereby removing the responsibility from any overconscientious Sanctuary Warden. It would mean recalling and destroying the previous edition, which had been printed at some expense, but one really cannot foresee everything.

I closed and locked my office door, removed my suit and spread it near the heating panel to dry. Fortunately Dacron sheds moisture fast. I made myself a hot toddy from my butcherblock bar. As I drank it I debated whether to confront Darrell with the enormity of his conduct in possessing a key without my sanction. I decided to affect that I had not noticed this detail but to have a key cut for myself forthwith.

As a result of all this I was an unheard-of fifteen minutes late for the Recapitulatory Survey Meeting.

24

I ORIGINALLY conceived the Recapitulatory Survey Meeting as a breakfast meeting, that great American invention for getting at the day's work before the day has actually started, even if most of those attending are still half-asleep. Darrell ruined the effect by turning up in pajamas, dressing gown and slippers. Thereafter I moved the event to mid-morning.

Even so it was all but impossible to secure one hundred percent attendance. Some wretched, uh, scientist would be absent, and when later instructed to provide an adequate written excuse would come up with an unconvincing tale of an experiment which had just reached a vital stage which to neglect would spoil it. As I always told these men, they should look at their Monthly Schedule of Meetings —heaven knows these were circulated far enough in advance, on the second Tuesday, unless it happened to be a five-week month, in which case it was the third Tuesday—they should look at their Schedules and plan their experiments around the various Meetings. Some malcontent had the gall to suggest that it should be the other way about, that the Meetings should be scheduled around the experiments. I believe this man is now earning his livelihood somewhere in Wyoming.

How in the name of sanity anyone could imagine it possible to maintain properly and orderly administrative procedures if these were to be subordinated to the irregular and slipshod habits of people like that? I know there is a legend that system and precision are the worft and wep—I mean weft and warp—of a scientist's being, but I can assure you, dear Dr. Ampiofratello, that the reality is very different. Why, one of these creatures once attempted to excuse his absence from a Recapitulatory Survey Meeting by saying that he had been working all night and had gone home to catch up on his sleep. I pointed out to him that there was no budgetary provision for that sort of thing and that he would certainly receive no extra pay. Moreover, since he had kept the lights burning all through the hours of darkness he had directly disregarded my five-page memorandum on energy saving—I think the code number is 8/76 a 305, or perhaps 306—which I held his signed acknowledgment of having received, read and understood.

Some of these people are distinctly odd in other ways. We had one fellow who went around carrying an expensive-looking musical-instrument-type case which made people assume he was an amateur of the oboe, or bassoon, or some such. One day the case accidentally flew open and proved to contain an electric whip. I had a very difficult time persuading him to resign.

Yes. I regard the Recapitulatory Survey Meeting as by far the most important of all those on the Monthly Schedule. Oh, I would not for a moment downgrade, say, the Great Little Economies Session or the Board of Departmental Development Techniques, although this called down on me one of Darrell's characteristic outbursts:

"You are less use than a wet dream. With infinite toil and cunning I succeed in locating a few brains that have so far resisted the anesthetic, and you have to spray them with your administrative DDT. Leave us to develop ourselves, won't you?"

I admit that in this case I was remiss in not checking the acronym before naming this particular body, but otherwise I feel his comment was typically anarchic.

I will also stoutly defend the Aesthetic Review Committee, the Intensive Usage of Productive Space Panel, the Interdepartmental Psychological Reconciliation Seminar or the Community Relations Conference. This last is especially unpopular with the, uh, technical staff, since it involves an annual Open House after which the number of requisitions for replacement of broken or st—uh, mysteriously missing equipment, not to mention the overtime bill for cleaning up bubble gum, spilled ice cream cones, and plastic and metal containers for portable nourishment and aliment, increase to an alarming extent. As I point out and point out, where, in these populist times, should we all be without good Community Relations, which, apart from anything else, are such an essential factor in obtaining Federal Funds.

But the Recapitulatory Survey Meeting is an excellent way—indeed, sometimes it appears to be the only way—to find out what, if anything, is being achieved by our serried ranks of highly qualified and highly paid—well, fairly highly paid—uh, scientists. God knows I have done everything possible to ease the strain on these people. I have even enlisted the aid of their secretaries, as the following circular letter bears witness:

> Dear Dickstacheler:
> Attached is a specimen of the Non-Progress Report which is submitted to the Administrator each week. Due to the nature

of its source data it is possible to request a recheck of the totality of its correctitude, but inside standard googolic dimensions it may be accepted as textually valuable. It visualizes the ebb and flow of new, about-to-be-new, ongoing, backgoing, finalized and irreclaimable activity in The Dickstachel Research Institute so as to provide reasonable factors of Boolean symmetry. It also provides certain synergistic analogs for the purpose of fiduciary evaluation.

The cooperation of the Secretaries of The Dickstachel Research Institute is vital in meeting the weekly deadline of 1000 hours each Monday. There are five hundred thirty-two scientists at work in The Dickstachel Research Institute. A moment's pondering will convince you of the vast task represented by the gathering of this mountain of bits. I know that your loyal contribution will be both regular and timely.

I was never wholly satisfied with this letter. It was written by an assistant-on-trial of mine who did not work out. To me it conveyed a certain lack of confidence both in itself and in the quality of the data which it was supposed to elicit. Moreover I must confess that it could have been couched in more intelligible language. Immediately after its circulation I was on my way to my personal washroom when I was confronted by a determined but somewhat distraught-looking woman who said to me, quietly and courteously:

"Dr. Tillevant, would you be so kind as to do me a small favor?"

There is nothing so trying as idle chat when one has delayed one's visit to one's personal washroom beyond the point of tolerable comfort. Despite this, I gave her my kindly smile and answered:

"My dear girl, you have only to ask."

She then brandished a copy of the document and inquired in a very trumpet-like fashion:

"WHAT THE HELL IS THIS SUPPOSED TO MEAN?"

This was a most unfortunate incident, because I had only the vaguest idea what the hell it *was* supposed to mean. My assistant-on-trial had brought it to me for approval as I was on the point of setting out for Rio de Janeiro to attend the international conference of the Associated Senior Statistical Hierocrats of Latin Europe, at which

I was to read a paper on Role Development. Here is another unfortunate acronym, but in spite of that it is a most important organization, and I was not unnaturally more preoccupied with the final revision of my paper and the validity of its translation into French, Italian, Spanish and Portuguese than with the administrative details which, however close to my heart they normally were, at that moment appeared to me somewhat mundane.

I sidestepped the issue by wagging a playful forefinger at my interlocutor and saying:

"Now, now, you mustn't ask me questions like that."

I then stepped nimbly around her and vanished through the door I had been seeking. While waiting until it seemed safe to emerge, I indulged my historical bent by speculating how men in skintight buckskins in the Regency period used to manage on their visits to the privy. I also made a mental note about the piped-in music, which had switched itself on a moment after I entered and was certainly going to switch itself off a moment before I left. Likewise the programming. "The Londonderry Air" is very soothing at such moments, but "The Irish Washerwoman" is merely disruptive.

On the following day the lady in question resigned. It seemed to me an odd decision, since she was within two years of retiring on pension; but I trust no one will term me a male chauvinist pig when I say that it is impossible to follow the workings of the feminine mind.

To return to the specific Recapitulatory Survey Meeting which I was in the process of describing. I must say that when I entered the room I detected a rather ostentatious air of hostility. Two departmental heads were playing ticktacktoe; two more were solving the acrostic puzzle from the previous Sunday's *New York Times;* and there was a fellow entertaining some of his colleagues by putting a string up one of his nostrils and pulling it down the other, a practice which, while I would not for the world seem guilty of any ethnic slur, I shall always wish had remained within the bounds of the East Indian subcontinent, since I cannot accept that it is a desirable addition either to the Higher Thought or to the lifestyle of our great country, which numbers among its illustrious sons the inventor of the Kleenex.

I explained my tardy appearance at the Meeting by inventing a long-distance call from Washington, a word which even in these days retains some of its lofty aura, although of course a long-distance call from Washington could equally well originate either in the Pentagon or in Mama Rosa's Pizza Parlor. Up to that time Darrell had not thought fit to honor us with his presence. As it was through his good offices that I was there at all, I affected not to notice the empty chair. He wandered in, however, a few moments before I reached the item on the agenda dealing with the Stringhinken Experiment, of which he was the nominal head.

The Stringhinken Experiment, I should explain, had been entrusted to The Dickstachel Research Institute by the highly prestigious Stringhinken Corporation, which manufactured Burpine, a remedy for acid indigestion, somewhat less prestigious, selling as it did number three in the ratings. In an endeavor to reverse this state of affairs the corporation had redesigned the product, which was about to appear in the form of lifelike colored tablets molded in the image of male and female stars of professional sports, television, itinerant but affluent professors of artificial religion and the like, all of whom had agreed to participate in the elaborate advertising campaign then in preparation. Parenthetically I would add that this refurbishment was an outstanding success, no doubt attributable to the many levels on which it could be regarded.

However, in order to provide a solid medical and, uh, scientific background the Stringhinken Corporation had devised a Test which consisted of feeding an identical overrich diet to two groups of volunteers. One of these groups would be dosed with Alka-Seltzer and the other with Burpine. The fact that the Burpine recipients all had the digestions of ostriches, while the control group was exclusively composed of chronic dyspeptics, was purely coincidental, since they had been chosen by computer, although it had been necessary to issue rather detailed instructions to the programmer.

To ensure impartial surveillance of the experiment, a small unoccupied area of The Dickstachel Research Institute had been fitted up as a kind of combination gourmand restaurant and hospital, with a recreation room where television might be watched and sedentary games such as Scrabble, bridge, or punching buttons and watching the results on the television screen might be played. At the start of the experiment at least, all the volunteers were ambulatory, but they were not encouraged to take any exercise other than to pass from dining room to recreation room to dining room to dormitory.

The Stringhinken Experiment was not without its extraneous tensions. Despite our utmost attempts at secrecy, the fact that some kind of medical or physiological test using volunteers was in progress had leaked out, and a government snoop—I really should not have said that. The dreadful thoughts that come into one's mind when one is a little below par—well, I don't care. He *was* a snoop. Or, as Darrell put it—and for the only time in my life I agreed with him:

"Some damned little man with a clipboard—"

There were no Federal, State or Municipal Funds involved. The Stringhinken Experiment was a glorious example of that undaunted spirit of private enterprise which—which—

No, nurse, please don't trouble yourself. I'm perfectly all right, I assure you. Heh-heh. There. See? I'm laughing.

I'm laughing at the reception this snoop got when he actually had the audacity to penetrate into the Stringhinken Wing, as that part of The Dickstachel Research Institute was ultimately named—after all, the fee for the project was extraordinarily satisfactory. He started to put leading questions to some of the volunteers, and bless their hearts they one and all assured him that they had never had it so good. After that they told him in chorus to fuck off, which he did, thank goodness, before he could start asking inconvenient questions about the fact that half the volunteers were men and half of them were women. There is no denying the fact that an overrich diet over even a couple of weeks does tend to arouse the passions as well as the bile.

The Final Report had of course already been written—I prepared it myself—and only awaited the lapse of the eight-week Test Period, of which there were still five weeks to go, before it could be dispatched to the Stringhinken Corporation. Nevertheless I felt it essential that weekly reports in due form should be prepared so that they could be properly included in the Archives; but in this essential, as in so many others, I found Darrell extremely reluctant to cooperate. Judge therefore of my surprise when, after making his belated entrance, he laid before me with a deferential aspect which should have warned me what purported to be the latest Statistical and Medical Return. My surprise quickly turned to horror when I read:

THE STRINGHINKEN EXPERIMENT
Statistical Summary for Week 54, 1492
NOTE: Some totals may add to 100%. On the other hand. . . .
.82 of a biologist currently observes .7 of a volunteer every 19.692 minutes. This is a considerable rise in output since last year, when .94 of a biologist observed only .6 of a volunteer every 23.078 minutes. Further possible increases in productivity are being sought in our Research Department, located on the northeast corner of the filing cabinet, next the philodendron.

An immediate problem is the disposal of the .3 of a volunteer that remains untreated. He is most indignant about this, and we have to agree that the place looks very untidy with all those recurring decimals lying about. Even allowing for wastage in cutting, trimming and packing it is difficult to see how this residue can be meaningfully minimized.

.00001% of our volunteers is a member of the Stringhinken Spoilers, world's first senior citizens all-girl Rugby football team. 2½% of our volunteers have been deducted for cash. 32.6% of our volunteers have names beginning with K. 67.4% of our volunteers do not have names beginning with K.

Runners at Belmont: 1. Stringhinken, paid $7.80. 2. Stringhinken, paid 50,000 lire. 3. Stringhinken, failed saliva test.

When I had finished glancing through this disgraceful document I directed at Darrell a look which must surely have conveyed the outrage which permeated every fiber of my being, coupled with a menace of things to come such as I imagine the countenance of the late Adolf Hitler would have expressed if someone had whistled the "Internationale" during a reunion in the Lowenbrau Bierhalle.

Darrell, however, was staring ahead of him with the unfocused expression of one who is pondering an aphorism by one of the ancient philosophers.

25

You will readily perceive, dear Dr. Ampiofratello, that if Darrell was capable of perpetrating monstrous japes such as the one I have just described at a time when my nominal control of him at least gave me opportunities of personal confrontation during such times as he was pleased to favor The Dickstachel Research Institute with his presence, there was absolutely no limit to the graceless, tasteless effrontery which could be expected of him when he was several thousand miles away and, from early morn to dewy eve, roaring drunk on the native liquor known as Whammo.

Apart from his degrading postcards—although I must confess that from time to time, when I needed a few minutes' relaxation from the pressure of work, I derived quite a deal of amusement from surveying the imaginatively exaggerated female contours depicted thereon—apart from these, if one had not known him as well as I did one might have imagined that his first full-length so-called report represented an absolute nadir. But I did know him as well as I did —no one knew him as well as I did better than I did—and I was convinced that if a second full-length report ever arrived it would represent a degree of ignominy which might well rock The Dickstachel Research Institute to its fourth basement. When the fell document arrived, my premonition proved only too well founded.

A more irrelevant, subversive paper, full of ideas so reactionary that some of them might almost be thought advanced, I hope it is never my fate to peruse. Not only to peruse, but to convey to the Trustees—and how I was going to do that, despite the notable diminution in my feelings of respect for them since the episode of the bugs, I could not imagine. Here it is, in part:

> Most Noble, Grave and Reverend Signors, and of course that includes Bessie—hiya, Bessie—and La Signora Stahl.
> I think that's how the quotation goes, but I will ask you to

forgive any inaccuracy, as my access to reference sources is minimal here in the rain forest. Things look different here in the rain forest, and I am going to give you the benefit of a few of my random thoughts as with one eye I look at civilization in perspective and with the other at my happy, laughing, primitive hosts. And hostesses, of course. There must be many remunerative jobs waiting in the Old New World for these last.

I am seriously thinking of going native, or these days I suppose one should say going local. Imagine me spending the rest of my days in a fog of Whammo and sex, till I finally discover at what point of advanced age the drive slows to a standstill. An enthralling project, eh, Tilly, little man? Think you could rustle up some Federal Funds for it? By the way, did you ever stop to think where Federal Funds come from? They come from you and me. Why, goddammit, Tillevant, I'm paying part of your salary. I'm even paying part of my own salary, that's how moronic this thing can get.

But lest you think I am irretrievably sunk in carnal sloth, let me to weightier matters. Let me give you my ultra-longshot, widescreen view of the knee-jerk civilization of my native country, which I would love with such passion if only she did not go to such infinite pains to make me puke. America is no longer a beautiful virgin with a queen's dowry, but she is decidedly an attractive rich widow, though Merry, hardly. Can we not find her a worthy new husband who will protect her from the hordes of beggarly para-humans who spit upon her in the very act of robbing?

Let us, in a spirit of brotherly love, consider the matter of education, or "what you don't know will get you into college." Education, that withered crop yielded by today's defoliated groves of academe, wherein day and night howl the mongrel dogs which defile the roots of the tree of knowledge. What is its purpose? Is it to provide inner strength, intellectual striving, wisdom and serenity? Verily, no. Its purpose is to enable a living to be earned. The higher the education, the higher the living. But that is not education, it is technical training and nothing more; and that is what it should be called.

We spend billions of dollars—oh ye suffering payers of imposts—to buy machines for the dispensation of portion-controlled pellets of knowledge in plastic bags that need only be popped into a pan of boiling water to provide approved food for addlepates. Our teachers, with their precisely formulated degrees in education (yick) have become machine minders, when they can spare time from distributing the free-lunch vouchers or calling for psychiatric reports.

What memories our little dears will have of their schooldays. Can't you imagine them reminiscing fondly about the Bunker-Ramo keyboard they learned to operate in second grade, and how they were sent to the principal and reprimanded (within the limited bounds set down in the manual) for stuffing a gift apple into the interstices of their automated multiple-choice tester? Dear old golden rule days, even if the apple was stuffed with acid or dynamite. Maybe it's better to assassinate a machine than a human—if you can call educators human. Because for god sake, we don't got no teachers no more. All we got is educators like on who you can practically see the pushbuttons, just the same as what they really was machines. May they all be cast into the wilderness and feed upon the flesh of foxes.

Where are the Mr. Chipses and the Misses Dove, dear old fuddyduddies who were somewhat capable of knocking or even persuading into all but the most hopeless material a reasonable amount of knowledge such as would distinguish them from the untutored savage AND ALSO such basic manners, comportment and inner resources as would entitle them to mingle socially with their opposite numbers in the comity of polite nations. Where are they? On a picket line, defying the law which in their own persons they're supposed to set their pupils an example of observing.

How foolish is our insistence that no one be kept back a year because it might give the lazy little sod a trauma. We have forsaken the Biblical injunction, "Know ye not that they which run in a race run all, but one receiveth the prize?" (I Cor. 9:24). Instead we accept the Lewis Carroll pronouncement: *"Everybody* has won, and *all* must have prizes." It was the dodo said that, and you know what happened to the dodo. He got ate up by hungry sailors 'cos he didn't have no defenses.

Unless—improbable—your Leader of Community Thought today has gone out and sought knowledge to satisfy some inner craving, he has no more knowledge of the ancient sages than had an eighteenth-century fishporter. Thereby, whatever the size of his sexual equipment he is only half a man. I cry—how foolishly, how vainly—for a return to the classics, in excellent translations at least, though why not in the originals? Why not teach Latin and Greek again? Certainly Latin, for its taut laconicism that disciplines thought; and I plead for beauty-revealing Greek. A man schooled by solid-based scholars, not by exponents of the latest theoretical fad having a half-life of thirty months, could grow in psychic stature and withstand the adversities of life. Is modern sociology any competent substitute for Pindar or Horace? And let the children begin with it early, as they used to do, and let it be spread over all their years of school. Neither prate to me that this is beyond the reach of the mass of the infant mob, which can barely stumble through a bastard version of their native tongue after twelve years of grade and high. A withered fig for all such. They stop the way for their more fully-cranium'd betters.

You think I'm crazy? Whom the gods would destroy, they first make sane. You'd like to declare me a nonperson? I shall still be ahead of the mass of humanity, who are nonpersons by nature. There are many gods, my friends, and the one that made the human race rushed the model onto the market to beat the competition. It should be recalled for rectification of faults. Look around you at the results of all that grunting and heaving. No wonder we have a throwaway civilization. It was evolved by throwaway people.

    Who knows how many towering geniuses
    Lie at the base of mankind's peniuses?
    But it's mainly the fools that get out.

It is undeniable that the para-human mass is a gigantic *lapsus lingam*. Let us forget about the perfectibility of man. And woman. Both have proved themselves imperfectible, at least by outside agencies. We need to self-start, to have the inner itch that only we can scratch.

Man is still but a little child hammering dents in a Hepplewhite table. "Thou hast made him a little lower than the angels" (Psalms 8:5). That says not much for the angels. Man's chief virtue is that he is biodegradable—and the embalmers have spoiled that. *Cogito ergo sum.* But ninety-five percent of the population never thinks from the first slap on the behind to the final application of pennies to the eyes. Or has that been mechanized?

A piddling fraction of the billions we squander on dolts and dunderheads would suffice for the nourishment of our best brains, on whom in the final event our survival must rely. So can we begin to rebuild a race depending on its own intellectual muscle rather than leaning and wailing on the shoulders of psychiatrists or even falser prophets here now and to come; and least of all upon governments made up of men and women as narrowly quote educated unquote as any of the miscellaneous spitballers who elected them; people who to solve or to leave unsolved their own personal problems have recourse to the same meretricious and ineffective means as those bemused dumbbells whom they are supposed to be governing.

Governing? Government itself these days consists of leading from behind after a careful study of the entrails of battery-farmed chickens to reveal the wishes of the governed. Government that achieves nothing, cures nothing, and, like the declining Romans, in its lust for re-election hands out ready-baked loaves to a populace overindolent to knead and bake a dole of flour. For each of our ills there is a Government Department, costly beyond belief and housed in a pretentious building with a leaky roof; and emitting foul clouds of the Civil Service gobbledygook which has replaced the Mass in Latin as a means of hiding truth. But while we pass—and reverse—panic legislation to save the ecology, why do we not rather send into the streets janissaries armed with rawhide whips to scourge the oafs who toss empty beercans into flowerbeds?

Ripeness is all, but there is no longer time for anyone to

ripen. Governments and Boards and Commissioners of all kinds deliver our young in a state of controlled arrested development, like gas-ripened tomatoes.

Quelle bitchup. I tell you, all of you, it makes me downright ashamed to see all these UN delegates from the developing countries looking so well-groomed and acting as if Talleyrand had trained them in diplomacy. And us? We look like a bunch of sandhogs wearing their first store-bought suits. Isn't it strange that after only sixty years Russia has dropped the cloth-cap image? Her diplomats look as bourgeois—as aristocratic, even—as the Versailles Peace Conference. And us? In the same time we've obstinately descended from silk-hatted Harvard scholars to bejeaned peanut vendors. And we think we're so great. What do we suppose other people think of us? If we don't know we just aren't listening, now we keep turning our ass to all points of the compass for the rest of the world to kick.

Let us recapture our belief in the individual, and help the individual recapture his belief in himself. Self-belief, my friends, that is one of the keys to our survival. Right now we do not believe in anything. And this is why we cannot any longer win our wars—because we are fighting against people who do fiercely believe their inhuman creed, yet who have already departed from their basic, untenable doctrine of equality so far that honors and scarce goods are heaped upon their most intelligent achievers. It is only a question of time before those countries which most lately follow in the steps of the master practice the same abandonment.

God help us if in our present state we ever have to fight the father of all these devils, as we have already fought and lost against his spawn; for we believe that machines will bring us victory. But it is not machines that win wars, but men. When the battering rams have broken down the gates, when the massed artillery has ceased its barrage, when the unmanned missiles have dropped their atomic warheads, then is it that the men—the poor bloody infantry—must go in to mop up. With short swords against bronze shields, with bayonets against cloth-shrouded bellies, with lead suits and radiation detectors against other lead suits and plague germs developed, as other weapons of yore, in spite of celebrated treaties. And if we do not look to ourselves it will be a mopping up of the soft-bred and the pacifier-mouthed against the iron-souled fanatics; and the odds will be too great.

Perhaps we shall not have to fight; not with martial weapons. On my bad days it seems to me that they are getting all they want by patience and the tongue, a little chip here, a little softening, a little undermining there. Just an iota a day, quite painless, quite unnoticeable, except that every day is a little nearer to the one when the walls of the temple that our fathers builded shall be rent, and at first slowly and then with a great roar the walls and the roof and the pillars thereof shall come stunningly upon us and all our lives.

Do I sound like Savonarola? Shall I return and exhort you all to bring your automobiles and TV sets and down-padded garments and tennis racquets and limited-edition ceramics and silver medals and snowmobiles and Louis Vuitton bags to Times Square and fling them onto the mighty bonfire that shall flame there as expiation? How wonderful that would be, with all the picture tubes imploding and all the gas tanks exploding and the stench of burning feathers and roasting leather, and the groans of the penitent and the wail of the police sirens. But no, duckies. It is not I, but a greater than I, who will never come after me, that will wipe the smile from jesting Pilate's face. Pope Alexander VI caught up with Girolamo S., and the cops would catch up with me, and I have no taint of martyr's blood. And the zest of the Whammo is growing faint within me, and it is half an hour before my next bowl is due. But nevertheless, *in Whammo veritas.*

Not only *veritas,* but *mirari.* For last night, as I lay on my pallet, I and my temporary handmaidens having all done our possibles, methought I did see a clearing in the forest, on each side of which did sit an opposing native tribe, each intent on genocide.

And the first tribe shrilly chanted to the rhythm of its drums: *co*cacola, *co*cacola; and the second, *pep*sicola, *pep*sicola; and the third, *doc* torpepper, *doc* torpepper; all of which rhythms, though antagonistic in purpose, were conformable in beat. But the fourth tribe, deeply and gutturally voiced, chanted to a different and terribly disturbing cadence, *un* cola, *un* cola.

And when they had sufficiently maddened themselves with their ancestral chants they did all fall upon each other, stunning their enemies with hurled books of great weight; and the name of each book gleamed upon it in letters of golden fire: MARKETING STRATEGY; but the outcome of the battle saw I not, for a sweet sleep fell upon me; but I wis that I slept with a smile upon my lips, for had I not been benisoned with a vision of the sweet ways of Home? And do not object, oh nitpicking little Tilly, that the rhythms I heard consorted better with the jungles of Africa than those of the Amazonian rain forest.

Speaking of which, don't you want to know what it's like in the rain forest? Oh, you know what it's like already? You've all been to that little corner of the Natural History Museum where it's green-dark, and the foliage makes you feel cool on a humid summer day even though there isn't any air conditioning, and there are soft taped noises of birds and small animals; and also a largely naked figure of an Indian eternally holding his loaded bow ready to shoot, and eternally resisting the temptation to loose off at the passers-by.

Well, you don't know what it's like, not even if you have visited that green-dark corner of the Natural History Museum, which you probably lie in your teeth if you say you have. It's not like that at all, in spite of the well-informed and highly-skilled efforts of the people who set up the exhibit. And the big difference is that in the real rain forest it fucking well *rains*. It rains every day from May to September, and also from October to April.

This is not the kind of rain that simply makes you wet outside. It is the gods peeing on their handiwork. It soaks inward until you can feel the fungus growing in the hollows of your bones where the marrow ought to be. I intend to leave my bones to science. I have no dobut they will discover seventeen entirely new kinds of antibiotic inside them. You could wring out the trees and vegetation like washed socks; and the ground beneath your feet is like yard upon yard of newly-chewed bubble gum. This is the kind of rain that gets inside unopened cans of beans. It warms and chills your skin in the same nanosecond, it covers you with glutinous sweat even as you shiver.

This rain is, I do believe, causing a dark green moss to grow upon poor Laura Milton's skin, the only kind of fertility she will ever know. No, I am wrong. It is but the ghastly light that filters in from above and changes the tint of the fuzz upon her cheeks.

The only way to keep from losing your mind in a brimming spoor is to drink and screw. What homely remedies, universal panaceas, effective in Ventrivia as in Vinton, Iowa. Oh, and to laugh.

I have already commented on the sinister quality I thought I detected in the quality of Cosamo laughter. I was right. They do not laugh because they find everything funny, they laugh because everything around them, every last detail of their surroundings and their lives is so unrelievably, bloodily, hoggishly, stinkingly, leprously, loathsomely awful, terrible, beastly, brutish and nauseating, and there is not a single goddamned thing they can do about it, except to up stakes and move.

And they dare not do that.

26

I HAD just read this last ominous sentence, and was preparing to absorb its dire implications, when my secretary reminded me that it was nearly time for a meeting at the offices of Bocks and Glasse, the architects of The Tillevant Building. I hastily thrust Darrell's report into the center drawer of my desk and sallied forth on this much more pleasant assignment.

Bocks and Glasse of course is the firm whose splendidly identical towers, like rectangular phalluses, adorn so many of the avenues, boulevards and cross streets of so many of our revitalized urban areas, lending such praiseworthy uniformity to the face of the land that the amount of readjustment required of the traveler on arriving in a strange city is becoming less and less. Thanks to Bocks and Glasse and their followers we may feel instantly at home even in the rejuvenated cities of Europe, whose untidily variegated architecture from the feudal past is by degrees being eliminated one step ahead of the preservationists.

Construction of The Tillevant Building was already proceeding with laudable speed. At intervals of what seemed like only a few minutes, hundreds of blasting charges reverberated from the old apartment buildings and sent indicator dials swinging wildly and microscope slides and flasks full of experimental liquids crashing from shelves and tables onto the hard floor of The Dickstachel Research Institute itself. There was a certain amount of protest from the, uh, scientific staff, but I pointed out that in such a cause we must all suffer—I could even hear a certain amount of muffled explosion in my very office at the far side of the original buildings —and a minimum of ingenuity was required to overcome these temporary inconveniences.

"Fiddles," I said.

"How's that again?" they said. The way in which these people reveal their illiteracy once they are jarred outside the edges of their own little specialities is extraordinary.

"Fiddles," I said again. "And shockmounts."

It is rather odd that if one says "Fiddles and shockmounts" three times in succession one tends to become convinced that there are no such words. Be that as it may, while they understood the shockmounts and, albeit rather gloomily, set about surrounding their dials with springs and foam rubber, I had to explain to them that fiddles, in the sense in which I was using the word, were wooden contrivances used in a storm at sea to prevent the crockery and so on falling off the dining table. The maintenance department of The Dickstachel Research Institute was thereupon put to work making a variety of curiously shaped objects for this purpose; and a pretty bill they sent in for it, while the more disaffected members of the staff developed a curious liking for whistling or humming the "Sailor's Hornpipe" not quite outside the range of my hearing.

Slice by slice, the massive outcrops on the site of The Tillevant Building disappeared with relative safety, save when the contractors omitted to put enough wire mats on top of the blasting charges. On these occasions rock splinters of some size flew through the air, breaking apartment windows and menacing the health and future of passers-by, one of whom I believe succumbed to his injuries. Various abortive attempts were made to claim damages from The Dickstachel Research Institute, but as the responsibility was clearly the contractor's our lawyers had little trouble disposing of them, and few of the litigants had the necessary funds to commence amended proceedings.

I must confess to some disappointment that there was no old building to be knocked down. A wrecking ball is such a splendidly priapic thing. If only someone had thought of a way to use two at a time—

To anticipate somewhat, when this part of the work was over I spent a good deal of time among the sidewalk superintendents. Indeed, I had a special window with a lockable shutter cut in the fence for my exclusive use. When I tired of gazing into the mysterious pit in which the foundations of The Tillevant Building were becoming a reality, I would cross the street and gaze upward to where, though in truth it was still an empty space, I could distinctly see the spot where my new penthouse office would look out towards the splendid Palisades, studded with even more splendid high-rises; towards the far-off, affluent tip of Long Island; towards the mountains of New England and the far-off coasts of Europe. There in due course would I sit, brooding like Zeus.

Alas, alas.

However, the present meeting with Mr. Bocks was not directly concerned with The Tillevant Building, but rather with the details of the holiday ranch house, with tennis court and sauna, which Bocks and Glasse had most kindly undertaken to provide on a choice site in one of the more watered spots of Arizona. I spent a most enjoyable few hours thus occupied, and even my wife chimed in pleasantly.

Alas, alas, alas.

27

NEXT DAY I was so busy with a thousand and one vexatious details that I literally had not a moment to myself in which to continue reading Darrell's latest report. First I had to deal with a wild-eyed scientist who wanted to go as much as three hundred fifty dollars over his budget without attempting to fill out a Supernumerary Requisition, although this form, which had been simplified to the very utmost with due consideration for the peculiarities of this strange race, consisted of only three pages and the five copies were of the integral-carbon type which eliminates manual interleaving, costly though this concession was.

I was also involved with the Chairman of the Arboreal Subcommittee of the Aesthetic Review Committee over the question of whether to plant flowering cherry trees or evergreens in the landscaping of The Tillevant Building. The Subcommittee's choice had been for evergreens, although I had clearly indicated my preference for cherry trees. Their reason, which I could not help feeling displayed an unwarranted mistrust of the fine community relations which we have built up with the even finer people who live on the cross streets adjacent to The Dickstachel Research Institute, was fear of vandalism. I have to confess that the morning after the cherry trees burst into delicately tinted blossom they were found to have been sprayed with paint of a peculiarly revolting shade of purple, but no doubt the miscreants who committed this antisocial act had only recently moved into the area. That, however, was in the future, and right then, while it is at no time my custom to interfere with the workings of those to whom I have delegated important matters, I had to spend a full ten minutes persuading the Chairman of the Subcommittee to point out to the Subcommittee that it would be as well if they would voluntarily reconsider their decision.

As if that were not enough, some kind of a cross-up had occurred in the internal telephone system. I found that I was constantly answering calls emanating from the Materials Receiving Dock, in a variety of voices suggesting that the employees working there were entirely composed of high school dropouts and escapees from maximum security prisons. Contact with persons of this ilk is extremely damaging to my psyche. The common man and woman is frequently so very common.

I made a note to take up the matter not only with the Engineering Department but also with the Personnel Department. I know that it is the duty of all of us, and particularly of those of us who are entrusted with obtaining Federal Funds, to give a helping hand and a quite disproportionate wage check to perpetrators of violent crimes who have subsequently been vouchsafed two-way fireside chats with the Almighty, persons whose entire educational career has been passed in a state of self-induced catalepsy, and any person whose intelligence quotient can by a violent stretch of the imagination be considered to read above zero; but the Engineering Department should have repaired the telephone instantly—instantly, and the Personnel Department should have sequestered our quota of lame ducks on their own pond where some of them could weave baskets for the others to score goals in.

I say I made a note of this, because I was so extremely pressed for time that it was only by seconds that I managed to board the airplane that was to take me to San Francisco to attend the East Coast Administrators' Conference.

Before leaving for the airport I hastily dropped some papers into my briefcase, among which I included Darrell's report. I intended to read and work on these during the flight. Well, as a matter of fact some inner urge compels me to admit that I did *not* intend to read and work on these during the flight. I took them with me to provide some substance to the story I had instructed my secretary to tell anyone who might come moaning to her about an apparent lack of reaction to his or her latest memorandum. I was well aware that comments had been made, and not merely by Darrell, that when there was a conference in the offing, the work of The Dickstachel Research Institute invariably took a back seat. I had even overheard a rather acid inquiry as to why a conference of East Coast Administrators should be held on the West Coast, but my goodness, people with such limited thinking fail to realize the extent to which a complete change of venue limbers up the mental muscles. And paradoxical as it may seem, the more relaxing the ambience, the more stimulating the results. Where do people want us to foregather? Pittsburgh?

Besides, what about the brilliant discussions which follow, which often follow, which sometimes follow, which occasionally follow, which have been known to follow the papers which are read at these affairs?

Moreover I do not mind confessing to you, dear Dr. Ampiofratello, though I would not wish it to be generally known, that these occasions provide unparalleled opportunities of getting early knowledge of changes which may be in the wind. Someone may be moving up, or taking early retirement; and while I am proud—proud—to be Administrator of The Dickstachel Research Institute, should Fate call me to some larger sphere of activity I would never shirk the call of duty—bearing in mind such questions as tenure and pension rights—and how can I do that if I only learn of the vacancy after all the infighting is over?

Be that as it may—and it certainly is—by the time I had eaten the filet mignon and drunk the patriotic champagne—though I shall always prefer imported—and watched the movie—and as I say, I attend very few cinematographic displays and I was surprised at certain sequences which these days, even without an X rating, seem to be considered suitable for a mixed audience which may include small children—where was I? Oh yes. When I had done all this I really was in no mood to do anything in the small time remaining before we landed but watch the stewardesses as they moved up and down the aisle, involuntarily undulating to compensate for the slight turbulence through which we were passing. I had paid my fare—or rather The Dickstachel Research Institute had paid my fare—and I was entitled to my, or rather their, money's worth.

And of course after I had arrived at the Mark Hopkins and registered and received the name plaque for my lapel—and by some unaccountable oversight I omitted to observe until the Conference was over that they had spelled my name with one l—by then it was time to attend the Welcome Cocktail Party. When that was drawing to a close I found that I was quite hungry again, so I joined a cheery and influential group for dinner downtown. There were a couple of guys from foundations, and a pretty senior representative of Health, Education and Welfare, and a woman from the Environmental Protection Agency, not bad looking either if only she hadn't been wearing those darned glasses with three-inch lenses. She had quite a figure too—I simply cannot get excited about these fashionable gals you can hardly see sideways—and I made a point of sitting next to her, because I had it on my conscience that The Dickstachel Research Institute hadn't been getting nearly enough assignments from the EPA.

I really felt that I was cutting quite a swath in more directions than one. After all, if one is living in the times one lives in, one might as well live in them, don't you think, dear Dr. Whatsyourname? Oh dear, oh dear, that was quite a night, except that after we'd all gone back to the hotel and had a few drinks at the bar, around ten o'clock when I was just feeling sufficiently primed to pop The Vital Question she went off with another woman. One never knows these days, does one?

I was so frustrated that I went up to my room and actually turned the TV on. I refuse to allow TV in my home, although I believe one can get some quite hot stuff on cable TV, but that would only give my wife another handle. Anyway, I found I was watching some kind of dramatic production in which two men were arguing with each other, but one of them mumbled and the other seemed to be suffering from facial paralysis, so I turned it off after a minute and went to bed.

Frankly, I had quite a hangover quite next morning. Although I usually find it so inspiring, I could hardly raise the energy to stand up and join in reciting the Maslovian Creed. This is a very beautiful compilation from two of The Sources. It runs:

> An organization is a composite of a variety of individuals with different personalities who have their own individual need-disposition and goals.
> Basic physiological needs
> Safety from external danger

> Love, affection and social activity
> Esteem and self-respect
> Self-realization and accomplishment
>
> Individual organizational systems must function within the context established by the societal environment. Society is a hard taskmaster. It demands strict adherence to the context established by it. Deviants and mavericks, be they organizations or individuals, are quickly cast aside.

Harsh as its closing words may seem, do they not contain one of the great truths of all time? And yet how lovely, how tender is the opening, what infinite promise of protection follows. "Love, affection and social activity." And if those there be who will object that the mere recital of The Creed solves nothing, that the vast majority of those who recite it do not believe in more than a fraction of its contents—is that the fault of The Creed, and what difference is there between it and other creeds? When I sat down again I was already feeling better, though it was not until well into the second paper that I was really able to pay attention.

The subject was "The Sociometric Conduct of Value Analysis Seminars," and as the healing balm of the grand old phrases flowed over my psyche I began to feel a better man both physically and spiritually. Core activities . . . Significant constructs . . . Horizontal plurality. Such beautiful words. And then during the afternoon session, what a stiffening of the sinews and summoning up of the blood as the speaker told of battles won and lost in the wars of the human relations experts against the industrial engineers.

The evening was spent in rehearsals for my own paper, on "Decisioning," which I delivered on the following day. With all due modesty I must say that it was the outstanding event of the Conference. It was what is known as a multi-media presentation, including spoken commentary, a live cast and slide projections of sociograms with arrows going in all directions—straight arrows, curved arrows, angled arrows, triangles in circles, circles in triangles—my word, they were exciting. The whole thing was topped off with a live dramatic visualization of an Accomplishment Atélier. I know this is the age of the anti-hero, but nearly all my characters were heroes or heroines.

There was the Formal Leader—a striking woman in high-heeled boots, with a chin like a meat cleaver. She had a background with IBM and was working on her own as a consultant. Then there were the Informal Leader, the Task Leader and the Social Leader—splendid types, all of them; and to round out the picture there were the villains—the Isolate and the Maverick. They raised boos from the audience as loud as the cheers which had greeted their nobler colleagues. I had had some little difficulty in finding anyone to play these thankless parts, but I managed it somehow. Oddly enough, both of them looked rather like Paul Darrell.

I was flushed with triumph when I attended the Farewell Cocktail Party that night. As I wandered from group to group, congratulations continued to shower on me from all sides, until I encountered Dr. Keinkoje, magnificently drunk. I knew Dr. Keinkoje well—he was Administrator of the Ulysses S. Grant Research and Rehabilitation Complex—but I did not manage to dodge fast enough. He had just finished patting my Formal Leader on her formal and indignant rump, muttering loudly:

"Full of power tonight, full of power."

He caught sight of me and continued:

"That's not all I'm full of either, and as for you, Ram, my boy, you're always full of it. Let's you and I do a pee together."

Since he had laid a heavy arm across my shoulders I had no alternative but to accompany him, although he was reciting all too audibly:

> "If you've never been the lover
> Of the landlady's daughter
> You cannot have a second piece of pie."

He then fell silent until we had reached our destination; but when we were facing our respective camphor-perfumed receptacles he broke out again.

"You know, Ram my boy. Of all the inflated charlatans here present. There is one. Who. Beyond all perad—perad—doubt. Would. If there were a championship among us for the title of Chief Pharisee. Win it by a country mile."

His pause was filled with the musical ring of liquid striking porcelain. He seemed to be awaiting some comment. All I could manage was:

"Oh?"

"You may well say Oh. You may well say it. I suppose you have no idea who our uncrowned king is?"

"No, I haven't the—"

"It's you, Doctor Tillevant. You."

He was between me and the door, so I could not escape.

"You take all this horseshit for gospel. The overall societal environment. Dynamics. Network feedback. Social integration in terms of interpersonal intimacy. Decisioning. Decisioning indeed. For Christ's sake, Tillevant, don't you know that decision is a noun, not a verb?"

The venom with which he said that—

"Management systems designed to give the purblind mediocrities a chance of edging out the undiplomatic crackerjacks who won't be called in until the bollixing an almost or quite fatal stage. Committees. Committees. Show me the minutes of the committee that wrote the *Iliad.*"

The heresies—the blasphemies—bounced in doomsday fashion off the white tiles. I had finished long ago, but all this while he continued to urinate. He was a big man, but the size of his bladder must have been incredible.

"At least half the major corporations in this country—this country? Everywhere. At least half of them are running on their own momentum. Who built up Gessler Hotels? Bill Gessler. Who put them on the slides? Committees. Who built them up again? Lou Bildersheim. Who created Proton Corporation? Harry Wechsler. Who let the stock run down sixty-two points? Committees. Who put Proton back where it belonged? Jimmy McCracken."

At the same time that I was listening to this I had that old nursery rhyme running through my head, which was already spinning with the drinks and this brutal unprovoked attack, and the boom-boom-boom of his voice reverberating from the shining walls.

"Ding dong bell,
Pussy's in the well.
Who put her in? Little Johnny Green.
Who pulled her out? Little Johnny Stout."

"For Christ's sake, man, how important do you think we and our forms and our systems and our pseudo-psychiatry really are? All this societal shit—it's just designed to soothe a bunch of dimwits into playing ball with each other. When I get two guys who don't resonate, know what I do? I lock them in a room and leave them to fight it out. It works. And it's a helluva lot cheaper."

He seemed ready to go on for another ten minutes, but suddenly he stopped, did up his pants, glared at me and left. I had no desire to accompany him. In any case my zipper had jammed.

28

YOU WILL realize, dear Dr. Ampiofratello, what a shock my nervous system received as a result of my involuntary dialog—or rather, to all intents and purposes, monolog—with Dr. Keinkoje. A dreadful man. The administrative equivalent of Paul Darrell. I shuddered as I imagined some nightmare organization in which the two of them were teamed up. What I found so unbelievable was that the Ulysses S. Grant Research and Rehabilitation Complex has the highest percentage of permanent cures in the country.

I did not even return to the Farewell Cocktail Party, but packed my bag, went straight out to the airport and returned to base on a plane which owing to the lateness of the hour was of the variety known, I believe, as a Box Lunch Special. I will not elaborate on that; but in all the circumstances I was so preoccupied in enjoying and dismissing all the brilliant and crushing rejoinders which, now that it was too late, flowed through my mind that I did not even think of doing any of the homework I had brought with me.

Certainly the last thing I could have faced was that confounded report of Paul Darrell's; and the whole of the next morning was occupied with a positive vortex of detail. Things slacked off after lunch, however, and around three o'clock I picked it up from the suspenseful line at which I had been forced to abandon it:

>   . . . And they dare not do that.
> You'll remember that when your friend Canon Smurge tried to find out what had become of the hordes of missionaries who had passed that way, the answer was: "They go mountains," accompanied by screeches of laughter. Well, Tilly, I put the same question to Harry, and I got the same answer and the same screeches. But where the worthy Canon had taken this for gross irreverence and had packed up and left in a huff, I was hammering away at my theory that just as white and not black is the color of mourning in China, so laughter for the Cosamo has quite the opposite meaning to what it usually has for us. Frankly, this ceaseless cachinnation from morning till night is getting on my nerves. It's like being locked up in an echo chamber with a canned applause track and not being able to find the switch. So I continued to ply Harry with remorseless questioning. I think the old bugger rather likes me—

Confound Darrell. That vibrant charm of his even gets to hairless pygmies.

> —rather likes me, and around two in the morning he suddenly sobered up and said:
> "See here, Darrell, I think you're a pretty right guy, and I'm going to tell you something."
> He stared distastefully at what was left of his drink, and poured it slowly on the floor of his hut. A kind of libation, maybe. The ground is pretty well saturated the whole time, and the Whammo just formed a pool and sat there. If it was a libation, it looked as if it had been rejected. Harry went on:
> "Darrell, it's the damndest thing, but no one who goes to the mountains ever comes back."
> I was pretty shook. Harry had never spoken anything but

pidgin English. With no warning, he'd gone over to everyday American to make the kind of doomsday announcement that ought to be accompanied by bodeful music. I wasn't going to spend time right then asking him where he'd learned his enlarged vocabulary. I stuck to what he'd used it for.

"Whaddya mean, no one ever comes back?"

"Whaddya mean, what do I mean? I speak English, don't I?"

He got up and rummaged at the back of the hut. What he found was a box of Havana cigars with about a dozen left in it. I took one—it was in surprisingly good condition—and we sat puffing for a while. Then Harry said:

"Look, there are legends about this thing, oh, from way back. Not only the missionaries, but our own people. Every so often some of them would decide they couldn't stand this hellhole any longer. They'd head for the mountains. You've got a line like that, haven't you?"

"Head for the hills."

"Hills, mountains, who cares? They'd go scouting, promising to send back messengers. Nary a messenger. There was one party went in my father's time. I was just a kid. Didn't get my first issue of women till a couple years later. I remember waiting for news, all excited. Day after day. Nothing."

"Maybe—"

"Maybe what?"

"Maybe there's a very good place beyond the mountains. So good that everyone forgets the folks back home. No messenger could bear to come back, even for a while."

He looked at me sideways.

"Yeah. Maybe. But there's this. Three, four years ago another party left. Oh, when I took over the chief's job after my father died I set up a tabu about that kind of thing. Young. New broom. But by then I'd lost my youthful enthusiasm. I thought, what the hell, maybe the luck would change. So I let them have a few pigs they could drive before them for food on the way, and off they went."

He looked sadly at the one-inch butt of his cigar and dropped it into the slowly draining pool of Whammo. I'd have thought that stuff had enough alcoholic content to catch fire, but it didn't. I prompted him:

"Off they went. And—?"

"And they never came back. But—now get this—some of the pigs did."

I was going to make some stupid crack when he went on:

"I thought those pigs didn't look too good, but I put it down to their having had a hard time traveling, and they'd soon pick up on the plentiful and healthful diet provided by their native rain forest. Some of our folks killed one—I don't know why, our own pigs were quite a bit fatter. Maybe they were drunk," he said, lifting another bowl. "In no time at all every one of the people who'd eaten that meat came out in sores. Some of them died pretty quick, others—didn't. They just hung around, getting worse, till finally I had to put it to them that everyone would be just as well off if they cleared out and started a settlement on their own."

"And did they?"

"They did, though I had to use my chiefly authority. It was kind of hard on them—they were getting so they could hardly feed themselves—but what the hell, for all I knew they were contagious."

"Were they laughing?"

"They were laughing."

Well, that confirmed my theory, but frankly, Tilly old pal, when I imagined that group of sick and dying people drifting off through the sog with a trail of unearthly hoots growing fainter as they got farther away, I got a malarial shiver. Harry went on:

"I had a bigger problem than them, though. The rest of the mountain pigs started to come out in sores, just like the people who'd eaten one of them. All those pigs wanted to do was lie about, so they didn't take much rounding up, but after we'd killed them I had the devil's own job keeping our people from eating the flesh. I didn't know what to do with the carcasses. Didn't want to bury them for fear they'd infect the ground.

Couldn't burn them—ever tried to burn anything in the rain forest? Finally we threw them in the river. They drifted downstream and I guess poisoned the water."

He took a big swig.

"Poisoned the water," he repeated with an evil grin.

I took a drink myself. I thought it would make me feel less sick than what he'd been telling me. Then I said:

"Downstream. Haven't any of your people ever started the pursuit of happiness in that direction?"

He laughed. Not the regular Cosamo laugh, but a kind of gutsy chuckle.

"Downstream, friend Darrell, and astride of the only practicable trail, is a warlike tribe known as the Bellaki. Hell, you must know all about the Bellaki. You had to come through their territory to get here. How did you do it?"

"I'll tell you some other time."

"O.K. Anyhow, the Bellaki don't like people invading their territory. We Cosamo are a peaceful race. Or maybe we're just yellow."

He squinted at his dark-skinned forearm.

"Is that funny?"

"Not very."

"Anyway, we can't fight worth a row of beans. Yes, some of us have tried downstream, but again no one came back. So here we are, and here I guess we stay, getting more and more inbred till—curtains."

For some time now our nightly rations had been waiting outside the hut. Occasionally one of them would stick her head inside and, at a sigh from Harry, decorously withdraw. Now Harry, who had been brooding since his last remark, clapped his hands. Two girls came in and he stood up, frowning at me.

"Life's very simple really. It all comes down to drinking and fucking. And of course laughing like hell when things get absolutely unbearable. Goodnight, Paul."

I sent my two away. I felt I was going to be impotent for quite a while. Besides, I wanted to plan my next move. Tilly, I'm going to prove out a theory about this mountain sickness.

Pretty soon I go mountains. I know that's outside my brief, and anyway I'm reversing myself, but you know what you can do if you don't like it. And another thing you won't like, Tilly boy. When *I* go mountains, I come back. Bimeby I send you plenty more big palaver.

29

THE ATMOSPHERE of the Trustees' meetings had in part reverted to normal after the bugging episode, although it could never be quite the same. I had decided that it was useless to worry about the effect of Darrell's reports. I simply instructed my secretary to Xerox them (standing unobtrusively behind her to make sure she did not run off more than the authorized number of copies) and myself laid one at each Trustee's place at the conference table.

The reactions were, as one might have expected, mixed. Mr. Haversham perused Darrell's variegated prose with much puffing and grunting. Mr. Krebs whistled at the more purple passages. Mr. Morwitz, perhaps as a result of his legal training, left his countenance absolutely blank and evinced no audible reaction. Ms. Kalman seemed to find a good deal of private entertainment in much of the text; and Mrs. Stahl, after a feeble attempt to cope, pushed the sheets away from her and engaged in a conversation of the "wuzzy-diddums" variety with little Donzel.

They all finished around the same time. Mr. Krebs spoke first.

"This guy is nuts."

Mr. Haversham replied:

"Of course he's nuts. That's what we pay him for."

"Yeah, but we don't pay him to tell us to run the country."

"That might be a fringe benefit. One of these days he'll be running for President on an independent ticket."

"He'd never get elected."

" 'E can do wot 'e likes ser long's 'e gits back sife," Ms. Kalman said, staring at the last sheet of the report.

"Oh dear." Mrs. Stahl fervently hugged little Donzel. "Is Mr. Darrell in danger?"

"Donchu worry, ducks. Our Paul can look arter 'imself. Whachu fink, Dr. Tillevant?"

By now I had managed to convey to her my distaste for being called "ducky."

"Oh, undoubtedly, undoubtedly," I said. I was unable completely to hide my lack of enthusiasm. She glanced at me sharply and looked away again.

"I have a suggestion to put before the Board," Mr. Haversham said. "This young man is far too valuable to the Institute for us to fire him. But there is no question he needs a lesson in manners. Perhaps the Board will leave me to administer it?"

I thought sadly of the cables of instant recall that Mr. Haversham had drafted and scrapped. So, I believe, did Mr. Krebs, with whom the phrase "prurient little minds" evidently still rankled.

"I should like to be in on that," he said.

"I think it had better be left to me," Mr. Haversham told him firmly. Mr. Krebs shrugged sulkily, and the Meeting ended on that note.

30

You will readily understand, dear Dr. Ampiofratello, from my account of the stresses and strains of those months, that I really needed a holiday. Unquestionably I had been overworking. There were moments when I felt that there was nowhere to go but down. For example, my photograph had not appeared in *Questionmark*, the house magazine of The Dickstachel Research Institute, for two consecutive months.

But with so many matters being referred to me for decision, not only in connection with the day-to-day administration of The Dickstachel Research Institute but with the host of problems which now arose over The Tillevant Building, I felt quite unable to allow myself the rest and relaxation which were my due.

If I had only been able to find some reliable Number Two who could have been trusted to behave with reasonable efficiency in my absence, things might have been different. I had made many attempts to find a strong right arm, but I found that nearly all the people I hired on trial were anything but that, while the few who it seemed under my careful training might have filled the bill showed strong symptoms of becoming not only a right arm but an entire body, and in my own interests had to be fired as promptly, if not more so, as the others.

Nevertheless it was about then that I mailed a coupon which formed part of an advertisement in a little magazine which I sometimes pick up from a newsstand when no one is passing. You may possibly be acquainted with this publication. Its name is, uh, *Jock.* I have two years' back issues which I have personally filed in a special cabinet in my office, fitted with a lock whose combination is known only to myself. The cabinet is generally thought to contain secret projects for the Navy.

Dear Dr. Ampiofratello, I would not have you think for a moment that it is from any concupiscent motive that I peruse this journal. It is simply that I feel it my duty to be aware of everything, or as nearly everything as is possible for one man in these information-glutted times, that is being thought and done in the contemporary world: the little good and the much evil, in the hope that in its own small way, by inquiring into special problems of psychiatry, behaviorism, biology, sexology, sociology, mental pathology, malnutrition, political corruption, terrorism—where was I? Oh yes—that in short, over this vast and admittedly remunerative field The Dickstachel Research Institute might be able to initiate new projects which would render the world, and particularly the Third World, whose possibilities for the outpouring of Federal Funds seem to me to have been scarcely tapped —render the world more capable of living up to those inspiring principles so eloquently set forth by the founding fathers.

Let me think what it is that I was thinking of. Ah, I have it now. I was explaining why I read *Jock.* Well, frankly, because I got a kick out of it. Now this advertisement was inserted by an establishment called the Weird O Ranch. It read as follows:

A NEW KIND OF VACATION

How about something NEW-W-W this year? A DIFFERENT vacation in the healthy heart of go-as-you-please Nevada. What's your specialty? Horses? Dogs? Goats? Plain old-fashioned boys and girls? Or maybe something a trifle more sophisticated. At the Weird O Ranch *you* crack the whip and see what jumps. If you're undecided, ask our Activities Director. Man, the activities he directs. Don't be shy talking to him, he'll understand. Have a Nevada Arrack in the bar, or lap free Perrier Water from the fountain in the forecourt. Swim in our two pools—one unbearably hot, one at 34° F. Rent any equipment you want, from cycle chains to open razors. Mail coupon for sixteen-page color brochure today. All major credit cards honored.

Much as vacations were in my mind just then, and much as I yearned for something different, something told me that the Weird O Ranch was not really the sort of establishment that it would be, shall we say, prudent for me to attend, even in the most detached spirit of, uh, scientific investigation. It is an inflexible rule of The Dickstachel Research Institute that all personnel without exception before going on vacation must leave an address where they can be reached should an emergency arise. While I felt that my patronizing an ordinary dude ranch might give rise to some ribald comment, since I am by no means an accomplished equestrian, there was no doubt in my mind what would be the reaction if it ever got around that I was vacationing at a spot with such an uncompromising title.

Despite this I mailed the coupon, although it meant that for some ten days afterwards I had to be in my secretary's office when the mail finally reached it. What with the dilatoriness of the post office and the increasing lethargy which besets our internal messenger service every time they receive a cost-of-living bonus, it is often lunchtime or even later before my letters arrive. During this period, therefore, I had not only to rearrange many of my appointments, and even set the Recapitulatory Survey Meeting back to begin at the normal closing time, which occasioned many ill-natured remarks from those who are supposed to be my colleagues, but I also had to go without lunch.

I was under no obligation to create an eager-beaver image by having lunch sent up from the executive dining room and consuming it at my desk, a custom which I abhor. Still less did I wish to appear trendy by brown-bagging it. I ate my last brown-bag lunch shortly before I left college, and I had no intention at that late date of returning to the practice by way of flaunting an inverted status symbol. For all this while, therefore, my favorite Rinaldo's knew me no more. I of course used the executive dining room only when entertaining visitors from Washington—an economical gesture which I am sure was favorably reported.

No doubt my secretary noticed this departure from my normal routine, but apart from a flick of the eyes on the first day she was too well trained to make any comment. At one time I had an English secretary who at that period was very status-indicative, but she made me feel so socially inadequate that I had to fire her. I could, I think, rely pretty well on her successor's discretion outside her office, since from time to time I induced certain junior members of the clerical staff, who subsequently proved unsatisfactory, to, uh, well, to pump her. The results, I am glad to say, were always to her credit.

She came from New England, however, and was rather blunt. Once when I had to instruct her to cancel all appointments since I was about to undergo dental surgery on an emergency basis, she rendered this as:

"He's going to have a tooth out."

It is very difficult to obtain satisfactory clerical staff these days. One of the juniors to whom I have just referred—she resembled a startled faun with acne—positively refused the assignment, stating:

"The Bible says, 'Thou shalt not go up and down as a talebearer among thy people.' "

I wish people would not quote the Bible at me. It is a most unsuitable work for today's competitive environment.

As it happened, my secretary was herself at lunch on the day when the eagerly awaited document arrived. I was therefore able to abstract it from the pile without her knowledge. It was, I was happy to note, in a decorous manila cover which bore only a post office box as return address. I took the unusual step of closing my door before slitting open the envelope.

My word.

Well, really, dear Dr. Ampiofratello, even when I think of it after this lapse of time, it seems to me that not even you, who have been familiarized with, and have lavished your almost priestly compassion upon, the deepest abysses into which the human soul can sink—even you surely can have no conception of the contents of that vile booklet. I will spare you the details.

Time for my injection, is it, nurse? What are you smiling at? Oh, you just feel happy? That's right. I always like to have happy smiling faces around me. Don't be alarmed, that was just a friendly pat.

Let me see now. I was just about to tell you some more about the publicity material of the Weird O Ranch. Now I am sure you are familiar with some of the revelations of the Victorian age in England, when it was possible to rent or purchase children of the lower classes, when members of the nobility had to remind the authorities of their privileged position to avoid being haled into court for this or that—particularly that. I am equally sure that as part of your basic training you have read the works of the Marquis de Sade. In our own time, you have no doubt perused every word of those itemized newspaper accounts of the manners and customs of that part of Forty-second Street between Seventh and Eighth avenues, as revealed in those masterpieces of investigatory journalism for which we can never be sufficiently thankful to the First Amendment to the Constitution. I merely refer you to these sources to save time.

Suffice it to say that all this, plus the benefits of the most modern, uh, technology, were described and pictured in full color in the sixteen glossy quarto pages of the brochure of the Weird O Ranch. On the back cover, amid a profusion of simplified gothic lettering and calligraphic flourishes, their guarantee appeared. It reproduced the million-dollar performance bond which had been lodged with the Bank of the Republic of the Delectable Islands. Above all it detailed the solemn oath which was exacted from every member of the staff to maintain a secrecy as to the names of the Ranch's patrons which should resist even the importunities of investigative journalism and the open-mouthed requirements of the Freedom of Information Act.

In the early years of this century the Everleigh Sisters of Chicago issued an illustrated catalog extolling the merits of their extremely high-class brothel. I have never seen a copy, but from the description I have read it appears to have more nearly resembled the innocuous brochure of a Grand Hotel of the period. When I reflect that for issuing this innocent publication the Sisters were promptly closed up, it seems to me that we have indeed come a long way, baby, if you do not mind my so addressing you, dear Dr. Ampiofratello.

I think I have said enough to make you understand that this opus left me in a somewhat ambivalent mood; but somehow I doubted whether I should ever have the courage to spend my next, or indeed any vacation in that part of Nevada.

With some regret, I locked the brochure in the Navy cabinet and went off for a late lunch at Rinaldo's, where I was most flatteringly welcomed as a returned wanderer.

31

WHATEVER I may be accused of, at all events it cannot be said that I lack ideas or, until the night of the Catastrophe, energy with which to put them into practice. I would not tell this to another living soul, dear Dr. Ampiofratello, but many of my most scintillating inspirations come to me when I am on the john, and it was there, early one morning, that I was vouchsafed a concept which caused me to stand up rather prematurely with a triumphant shout. I hastily resumed my seat and began to work out the details.

In a word, I was going to make, or cause to be made, a documentary film portraying the intricate tapestry which, woven by so many skilled and loving hands, comprised the pneuma, the esse, the ana, of The Dickstachel Research Institute. Technicolor it would have, and wide-screen, and Dolby stereo, and—crowning it all—a voice-over commentary written by Rameses P. Tillevant, Ph.D., LL.D. (Hon.), M.B.A., M.S.S., Administrator of The Dickstachel Research Institute.

As I have said, I rarely attend cinematic entertainments. Additionally, you will have gathered by now that I have a certain disdain for the merely, uh, technical side. It was not, therefore, until I began perforce to associate with the mechanics whose grateful task it would be to make of my dream a living thing that I learned the names of these devices. At that moment most of them were but hazy details in my mind. The one thing that stood out clear as lightning's summer ray (Kipling) and on which I was irrevocably determined was, putting it bluntly (and I am sure you know that when the chips are down I can put things very bluntly) if anyone was going to do the talking it was me. I. Me.

Well, anyway, the next step was to, as the saying goes, sell the idea to the Trustees. I did this, needless to say, with all my wonted eloquence. Indeed, I outdid myself, for I verily believe that the divine afflatus was upon me, and when I sat down I positively had to make the coarse gesture of mopping my brow. I even went so far as to pop a tranquilizer into my mouth under cover of taking a sip of water, although in the ordinary way I am scared of side effects. Oh, I would not hurt your feelings for the world, dear Dr. Ampiofratello. I am well aware that under your highly qualified supervision whatever medication I am now receiving can only have the most beneficial results.

At the start the Trustees were alarmed over the probable cost of the project. I quite easily overcame this objection by pointing out that it should be quite easy to obtain a Foundation or even a Federal grant for such a worthy educational project; and that the film would be a powerful tool for eliciting grants, donations, bequests, subscriptions, contributions from many hitherto untapped sources. Why, with proper handling the revenues simply from Friends of The Dickstachel Research Institute, Inc., whether Individual, Family, Sustaining or Life, could be confidently expected to swell to an annual total outstripping the income of any Friends of Anything Anywhere.

I also expanded on the national exposure which would result from showings on the Public Broadcasting Service television network. Mr. Haversham raised an objection:

"They'll want it for freebies."

"Quite so, Mr. Haversham, but let me point out that the script will contain an eloquent appeal for viewers to send in even the smallest contributions—as little as twenty dollars. *Mony a mickle mak's a muckle,* as the Scots say, and this will in no way weaken the force of the appeal which will be made at some other point for a generous loosening of the pursestrings on the part of our wealthier supporters."

"I don't know how many twenty bucks you're likely to get out of it. Any time I turn on that channel by mistake there's some creep playing the piano. Who the hell watches that stuff anyway?"

"What's wrong with playing the piano?" Mr. Morwitz interposed. He is as it happens a well-known amateur. To avert impending strife I hurriedly raised another point:

"We could have an auction on the air. It would cost us nothing —we would ask well-known people to contribute in kind—and the idea's always successful."

"Yeah, I guess these people appreciate the chance to clear out their attics in exchange for some free publicity, although that gets me back to where I started. It isn't like you to come up with an idea that has so much in it for other people. Still, talking of clearing out attics, maybe we could get rid of some of the junk that's lying unused around this place, huh?"

This rather touched me on the raw. I have to admit that there had been certain projects—the Investigation into the Possibility of Modifying the Hereditary Characteristics of the Sheep Tick with a View to Self-Destruction, and the Statistical Analysis of the Incidence of Sexual Precocity among Underprivileged Children in the Outer Hebrides, for example—which somehow gave rise to the purchase of a considerable amount of equipment that for various reasons was never used for its original purpose and, because it had been earmarked for these specific applications, could not be transferred to subsequent undertakings. It was all rather complicated, from the administrative viewpoint. Moreover the projects themselves were rather a sore spot. We had to abandon the Sheep Ticks because we were accused of upsetting the balance of the ecology, if not of outright genocide, and the Hebridean project was aborted because the sturdy but reactionary islanders not only refused to admit that any of their offspring were underprivileged but routed our fieldworkers by hurling chunks of granite and manure. The present situation was saved by Mrs. Stahl, who asked:

"Would the Trustees appear, Dr. Tillevant? I do hope so. I've always wanted to act in a film."

Ms. Kalman said nothing, indeed I thought she looked rather alarmed; but Mr. Haversham said firmly that nothing would persuade him to make a fool of himself in front of a camera. Mr. Krebs and Mr. Morwitz supported him in this; though from the way in which all three gentlemen straightened their ties and smoothed their hair I deduced that they would need a minimum of persuasion; and indeed, after I had rhetorically asked them what they thought The Dickstachel Research Institute would be without its Trustees, the project was approved *nemo contra*.

The matter being thus happily resolved, I threw myself into the realization of my dream with all my wonted enthusiasm. Needless to say, the field was virgin to me, although I do happen to have in my desk at home a number of partially written manuscripts which in happier days—Nevertheless, after the success of my first dramatic production, "Decisioning," I was full of confidence.

I had also, of course, to obtain competitive quotations for the actual, uh, mechanical aspects of the production. Of the many preliminary interviews which I conducted, the briefest was with a fairly young person of on the whole male appearance, whose swirling black cloak, scarlet-lined, only partially obscured its cliché faded jeans and unkempt sneakers. From under its huge and I imagine expensive billycock hat its fine but colorless hair escaped in all directions, drifting at times over the enormous gold-rimmed spectacles through which it peered at me with eyes rendered almost equally enormous by the magnification of the lenses. I cannot believe that a person who looks like that knows anything about anything.

Addressing me as "Dad," and eking out its limited vocabulary with innumerable "You knows" and other outworn phrases, this creature replied to my searching questions as to its abilities and experience in a distrait manner which led me to believe that its thoughts were in some other, opium-derivative world. From its clipped and disjointed utterance, however, I managed to disentangle that it relied heavily on hand-held cameras, that its studio facilities consisted of loaned space in a pirate tape factory, and that its only completed film to date was a so far unreleased biography of the Manson family. I terminated the proceedings as quickly as possible, but was unable to avoid an indignant though inarticulate demand for my reasons for not awarding the contract on the spot.

I was in fact forced to activate the under-carpet switch which acts as an emergency signal to my secretary. She is, as I have previously indicated, a big girl, and after she had stood silently in front of the person for a few seconds this ghost from the sixties dematerialized into whatever uncertainties the present might hold for it.

The other representatives whom I interviewed were in the main a clean, well-groomed lot wearing suits from Brooks Brothers or Bloomingdale's. I had little difficulty in compiling a short list of outfits all of which seemed highly qualified, uh, technically, and which I felt would be prepared to furnish acceptably comparable quotations. Where time and again problems arose was that we could not agree on the script. It was only in rough form at that stage, of course, and because of the press of other work I had not got very far with it. Only four pages, in fact; but it was a very extraordinary thing that everyone who looked at those poor little four pages said that they were, uh, technically impossible. Most of them were very diplomatic to start with—one man said it was twenty years ahead of its time—but the last fellow I saw started to laugh halfway down page one and fourteen lines later was almost hysterical. Then he left, saying that next week he was due for open-heart surgery and his doctor had told him to take it very easy until then.

Frankly, I felt pretty discouraged. But I was determined to get what I wanted, even if I had to direct and edit the film myself, aye, and compose, orchestrate and conduct the score, if it came to that. To tell the truth—and that is what I feel an irresistible desire to do—I rather hoped it would not come to that. As I expect we have all noticed, there are only twenty-four hours in a day. Besides, for example, I must confess to a slight inward qualm at the thought of the possible reactions of the New York Philharmonic Orchestra when I first shook a baton at them. After all, that is something quite different from beating four-four time in front of a mirror, a matter of which I do have some experience.

As I sat considering the unexpected turn of events and fitfully scribbling at page five of the script, my secretary advised me that the representative of Zeeta Productions, the last company on my short list, was waiting to see me. So depressed was I at that moment that I almost pleaded an unforeseen emergency which would prevent me from seeing this person. Ah, how different things might have been had I followed this impulse. Instead I muttered "Very well" and composed my face into an expression of judicial welcome.

My secretary then appeared in the center of the doorway, raised her right arm in a somewhat dramatic fashion, and announced, as if emceeing a variety show:

"Miss—*Greta*—LOVE."

She then vanished like a conjuring trick and was immediately replaced in the doorway by the most beautiful woman I have ever seen. God, but she was cosmetic. More than six feet tall was she, with longer legs than ever waved on a Las Vegas stage, a ballerina's arms, and hands that I could have loved not only by the Shalimar but by the banks of any river you could name. Ah, fateful quotation. For those hands were destined, as the old song continues, to crush out my life, then wave me farewell. Had I but known, had I but known. But at that moment I was too entranced, as she swayed forward in a way which emphasized the bountiful promise of her breasts, with soft draperies that stroked her rounded thighs and clung to the sweeping curve of her calves—I was too entranced, I say—I was too entranced—

Nurse. My palpitations are coming on again.

Thank you. I think I will sleep a little now. To sleep, perchance to dream. . . .

I am awake again now, I think. Let me see, let me see. Somehow I managed to stand up and induce this incredible houri to render by caressing it with her haunches my Chippendale chair forever sacred. Somehow, although my speech had developed an unwonted impediment, I managed to parley with her on the mundane transaction which had brought her, so beautifully, there. Mundane, do I call it, that transcendent concept which until that moment had seemed to me to out-Odysseus the *Odyssey*. Ah well. Helen—Paris—the man, not the city—am I the first to be thus besotted? No, indeed. But I will be calm, calm.

Bashfully I slipped into her lovely hand the sheets on which I had inscribed my tyro's stumbling words, and waited tensely for her condemnation. But when she raised her enormous blue eyes, fringed by silken lashes which, even though they were palpably artificial and even though my reeling senses were not so overcome but that I could distinguish that one set was a full sixteenth of an inch shorter than the other—when, I say, she thus looked at me, I read only admiration, and the words she said were these:

"Wha, Doktuh Till'vant, Ah think this's puhfectly splayndid."

Oh, that Magnolia Soulangeana voice, that double-cream accent. When, entranced, I listened to her modestly proffered suggestion that if Ah wouldn't take't wrong—I beg your pardon, if I wouldn't take it wrong, the boys back at the studio would just love to put forward one or two teentsy-weentsy thoughts of their own, what could I do but agree? When the revised opening came back to me I was unable to recognize in it any minute vestige of my original work, and indeed although I pressed on with my own manuscript to the very end, the entire script underwent a like sea change. But so profound was the hypnotic state into which Miss Greta Love consistently soothed me that for her dear sake I raised not the smallest query. So skillful was her dialecticism, so mesmeric her dialect, that she persuaded me that the contents of the simulated-leather folder which she laid before me represented only the smallest deviation from the course I had charted. It was not until much later that I recalled the elementary fact that a variation of even half a degree in a missile's course, if sufficiently protracted, will result in a landing on, shall we say, Mars instead of Venus. The aptness of this particular illustration would in due course be borne in on me.

On one point only was I adamant. I, and I alone would write and deliver the commentary. I fancied that I detected a shade of disappointment—even a hint of moisture—in those lovely eyes when I delivered this fiat; but I held firm, and my will triumphed though my heart was sorely troubled. When I speak again some of this epic recitation, dear Dr. Ampiofratello, I know you will recognize the essential correctitude of my decision.

I must say that I was a little surprised, nay alarmed, at the size of the bottom line when I received the Zeeta Productions quotation. Putting it bluntly, it was the highest of the lot. But I felt that it was neither the time nor the place for cheeseparing. Some little problem I did anticipate with the Trustees; but I had the happy idea of inviting Miss Greta Love to be present, ex officio, at the meeting which sanctioned the expenditure. Messrs. Haversham, Krebs and Morwitz were, so to speak, sunk without trace; Mrs. Stahl was too lost in dreams of becoming an actress to object to anything; and Ms. Kalman spent the time looking alternately at Miss Love and myself with a very peculiar expression on her rugged countenance.

But I anticipate. At the end of this, our first encounter, I invited, though with some inward trepidation, Miss Greta Love to accompany me to Rinaldo's for lunch. What joy when she accepted, although she did murmur:

"Wha, Doktuh Till'vant, suh, *Ah* was about to invaht *yuh.*"

I laughingly brushed her suggestion aside. What cared I on whose expense account the meal was entered.

As I followed her out of the office her hindquarters clashed together like cymbals. As I passed between the tables at Rinaldo's I heard all around me a low rumble of masculine approbation like great boulders on a beach beleaguered by the breakers of a wine-dark sea.

And when she ordered lunch, she made it sound like foreplay.

32

IN THE delirium of the creative ferment and the storm of amatory passion which had engulfed me, I had, understandably but nevertheless reprehensibly, omitted to peruse Paul Darrell's latest report, which had now been languishing in my desk for several days. I realized this while I was wrestling with the childproof opening of a jar of kelp one breakfast time. I made it my first business to go through this screed. Even at a distance of several thousand miles it was dangerous to neglect Paul Darrell, and as I picked up the sheets disfigured by circles of dried mold I wondered what fresh enormities they contained. Putting it bluntly, I was in for quite a shock.

PROJECT BAREBALLS
subsection 14
gfkh 3927/a. PFR .06

Ye ladies and gentlemen of Dickstachel/Who sit at home at ease/Ah little do you think upon/The dangers of the rain forest. As I told you in my last, if you've taken the trouble to read it, my last rap with Harry had given me a theory why folks who go mountains no come back, and I was going to prove or disprove it come hell, high water and any number of cables-in-a-cleft-stick telling me not to.

Harry did his best to stop me.

"Paul, you're out of your mind."

"I was born that way. Too late now."

"Don't you ever listen when I talk to you? Nothing ever came back from there except half a herd of very sick pigs."

"Sure. But nobody ever went there who was first-chop research witch-doctor with little black devil-box he go cluck-cluck."

"Ah, shaddap."

"By the way, Harry, you never told me how you learned to speak American."

"If I tell you will you promise to drop this fool idea?"

"No, but tell me anyway."

He sighed.

"I learned it from an anthropologist with a broken leg. We did what we could for him, but he had to stick around here for quite a while, especially as he had a dose of fever before he could walk good. He wasn't a bad guy, for an anthropologist. He left me a couple of books and a dictionary. They've pretty well fallen to pieces by now with this damned humidity, but they helped a lot. Maybe I'm a natural linguist or something."

He pulled some yellowed pages from a tin box and handed them to me. Part of an English-Spanish dictionary, part of *The*

Story of Man, by Carleton Stennis Coon, and the first two-thirds of Agatha Christie's *Thirteen at Dinner.*

"Listen, Paul, can you for Chrissakes tell me how that one comes out?"

"Harry, I'm sorry as hell, but I never read it."

"Goddamn. Now I'll never know. Once a year I read what there is of it to the boys and girls, and we all guess whodunit. Oh well."

He got out the cigars and looked sadly at the few that were left.

"He gave me those too," he said, and offered them. I tried to refuse, but he insisted.

"You still going?"

"Sure."

"What we going to do with the rest of your party?"

"Be nice to them till I come back."

"You ain't coming back."

"Don't start that again."

"Will you do me a favor?"

"Depends."

"Take that godawful Milton dame with you. She's wrecking my men's morale."

"That's a helluva big favor."

He looked at me dumbly.

"Oh well. Just to please you."

So we leave at dawn.

Next evening.

Tragi-comic interlude, Tilly boy.

Yesterday we pushed on to the edge of the rain forest, Laura Milton and I and our bearers. Harry had given six criminal types the option of going with us or staying in jail. Laura spent most of the day telling me why she had no wish to be regarded as a sex object. Now you know as well as I do—or perhaps you don't—that when a woman starts talking like a forty-year-old Victorian spinster she's desperate to get laid. I have a kind heart, Tilly, though you might not think so. Came evening, we had eaten our tinned food—every mealtime I think of you stuffing your belly at Rinaldo's—and it was time for bye-bye. I walked over to Laura's tent, lifted the flap and looked at her. Moonlight was flooding in. Laura looked back at me. Neither of us said a word. But you know, Tilly, I couldn't. I simply couldn't. After a minute I dropped the flap and went back to my own tent.

All today she's been very silent. I am so sorry for that girl I could cry. Imagine what it must be like to be so absolutely devoid of the necessary that in the whole of your post-pubescent life no man has ever got it up for you.

Next day. Thursday, or maybe Tuesday.

We're on a grassy plain. I should say the mountains are about thirty or forty miles away, though it's difficult to judge. The cachinnation of the bearers had got so unbearable—ouch—that I told them to drop back till they were almost out of earshot. Obviously they're scared. I taped film badge meters on their chests first, pinned one on me and gave Laura one. No funny cracks, please. I also dug out the Geiger counter and checked it. So far, nothing. Maybe tomorrow.

Friday, or maybe Wednesday.

Around mid-morning the Geiger started to cluck at long intervals. I sent the bearers even further back and told them to make camp there. Laura and I went cautiously forward. After a couple of hours the clucks were coming noticeably faster, though nothing to worry about; but they went on speeding up till halfway through the afternoon, when I realized that the film badges were certainly doing their job. We decided to go back to camp and hassle out what to do next.

In the morning Laura was nowhere around. I went forward on yesterday's trail. Not a trace of her, even through the glasses. Finally, when I judged I'd reached the point where we'd left off the day before, I imagined I could j-u-s-t see a little pinpoint moving, way ahead. Christ, Tilly, what could I do? If the radiation level continued to rise the way it had been doing, she was well into the lethal zone. If I'd gone after her I'd never have got back. I don't think I'm over the safe amount myself, but time will tell.

SUMMARY AND CONCLUSIONS.

1. The Dickstachel Research Institute is now short of one highly competent senior technician.

2. Somewhere in those mountains is an unbelievably powerful source of radiation. I have no idea what it is. I suppose most probably it's a freak concentration of radioactive material—a practical joke on the part of Old Mother Nature, as you so frequently and disgustingly nickname the cosmos. If you want to indulge in an s.f. cliché—and you would—perhaps the relics of a super atom bomb dropped by Visitors from Outer Space when no one was looking. But there is no way—no way —of investigating more closely. Even at that distance—I repeat, thrity or forty miles—the warning devices were quite sufficiently activated, thank you very much. No way, even with lead suits, and you couldn't wear one in those temperatures even if it was air-conditioned, and then you'd have to have more people to look after the air conditioning, and—no, it would all get too complicated. Unless of course you were riding a self-powered vehicle. But you wouldn't need to ride it, you could use an adaptation of a lunar landing module, remote-controlled, if the gear would stand up to that unknown degree of radiation. Oh hell, it will have to wait till I get back stateside.

But get this, Dr. Tillevant, and get it very loud and clear. It is the duty of The Dickstachel Research Institute to broadcast this information at once for the benefit of all explorers, prospectors, religious maniacs and particularly all airplane pilots. For all I know, that mountain range accounts for a number of planes that have disappeared without trace. For all I know, the bones of Ambrose Bierce are lying there, phosphorescent in the night. But tell them, damn you, tell them.

My God. What a way for a girl to commit suicide.

33

Dear dr. Ampiofratello, you may recollect the late President Truman's unrestrained wrath when the equally late General MacArthur expressed his intention of crossing the Yalu River. I am incontrovertibly convinced that my own wrath was no less when I had finished reading Darrell's latest effusion; but whereas the President could and did fire the General on the spot, I could not fire Darrell till he got home, and quite possibly, in spite of his lunatic reports and reckless endangerment of personnel, not then.

I felt so helpless that I was reduced to a fantasy of a great public anti-Darrell movement, with tables piled with petitions for signature and signs saying STOP DARRELL NOW all along one block of Fifth Avenue. The vision faded when I recalled the ineffectiveness of similar efforts and realized that my enemy would doubtless counter on the other side of Fifth Avenue with similar tables and signs saying STOP TILLEVANT NOW.

Darrell had lost one of the most conscientious and faithful servants The Dickstachel Research Institute ever had. She had been with us from the beginning, and during all those years there was no single instance—I am positive of this, because I had my secretary check it—no single instance where any of her reports had been after deadline; indeed they had frequently been twenty-four hours early. It is practically impossible to find personnel of this high caliber. Her place might be filled, but Laura Milton was probably irreplaceable. Why, oh why had I put at risk this stalwart supporter of administrative principle?

There was another point. The claims for employers' liability insurance, group insurance and so on, would impose a considerable additional burden of paperwork on my insufficient and overworked staff; but this in itself might be turned to good effect when I next beseeched the Trustees to ease the pressure. What concerned me most was that the mere fact that these claims were being submitted might lead to an increase in the already unconscionably high premiums. This of course was one of the last things which one could expect Paul Darrell to have considered. Yet blameworthy as he was in not making an accurate extrapolation from the wretched girl's behavior, which by the evidence of his own report he had noticed, so that he should have watched more closely the property of The Dickstachel Research Institute—blameworthy as he was, I felt that Miss Milton herself should have considered more carefully the administrative problems which she was causing by committing suicide.

I wondered if it really was suicide. Perhaps it was murder. I believed Darrell was capable of anything. But how could it be proved, particularly in the absence of a corpse. I had a very clear picture of Darrell digging a shallow grave with an entrenching tool—or a deep one if you come to that—in spite of his apparent superficiality he was always thorough. But how were we going to locate an unmarked grave on the edge of, or more probably within the tangled vegetation of—that is where I should have put it—the rain forest? We certainly could not expect Darrell to lead us to the spot; and if you come to that, murder would be even worse publicity than suicide so far as The Dickstachel Research Institute was concerned.

There was also the question of those damned mountains. If Darrell had not been so hysterically imperative in his demand that I "tell them" I should, admittedly at some risk, have kept the whole thing quiet until his return, so that at least there would have been nothing to dilute the publicity attendant upon the successful completion of The Tillevant Project. But if I now started to send out press releases about radioactive mountains I could foresee the speedy transformation of The Tillevant Project into The Darrell Discovery—and a more useless discovery I could not imagine. Even if Darrell had accidentally stumbled on some fantastic reservoir of uranium, or plutonium, or whatever the wretched stuff was, what good was that if no one could get nearer than forty miles?

As for disappearing airplanes, that was a quite unsubstantiated theory. Airplanes are perfectly capable of disappearing without such adventitious help. For all I knew, the mountains were perfectly ordinary mountains and the planes had disappeared by the simple process of hitting them.

For all I knew, Darrell's equipment was malfunctioning, possibly due to the extremely damp local conditions, although I had to admit that the film badge readings rather set me back. A film badge is not subject to malfunction. That at least is what I was assured by a member of the, uh, scientific staff—*not* Darrell—when I began to wear my own film badge. I wear this the whole time, and check it constantly, both inside The Dickstachel Research Institute, although our Radiographic Department is safely, I hope, underground, adequately, I trust, shielded, and in any case I never go near it—both inside and outdoors. The whole time. Well, no, not in the shower, of course. I even pin it to my pajamas, assuming that it will continue to function should I have cause to remove these during the night, although in recent years such occasions have become increasingly rare—but I wander.

On top of all that, Darrell had included with his frivolously worded report several sheets of calculations and, uh, technical description which he had marked for the personal attention of our chief radiographer. I could not, thank God, make head or tail of these, but I supposed they constituted some kind of firm evidence. My first impulse was to put them through the shredder, together with the report itself. I was dissuaded from this course by the fact that all incoming mail at The Dickstachel Research Institute is numbered and registered in a leatherbound ledger which forms an unquestionable record of such mail having been received at The Dickstachel Research Institute. It is not necessarily opened, you understand, or I would not have had my Nevada correspondence sent to my business address.

There have been many complaints that the delay this causes, coupled with the other factors to which I have previously referred, means that mail is not received until the following day, or even the day after that; but I always quash such mutinous comment by pointing out that this great country of ours is growing toward adult status. In our infancy we acquired the dubious reputation of being a land of hustlers—a word which itself has since acquired a reprehensible secondary meaning—but in this day and age, when the Manhattan telephone directory alone contains some fourteen pages of Federal, State and City Government listings, and other cities throughout the land doubtless boast a proportionate number, it is high time that we began to comport ourselves in a manner befitting our advancing years.

We are beginning to learn. It can take as long as three weeks to obtain from one of our major corporations a reply to a simple written inquiry; we are beginning to give an entirely fanciful interpretation to delivery dates; but we still have a long way to go before we realize that Method is paramount, that Method is greater than all of us, that Method will endure after all the ephemeral mayflies of an earlier tradition and indeed we ourselves, the High Priests of Method, have passed away.

There I sat at my desk, now taking a whiff of oxygen and now checking the time in Genoa—a very lovely city, I have always understood, which I hope to visit someday. When I had spent some two hours thus reflecting upon the beauties of Method I realized that in Method itself lay at least a partial solution to my problem.

I scribbled a note bearing every appearance of haste and saying, "Please let me have your written recommendations on the attached at the earliest possible moment." I enclosed this and the relevant sheets in one of our Internal Mail envelopes and inscribed thereon, "For the eyes of Dr. Zenko only. Urgent." I then waited till after the last Internal Mail collection of the day had been made and put the envelope in the appropriate tray. I was confident that it would not reach our Radiographic Department until late the following day, or perhaps even the morning after that; and since Dr. Zenko was leaving that very night for a conference in Mexico City and would be away at least ten days, while it would doubtless take him some little time to prepare his recommendations in due form and transmit them to me by the same leisurely route—oh yes, I had certainly gained myself a useful breathing space, and who knew what the situation might be by the time Dr. Zenko's recommendations lay on my desk?

And then, it would take time to consider them fully, and I could always summon him for a verbal discussion, the date of which, owing to my many engagements, might be some further days off; and then of course as a result of that discussion it would probably be necessary for him to revise his recommendations, and that would mean a few more days gained. Oh, there was no end to the ways in which I could keep the iron, if not hot at least tepid, until Darrell's return, thereby maintaining the relative importance of his mountains and my pygmies.

It was thus in a carefree mood that I came to work next day. Before entering The Dickstachel Research Institute I paused and spent a moment or two—well, half an hour actually—watching progress on The Tillevant Building. The steelwork had been topped off—I believe that is the correct, uh, technical term—and the outer facing was well advanced. In order to obtain these results the overtime bill was not inconsiderable—as a matter of fact it was astronomical—but I was confident of my ability to attribute the major part of the cost overrun to inflation, even the most unpleasant phenomena may have their beneficial side, and I was determined that The Official Opening should take place as planned. I had cabled Darrell to remind him of the importance of his return before then, with, of course, his selected band of pygmies. I would much prefer to have had the pygmies without Darrell, but there it was.

In spite of my utmost endeavors, which included two most unpleasant interviews at which both the architects and the contractors were present, I had been unable to get these slothful and obstinate people to budge from their position that it would be impossible to complete the entire building by the date of The Official Opening. It is really incredible how, in a country whose name was once synonymous with hustle, people are more and more behaving like sleepwalkers. However, they had guaranteed that the entrance hall, the first-floor washrooms and the reception foyer would be finished, together with the exterior canopy and the entrance roadway, and that the landscaping would be installed. This was really all that was necessary for the ceremony; and by placing RESTRICTED AREA signs, reinforced by armed Sanctuary Wardens, at all points leading off the reception foyer, anyone who might be expecting a conducted tour could be gently led back to the canapés and punch.

I had another reason for humming a jaunty tune, for this was the day on which would commence the filming of *Discovery*, as my documentary epic was entitled. The actual directing would be in the hands of a rather objectionable person named George Langston, who was already indulging in his favorite tantrum of retiring into a corner and beating his head against the wall; but my dear Miss Greta Love had promised to supervise the entire undertaking as Executive Producer, and I was therefore looking forward to being in her company on many occasions during the ensuring weeks.

Security had been considerably relaxed—in fact it had been totally suspended—for the occasion, although of course all employees of Zeeta Productions were supposed to wear identity plaques, a requirement to which they paid but nominal attention. Equipment of all kinds was already pouring in to The Dickstachel Research Institute —cameras, lights, reflectors, mikes, clappers—you see I was quickly picking up the jargon; heavy cables were snaking about the floor, and the junior members of the crew, with compressed lips and sinister expressions, were manhandling these now into one place, now into another, as George Langston, addressing his underlings in a restrained voice expressive of courteous enmity, changed his mind and then put it back again. Progress was not as rapid as it might have been, since members of at least four unions were involved, none of whom was on speaking terms with the others.

Thrilling as all this was, to me the culminating moment of this opening session—and indeed of all the others—would not occur until Miss Love arrived. And here she came now, the dear girl, as lovely as ever in the morning sunlight. Hastily I took from my secretary, who had been holding it for the past fifteen minutes with an increasingly sour expression, a bouquet of rare orchids, with its silken ribbon. I presented this with all the grace and charm of which I was capable, and she accepted it with bewitching languor, while the principal staff photographer of *Questionmark,* the house organ of The Dickstachel Research Institute, recorded the scene for that publication and any of the outside media which could be persuaded to pick it up.

Photographers are all alike, and we had to repeat the scene several times until the bouquet, my grace and charm, and even Miss Love's bewitching languor were becoming a little shopworn. When we could again give our attention to the main matter in hand we found that a temporary work stoppage was in progress, if that is not a contradiction in terms, over the question whether the pictures ought to have been taken by Zeeta's own still photographer. In order to restore harmony we went through the motions some half-dozen times more, at the end of which the condition of the bouquet was such that there was really no alternative to throwing it into the nearest trashcan.

When later we came to shoot, as the photography process is termed, a typical Trustees' Meeting, we experienced maximum cooperation. Indeed, almost our only problem was in dissuading each of the Trustees—except, oddly enough, Ms. Kalman—from leaning forward or twisting around at the most painful angles in order to hog, as the expression goes, the camera and upstage—another professional term borrowed from the theater—everyone else.

I wish I could give the same high praise to the, uh, scientific and technical personnel of The Dickstachel Research Institute. From the very first announcement of *Discovery,* the grapevine brought me ominous rumblings about unnecessary interruptions of routine. I ignored these, since the contract of each and every one included a clause binding the beneficiary to obey any reasonable instructions from Higher Authority. But when we actually began shooting I was aghast at the maniacal glares which were directed into the lens, as the optical portion of the camera—but I expect you know that already, dear Dr. Ampiofratello. Had these bellicose grimaces—which George Langston, despite his undoubted directorial prowess, seemed unable to sweeten—had they actually appeared in the final version, the image presented to the public would have been that The Dickstachel Research Institute was entirely staffed by scientists mad in both senses of the word.

It was not until Miss Greta Love, in her capacity as Executive Producer, personally appeared in each man's cubbyhole—uh, office —that the situation was not only ameliorated but transformed. Indeed, there was a most ludicrous effect in one day's rushes, as the hastily printed and unedited scenes taken on the previous day are called. The face of the man in question bore the all-too-familiar wide-eyed snarl until about halfway through, when it suddenly changed to a look of calflike yearning tinged, I am afraid, with positive lechery. It took very little deduction to establish that at that point Miss Love had, without previous warning, appeared behind the camera. In the final version of this scene, George Langston had managed to eliminate the lechery and somewhat tone down the yearning; but I am forced to admit that the film as a whole presented our, uh, scientific staff as somewhat too visionary in appearance. Even the females, whose hostility Miss Love only seemed to intensify, bore the same dreamy look, by virtue, if that is the right word, of the fact that we finally shot them after Darrell, curse him, had returned, and he took her place behind the camera.

In spite of that, those were halcyon days. Halcyon.

Ah well.

34

THERE WAS, however, one thumb in the soup—Darrell's latest report.

TO BE FILED AFTER SUCCEEDING REPORT
BUT BEFORE BREAKFAST.

Here I come, ready or not. Make ready to break out the bunting and champagne, or if funds are thin never mind the bunting. Operation Bareballs is about to reach its triumphant conclusion. I am bringing with me, in accordance with your revered instructions, the world's first performing troupe of non-pubic-hair Cosamo, headed by their very own Chief. The non-stop laff riot from the world's soggiest rain forest. Absolutely no deception. No razors, no tweezers, no depilatories. Men, women and children exactly as Old Mother Nature made them. SEE the levigate pudenda. SEE the hairless testes. The miracle of the ages displayed for your instruction and delight. For only fifty cents extra you may touch these genitary marvels with your very own fingers at your very own risk—the management accepts no responsibility. HEAR the happy laughter of these unique physiological quirks. TASTE their native drink—a mere ten dollars the bowl. Warranted to cure the vapors, the megrims, sterility, fertility, virginity and infinity. Walk up, walk up. Just about to begin.

It's on your own head, Tilly. Personally I think the Cosamo should have been left alone. It's not so much the effect civilization will have on them, it's the effect they're likely to have on civilization. Still, Harry's a great guy. Shouldn't wonder if he ends up on the cover of *Time*. Maybe as Man of the Year, even.

I was very touched by the reception he gave me when I walked back into his village. He hung back a bit at first—told me afterwards he thought I was a spirit—but he soon showed true chieftain's courage and came forth to parley, ghost or no. When he found I was real he stopped laughing, put his arms around the small of my back—about as high as he could reach—and hugged me. He's surprisingly strong, and he has a very hard head. When I got my breath back he asked me if I'd brought Laura Milton too. I didn't go into details. I simply told him No, and he stopped laughing more than before.

Then he got a bit worked up in case I was going to develop what he called the pig-sickness. I think this was partly on my account—he does seem to think rather highly of me, Dr. Tillevant. The feeling is mutual, because any guy who can hold his people together in such difficult conditions and keep their love and respect—excuse the dirty words—has to be pretty special. If memory serves me well it would be hard to find many such in the great world outside the rain forest.

But partly it was because he thought it might be contagious, and naturally he didn't want his people to get it. After all, spreading the pig-sickness among a simple and Alorra-fearing people would be too syphilis-and-Captain-Cooke, wouldn't it? More about Alorra soon. I was able to reassure him, in fact I incautiously showed him my film badge, which impressed him so much he asked me for a whole lot of them so he could make a government issue.

Anyway, after the first raptures of reunion were over I had to point out to Harry that it was time I got down to business, and how about letting me take blood samples and all that jazz, and oh, by the way, I was hereby extending a cordial invitation from The Dickstachel Research Institute to him and a selected group of his fellow countrymen to enjoy an all-expense paid vacation in the United States, including deluxe hotel accommodations, use of tennis courts, a guided tour of Wichita, Kan., all gratuities and round-trip transport. And he of course would be the guest of honor.

The whole idea shook him up pretty bad.

"Hell no. My people. How can I leave my people?"

Thereby echoing to an amazing degree the official last words of the younger Pitt, although there is another version which goes:

"I think I could eat one of Bellamy's pork pies."

Harry absently caressed the rump of a passing female, who obediently stood still for the purpose, and went on:

"As for letting you take some of them with you—how do I know what I'd be letting them in for? It isn't that I don't trust you, Paul, but the characters who come through here from time to time—they're such a weird lot. And they seem to grow weirder and weirder."

I made no comment on this unsolicited testimonial.

"Besides, Paul, what I can't understand is why, if the outside world is so great, why doesn't everyone stay there? Why do they have to come out to this mudsink? Why can't they leave us alone?"

To this heartfelt cry of a large part of the human race, from the Japanese when Commodore Perry dropped anchor to the latest married couple afflicted with visiting relatives, I had no answer either. Well, I did think of explaining that all of us except certain residents of Tennessee are descended from monkeys (descended is right) but there was no time to give him a crash course in Darwin. Besides, I thought it would hardly strengthen my case. So I started to hand him a line about this being an Important Scientific Project. You'd have been proud of me, Tilly, you really would. Except that I started to overdo it and tell him how The Dickstachel Research Institute spent all its time helping to make people healthier, happier and wiser, and this was part of it.

"Paul, you don't believe that."

I switched to telling him that if I returned home with my mission unfulfilled, or only partly fulfilled, I should be in plenty of trouble with the Chief of my tribe. That's you, Tilly. Doesn't it make you feel grand? It registered well with him too. He sat quiet for a while. Then he asked that familiar question—he was coming out with all kinds of echoes of the Western world that night:

"Paul, what is it really like?"

When you're drinking with a friend you don't want to tell him important lies. Besides, he wouldn't have believed them. He'd already tripped me up when I came out with the one little one that could be excused as loyalty to the people who pay my salary. So I started to tell him about the things I thought would appeal to him. Like Southern Comfort and easy women. I guess I was tired, or I'd have chosen something less obvious. He said:

"If I never had to get drunk or see another woman, it couldn't come a moment too soon. For Alorra's sake, Paul, if you people have to spend all your time drinking and fucking it can't be any better than it is here."

And I hadn't even mentioned pot and heroin, because the Cosamo are very decent people. But it was at that point that by chance I hit on the right bait. I told him that Out There he could have all the cigars he wanted and that he could not only get a clean new copy of *Thirteen at Dinner* with the solution in it, but also the other seventy-odd thrillers from Christie.

And do you know, that did it. He said he'd come, and take six—count them, six—of his subjects with him, so long as he chose them himself. I said O.K., so long as there were some of each, and we shook hands on it. I had no idea what he proposed to do about running the tribe while he was away, but that was his headache. As it turned out, he appointed a Council of State —two guys and a gal who I happened to know didn't like each other very much. Well, when I say gal she was forty and toothless. He had a very odd look on his face when he pointed them out to me.

For the next few days I was busy taking routine samples—for which fell activity Harry told me with an absolutely poker face Alorra had granted a special dispensation—preparing ammunition for the return journey through the territory of the warlike Bellaki, and packing up generally. Harry and his hand-picked laboratory specimens were packing their own baggage, which consisted entirely of outsized containers of Whammo, and the Council of State held its inaugural meeting, at which the proceedings seemed to consist of pointing derisively at each other and laughing, another indication that, innocent as the Cosamo are when left alone, they could very easily adapt to the manners and customs of contemporary civilization, particularly at election time.

On the morning of our departure we rose at dawn, After a hasty breakfast I started for Harry's place, but he was already striding through the village towards the temple of Alorra, which he reached without seeing me. I let him go in without hailing him—my motto is always not to interfere with sleeping dogs and persons bent on their religious occasions—but while I was waiting for him to come out again I fear I was overcome by vulgar curiosity. I'd been havering with myself whether I would or whether I wouldn't poke my nose into an aspect of the Cosamo which had absolutely nothing to do with my official brief. Such superficial study as I have done in comparative religion has only convinced me that all the existing theories are wrong. My private view is that the only way to find out anything about the superscientist who let off the big bang which started the universe—which may very well have been a technical error on his part when he was conducting another experiment—the only way to find out anything about him, her or it is by dying, and maybe not then. Also I didn't like the way the Cosamo used the temple of Alorra as some kind of place of punishment. They had been very decent to me, I was sure I had seen them at their best, and I really didn't want to see them at perhaps their worst.

But for some reason, at that moment I felt the urge to act like any gaping tourist and take a look inside. Harry wasn't laughing when he came out, and he kept silent until, as gently and politely as possible, I told him what was on my mind. Then he had such a fit of sinister merriment he had to lean on a tree to keep from falling over. When he felt a little better he said:

"Paul, are you sure you can take it?"

And I, being young and foolish, said:

"Why not?"

Between paroxysms of mirth he gasped out:

"You'll find out. Yes. Go ahead."

"Should I take my shoes off, or wear a hat, or something?"

"It would be nice of you to strip off first."

Already doubting myself, I did just that, and he came with me, closed the door and stood, as far as I could tell, right behind me. He probably had some idea of catching me if I fainted, which was kind of him, because he'd already had one dose of religion that morning. I didn't faint, but in the first shock I certainly swayed dramatically.

It was pitch dark with the door shut, except for one beam of sunlight through a hole high in the wall. A natural spotlight, shining full on the face of Alorra.

A very, very old face, carved in wood which time and climate had cracked in many places, like wrinkled skin. Carved, moreover, in a Laugh. The most horrible Laugh I ever hope not to see again. Neither Dürer nor Bosch could have come near it. When Zeus laughed at humanity, I imagine there must have been something kind in it at bottom. When Mephistopheles laughs, well, that's nearer to it but he laughs because he's a bad boy who enjoys pulling the rug out from under people. But the Laugh of Alorra is simply a sick satire on the utter uselessness and idiocy and purposelessness of all things; and whoever carved it long ago, as the deathly rain pattered and dripped from the trees, was a highly perceptive genius making the ultimate comment on his world.

I suppose if you are born and grow up a Cosamo you develop some kind of immunity; but Harry was right. I couldn't bear to look at the Laugh of Alorra for more than a couple of minutes. By that time my eyes had adjusted enough for me to see that the rest of the statue was quite recent, and painted as fine and

163

beautiful as the contemporary Cosamo artists could make it; and that there was nothing else in the hut, either on the walls or the earthen floor, or any decoration. But I'd had enough. I turned to where I could now dimly see Harry and said:

"Let's get out of here."

Once away from the Laugh, even the rain forest looked good. I can't have looked too good myself, though. Harry shook his head:

"I tried to warn you, my friend."

"That's O.K. I'll be fine in a minute."

As we walked back through the village Harry told me that yes, the tradition and the legend is that from time to time the body of Alorra must be renewed, and that one day an artist will be born so supremely gifted that the body he gives Alorra will cause the Laugh to fade; and when that happens the rain forest will turn into a beautiful place, and good to live in, and laughter will become infrequent and gentle. I seem to have heard something like that before, and that legend also has been a long time coming true. But you see, Tilly, your friend Nugent-Nugent was not wholly accurate in his account, and he had missed the point of the story, which far better men of his profession are also wont to do.

We set off soon after that; but Harry had to make his farewell speech first. He told the Cosamo, assembled in the center of the village, to be good boys and girls and when he came back he would bring them the solution to *Thirteen at Dinner*. Except for the Council of State, they were all laughing so hard that he was rather difficult to hear; but they stopped when he spoke of coming back, though that was when the Council of State started.

Two days' march brought us to the border of the Bellaki country. Everyone tensed up and of course the noise was deafening. I'd taken Harry's word for it that the Cosamo were poor fighters, but they certainly were lousy reconnaissance troops. You could hear them for miles. I said to Harry:

"Lookit, why are you worrying about the Bellaki if you have Government protection?"

He gave me a long, and for him nasty, look that removed the last tattered shreds of my naiveté. So I passed out the ammunition. Everyone had plenty, and when the Bellaki appeared, strung out along the edge of the trail, blowpipes poised, we had no trouble. Into every outstretched hand was thrust an eight-by-eleven picture of Farrah Fawcett-Majors, and as each man got his he ran off highly delighted.

I forgot to tell you, Tilly, that that was how we got through on the way in, except that we used Ellen Burstyn.

The Cosamo couldn't have cared less about the pictures. They gave them away right willingly.

Well, tomorrow we shall reach town. There was rather a problem today, because I felt it was time to start handing out loincloths. South Americans are a good deal more conventional than people back stateside. The Cosamo cooperated in the end, but they complained of chafing.

Will mail this as soon as I get in, and probably one more before we leave by air. There now. Aren't I behaving nicely? Love to all.

35

WELL, DEAR Dr. Ampiofratello, I really did not know what to make of that last rigmarole of Darrell's. Peculiar tribal gods, unorthodox methods of warfare, so many unjustified innuendoes about so many things—but it was painfully clear to me that he was returning safe and sound to the land which unfortunately gave him birth—and how I wished one of those poisoned darts had got him, though I suppose he would have had the antidote ready, curse him —and that if Darrell's psychological insights were correct, and they probably were, the Cosamo themselves were a more complex problem than Nugent-Nugent's more superficial approach had led me to expect.

What with that, and the fact that someone had stolen the clock off the wall of the reception foyer of The Tillevant Building before it was even officially open—and besides that Dr. Zenko was proving extremely obstructive—or rather, much too cooperative—over those alleged radioactive mountains, and kept urging me to release a statement, so that I was at my wits' end to invent new pretexts for delay, and I was terrified that he would ignore proper administrative procedures and telephone the *New York Times*—and the previous night my wife. . . .

Well, anyway, at that moment I felt that everything was getting rather too much for me. I simply had to, so to speak, back off a little so that I might view things in proper perspective and return strengthened to the fray. In fact, I determined to take the afternoon off. And that led to one of the most embarrassing incidents of my career. There was worse to come, but at the time I certainly—as a matter of fact, I determined to go out and get drunk.

I had never made such a decision in my life before. I had *been* drunk—well, *rather* drunk—at certain official events, because it is not always possible without giving offense to avoid the excessive bonhomie which one is prone to encounter on such occasions, but not to the extent of walking crooked or slurring my utterance, so that my being rather drunk was more in my mind, and I am sure no one else noticed, at least I hope not, oh of course not, because by that time everyone else was a little on also, except for those people, and there seem to be more of them every day, who spend the entire evening on Bloody Marys made wholly of tomato juice. I suppose that would be a good thing for me to try, only I loathe tomato juice. White wine is very fashionable just now, but it always gives me acid indigestion.

In view of everything, perhaps I was subconsciously influenced by the Cosamo viewpoint that there are only two things which make life possible on this barely habitable planet. Drinking and f—, uh, sexual intercourse. Unfortunately heavy drinking always gives me pains in the guts next day, and the other thing gives me palpitations, although at my last physical checkup I was assured that there was nothing wrong with my heart. But I was feeling so *low*—

Well, anyway, the one thing I am *not* is a solitary drinker. If I was going to spend the afternoon, and maybe the evening, getting drunk, I was certainly going to find myself a drinking companion. And as I sat at my desk, now admiring the mellow shine on my Duncan Phyfe bookcase, now making a note to reprove the head cleaner for leaving a spot of tarnish on my Charles I pencil bucket, now taking a whiff of oxygen and wondering whether I might not be just as well off getting high on that, though it is not the same thing, and besides I felt that if I asked anyone to join me in sniffing oxygen it might seem a little unorthodox, though not glue, but really people who sniff glue—

What I actually had in mind was that I wanted to get drunk in the company of a beautiful woman.

And the only beautiful woman I could think of just then was Miss Greta Love.

As a matter of fact, around that time Miss Greta Love was almost all I could think of. Whatever important administrative problems I might be concerned with, such as effecting some meaningful reduction in the excessive amount of costly toilet paper used by the employees of The Dickstachel Research Institute—or of installing coin-operated dispensers—in another part of my mind Miss Greta Love was always present. I make no excuse for this. Infatuation has entoiled many a famous man.

By good luck, Miss Love was at that very moment in the building, acting in her capacity as Executive Producer. It was but the work of a moment, using the internal telephone system, to touchtone the number of the department where by coincidence I happened to know she was functioning. With only the slightest quiver in my voice I asked her to lunch. She had lunched with me several times since that first occasion. But this was going to be different. Hence the quiver.

Her response was delightfully frivolous.

"Oh wow," she said, and then, "Ah'd love to."

Dear girl. Oh wow, indeed. It was not till some considerable time afterwards that it occurred to me that her use of the expression might not have been intended to express heartfelt joy.

We went, of course, to Rinaldo's, but I departed from our usual custom by suggesting that we have a drink at the bar instead of at the table. I thought I detected the faintest tinge of surprise in her acceptance. There were two adjoining places fortunately vacant, and by sitting a little sideways I was able to appreciate the beautifully symmetrical patterns which her hindermost, thus placed on the somewhat inadequate circular seat, created. We began with very dry martinis with a twist, in glasses exquisitely frosted. Cesare, the bartender at Rinaldo's, is a handsome young man who learned his art at some of the best-known luxury hotels in Italy. I have drunk many good martinis, but Cesare's were the only ones which I could unhesitatingly call perfect. It is a very extraordinary thing that such a native American invention as the martini has to go abroad to become consummate.

Cesare had large, soft, dark eyes, and when he mixed a drink he looked upon his work as if it were a Cellini cup. Unfortunately he tended to look at beautiful women in the same way, but he discreetly withdrew his gaze when he found my eyes minatorily fixed upon him. After the third martini we went in to eat. Miss Love had veal scaloppini, I had spaghetti. The sauce was not overgenerous in amount, but there was a great deal of spaghetti, and I ate it all to provide a sponge for the serious drinking ahead. She began to speak of *Discovery*, but I held up a hand.

"Not this afternoon, my—my dear. This afternoon I am devoting to unashamed escapism, free of all mundane cares. Who knows what may happen ere midnight?"

I hastily ate some more spaghetti. Perhaps I was going too fast. Miss Love's enormous eyes momentarily grew even larger.

"Wha, Mistuh—Doktuh—Till'vant, Ah'd never have thought it of yuh. Yuh've always seemed so daidicated."

I gave her my philosophical smile, although I fear it was dimmed by a partially uningurgitated thread of spaghetti.

"Ah, Miss Love," I said. I thought it might be too soon to call her "my dear" again. "Ah, Miss Love, you of all people must understand the terrible drain that creative responsibility imposes on the psychic reserves. Surely you must sometimes feel the need to recuperate—to be for a while free of the everyday world?"

She slowly nodded her lovely head.

"Ah sure do, Doktuh Till'vant."

"Can't we stop being so formal with each other—Greta? Why don't you call me—Ram?"

Here let me interpose, dear Dr. Ampiofratello, that I have never been at all satisfied with the given names which my parents bestowed on me. Rameses has always struck me as *outré*, and surely to goodness there could not be a less *outré* person than I, although of course it was the name of several kings of ancient Egypt, a thought which has sustained me on many occasions. My middle name, for which I always use an initial, is worse. Much worse. My father chose it. Goodness knows how much he had to pay the officiating clergyman to dub me Penis. Save to meet the inexorable demands of certain official documents, I have never revealed this to a living soul. That I am doing so now is, I suppose, merely part of the catharsis. But I was certainly not going to ask Miss Love—Greta—to call me Penis. At least, not until we had for some time known each other much more intimately. Rameses was too lumbering, but I had high hopes of the diminutive form, Ram, with its potent but not explicit overtones.

"All right—Ram," she breathed. Ah, never had I expected to hear the syllable pronounced in tones of such blandishment.

I was not quite sure of the next step, so I drank some more of the bottle of Bardolino which we were sharing. In choosing it I had overcome a spendthrift impulse to order champagne, expense account or no, although the mere idea of champagne made me think of bathing my lovely companion in it. Domestic, of course.

"Bardolino," I ventured, "Bardolino is an excellent wine to go with Italian food. Its sharp dryness counteracts the occasional over-richness of the cuisine."

"It certainly does—Ram."

"It is an Italian wine, of course."

"Yes. Ah suspected that."

"It is interesting how well some things go together. Italian wine with Italian food. French wine with French food."

This had seemed a promising line of attack. I was going to add to my list of things that went well together "You and me" but when it came to it I could not get the words out. This rendered my immediately preceding remarks, even to my ears, banal.

The ice cream came. Spumoni, with its concentric circles of different colors. I had the brilliant idea of comparing one of the colors with her lovely eyes, but on checking I found that our portions were bright red, arsenic green and dingy chocolate. So that did not work either. I was sure that I had been going too fast. Perhaps some fatherly—or rather, avuncular—or rather, cousinly—sympathy might provide the correct intermediate speed.

"Tell me, Greta, even these days, as a woman do you find it difficult to be accepted in an executive capacity?"

"Wale, sometimes Ah do have to flutter mah eyelashes a little."

"Not at me, I hope," I said, not knowing in the least whether that made sense. At that moment she did flutter them, with the result that I put my elbow in the spumoni. As I was wiping myself off I had a really brilliant idea.

"Tell me, Greta"—that was the second time I had used that opening—"what do *you* do when you need to escape?"

Even as I said it, it sounded like a line from a commercial: "What do doctors do when constipation strikes?" She opened her mouth to say something, but for some reason I am quite sure that what she did say was not what she had originally been going to say, if you take my meaning, dear Dr. Ampiofratello.

"Whenever Ah can, Ah go skiing."

Skiing, indeed. The very idea of jumping off the edge of a precipice onto a slippery slope makes me ill. Besides, she might break one or both of those beautiful legs. Thinking of her beautiful legs made me think of her beautiful knees somewhere there under the table. I swigged the last of the Bardolino and made a lunge for them. They did not seem to be there, and my momentum nearly carried me off the edge of my seat. When I had recovered I said:

"I'll tell you what. Let's go some place else and have some brandy."

I was rather proud of that. It seemed to me quite forceful, and in a colloquial style which was worlds away from my normal style of speech. But to my horror she demurred.

"Wha, Ah'd lurv to, but Ah really shude have a word with George Langston about that sequence with the labor'try rabbuts—"

"Toh, my dear young lady," I said, although I knew that it was most important that the rabbits—prize-winning pets specially imported for *Discovery*—should be filmed *before* we went to work on them. "Toh. Tomorrow will do for that. This afternoon we are to be free. Carefree and happy."

I was standing up by then, and suddenly I did feel carefree and happy once more. The necessity for immediate action had passed, and I was sure that as the hours wore on my luck would improve. She gave an enchanting little shrug and an enchanting little laugh, although as I look back on it that laugh was rather odd, really. She said:

"Wale, O.K., Doktuh Till'vant, yuh're the boss."

"I certainly am," I said, "And remember, please—Ram. Ram."

"Ram, theyun," and she squeezed my arm. She actually squeezed my arm. I rather wished she had waited until we got outside, because at Rinaldo's they know who I am. But oh God, I could have raped her on the spot, for the drink was in my blood and my terse was hard and painful. There was a good time coming, I was sure of that. I call it my terse because I could hardly call it my penis, could I now? Terse is a good old English word derived from the Latin *tergere*, to rub off, and thus more accurate in any case.

We went to Brannigan's, a little place on Lexington that I knew of. From their talk it is frequented by radio people on the verge of retirement, sighing for the good old days. The management knew me by sight, but unlike Rinaldo's they did not know who I was. In the taxi I held out my hand and she took it, and we simply sat there, motionless on the cross street while the lights changed and changed again and the intersection remained blocked by cars and trucks trying to get across and not making it, and the neon figures on the meter clicked up and clicked up, and although Greta was holding my hand the sight of those figures was most anaphrodisiacal, and my terse went down again.

We drank brandy, slowly, for an hour. I thought that another good line of approach might be to tell Greta of my unhappy childhood, but I found that she was telling me of her unhappy childhood instead. Her parents had split up while she was five or six. They hated the sight of each other so much that one of them had gone to live in California and the other in Florida, about as far apart as they could get while enjoying easy winters. They had equal custody, so she had done a good deal of traveling before she was out of her teens, and she had come to dislike her parents almost as much as they disliked her.

"Poo lil girl," I said—you will understand, dear Dr. Ampiofratello, that I intended to say "Poor little girl," but that is the way it came out. "Poo lil girl. No father to love you and make you love him, eh? Is that why you're going around with a baldheaded old bugger like me?"

I have no idea why I said that. It was not at all the effect I had been striving to produce ever since twelve forty-five, it then being around three. But:

"Oh no," she said. "I think you're rather sweet really."

Now you will see from this what a very lovely person she was, inside as well as out. No one had ever called me rather sweet before. In fact no one had ever called me any kind of sweet that I could remember. I am a tough man, Dr. Ampiofratello, as you must have found out by now, but tears came into my eyes.

"Poo lil girl," I said again, and patted her hand, but it was not there and I patted the butts in the ashtray instead. While I was wiping the ash off with my napkin I continued—in retrospect I fear rather lachrymosely:

"All alone in this harsh world of business with no one to protect you from being regarded as a sex object."

I must have had some confused memory of Laura Milton when I said that, though a less congruous juxtaposition. My God, you couldn't compare those two women. She replied:

"Wale, Ram, if no one ever regarded me as a sex object Ah wouldn't have much fun, would Ah?"

Here, clearly, was my cue. But at that precise moment I remembered something.

"Good heavens," I said. "Good heavens. We must go at once."

"Why?"

In parenthesis, Dr. Ampiofratello, as the afternoon went by it seemed to me that her Southern accent was becoming much easier to understand. I supposed it was a question of practice. To my ears at least it sounded as if instead of saying "Wha?" she had distinctly said "Why?" But this was no moment to worry about that.

"Come along," I said, "Come along. You'll soon see why."

I was proud of myself as I walked out, so straight, with hardly any need to think where the next foot went. Three doors north from Brannigan's there is a very high-class fruit shop which for one week in the year, and for one week only, sells pomegranates, or, as the French call them, *grenades*. By either name this luscious fruit conjures up for me the most provocative images . . . of languorous decadence . . . of the perfumed East . . . or of martial triumphs, heroic guerrilla action . . . I am well aware that of these *grenades* the French merely make an innocuous syrup known as grenadine. At all events, the store tends to have sold out of pomegranates by the middle of the week, and here it was already Tuesday. But thank goodness they still had some left.

"Give me six," I said. "No, twelve."

In a cooler moment I might have remembered that I can never eat more than half a pomegranate at a time without suffering from diarrhea, and that I should have to store the rest of the consignment in the crisper compartment of the refrigerator. My wife always makes a most unreasonable fuss about cluttering, as she is pleased to call it, the crisper with my grotesque gourmeterie, as she terms it. But just then the desire was strong upon me to contemplate at long leisure this Oriental evoker of plashing fountains and doe-eyed unemanicipated houris.

As I put the bag under my arm and turned to go, I found Greta standing there, smiling in her most alluring fashion.

"Good heavens," I said. "Good heavens, Greta. I had forgotten all about you."

I realized immediately afterwards that this was not really the most courteous thing I could have said in all the circumstances. I sought to explain away my gaffe, but the dear girl laughingly waved away my apology.

"But," I said, "I must certainly make you amends for such a faux pas. Taxi!"

Normally I have some difficulty in attracting the attention of taxidrivers, but on this occasion one pulled right in to the curb from the center lane, to the vociferous disgust of other drivers. I turned to wave my fair companion into the vehicle, but she hesitated.

"But where are we going?" she said, with a merry laugh, which even through the buzzing in my ears sounded like an arpeggio on a celeste.

"Aha," I riposted. "That's *my* little secret."

I then gave the driver the name of a watering hole in the vicinity of Grand Central where they make the world's best stingers. This place is my own personal discovery, and I am not going to reveal its name and exact location even to you, dear Dr. Ampiofratello. It is called Amenity II, and it is on the West side of Madison Avenue between Forty-first and Fortieth streets. The passing lights from the store windows—or do I mean the lights from the store windows we passed?—anyway there was enough light inside the cab for me to get a perfect view of my Greta's beautiful knees, simply begging to be squeezed. So I squeezed them, or rather I tried to, but that damned bag of pomegranates was most unwieldy and I ended up by squeezing one of them instead, which was rather ripe. This was frustrating but undeniably humorous, and in fact I had not stopped laughing by the time we arrived at our destination. When we detaxied the driver said to me:

"Enjoy yourself, Mac."

I thought this was benevolent of him, although normally I detest taxidrivers who call me Mac. I turned back and added another twenty-five cents to the tip.

As I have said, the stingers at Amenity II are excellent. Excellent. After the third one I felt sufficiently recovered from the recent interruptions to resume my role as Lothario. But at that moment I recollected that I had never imparted to Miss Love the details of my unhappy childhood. After all, I had listened to hers. Why should she not listen to mine? As you know, dear Dr. Ampiofratello, my motto is Method and System in All Things.

It is indeed a sad story. When I had attained the tender age of only twelve years, my father heartlessly deserted both me and my dear mother. He not only made opprobrious remarks about her sexual incapacity, but stated that his experience as a parent had done nothing to allay his natural dislike of children. His new love was an unattractive female of good family (the main stem were stockyard millionaires, but she was of a collateral branch). I know she was unattractive, because she was present at a meeting which my dear mother, in a fruitless attempt to effect a reconciliation, had arranged, despite the fact that only a few weeks before the breakup she had said to me:

"I'm worried about your father's health. It's so good."

My dear mother, who was deeply religious, deeply religious, was quoting various verses from the Bible, ranging from the simple commandment against adultery to such stirring admonitions as the undertaking which had been made on his behalf at baptism to renounce the sinful desires of the flesh. While my dear mother was thus occupied, this terrible woman suddenly sat on my knees, flung her arms around me and began to make love to me in the most abandoned fashion. I, a mere boy of twelve, and she my father's mistress at that. Besides, she was much too heavy for my frail frame, and very bony; although since, in daydreams—needless to say, this finally disrupted the proceedings, and after my father, who smelt strongly of whiskey, had stopped laughing, both these people vanished forever from our ken.

My dear mother was therefore compelled to go to work in order that we might have bread; although since she carved out for herself a successful career as a fund-raiser for various worthy causes which did not inquire too closely into the percentage of receipts retained as expenses, our menage was not altogether ascetic. My talent in that direction is, I suppose, hereditary.

During the years that followed, and particularly in my teens, my dear mother lost no opportunity of impressing on me the tenets of the Christian lifestyle, particularly in regard to the sins of the flesh. My dear mother and I were very close during those years, very close. It was not until some later time that I realized that my dear mother was a castrating old bitch, do you hear me. A CASTRATING OLD BITCH.

I'm sorry, nurse. I apologize. Yes, I will keep my voice down.

As a matter of fact, at that point I had to give a similar undertaking to the barman at Amenity II. It was probably because of this that Greta suggested that as the hour was late it would be as well to leave, especially as we both had work to do next day. The thought passed through my mind that my preoccupation with Method and System had unwarrantably interfered with the real purpose of this exercise. But at the same moment it occurred to me that after all things were proceeding to their logical conclusion. I put my bag of pomegranates under my arm again, motioned to Greta to precede me, and walked out with a gratifyingly firm step, although I had some little trouble in opening the door. This was easily accounted for by the fact that Greta had already opened it and was holding it for me.

We again had little trouble finding a taxi—my luck was certainly in that night. In fact there were two taxis, and Greta suggested that we take one each.

"My dear young lady," I said, every inch the gallant knight, "you cannot possibly suppose—you can not possibly suppose that I would allow you to return home unescorted. The dangers that lurk in the highways and byways of Manhattan—"

"Oh, but I get home at all hours when I'm filming."

"Alone?" I said, in my most insinuating manner, and then, fearing that I had been guilty of an unpardonable double entendre, I added, "Come, come, I insist," and I had my way with her. Dear me, there goes another.

I was not able to achieve very much during the ride, as my pomegranates were becoming more and more unmanageable. I realized to the full my stupidity in purchasing such a large quantity. For a moment I even contemplated offering several to the driver as a gratuity, but I felt uncertain how he would receive them, and the other course—leaving them on the seat—went against my inflexible, if outmoded, axiom, Waste not, want not. While I pondered these alternatives we reached Miss Love's residence.

She lived in one of those apartment buildings on Third Avenue with an exterior of white brick. Somehow they always remind me of the interior of comfort stations, though not so highly glazed. Despite the protests which she continued to utter in a voice which, if the idea had not been so improbable, I should have thought contained stifled giggles, I insisted on accompanying her across the sidewalk and through the revolving doors, under the eye of a concierge at whom I was forced to direct one of my most authoritarian looks of reproof, since his countenance was by no means as, uh, wooden as the countenances of such persons should be.

Even at this point Miss Love attempted to bid me farewell. It became necessary for me to remind her of the dangers of potential rapists hiding in elevators, and even though she assured me that the building was equipped with twenty-four-hour TV security, I pointed out that modern, uh, technology was subject to unpredictable failures and that even if the cameras were working, who knew what might happen before the guard, who might well be taking his coffee break, could reach her?

By much the same argument I followed her into her actual apartment, clutching my bag of pomegranates in both arms. I had some idea that if the dangers I had been postulating became real, the fruit might render good service as missiles. After she had switched on the light I gratefully lowered my load to the floor and sank into a chair. She looked at me for a moment with her eyebrows raised into a most charming inverted V, said:

"I'll get you some coffee," and disappeared.

"Oho," I said to myself. "She has gone to put on something more comfortable, as the saying went when I was, alas, younger."

But she reappeared with suspicious promptitude, wearing the same clothes and holding a mug in each hand. As I surmised, the coffee was instant, a fluid which I abominate. After the first sip I put the mug on a small table with a grimace which, as she had her back to me, Greta fortunately did not see. She sipped at her own mug, put it on another small table, and reclined at full length on a sofa. From this vantage point she regarded me with an expression which, it seemed to me, conveyed perplexity. It was clear to me that the moment of truth was at hand. I began to sweat heavily.

Figure to yourself, dear Dr. Ampiofratello, how enticing she looked, thus recumbent. That lovely face, with its soft golden hair, those enormous eyes, generous, sensual mouth a little open; her swelling breasts, biding the arousing hand of a lover; nearer the storm center, her well-curved buttocks ready for the sterner pinch; the undulatory line of her whole body, the lush molding of her thighs and the long curve of her legs, subtly emphasized by her high-heeled boots. I wondered if she wore them in bed.

Now it seemed that she had reached a decision. She raised a hand to her bosom, curled a finger around a shining ring that lay there, and pulled it slowly downward. Moment by moment I could see, first the pale ivory of her breasts and then the lacy outline of her brassiere—

And my terse, which had been going up and down all evening like a mining stock, now shrank till I feared it would recede wholly into my scrotum.

As Defoe makes Moll Flanders say, I began to see the danger I was in.

I was a married man.

I was about to break—if my instrument would let me—the most sacred of all vows.

To betray my wife.

Supposing she found out?

Besides, the girl, in her generation, was doubtless accustomed to what I believe are known as one-night stands. To the most casual of contacts. How did I know what poison she might carry?

I looked at my watch.

"Dear me," I said. "I had no idea it was so late. I must go."

She pulled up that shining ring much faster than she had eased it down, and swung herself off the sofa. I think she was laughing a little. I shook hands, hoped I had not tired her, thanked her for a most enjoyable evening, and left.

I had gone only a few steps along the corridor when I stopped short.

I had forgotten my pomegranates.

It might be a full year before I could buy another supply of these fantasy-provokers. There was only one thing to do. I retraced my steps and rapped on the door.

"Excuse me. My pomegranates."

She gave a little sigh, and fetched them.

"Thank you."

I did not use the elevator. For some reason it seemed to me that I needed exercise. I found the door to the stairs and began to descend. On the second flight I stumbled, opened my arms to steady myself, and dropped the bag. Floppily, squishily my precious burden rolled down the steps, a few surviving to lie in the dust of the next landing. With tears in my eyes, I continued down, holding tightly to the handrail and tiptoeing carefully around the relics of what must have been a disgracefully overripe batch of fruit.

When I emerged into the lobby the concierge seemed surprised at more than my unorthodox entrance.

"Leaving so soon, sir?"

I did not see that it was any business of his, but I replied: "Yes. Yes. I, uh, have an important appointment."

I looked at my watch. It was twenty past one.

And there were no taxis.

36

To such a perceptive man as yourself, dear Dr. Ampiofratello, I need hardly expand on the truly miserable condition in which I found myself on awakening next morning, and therefore I will not do so. When my clock radio, which I always keep tuned to WNCN, went off, the station was playing determinedly cheerful thirteenth-century music which appeared to consist entirely of a breathy male alto and some person persistently striking a tabor, or small drum. This is by no means the best treatment for the kind of headache from which I was suffering. I had slept only intermittently, and in my waking spells had experienced the illusion of floating several inches above the bed, a form of levitation with which I could willingly have dispensed.

In addition to my physical pain, it soon became apparent that my potations of the previous night had by no means been the waters of Lethe, which in classical mythology was a river of Hades which caused forgetfulness to those who drank of it. The recollections which now came to me were such that I heartily wished I were one of that class of person who on such occasions enjoy the mercy of mental blackout.

My manifest destiny seemed to be to make an idiot of myself. How could I have proved myself such a poltroon? At the very moment when victory—and Greta Love—were, if not literally within my grasp, so close that I had only to reach out my hand, I had drawn it back. I cast a reproachful gaze on that cowardly hand, which was shaking a good deal. Not only had I cast away the fruit of many hours' labor, as well as the price of all those very expensive drinks, but how was I going to comport myself on the next occasion of meeting my inamorata? Useless would it be for me to draw around me the awe-inspiring mantle of my official position. Between her and me there now lay a shameful secret. Would it remain so? Could I trust to her discretion? With the memory of all that we had not been to each other, could I face the ordeal of working side by side with her on the completion of that epic of the cinema, that creative triumph of my own artistic *alter ego,* or other self, on the wings of which my spirit, freed from the trammels of the everyday, could soar? And apart from that, I had the most appalling pains in my bowels.

I cautiously turned my gaze towards my wife's room. The door was open, the bed empty and unused. So had it been when, after a terrifying walk in which every doorway held a potential assassin and the only taxi I saw was already engaged, I had finally reached home. At the time I had been too preoccupied to ponder why my wife was absent from the post of duty, but now, as the Burpine took effect, I began to speculate with ever growing hope on the reason for her staying out all night.

It was entirely on her account—no. It was largely on her account —no. It was partly on her account, to my sense of the old-fashioned faithfulness, the extramarital chastity which I owed her, that I had so ignominiously deserted the field of conquest. If indeed she had spent the night in a lover's arms, well and good, astounding as that statement may appear; for it would, I felt, relieve me of those obligations which, in my view, dissolve if not mutually observed.

Thus delivered I could resume the chase, and this time I would bring down the quarry; for, as my bowels ceased from troubling and my stomach was at rest, I realized that my infatuation was still upon me and that if I, Rameses Penis Tillevant, Doctor of Philosophy, Honorary Doctor of Laws, Master of Business Administration, Master of Social Service, could successfully explain away to visiting potentates from Washington the many equivocal things which I *had* successfully explained away to visiting potentates from Washington, why, I could certainly perform the same feat when it was merely a question of overpersuading for the second time a woman, however lovely, who was bound to me, or rather to The Dickstachel Research Institute, by a contract which contained a unilateral cancellation clause for unsatisfactory performance; although, come to think of it, the unsatisfactory performance had been all on my side.

I was rather dashed to discover a note taped to the refrigerator door which stated that my wife had gone to nurse her sister, who was suffering from a severe attack of influenza. A telephone call quickly established that she was indeed at her sister's, and a series of soprano sneezes in the background confirmed that that lady was certainly afflicted with a notable respiratory complaint of some kind or other.

I made a light ginseng breakfast and set off for work. I was not cheered to find on my desk, among other unpleasant things, two cables from Darrell. As I had instructed her always to do, my secretary had arranged these in date order, with the earlier one on top. It said:

IMPOSSIBLE OBTAIN PERMISSION COSAMO MIGRATION STOP TRIBE IS PROTECTED BY MUDDLEHEADED VENTRIVIAN HUMAN RIGHTS COMMISSION WHICH ALTHOUGH IN JAIL MAINTAINS CONTACT WITH LOCAL UN REPRESENTATIVE WHO IS BLOODY FOOL AND WILL NOT ACCEPT TRANSLATION OF VERBAL STATEMENTS BY EACH MEMBER OF PARTY OF EAGERNESS TO LEAVE STOP INSISTS SIGNED DECLARATION OWN HANDWRITING IN QUADRUPLICATE STOP COSAMO CANNOT WRITE STOP CABLE FULL STATEMENT SCIENTIFIC IMPORTANCE OF PROJECT AS IT AFFECTS POLLUTION POPULATION CONTROL WORLD HUNGER ECOLOGY LIBERTE EGALITE FRATERNITE AND ALL THE OTHER HOGWASH YOU SPOUTED AT ME BEFORE I LEFT STOP INCLUDE STATEMENT FROM WHITE HOUSE OF PEACE ON THE EARTH GOODWILL TO MEN AND EXPLICIT THREAT OF LOAN CANCELLATION STOP OTHERWISE ABORT WHOLE PROJECT STOP COSAMO ARE LITERALLY LAUGHING THEMSELVES SICK SUPPLIES OF WHAMMO ARE NEARLY EXHAUSTED AND SO AM I BEST WISHES DARRELL

The second cable, unsigned, said:

NEVER MIND BOANERGES HAS FIXED IT

The trauma which I experienced on perusing these two documents was such that I inhaled oxygen continuously for five minutes before discovering that the cylinder was empty. Despite the fact that if I had actually been inhaling pure oxygen for such a length of time my lungs would presumably have been burnt to ribbons, I immediately rang for my secretary and rebuked her severely for neglecting to ensure that the supply had been replenished. This exercise of my undoubted authority—she is not a member of any union, a decision to which she has adhered in spite of social ostracism in the canteen —this, I say, plus the psychic reinforcement which the rampart of my desk always provides me, strengthened me sufficiently to consider the ominous implications of that second cable.

"Boanerges has fixed it," indeed.

That did not surprise me. Boanerges, I was sure, was still capable of fixing anything.

Boanerges, son of thunder.

37

BOANERGES WAS my roommate at college. His real name was Simon Richmond, but he preferred to be called Boanerges. He was of rather less than medium height and possessed immense stores of restless, darting energy, save when he would lie on his bed for a whole day or two days at a time, eating nothing and drinking only the milk which he made me bring him. The top of his head was almost spherical, an impression heightened by the fact that in profile his forehead described a convex arc.

He was a pioneer of the practice of wearing sunglasses on nearly all occasions, even in the almost total darkness of cocktail lounges, as a protection not from light but from the disparaging appraisal which he believed other people made of him. Through their murky lenses one could sometimes see Boanerges making an equally disparaging appraisal of oneself, his gaze shifting rapidly from side to side. When he occasionally removed his glasses to rub his eyes, which were long and narrow, the pupils a faint green, one received a faintly reptilian impression.

Boanerges had overwhelming charm, which in his self-chosen role of *enfant terrible* he remorselessly exploited, so that people whom his careless disregard of detail had placed in the most embarrassing predicaments would always after a while forgive him. Once he arranged to meet a girl on the southwest corner of Times Square for a cafeteria lunch, and slept peacefully until well after the appointed hour. When she called him to complain that she had nearly been arrested for loitering, he told her to take a taxi to the Plaza Hotel, where after some further delay he treated her to a meal which temporarily bankrupted him. At the coffee and crème-de-menthe stage she apologized for having disturbed his slumber and refused to let him pay her taxi fare.

This sort of thing left him constantly short of money, in spite of the considerable amounts which passed through his hands from long-suffering relatives and as the proceeds of the many slightly questionable business enterprises on which he embarked with immense enthusiasm and of which he tired with equally immense enthusiasm. Where ordinary people would have taken a taxi, he rented a chauffeur-driven Cadillac; and his idea of a wedding present for an almost casual acquaintance was a heavy Georgian silver tray rather than the thinly plated salt and pepper shakers which would have been more than adequate. I could not help contrasting this profligacy with my own enforced expertise in squeezing two cups of tea from one teabag.

His dubious entrepreneurism included financing a rumrunning service to one of the Moslem states. This was very successful until the entire fleet—a rather battered World War II submarine chaser—was sunk in a gun duel with the local Coast Guard, or whatever it is that these countries have. He also helped to capitalize a new manufacturer of rubber goods who failed within a year because of the porous nature of his products; and he once made quite a sum by writing the prospectus for an oil company of the type whose stock is sold in boiler rooms. He was paid in shares which he disposed of at a high figure before the boiler burst.

All this of course was before the high seas were congested with rusty tubs full of marijuana, before the pill, and before the Securities and Exchange Commission became as pedantic in the exercise of its functions as it is today.

Boanerges' hobby, of which he never tired, was rooting out incidents which the parties involved would have preferred to remain unknown. He claimed to have, as he expressed it, "something on" everyone from the President of the University down to the porter who put out the garbage; and, as will soon become apparent, his tentacles extended far beyond those particular environs. Whenever he came into our room with particularly bright rays shooting from his dark glasses I took it for granted that he had made some new discovery. He was a member of no fraternity, and games of all sorts were anathema to him; but the President of Phi Beta Kappa or the head football coach, even if accompanied by others, would nod to him on campus, albeit with a certain uneasiness.

Until the incident which I am about to recount, he "had" nothing on me, for those were the days of my innocence; but one evening he found me sitting on my bed with my head in my hands. He ignored me for a while and occupied himself by putting the third record of Bach's *B Minor Mass* on his 78-rpm record player and repeating his favorite forty-two bars until I looked up and said:

"For Christ sakes turn that off."

He removed the record and, with characteristic clumsiness, dropped it on the hardwood floor, where the shellac broke into many pieces. He gathered most of them up, dropped them in the wastebasket, and said:

"That's a first-rate impersonation of Rodin's *Thinker,* but you're not equipped for it."

"I know I'm not," I said—no, I think I sobbed. "I'm going to flub."

He picked up the eighteen-inch cigarette holder which was one of his affectations, fitted into it a cigarette which looked extraordinarily small by contrast, flicked his gold lighter and sat smoking and looking at me for a while. Then he said:

"No, you're not."

"I am. This stuff simply isn't for me."

"I tell you you're not. And if I tell you you're not going to flub, you—are—not—going—to—flub."

He stood up, grinding shellac particles into the floor, dropped a ten-spot on my knees, and added:

"Now run along and get me another record before the store closes."

I went. It was a menial task, but Boanerges was fond of giving menial tasks to people he intended to help. I ran all the way and nearly dropped the fragile parcel in handing it to him. He took it with a grunt, opened it, put the disc on the turntable and went on playing the same forty-two bars for the next half hour. I could cheerfully have broken the record over his head.

No one in his right mind would have given me a degree on the work I turned in; but when the list came out my name was on it. At the very bottom, but it was there. Boanerges was only three places above me, but then he never worked. I turned around and saw him standing next me.

"I got it! I got it!"

He dropped fifty cents into my hand and said, "Go get me two packs of Luckies."

The only clue to the whole affair was the look of hate in the Dean's eyes when he gave me my sheepskin.

That was my M.B.A. I worked in my spare time for my M.S.S. and got it fairly easily, because by daily practice in the job I was then doing I had acquired by rote a goodly fund of those meaningless clichés which facilitate the misuse of billions of dollars every year.

My goodness. Such dreadful heresies. I must be going out of my mind. Supposing someone were to take me seriously? I *must* guard my tongue.

Oh, is it time for my injection, nurse? Very well. Another prick. No, no, I meant the needle, of course. Thank you. Now I can go on.

My Doctor of Laws was the last degree I received. At one time I hoped there might be others, but now I suppose . . . In any case it was honorary, so I did not have to work for it, or rather I do not count as work the favor I was able to do the President of that small Western college by giving him some elementary instruction in the art of fund raising. Before then his position was very shaky. I feel it is the duty of everyone to share specialized knowledge with the less fortunate.

But that was preceded by my Doctorate of Philosophy. Right from the start I found myself in difficulty over my dissertation. To begin with, I could not think of a subject. That problem was perhaps less common then than it is now, but every time I faced it I came to the laughable conclusion that everything had already been done. Moreover, when I did have one or two tentative ideas I paled before the amount of research which would be entailed. The prospect of long hours fingering index cards in the New York Public Library, many of them in the painstaking calligraphy of a long-gone generation, their corners either vanished or flaking away at a touch—one's desperate efforts to think interrupted by the happy laughter of the more emancipated members of the staff—then sitting at those shabby oaken tables among rows of the most depressing-looking people . . . it was enough to make me move to Boston, though I should still have to scrabble in those damned books. And yet that degree would be worth a sizable increment in my annual honorarium.

It was in that despairing mood that I bethought me again of Boanerges. It was not that I thought he could actually do anything about it—well, that is not true. I did think he could do something about it, and I was certainly going to put the matter to him in such a way that if only for old times' sake—I had come far as a survivor since I left college.

Boanerges was then a vice-president of a leading public relations firm. When we met, by the information booth in the concourse of Grand Central Station, he looked reassuringly prosperous. As we paced among the anonymous wayfarers, of whom there were but few, for it was a Sunday morning, I explained the matter to him in as low tones as were compatible with intelligibility. When I had finished he said:

"I want some oysters."

Then he set off at a brisk pace for the Oyster Bar. Without speaking, he consumed with relish several dozen of these revolting mollusks, while I nervously sipped a cup of coffee. When I had finished he handed me the bill, still in silence, and departed.

Exactly one week later I met him by appointment by the newsstand near the Eighth Avenue entrance of the Port Authority bus terminal. He handed me the key of a luggage locker and said:

"Change the name on the front cover, bring the arrangement of the footnotes up to date, and get me a Sunday *Times*."

He put the paper under his arm—its weight set his small figure off balance—and left.

I had some difficulty in locating the locker, as he had not told me which bank of these useful devices it was in. It proved to be downstairs, near Ninth Avenue. Inside was a well-filled nine-by-twelve envelope. With a fast pulse I went home, locked myself in the bathroom and ripped it open. It contained a dissertation by one E. Pippington Briggs, dated several years earlier, at a college far removed geographically from the one with which I was then concerned. Though time had yellowed its pages, the text was admirable.

You will not think me ungrateful, dear Dr. Ampiofratello, when I say that there still remained a considerable amount of toil for me to perform. I had to copy the entire document in longhand before handing it to my secretary to type, and there was also the question of modernizing the style of the footnotes. Fashions in these essential addenda seem to change faster than I should have thought possible. However, with the aid of the latest edition of the *Chicago Manual of Style* I eventually accomplished this wearisome task. I then had to devise some means of disposing of the original.

At first I tried tearing the sheets up small and flushing them down the toilet, but as the paper was nonabsorbent it displayed a disappointing tendency to float and remain behind after the turbulence had subsided. There was also an evident risk of blocking the plumbing, apart from giving my wife the impression that I was afflicted with dysentery.

I therefore decided to place the torn-up sheets in the smaller size of grocery bag, staple the top shut, and drop them down the apartment house incinerator. (The larger-size grocery bag would have jammed in the shaft.) It was difficult to find a sufficient supply of these smaller bags in the broom closet, and I was forced to make many unnecessary purchases merely to obtain these. Not only was this expensive, but my wife's curiosity was aroused by my sudden appetite for such items as potato chips, salted nuts, pretzels and the like, none of which I wish to eat again as long as I live. On one occasion she asked me if I was pregnant.

Even so the project took a considerable time, as the incinerator broke down at least twice a week and of course I could only make these little trips when my wife was visiting her sister, attending her art class or watching a movie in a cinema—a form of evening entertainment less hazardous then than it is today.

Indeed, from the first moment of setting pen to paper, the whole project had to be shielded from my wife's prying. She knew better than to interrupt me when I was working, but I strongly suspected her of having obtained a duplicate key to my desk, and I was forced to purchase and install a new set of locks, although I am most unhandy with a screwdriver.

All this was a great nervous strain, but I was stronger in those days. I must confess that for some time after that I was apprehensive that E. Pippington Briggs might appear and accuse me of plagiarism, but in a chance encounter with Boanerges he told me that this unfortinate gentleman had been killed in a car accident before the actual award of his degree, a fact of which I think Boanerges might have informed me when he gave me the key to that luggage locker.

You may think, dear Dr. Ampiofratello, that I am making an unnecessarily elaborate presentation of these facts at a time when all over the country regularly incorporated organizations exist for the purpose of providing students with term papers and so on for a very reasonable sum per sheet; when persons who have been dismissed for cheating may either start a successful lawsuit or find themselves, if they have made enough money in after years to add munificently to the endowments of their alma mater, being eulogized and draped with laurels; and when Congress, with an eye to future voters, seeks to mitigate the harsh measures which have traditionally been associated with the academies for our armed services when some student or group of students, no doubt because of family or amatory troubles, departs from the way which is straight and narrow. But I remind you that things were different in my time, although I shall never forget that look of hatred in the Dean's eye.

The last time I saw Boanerges was by appointment opposite the gorilla's enclosure in the Bronx Zoo. He said:

"I'm going to Ventrivia. I need a thousand dollars."

The most elementary tact called on me to forbear from asking for reasons. Pure sentiment, the memory of old days urged me to grant his request. Besides, it had long been in my mind that Boanerges, who had so long claimed to "have something" on everyone he knew, now "had" a great deal on me. Much as I liked him, I should feel easier if he was out of the country. My checkbook was luckily with me. Under the cynical gaze of the gorilla I filled out a form for almost my entire balance. Boanerges took it wordlessly and marched off without even telling me to buy him a bag of official animal food. I departed in the opposite direction, only pausing to admire an exceptionally beautiful tigress who immediately turned her back on me, lifted high her tail and ejected far beyond the confines of her cage a stream of liquid so powerful, so glistening in the sun and, if I had been less nimble, so drenching.

"Boanerges has fixed it," indeed. Boanerges could no doubt fix anything anywhere until the police caught up with him. But was he in all respects the same Boanerges? For all I knew, the climate of South America may have some strange effects on a man's psyche. Was he as close-mouthed as ever?

What might he have told Paul Darrell?

38

IT WAS then that my first forebodings of personal doom began to steal upon me like mocking phantoms, snapping their fingers in my face and tiptoeing away. In due course their visits became longer, until I was hardly ever rid of them, and at the last—but I anticipate.

Do *you* ever have forebodings of personal doom, dear Dr. Ampiofratello? I am sure you do not. You are such a saintly man, such a tower of strength to me and, I suppose, to hundreds—thousands—of others. How jealous I am of those others.

Enough of reverie. I must now recount some of the myriad practical details which besieged me in connection with the first entry of the Cosamo upon freedom's shores. Darrell's accounts of their ceaseless outbursts of hilarity had rendered me somewhat apprehensive, but his theory of the cause, farfetched though it seemed, to some extent reassured me. I was certain that at the very first breath of our native air they would stop laughing.

I had many little ideas for enhancing their welcome. Each member of the party would be handed a paper bearing a translation into Cosamo of the immortal words of Emma Lazarus, which are engraved not only upon the Statue of Liberty but also on the rear wall of the escalator facing the exit from Customs in the center of the lobby of the International Arrivals Building at Kennedy International Airport, where they remain astonishingly appropriate, at least insofar as "huddled masses" disembarking from a jumbo jet.

I could no doubt arrange for a Welcome Wagon, flying the flags of the United States and of The Dickstachel Research Institute, to press upon our visitors specimens of the varied products of our inventive genius, such as genuine imitation maple syrup, Dan's Diaper Service, cola drink, decorative ceramic products and coupons redeemable at an immense variety of stores. The thought of flags naturally conjured up banners, and I at once determined to have several made bearing the legend "Welcome Cosamo" in their native language. I would suggest to the management of the various motels on the New Jersey border the desirability of displaying the same sentiment on their signboards, immediately above the "No Vacancy" announcement.

My brain was in fact teeming. The only problem I could foresee was obtaining a translator for what was admittedly one of the more esoteric dialects. I had no intention of asking Darrell, whose perverted sense of humor would probably have led him to furnish me with some deadly insult to our guests, the meaning of which I should not learn until too late. In this connection I was reminded of my wife's kimono, which bears Japanese characters meaning, so the salesperson assured her, "May The Ten Thousand Happinesses Grace Your Way," but which I am convinced a more impartial interpretation would render "Down with Trade Restrictions on Toyota and Panasonic." However, I—or rather, my secretary—succeeded in tracking down a lonely savant at the Smithsonian who was so overcome by this unwonted request for his services that he called long-distance, with tears in his voice, to thank me.

It was not until these preparations were well advanced that I remembered that I had no idea when to expect my pilgrims, as I now thought of them. With his usual pococurantism, Darrell had omitted to inform me of this essential detail, although on second thoughts this may have been intentional. His unhealthy and degraded animus against all forms of publicity might have led him to hope to slip into the country as unawares as the unusual nature of his cargo would permit. After several increasingly imperative requests he finally advised me of the date, which by the time I received his cable was only twenty-four hours ahead. My day was therefore spent in an absolute turmoil, not the least touchy part of which was the necessity for person-to-person communication between myself and Miss Greta Love in order that her crew might be at the airport with all their apparatus set up in plenty of time.

Since the slight embarrassment attendant upon our last meeting —uh, since that dreadful night—I had communicated with Miss Love only by internal memorandum or, if some emergency arose, by telephone messages passed through my secretary. In view of the immediacy of the present occasion I now sent another message courteously requesting her presence in my office. I was hardly able to meet her eyes when she appeared, but she was perfectly self-possessed. Her warm smile and her Southern accent were undimmed. I cannot imagine why I thought the accent had thinned out. It must have been the stingers. Thank heaven, she had reverted to calling me Doktuh Till'vant. Ram would have been deliberate irony—a very sword in my terse.

Our rendezvous—my God, rendezvous!—at JFK was set up with a minimum of words and she cymbal-clashed out, leaving me, I was convinced, with an incipient case of paralysis agitans, or Parkinson's disease, or shaking paralysis, or—dear me, I really must get a grip on myself. I mastered the symptoms with some difficulty, charged my secretary with making final reminder calls to the media and those members of the staff whom I had appointed to constitute my retinue, and went home to bed, as I should have to arise at an extremely early hour next morning. The ETA, or estimated time of arrival, which I had obtained from the company chartering the plane, was 6 A.M. Allowing for last-minute changes, windage, traffic jams, hijackers and, if you will pardon the expression, dear Dr. Ampiofratello, general ball-ups, this meant that everyone over whom I had any semblance of control should be on parade, banners ready to unfurl, leaflets ready for distribution, and any disengaged right hands ready for shaking, not later than 5 A.M. To be on the safe side I had issued instructions for 4 A.M. This meant that I myself had to leave my couch at 2:30 A.M., perform an extremely brisk toilet, though, I flatter myself, without detriment to the dapper and urbane aspect which I normally present to the world, and consume a hurried alfalfa breakfast before departure.

Since the traffic at that hour was light and there were no seven-car pile-ups, my trip to JFK was performed with unwonted celerity. In fact, after I had parked the car I found it was only 3:45 A.M. I made my way to the hangar where the charter plane would pull up. Here I found the contingent from The Dickstachel Research Institute in process of assembling. They seemed somewhat jaded, and I therefore distributed among them cordial greetings and several of my most inspirational smiles. I could do nothing about the fact that there was no sign of the media, but I was distressed to note that not a single representative of Zeeta Productions had yet put in an appearance.

At 4:05 A.M. precisely I instructed my secretary to go and telephone the studio, but after some time she returned with the chilling information that the only reply had been from an extremely discourteous night watchman. In point of fact she said that he was a rude bastard, but in view of the rather special circumstances I feigned not to hear this remark, and merely instructed her to continue telephoning at fifteen-minute intervals. She did this until 5 A.M., when she reported that the watchman was now using four-letter words and if I wanted any more calls made I could make them myself. Just then it occurred to me that there was doubtless some good reason for the delay, and I let the matter drop.

I do not know, dear Dr. Ampiofratello, if you have ever watched the dawn. This was the first time that I had done so, and I can assure you that a remote corner of an almost deserted airport is not the best place for the purpose. This particular dawn came up, not like thunder (Kipling) but like soup. I suppose it was the effect of air pollution. Reluctant though I am to reveal weakness, I must confess that even in so short a time my inspirational smile had dwindled into my philosophical one, and I was beginning to wish that I had been able to satisfy my conscience with a smaller time margin.

My watch creaked on, the veiled sun rose sulkily higher, and still there was no sign of Zeeta Productions. I was becoming seriously alarmed, and gathering up my courage to instruct my secretary to call the studio again, night watchman or no night watchman, when at 5:45 A.M. the crew arrived. At 5:59 A.M. they had their equipment at the ready. Simultaneously Miss Greta Love arrived. At 6 A.M., unfortunately, the plane did not arrive. Nor at 6:05 A.M. Nor at 6:10 A.M.

By 6:30 A.M. I was quite disgusted at the way in which, except for my secretary, the entire contingent from The Dickstachel Research Institute was milling around Miss Love, fetching her coffee, offering her cigarettes, jostling each other to light them, telling her feeble jokes—I am sure they were feeble, although she laughed her deep, sensual laugh at each of them—or simply, as in the case of our chief biochemist, looking at her in a way which I can only describe as vapid. Vapid. The word means "having lost life, sharpness or flavor; insipid; flat." Well, that is exactly how our chief biochemist was, looking at Miss Greta Love. Idiot.

No one was taking the slightest notice of me, their lawfully appointed and tenured chief. I moved away in search of the representative of Global Airlines, the inefficient, dishonest, conscienceless outfit which had thus reneged on its pledged word. Well, I know that ETA means *estimated* time of arrival, but for godsake if they couldn't estimate better than that what was the use of all those computers and weather stations and radar and so on? If all that, uh, technological equipment couldn't count more accurately, why didn't they take their shoes off?

I walked into the partitioned-off office of the representative of Global Airlines in a state of mind fit to make the Wright brothers arise from their graves and tear down the memorial at Kitty Hawk. I said:

"I am Dr. Tillevant, Administrator of The Dickstachel Research Institute. Your machine is now forty-one and a half minutes late. What is the meaning of it?"

She was a thin, taciturn woman, though not ill-looking. She said: "Equipment trouble."

Of all sad words of tongue or pen, these are the saddest that anyone dealing with an airline can hear. I snapped:

"Equipment trouble? What kind of equipment trouble?"

"Sea gulls."

"Sea gulls?"

"Yep. In the air intake."

How I wished I had brought my miniature oxygen outfit with me. My secretary had duly, if belatedly, replenished it, but it was miles away, in my desk. Well, that is what my wife gave me, a miniature oxygen outfit to keep in my desk. She had not had the sense to give me another miniature oxygen outfit to carry around with me; and if ever I needed oxygen I needed it then. I think I have made it clear that I am not, thank God, a technical man, but I read the newspapers when I feel strong enough, and I do know that when sea gulls, or sparrows, or baldheaded eagles get into the air intake the plane probably crashes and everyone on board is probably killed, besides which someone probably sues the airline for endangering a protected species.

I know Mr. Richard Bach wrote a very charming book about a sea gull, but as far as I am concerned a sea gull is a greedy bird which preys on defenseless fish and is as excretorily incontinent as any other bird. Besides, it must be pretty stupid to get into the air intake at all, after the long time airplanes have been around. I know if I am anywhere near an airplane I take very good care that *I* do not get into the air intake—whatever that may be.

When I had finished counting my pulse, which appeared to be 192, I said:

"Are you trying to break it to me that your machine has crashed?"

"Nope. Happened while taxiing. Ain't nobody hurt."

That was certainly good to hear, even if it meant that Darrell was still alive. While The Dickstachel Research Institute would of course have done right by its dead, even including Darrell, I had had a horrible vision of being landed with a pile of unclaimed coffins full of Cosamo, and we have had quite enough of that sort of thing in this country, thank you very much.

When I had finished counting my pulse again—it seemed to have gone down to thirty-three and a third, like a phonograph record, I said:

"What is the extent of the damage?"

"Hafta change an engine."

This woman was maddening. I could picture her delaying a regiment of redcoats while the spy they were hunting got safely away.

"How long will that take?"

" 'Bout three hours, maybe four."

"Oh my God," I said, and walked out. I had had as much as I could bear for the time being. I went back to my group and broke the news to them. They were visibly depressed, except for one man who sat down in a patch of oil and started to draw something on the back of an envelope. I learned indirectly that he was designing an anti-sea-gull device for air intakes, but I do not recollect that it ever came to anything.

The only other person who was unaffected was Miss Greta Love, who inquired:

"Wale, Doktuh Till'vant, wha time shall we make our noo appuhntment?"

"I don't really know," I said. It was the truth, even if feeble. I then instructed my secretary to go and see if she could obtain some new ETA, however illusory it might prove to be. She returned with the information that Global Airways had more than one airplane; that a second machine was available at the Ventrivian airport; that Darrell and party had been transferred to this machine, which had taken off without ornithological interference; and that, God willing, it would reach JFK in about two hours.

"In heaven's name," I said, "why couldn't she have told me that?"

"She says you didn't ask her."

"Toh," I said, and went for a long walk about the vastness of Kennedy International Airport. On my return I noticed that the media, which had been conspicuously absent all the time, were still invisible. That of course is one of the disadvantages of a free press. They go just where they choose and when they choose. The only occasion on which one can count on their being present is when they are distinctly not wanted.

However, the Welcome Wagon lady had just arrived. She explained that she had had a flat tire on the Belt Parkway and she was afraid that the ice cream cones were all melted. I was not sorry to hear this, as I consider the present fashion for eating all kinds of portable food while walking along the street is regressive. As a nation we are supposed to be growing up, not reverting to the habits of childhood, and there was no point in introducing the Cosamo to this particular custom in a way which would seem to carry the seal of approval of The Dickstachel Research Institute. Indeed, it occurred to me at that moment that an inquiry into the causes of this reversion to infantilism would be an appropriate project to which might be joined the habit of lying around the landscaping of public buildings, sitting on other people's front steps or, failing that, on the sidewalk.

Having made a note of this, together with the most likely sources of funds, I asked the Welcome Wagon lady to give me one of the least melted ice cream cones and, there being no chairs, lowered myself to the floor of the hangar to consume it. Well, I was hungry and my feet hurt.

When Darrell's plane finally touched down it caught us all unawares with the exception of my secretary and Miss Love, who personally filmed the machine as it taxied towards us. I confess that I had almost dozed off, although it was quite unnecessary for my secretary to shake me with such vigor that my top set slipped.

The plane was of a somewhat elderly type from which passengers debarked down a flight of steps which was rolled up to the door. Darrell was the first to appear. He looked thin, pale and tired, but I heard a stifled gasp behind me and saw Miss Love gazing at him —and gazing at him—and gazing at him. I had thought it would happen, but my heart was no less bitter.

I almost missed the first Cosamo because I was still looking at the place where Darrell's head had been, but I caught the little fellow on the second step down. He was very upright and dignified, and his face was calm. This, I supposed, was Harry, the Chief. The others followed, a little scared, I think, but oddly quiet, with faraway expressions. I was nearly overcome. Here was my great personal project almost realized, and yet as I looked at these small figures marching forward, a little awkwardly perhaps because of the unaccustomed loincloths, but with this strange remoteness upon them, I felt they were more than I could handle—that the hints in Darrell's reports—that perhaps I had stirred up. . . .

Nurse. Nurse. Help me, please. I think I am going to cry.

Not another injection. I am so sick of all these injections. Ouch. You don't give them as well as the other nurse.

I still feel terribly depressed, but I must go on.

Well, anyway, after the Customs and Immigration people had gone away Darrell and I shook hands, grinning at each over and over for the cameras—the media had appeared from nowhere, like jackals after carrion. I had invited them, I had wanted them to come but now I wished them to hell. Darrell looked at the banners and said:

"What's all that about? Cosamo can't read," and he stopped my people giving out the Emma Lazarus translations. I suppose it was stupid of me. I already knew the Cosamo had no written language, and I should have guessed that what the man from the Smithsonian sent me was synthetic.

I shook hands with each of the little men and I smiled at them, not my inspirational smile or my philosophical smile, I just smiled as kindly as I could, because all this must have been a great shock to them and I felt it was my fault. The faraway look was wearing off a little, but they were still quiet. The Welcome Wagon lady gave them their bundles of goodies, which I think frightened them a little until Darrell said something to them and then they seemed to understand that it was all well meant.

Darrell then made a statement to the media.

"I have returned considerably scathed to the poppied atmosphere of Western civilization. Let the cheering tenantry disperse, collecting their beer and red flannel at the North Lodge. You are all invited to a midnight beanfeast and hoedown in the Administrator's office of The Dickstachel Research Institute. Formal dress—jockstraps and G-strings."

They loved that, confound him and them.

There was an insistent demand for the Cosamo to remove their loincloths, which Darrell successfully resisted by an involved reference to something he called the Pubic Information Act.

Then we all went out to the chartered bus. The faraway look was going fast, and then we met the noise of the traffic, and that started the laughter. It wasn't very loud at first, but just then a car slammed into the rear of another car and the drivers got out and cursed each other, and that did it. The Cosamo really let rip.

I could never have believed that so few people, and such little people, could have made so much noise. Children at play were nothing to it. They dropped their bundles, and the jars and cans rolled all over the sidewalk, and people picked them up and walked off with them, and the Cosamo seemed to think that was even funnier.

Darrell got them into the bus and pulled the blinds down like covering a canary's cage; but as it drove off I could still hear occasional outbreaks.

39

FORTUNATELY I possess—or used to possess—a remarkable power of recuperation. Exhausted though I was after the welcoming ceremony, some reserve of adrenalin was already flowing when, after battling the full flow of noonday traffic, I re-entered my office. I found Darrell awaiting me there, although he was apparently asleep. No sooner had I ensconced myself behind my desk, however, than he opened his eyes, stood up, plucked from the floor several transparent bags and laid them in a neat row on the immaculate *eau de Nil* leather of my desk top.

He then said, indicating each bag with a forefinger:

"Cosamo nail clippings. Cosamo head-hair clippings. Cosamo

urine. Cosamo feces. Under laboratory conditions it will be possible to perform chromosome analysis—"

"Just a moment," I said. My eyes were irresistibly drawn toward the strange collection of human detritus. Particularly towards the feces. Trite though the comparison may be, I could not help reflecting how odd it was that the most advanced science should work with the same materials as the most primitive witch doctors. Also I knew full well that he had only brought these disgusting relics to my office because he knew they would, to put it bluntly, turn my stomach up. What was he trying to do? Build a shrine to the Chicago riots?

"Just a moment," I repeated. "I take it that these, uh, specimens have been brought from the, uh, ancestral home of the Cosamo?"

"Exactly."

"Could you not have taken similar, uh, specimens from our friends who have now arrived in this country, without the necessity of—" and I waved my hand at the row of garbage.

"I shall. But these represent the pristine thing, untainted by the by-products of our overcivilization. That's why I want to get at the chromosomes the minute I can."

"I have no dobut you will handle the matter with your usual efficiency. In the meanwhile—"

"In the meanwhile, where are these hapless hostages going to sleep?"

"Sleep?"

"Sleep. And eat."

Frankly, I had not considered it my province to act as groom of the chambers. However, I said:

"Doubtless their wants are simple. I will instruct my secretary—"

"Don't bother," he said wearily. "I've dealt with it."

"Oh. Well, where *are* they going to sleep?"

"In the new building."

"The Tillevant Building?"

"Oh, yes, The Tillevant Building. It's as bare as their own balls, but as you say, their wants are simple. I'm having some straw mattresses sent in, and a lot of pig products. They'll have to be cooked in the cafeteria kitchen."

I refrained from quibbling about the question of overtime for the cafeteria staff; but the hope was strong in my mind that our visitors would respect the virgin purity of their accommodations.

"Have you educated them in the use of the, uh, washrooms?"

"Yes, Tilly, I've done all that. Once they were convinced the stuff went where no enemies could get at it they seemed rather happy to be relieved of the chore of burying it. I'll say this for you—at least you had the sense to put in low pedestals."

I bowed my head in acknowledgement of this tribute, although in fact that was merely the fashionable design. Darrell said:

"Now what about these mountains?"

"I'm glad you mentioned that. I have been having discussions with Dr. Zenko—"

"I know. He tells me you've raised one damfool objection after another."

Darrell seemed to have accomplished a good deal in the short time after his arrival. I wished I had spent less time on lunch.

"Were those Dr. Zenko's words?"

"They were. What are you going to do, fire him?"

"Dr. Zenko is a fully tenured member of The Dickstachel Research Institute."

"And don't you wish he wasn't. Well, come on, Tilly. Two more planes vanished in that area this week."

"They did?"

"They did. Don't you read the papers?"

"Certainly I read the papers. The items in question had, uh, escaped my notice. You must remember, Mr. Darrell, that I was being called on to issue a statement in the name of and bearing the full authority of The Dickstachel Research Institute, which would have been founded on an unsubstantiated theory—"

"For Christ sakes, man, we'll work out some way of substantiating it. Transmissions from pilotless airplanes, perhaps. But sixteen people died there last week because of your pigheadedness. That makes you practically a mass murderer."

"I must ask you to moderate your language."

"If you don't put out a statement here and now I will string you to the nearest utility pole and plug your balls in. After that I'll put out my own statement without going through channels. Stuff channels."

I had no alternative. But at least I had succeeded in my objective—to get the practical reality of The Tillevant Project well publicized before this to me largely hypothetical story absorbed public attention. And I knew how to keep Darrell's name out of it. I summoned my secretary and began to dictate.

"Dr. Rameses P. Tillevant, Administrator of The Dickstachel Research Institute, announced today that according to a theory advanced by the head of the newly returned Cosamo Expedition—"

"Dr. Tillevant warns—"

"Dr. Tillevant cautions—"

When I had finished I looked at Darrell and hastily looked away again.

"Will that satisfy you, Mr. Darrell?"

"You could have worded it that way weeks ago."

"I am not disposed to discuss the matter further. By the way, Mr. Darrell. Those reports of yours."

"What about them?"

"I doubt if they have done you much good with the Trustees."

"The Trustees. That group of daytime insomniacs. I should like to see their EEG's. Any deviation from a straight line would be due to someone shaking the recorder."

"Nevertheless," I said, shrugging. "That second one in particular—"

"The one on education and such?"

"Yes. Why?"

"I thought it might act as a ladder truck to get at least one person off Cloud Nine."

"Mr. Haversham—"

"I abominate his reins."

From this view I could not wholly dissent, but I could hardly admit that.

"You have an unpleasant interview ahead of you, for all that."

"Oh—" he said. "That stuff they grow mushrooms on."

He held up two crooked fingers.

"In hoc signo vinco."

He snatched up his disgusting row of plastic bags and, much to my relief, began to leave. Then, much to my horror, he turned back, saying:

"Your friend Boanerges—"

"Ah yes. We were at college together."

"He told me."

Once more I inwardly shuddered at the thought of the confidences that might have passed between those two *enfants terribles,* now in process of becoming *veillards terribles.*

"How is the dear fellow? I haven't seen him for years."

"He's in fine shape. Practically runs the country, after the dictator. I'd have thought he'd be rolling, but he seemed to be, let's say, slightly insolvent."

"He always lived in open-handed style. What was his, uh, fee for—?"

"Five thousand dollars in Japanese yen. Said if it had been for you personally he wouldn't have taken a nickel, but screw the Institute."

"No doubt you will be putting in your detailed expense account in the very near future."

"Yassuh, boss, Ah sure will do that, yowsah, yowsah, yowsah."

"If you require any help with the, uh, classification of the, uh—"

"Don't worry, Tilly. I know what to call things."

"How did you, uh, first encounter our mutual benefactor?"

"I didn't. He encountered me. In the bar of the local Sheraton. I'd parked Harry and Co. outside town and was having a drink to cheer myself up. Incidentally, I've had a hell of a time, Dr. Tillevant, as if you gave a shit. He simply sat next me, said it was a fine evening —which it wasn't; he'd heard I was having problems and his proposition was thus and such."

"I see. He remembered me, then?"

"Oh yes. He remembered you!"

"You, uh, seem to have got quite friendly with him."

"As much as the time allowed. He'd be quite a guy—Boanerges, if he wasn't such a shyster."

In spite of my Honorary Doctorate of Laws I have had no legal training, and at that moment I much regretted my lack of skill in cross-examination. Somewhere in the armory there must be an innocent trick question which would get me the information I needed, but I simply could not find it. To say outright:

"Did Boanerges tell you that he once helped me get two phony degrees?"

That would have banished any doubts with remarkable celerity, but of course. . . .

Once more I tried to read Darrell's face, but I could not see in it any special accession of the derisive insolence which it usually bore during our contests. He seemed to have recovered from his anger at my dilatory behavior over his wretched mountains, and was looking into space in what for him was a positively dreamy manner. I sought for some words which would end the interview in at least an apparently reconciliatory way.

"Well, Paul, I am glad to see you back. I fancy you are just the same Paul as before you went away, but then I suppose I am just the same Tillevant. But let us always remember that whatever our personal differences, The Dickstachel Research Institute comes first."

I stood up and held out my hand. He leaned forward and took it, absently, but instead of going away, which would have provided a neat, if insincere, drop curtain, he leaned back again and said musingly:

"You know, Tilly, I'm damned if I can make the Cosamo out. There's something inside them that—something we don't—something—oh hell. After we'd got past the Bellaki they quietened down and were perfectly happy for the rest of the march. It had stopped raining, there was plenty of food, and there were no other human beings ahead of them for a very long way. They stopped laughing, they drank only token amounts of Whammo, they even stopped fucking for quite a while, and when they started again it was only when the mood took them. They were still happy after I parked them in the open country. But when this damned exit permit business came up, I had to take them into town. That's the way the bureaucratic mind works. I had to take them into civilization in order to establish once and for all that I wasn't going to be allowed to take them into civilization. Nobody had the flexibility—or the decency—to go out and see them. Oh no. The Human Rights people—"

"I thought they were in jail."

"On currency charges. They bought their way out the following week. But before that they'd insisted that the Cosamo come to them, in their acoustic-ceilinged offices, because that was where the electric typewriters were. And the Cosamo hated it. They started laughing as soon as they got into town, and in no time at all they were drinking and fucking away as if they'd never left home."

He broke off, rubbed his forehead and said:

"By the way, who was that lovely girl at JFK?"

I flinched, but explained briefly about *Discovery*.

"Oh Christ. No wonder everyone's behind on their assignments. What's her name?"

"Miss Love. Greta Love."

"Greater love hath no girl than this, that she lay down her body for a friend. Wonderful legs. And what's between them must be pretty good too."

"Really, Darrell—"

"Excuse me, Tilly. I forgot you were happily married. Well, anyway, the Cosamo quietened down quite a lot after they'd got into the plane, and even while we were taking off, which must have been pretty scary for them. But when we'd climbed some, and there were clouds below us, the inside of that plane grew quieter than the inside of a church on a weekday. And it stayed like that. We reached thirty thousand, and everything opened out the way it does, and there we were, in a void with no darkness. And the faces of the Cosamo got a strange, rapt look as if they were communing with their idea of the First Principle. They didn't lose it until quite a while after we'd landed. I don't expect you noticed."

"Yes," I said. "I noticed."

"You'd be hard put to it to find that look on the face of any one of a bunch of economy-class passengers with a window seat. It got too much for me after a while. I went and had a bit of nookie with the stewardess."

"Indeed."

"Yes indeed. She was quite a girl, though hardly up to the standard of your Miss Love. But my point is, for those few hours the Cosamo were alone. They'd forgotten the Bellaki and the mountains and the rain. Maybe they thought the whine of the engines was just some strange hypnotic music. And they were happy. For the first time in their lives, they were happy. If only there were some way of letting them live their lives out in that strange isolation . . ."

"Perhaps we could find them jobs on a space station."

"Oh-h. Tillevant, you are not enough. A space station. With Houston on the blower every hour on the hour. I might have known you wouldn't get it."

He was wrong. I had got it, all right, in those first moments of meeting the Cosamo. But it was something I could not afford to keep. It would have wrecked the career which I still thought I had ahead of me.

Darrell glared at me, picked up his plastic bags and went out slowly. He started to sing:

> "Wait till the light turns green, Nelly,
> Wait till the light turns green.
> If a truck hits you in the belly, Nelly,
> You won't be fit to be seen."

I wondered whether his sojourn in the rain forest had affected his mind. If so, it might provide an unexpected solution of my problems. Boanerges. . . .

I felt the need for a few minutes' relaxation. As an indication that I was deeply involved with a major administrative problem, I closed the door of my office. Then I removed from my desk a plain brown envelope bearing only a post office box number as return address, part of the day's mail which my secretary by some miracle of intuitive discretion had refrained from opening. I studied its contents closely.

So the Weird O Ranch was offering a Commuter's Special Weekend for only four hundred fifty dollars, double occupancy, airfare and limousine included, were they?

It was, in my present mood, an exceedingly tempting suggestion. I placed the literature, with its reservation form, in the Navy cabinet and carefully relocked it.

40

AT THIS point let me dispose of those wretched mountains once and for all. How grand that sounds. At one time it would have been quite natural to think of myself, Rameses P. Tillevant, Administrator of The Dickstachel Research Institute, disposing of a range of mountains by a wave of the hand or at most an instruction to my secretary; but that was in the early days of my association with Darrell. How different is my life today, when I have difficulty in disposing of an object as small as an unwanted tranquilizer.

The reactions to my carefully worded announcement were exactly as I had hoped. The public at large, sated with real and potential disasters and ardently following the fortunes of the most likely team to finish the season at the top of the National Football League, exhibited an attention span on this matter no longer than two consecutive news broadcasts. Various, uh, scientific organizations indulged in the usual acrimonious dissensions, which were somewhat hushed by the all-knowing though equally conflicting pronouncements of the various Government departments concerned. All these eminent bodies finally agreed that Darrell's own solution—signals from pilotless airplanes broadcast to ground receiving stations located at a safe distance—was probably the best, if not the only way, to prove or disprove Darrell's theory.

Unfortunately, the dictator of Ventrivia denounced the whole affair as another nefarious scheme of the Central Intelligence Agency, and stated that any flights by pilotless airplanes over his territory would be regarded as an invasion of his airspace. Such airplanes, he continued, would at once be shot down by the advanced-technology missile system which Ventrivia had recently acquired from the United States. It appeared unlikely that the impasse could be resolved even by such drastic measures as developing Darrell's pioneer campaign against the Bellaki and distributing to the dictator and his advisers lifesize inflatable figures not only of Farrah

Fawcett-Majors but of the Brothers Travolta. The matter was therefore discreetly allowed to drop, and pilots of aircraft already operating inside Ventrivia simply filed new flight plans which avoided the controversial area.

When the dictator had recovered his temper he realized that he was probably, so to speak, sitting on the richest source of radioactive energy in the world, a fact of which he was forcibly reminded by private and state entrepreneurs from all, so to speak, over. I see by the papers that he is still having an enjoyable time playing them all off against each other, although of course the fact that it is still impossible to survive after getting within, say, thirty miles of the wretched stuff is proving rather a stumbling block.

I have no doubt that Darrell could clear the whole thing up in five minutes if he would give his mind to it, but it is a little difficult to gain his attention right now, as he is far more interested in the post-Catastrophe situation.

41

I MUST now relate to you, dear Dr. Ampiofratello, some of the more untoward incidents which occurred during that traumatic period when the Cosamo were, in one way or another, exposed to the public gaze. I know that you must already be aware of many of these since they were widely reported by the media and were the subject of innumerable one-liners from such standup comics as were still able to wrest a meager living from their outmoded craft. We all remember, too, that TV sitcom (please pardon the jargon, but after all I was in showbiz, however briefly)—that TV sitcom allegedly based on the domestic lives of the Cosamo, which came to a speedy and disastrous end after a disgruntled makeup artist leaked the fact that the purported Cosamo were in fact white midgets in blackbody and freshly shaven for each episode.

Nevertheless I feel an irresistible urge to recount some of the more striking occurrences. Many of them I am convinced were due to

Darrell's carefree deviltry. Others I must frankly ascribe to the fact that even at that stage I was beginning to lose my grip.

It was obvious to my mind that the first thing for the Cosamo to do was to meet the Trustees. It was obvious to Darrell's mind that the last thing for the Cosamo to do was to meet the Trustees. He seemed to have some absurd idea that they should as far as possible be kept in their own quarters, which he said in a rather pointed way would have to be better equipped, and allowed out for comparatively fresh air and exercise, probably under armed guard, at such times as the nearest public park was relatively safe from the local equivalent of the warlike Bellaki. In support of this he again adduced his argument that the Cosamo should as far as possible be kept away from any features of the local environment which might alter their genes, or their hemoglobin, or some wretched thing or other.

"If we're really going to find out anything about them this is the worst possible place to do it," he said. "I'd like to take them out to Montana."

"My dear Darrell, what is the use of erecting a splendid new building—"

"That's what I say, Tilly. What *is* the use?"

I ignored this.

"The needs of so primitive a people must be few and simple. If you will submit a requisition for any additional items that you consider really essential, it will be given due consideration. By no means incidentally, you have not yet formally indented for those mattresses."

He seemed to be about to speak. I continued:

"As for your Montana suggestion, the transportation and continuing supply costs put it out of court. I must remind you, Darrell, that the Trustees have been extremely cooperative over the unforeseen expenses of your expedition, which are grossly over budget. Grossly. I am sure you will agree that the Trustees are entitled to see what The Dickstachel Research Institute has got for its money, and I am equally sure you will do everything possible to make the occasion a pleasant one."

I was about to give my persuasive smile, but in view of the expression on his face decided not to. He observed:

"You give me a low back pain that no orthopedic bed could cure. When your soul is condemned to the everlasting fires of hell, I hope you have to pay your share of the fuel bill."

The meeting duly took place in the Trustees' Conference Room. I had chosen this site partly because I felt that the Trustees would be happier on their own ground, and partly because I did not wish to arouse any comment on the rather bare condition of The Tillevant Building beyond the nearly completed reception foyer.

Darrell certainly turned his people out well. He had not been able to persuade them to bathe, but I gathered they had rubbed themselves down with grass, which I subsequently discovered he had obtained from the landscaping of The Tillevant Building. He had impressed on them several times how important it was not to guffaw in the Trustees' faces. To this end, for an hour before they came on parade he had been playing to them on his personal harpsichord, imported into The Tillevant Building at doubtless exorbitant cost, some of the works of Bach. They had evidently taken well to this composer, as their faces bore much the same faraway expression as they had done when leaving the airplane.

The Cosamo saluted the Trustees in traditional fashion, by striking the sides of their own faces with an open hand. The Trustees bowed and nodded at them rather stiffly and there was a short silence, broken by Mrs. Stahl.

"What dear little people. So they really don't—what a good idea. Now my late husband—"

Mr. Haversham, who evidently did not wish to hear another reminiscence of Mrs. Stahl's late husband, interrupted:

"That all seems satisfactory," he said with a certain vagueness. "Why don't we make them welcome with a drink all round?"

Darrell, who was absently sounding a tuning fork on the conference table, said:

"There's no Whammo left."

"Whammo. Ah yes, Darrell, I've been meaning to talk to you about that. Perhaps after the meeting. Still, let's try them on bourbon."

Darrell looked slightly alarmed, but shrugged. It was with apprehension myself that I passed around the first drinks, since although

209

on my instructions the liquors available for guests of The Dickstachel Research Institute were of the lower proof which rising costs of production have induced the manufacturers to put on the market, bourbon is still a potent refection.

The Cosamo, I thought, seemed disappointed at the size of their portions, which presumably appeared somewhat paltry to people who were used to drinking strong liquor in bowls. However, they took their glasses politely, rolled the liquid around their mouths, swallowed it and held out their arms for a refill before any of the Trustees had taken more than a sip. They repeated this process until the bourbon was all gone, although Mr. Haversham, by speeding up, adroitly managed to secure a second portion. To satisfy the repeated mute requests of the Cosamo I was forced to start on the scotch, then the gin, and finally the brandy. The other Trustees had long abandoned the unequal contest, but Mr. Haversham—before leaving he stated that he was damned if he was going to be outdrunk by a bunch of naked savages—insisted on having at least one, and sometimes two, portions of each variety of liquor as it came into service. For any visible effect it had on them it seemed to me that the Cosamo might as well have been drinking lemonade, which would have been much cheaper. Mr. Haversham, however, although his coordination remained good, became very flushed and talkative.

He nodded towards Harry and said to Darrell:

"Is this the guy who understands English?"

"Yes, it is," Darrell, with a peculiarly feline look, replied.

Mr. Haversham then embarked on a lengthy and, even to me, tedious exposition of the natural and acquired assets, talents and virtues of the United States and all that in them dwell. Harry listened to this with exemplary patience and good manners, only interpolating, when Mr. Haversham was stressing the richness of our great country:

"Plenty cowrie shells."

However, he did this in such an unobtrusive way that it is doubtful whether Mr. Haversham understood the remark, especially as he was now explaining our desire to protect, by every peaceful means such as vending arms but withholding troops, all those weaker peoples who were of our way of thinking. By a natural transition this led him into a history of our armed forces, in the course of which he paused to moisten his lips with brandy and resumed:

"You are, I take it, unacquainted with the expertise of the bombing airplane?"

Harry, whose visage during the entire lecture might have been carved out of lignum vitae, replied:

"Sure me know-um. Big bird him fly, shit eggs. BAM-BAM."

At this point Darrell, who I am convinced had been eagerly awaiting some such denouement, interposed with the excuse that it was time for the next in a series of tests and ushered the Cosamo into the corridor. Even through the closed heavy double doors of the conference room we could hear the strident laughter with which, at last freed of the unnatural restraint which had been placed upon them, the Cosamo made their editorial comment.

42

THEN THERE was that aborted tour of New York City. I was against this from the first. It only took place because I allowed myself to be overpersuaded by Darrell, who repeated his arguments in favor of outdoor exercise and mental diversion.

"Harry's smoking himself to death."

"His cigars smell excellent," I said. "Excellent. Anyone would think they were genuine Havana."

"Glad you like them."

"What, uh, what brand are they?"

"I forget."

"Perhaps you could spare me a sample."

"I'll make a note of it."

In the course of the next few days an envelope with a single cigar did make its way to my desk. The band had been removed, but it was unquestionably of Cuban origin. The presumption was that Darrell had added smuggling to his other unorthodox activities. However, I decided to make no direct comment on this.

"How do the other members of the party spend their time?"

"I've bought Harry all the Agatha Christies and he's reading them aloud and making them guess the solutions. They haven't got one right so far. But they can't do that the whole time, so they watch quite a lot of TV and that makes them laugh so much it's bad for them. And Harry reads newspapers and magazines to them too, and they all fall over with merriment, including Harry. So you see, apart from Christie they really have no healthy amusement."

Reluctantly, I gave in.

For the first time, Darrell allowed the Cosamo to sally forth without loincloths. Regardless of the ethical desirability of this decision, he should of course have made them wear sneakers since, lacking the street wisdom of the local practitioners of the barefoot cult, within a few yards of leaving The Tillevant Building several of the Cosamo had cut their feet rather badly on shards of beverage bottles strewn about the sidewalk by the fun-loving youth of the neighborhood.

Difficult as it is to arouse the interest of the hardened New Yorker by anything less imperative than a fragment of cornice falling ten floors onto his or her head, the strident laughter which arose from the Cosamo after this pedal mishap caused one or two passers-by to stop and stare. Of course, in moments what can only be described as a milling throng had gathered, foremost among which was an aged beldam with honed elbows—I am quoting Darrell's own words—who stooped myopically to the writhing forms and after careful inspection arose with the oracular pronouncement:

"Why, they ain't got no clothes on, the doity heathen."

She then struck out energetically in all directions with her shopping bag, but the high trajectory passed harmless over the heads of the Cosamo and landed on her fellow spectators. These good-naturedly forbore to return the blows but quickly shuffled her into the background and surged forward to inspect the other and more unusual feature of interest which the Cosamo presented. Not satisfied with looking, they proceeded to touching, many of them evidently having attained years of indiscretion at the time when touching was freely advocated as a means of ending all dissension between human beings. From the renewed peals of merriment which now arose from the Cosamo it was evident that they disliked this invasion of their privacy very much indeed.

I asked Darrell what he was doing all this time. It became apparent that for once he had been faced with a situation with which even he was unable to cope. I was so delighted to hear this that I forbore from further comment. However, at that moment a chance police car arrested its progress, and although that was all its occupants did arrest they dispersed the crowd with commendable promptitude. Making themselves heard as well as they could above the outcries of the Cosamo, they then discussed this further problem.

"Oughta pull 'em in for indecent exposure," opined the younger policeman.

"Ain't no such thing no more," his grizzled and frankly obese senior stated. "You never go to the theater or the movies?"

"Yeah, but them actors is a dirty lot anyway. This is for real."

"We pull 'em in, what happens? The judge cans 'em for twenty-four hours, or he gives 'em a talk on toilet training and lets 'em go. You wanta spend half a day in court, I'm phoning in sick. The air in that place is bad, man, bad."

"Well, we oughta do *something.*"

"You're too young to remember, but for a while there I useta be on the vice squad in Buffalo. Sometimes I'd get to watch the old burleycue shows, make sure the girls didn't take too much off. Didn't cost me a cent, neither. Some of them dames was beautiful, man, beautiful. 'N if you got to make a pinch, if you wuz any good you could make it a real pinch, in the right places, know what I mean? Nowadays they just start off stark, an' it's O.K. with everyone. But I don't see no artistry in that."

"Yeah, but we oughta do *something.*"

The Cosamo had stopped laughing and were gathered around the two policemen like well-behaved children with two favorite teachers. Darrell said to the older policeman:

"Excuse me, sergeant, but these people are members of a religious cult."

"Oh, they are. Well, that settles it. Sorry if you've been inconvenienced, sir."

"Yeah, but ain't we going to do *anything?*"

"Listen, feller, you've heard of the Four Freedoms?"

"They were before I was born."

"The Four Freedoms were invented by that great and good man, Franklin Delano Roosevelt. The second one goes, 'Freedom of every person to worship God in his own way—everywhere in the world.'"

"And that's the way they worship God?" the younger man said to Darrell.

"It certainly is."

"Jesus Christ," said the younger man, and got back in the car. Darrell took his charges back into The Tillevant Building to apply antiseptic and bandages to their feet.

Of course what he had told the policeman was not strictly true, but these days it very well might have been.

43

WE COME now to the appearance of the Cosamo—the genuine Cosamo—on television. I was against this also. The Dickstachel Research Institute was approached by one of the commercial networks—the one that was trailing the other two—and it did not require very much perceptiveness on my part to realize that our distinguished visitors would not be treated with the detached consideration which they deserved.

If it had been a question of the Public Broadcasting Service I should have reacted differently. I said as much to Darrell when we first discussed the matter. Incidentally, an additional cause for annoyance was that the network had contacted Darrell and not myself. I try not to be petty about these matters, but there is a right way of doing things and there is a wrong way of doing things.

Darrell reacted typically.

"Public broadcasting," he said, sitting sideways and to my horror putting his legs over the arm of my Chippendale chair, "under the guise of providing education, public broadcasting presents at enormous expense a string of superficial data aimed at people of less than average intelligence who just managed to scrape through high school and maybe not even that. Eighty percent of the program is forgotten before it ends."

"I disagree with you entirely."

"You would."

"And furthermore, please do not abuse that very valuable piece of furniture."

"Fetch more at auction than I would, no doubt." But he moved to an ordinary chair. "Come on, yes or no? Public would want us for free, but the network will pay us. Only scale, of course, but I might be able to bump them up a little."

I resented that "I" very much, but I controlled myself, and merely said:

"I presume they would want me to appear?"

"They wouldn't want you, but I can see they won't get the Cosamo without you. Turning into quite a ham, aren't you?"

"One man in his time—" I began.

"Goodbye, Jacques," he said, and left before I could finish the quotation.

On the night before the broadcast I developed influenza.

You can see, can you not, dear Dr. Ampiofratello, how in those months everything was working against me. I had a temperature of 104 degrees, not only the world but I myself appeared to be out of focus, and every time I tried to sit up in bed I fell over sideways. It was obviously impossible for me to make a personal appearance. All I could do was rent an (ugh) television set and hope that I would retain consciousness long enough to see what kind of an absurdity Darrell made of his temporary role as public relations representative of The Dickstachel Research Institute. At first I thought of nominating our actual public relations officer to take my place, but fortunately I remembered, despite my migraine, that Darrell loathed this man quite as much as he loathed me and that they were quite incapable of declaring even a temporary truce.

When I asked my wife to arrange for the television set she thought I was delirious. With the last vestige of my strength I convinced her otherwise, and presently a disgustingly hearty man arrived and set up the abominable contraption at the foot of my bed, meandering on the while about what a boon television was to shut-ins. Finally he said, "There you go"—an expression I particularly dislike—and departed, leaving the set on. I was able to close my eyes—indeed I could hardly keep them open—but as I had neglected to furnish myself with earplugs I was forced to listen to an elderly man saying that he was going to have lunch downtown, in accents which made it clear that what he was really going to do was learn the result of his recent biopsy. I called to my wife to turn it off but my voice was so weak that she, being in the living room paying the man, did not hear me, and I had to endure a full ten minutes of this blatherskite.

I was feeling a little better by the time the talk show which had hired the Cosamo began, but since these alleged entertainments purposely avoid announcing even the approximate time of appearance of their so-called attractions I lay there, grippe-bound and helpless, while an alleged comedian was allegedly comic, an alleged singer allegedly sang, and a deservedly famous actor was compelled with no preliminary warmup to plunge into an emotionally distraught speech from *Troilus and Cressida*.

Finally the person whose name the program bore, having disposed of three commercials for unclogging respectively drains, nasal passages and intestines, leaned forward, assumed an extremely sincere expression, and said:

"And now, ladies and gentlemen, we're going to have kind of a change of pace. I guess you've all heard of the important and valuable scientific research that The"—glancing at notes—"Dishtable Research Institute is conducting in connection with that little-known tribe who dwell in the rainswept forests of the Upper Amazon—the Cosamo. Tonight, ladies and gentlemen, in a strictly scientific spirit, and in order that you may learn a little more of the wonders of the world around you, we bring you the opportunity of meeting some of these charming and delightful people. They will appear before you"—slight choke—"unclothed, in order that you may see and marvel for yourselves at the unique physical appearance which they present. They have no"—he lowered his voice impressively—"pubic hair."

Unfortunately, he lowered his voice so much that it was to all intents and purposes inaudible, and some oaf in the audience called out:

"No what?"

One would have expected the person in charge of the program to be totally imperturbable, and in normal circumstances no doubt he was so. On this particular night, however, he was understandably a little nervous. After all, he had been entrusted with network television's first experiment with full frontal nudity—they had to do something to boost their Nielsen. He was pretty sure of his studio audience, but he must have had some doubts about the Federal Communications Commission, enfeebled though that body now appears to be.

Instead, therefore, of ignoring the hard-of-hearing oaf who had called out "No what?" and completing the announcement which had undoubtedly been prepared for him by five writers and seventeen lawyers, he lost his head and repeated in a stentorian voice:

"PUBIC HAIR."

At that moment, then, millions of bedrooms throughout the land reverberated with these words. Although I had the sound in my own room at a moderate level, my eardrums bounced. I also received the impression that the phrase had re-echoed in the airwell like a battle cry, and in fact my wife reported to me that the windows of many people who presumably had been watching other programs were being flung up and the occupants were peering out.

The person now very sensibly abandoned the rest of his script, threw out an arm and declaimed:

"Ladies and gentlemen, the Cosamo."

Led by Harry, and with Darrell bringing up the rear, the Cosamo then filed on stage. To everyone's surprise and disappointment they were all wearing loincloths. The producer, though young, perhaps had racial memories of "the old burleycue shows" to which I have previously referred, and had decided that it would be even better for the ratings if the Cosamo appeared in what was for them full clothing and removed it when the time came for the closeups.

Darrell and Harry sat down, and the lesser lights remained standing. The person then said, admirably retaining his very sincere expression:

"Ladies and gentlemen, this is Mr. Paul Darrell, Scientific Director of The Dishtable Research Institute. That is right, Mr. Darrell?"

"Quite right, except that it is usually pronounced Dickstachel."

I could see at once that these men were not going to get on. However, the person, with a certain doggedness, proceeded:

"Now, Mr. Darrell, would you outline for us so that we can all understand—just what do you hope to achieve from this project?"

I am sure that at this point Darrell overcame a strong temptation to reply: "Sweet fuckall." Instead, however, he recited the official purposes of the investigation with admirable gravity. But after he had been speaking for a few seconds it occurred to me that his style was not at all his own. In fact, it reminded me of someone I had encountered at some time or other. I first ascribed this to the slight mental confusion associated with a high temperature, but shortly after it became apparent that Darrell was giving a full-fledged impression of *me*, including a certain trick I have of rotating my right wrist to emphasize certain points. He even produced a very fair impression of my philosophical smile, damn him. In spite of the person's efforts to interrupt him, Darrell's voice rolled inexorably on in rounded periods which I should have been perfectly happy to employ myself.

But let us face the facts, dear Dr. Ampiofratello. The audience was not interested in sober scientific discussion. It wanted to get to the closeups of pudenda, male and female, bald or otherwise. What I can only describe as a gang of hooligans began a rhythmic clapping, with an equally rhythmic chant of:

"Take it off. Take it off. Take it off."

Affecting surprise, Darrell turned to Harry and made what was evidently a prearranged gesture. Harry shook his head. Darrell repeated the gesture, this time including the row of figures which was phlegmatically standing center stage.

The Cosamo were not going to take it off.

During our subsequent discussion Darrell and I agreed that, had they been allowed to come on stage in their natural nakedness they would have felt no qualms; but to be asked first to don a strangely shaped piece of cloth in order to conceal what the aliens among whom their lot was cast evidently considered shameful, and then to be asked to remove it in full view of some of these aliens whose only desire, it was apparent even to these innocents from the rain forest, was to gloat: that was more than the Cosamo could tolerate.

Modesty had been reborn in the United States.

Darrell looked at his balking charges for a moment. Then he turned to the audience.

"Ladies and gentlemen," he said. "Perhaps we have been taught a lesson. God bless you all. Goodnight."

He strode from the stage. With considerable dignity, the Cosamo followed.

44

THE NEXT regrettable incident occurred when His Honor the Mayor decided, for reasons best known to himself, to provide some kind of civic reception for the Cosamo. By that time I was looking rather askance at the Cosamo, who really were not turning out at all as I expected. To tell the truth—and to you, dear Dr. Ampiofratello, I could never do anything else—I am not sure how I *had* expected the Cosamo to turn out, but never in my wildest dreams—and I have had some pretty wild dreams, could I have imagined the reality. However, since the civic reception did reflect favorably on the activities of The Dickstachel Research Institute I was certainly going to attend it; and of course Darrell was there too. I was having altogether too much of Darrell's company at that time—another unforeseen consequence—and still a third vexatious feature was that Miss Greta Love was also present.

I do not mean to convey that the presence of Miss Greta Love was in itself vexatious—it could never be that—but I was hoping that by degrees it might be possible for me to efface the memory of my admittedly farouche behavior on a certain occasion which I have already put into this record. Having done so, perhaps by means of some extremely credible excuse which I had not so far been able to devise, it was my hope and indeed my intention to try, try, try again.

Any amelioration of our now somewhat formal relations was, however, made extremely difficult by the fact that not only was Darrell blatantly attracted to her—that was easily understandable—but she was just as blatantly attracted to Darrell, and in spite of what I suppose some people would think his good looks I found this hard to comprehend.

Darrell had such an offhand address, even with her, and really her own manners were so elegant that I should have thought she would have preferred the perhaps rather old-fashioned courtesy which I had on all occasions been only too happy to offer her. As you are doubtless aware, dear Dr. Ampiofratello, there is a school of thought which avers that a woman—any woman—likes to be thrown on her back. I really do not know about that. It is assuredly not a course of action which I should ever have attempted to pursue with my wife; and in the case of some women—for example, Ms. Kalman, I imagine that one would need to have achieved some degree of competence in one or other of the Japanese martial arts before one could successfully carry out such a feat.

The cold fact is that whenever at this blessed civic reception I attempted to move closer to Miss Love in order to make some pleasant remark I found Darrell standing in front of me, and if I moved around him I found that he had mysteriously moved too. It seemed to me that he was neglecting his duties as cicerone of the Cosamo just as much as Miss Love was neglecting hers as Executive Producer. At that moment she seemed to be telling him about some production or other in which she had been involved. The words "stinkeroo" and "had to rewrite the whole goddamned script" came to my ears—and in anything but her usual magnolia-like tones, at that. Since I did not know to what she had reference, I moved away, puzzled and disheartened.

Frankly, the civic reception struck me as a rather cut-rate affair. It took place in the open, on a raised wooden platform of a decidedly flimsy nature. There were no refreshments of any kind. The, uh, sanitary arrangements also were conspicuous by their absence, a fact which in itself was enough to cause me to abandon any attempt to re-establish communication with Miss Love, since I was, to use a vulgar expression, "caught short" and had to walk up and down the platform until the Mayor arrived, ten minutes late and looking as usual as if he expected at any moment to be impeached. Thereafter I could only shift from foot to foot while he read his speech.

Neither could I help criticizing the administrative side of the proceedings. The Mayor started to read from a speech intended for a conference of the American Blasting Association, and had got several sentences along before he discovered his mistake. His remarks while the correct script was being substituted were clearly audible over the public address system.

During this time the Cosamo had comported themselves in most exemplary fashion. Indeed their behavior would have put to shame many an audience at far more august public meetings. But the discipline which Darrell and Harry had imposed on them was evidently wearing thin. I cannot say that I blame them. They had been marshaled a full half hour before the official starting time, so that they had been waiting forty minutes in all. A cold breeze, bearing the usual accompaniments of flying grit and old newspapers, was sweeping across from Park Place, and quite possibly affecting their interior economies as well as mine. I know that I was suffering agonies. Agonies.

Now the weakest-willed among the Cosamo emitted a suppressed giggle. In a moment the discordant note of Cosamo laughter was audible in its most uninhibited manifestation. The Mayor stopped speaking and glared; but a few nearby spectators also began laughing, and the urge spread to many of the bystanders. The microphones picked up the sound and relayed it over a larger area. One or two lunchtime strollers at some distance reacted, and in their turn set off more. In an amazingly brief time the sound of laughter was spreading along Broadway and into the cross streets, drowning the traffic. Men who an instant before had been engaged in combative argument paused, chuckled, and almost at once were clutching at each other for support in their mirth. Others leaned weakly against store windows, many of which broke. Cars, taxis and trucks crashed into each other as their drivers caught the infection. I myself was screeching with abandoned hysteria, to the detriment, I regret to say, of my trousers. Darrell and Miss Love were holding on to each other in a manner which in other circumstances would have suggested some novel sexual technique; and the Mayor, after his first outraged reaction, was bent helplessly over the reading desk, only straightening up at intervals to apply a hand to his aching abdomen before falling into some even more convulsed attitude. From the Battery as far north as Astor Place the sound of unreasoned hilarity spread, and for all I know bid fair to envelop Manhattan and points north, before Darrell staggered to the public address amplifier and switched it off.

In the same directions that it had swelled, the laughter faded, and the normal snarls and growls of the city arose once more. Ambulances removed those for whom hysteria had been followed by heart attacks, insurance claims began to be filled out, and the first moves were made in the many lawsuits which, I regret to say, were leveled at The Dickstachel Research Institute, which was assumed by the prosecuting attorneys to be the legal guardian of the Cosamo, with whom it had all started. In the congested state of our legal machinery, the first of these suits will probably not come to hearing for several years, by which time with any luck many of the plaintiffs will be dead, leaving no issue. I myself, of course . . . In any case, there will be a nice legal point to resolve. Can one render oneself liable to damages for spreading laughter?

At that moment, however, I was not interested in such considerations. I had had enough. I hailed a taxi and went home to change my pants.

45

Yes, the multitudinous duties and anxieties that crowded upon me at that time were almost too much for one man to bear. Had I been able to step back and view things in perspective—although so heavily were the Furies ganging up on me that in stepping back I should probably have put my foot in an outsize can of paint. I could not possibly attend to everything with my usual painstaking thoroughness. In allotting priorities I suppose it was only natural that I should favor the two that were nearest my heart—the Official Opening of

The Tillevant Building and the world premiere of that socially significant motion picture, *Discovery*.

I had already booked the Grand Ballroom of the Louis Vingtième on Fifth Avenue, which I felt was one of the few luxury hostelries still retaining any cachet. Well, they had renamed the Grand Ballroom the Hustle Hideout, which I found pretty nauseating, but just as I made the booking they were switching back to Grand Ballroom, which I suppose proved something or other.

The next important consideration was, of course, the audience. If there were no audience there would be little point in having the premiere, heh-heh. Here was an unequaled opportunity for making the work of The Dickstachel Research Institute known to a large number of, putting it bluntly, well-heeled people who could not only be mulcted of exorbitant sums in return for their tickets of admission but a percentage of whom could subsequently be, again putting it bluntly, tapped for donations and bequests. I had no doubt I could rely on the Trustees to persuade or bulldoze some of their affluent friends to patronize the affair, but I imagined that, desirable as these would be, they would not necessarily impart to the proceedings that aura of sophisticated internationalism, and quite frankly of privilege, in favor of which I am, that one associates with the Beautiful People, if that is what they are still called, and with those who are at least on the fringe of showbiz if not actually in it, although of course in the latter case I should wish to filter them with some exactitude.

The trouble was that I did not know anyone answering to that description. In this dilemma it occurred to me that I had read somewhere of the existence of persons whose occupation it was to bring together other persons who wished to give notable parties and other persons of a notable nature who wished to attend such parties. I hope that is clearer than it sounds. I myself was not clear about the detail of these arrangements, and I had completely forgotten the names of the persons quoted in the article. Free association, at which I am normally rather good, merely produced, with aggravating recurrence, the name of the magazine *Rocks and Minerals*, which was so obviously absurd that I abandoned the attempt.

I therefore instructed my secretary to obtain the information for me.

"Without," I added, in an understandable excess of caution, "without troubling Mr. Darrell, who is extremely busy at this time."

She flashed a rather odd look at me and replied:

"I know who you mean. Willem van der Lust. He's absolutely the top man. My sister knows a gal who works for him, and she says—"

"I am far too busy to listen to gossip about your sister," I said. "Kindly get him on the telephone."

I intended to summon Mr. Willem van der Lust to my suite in order to apprise him of my requirements. Next day, after I had waited twenty-five and three-quarter minutes in his office, I was making a pretense of shaking his poorly manicured hand. I was forced to state my requirements in the brief intervals between telephone calls, which is one of the cruder ways of cutting a visitor down to size. When I had finished he twitched his nose.

"You want them to pay for their tickets?"

"Certainly. I thought of keeping it low. Say thirty-five dollars, or sixty dollars a couple. That would include refreshments," I added, as he began another twitch.

"Well, I don't know, I don't know at all. (Hello? No, Sharon, I can't get you in there. I-can-not-get—You know what happened last time. Well, send me a doctor's certificate and I'll see what I can do.) You see, Mister—Mister—what with the market and all there isn't as much money around as there used to be, and a lot of people— (Hello? You want *who* to come to your party? *Who?* And play just a couple numbers. Like Beethoven snartas, huh? Why don't you call his agent? You already did? So goodbye.)"

He put down the phone and stared.

"*Spivakov,*" he said.

He turned his long-lashed, peculiarly transparent eyes back to me.

"Like I was saying, Mister—Mister—these days a lot of people, it isn't enough they should get in free, they expect to be paid."

"But surely—"

"Y'see, it's not like you was a disco queen, or something Chinese —Chinese is very tchick just now—or even if you was a popular cause like children or bad kidneys. You're too general."

"Mr. van der Lust, the Dick—"

"(Hello? How are you, darling? Sure. For you I can get anybody.

Yeah. Yeah"—scribbling—"yeah, and her, too. Leave it to me. Have a *good* day.) Know who that was?"

"Frankly, I would prefer not to."

"That was—hey, ain't you the guy with those little people with the naked you-know-whats?"

"The Cosamo—"

"Why didn't you remind me? For you too I can get anyone. You know something? I got a nose for these things. Cosamo is going to be very tchick. You know something? People is starting to depilate."

"To what?"

"You know. To remove the—the—ah, please don't make me say it." He picked up the phone. "Karen? No calls till I tell you."

"Mr. van der Lust, in no circumstances are the Cosamo going to appear at this premiere."

"You crazy or something? They'll be the biggest—"

"I cannot guarantee their behavior. At the civic reception—"

"Oh yeah, that's right. But hey, they're in the movie anyway?"

"No. Yes. Uh—"

"So shoot some more footage. Put it in at the end. Spread the good word— 'Now you can see what you never saw on TV.' Waidaminit. Waidaminit."

He reached a slim folder out of his desk.

"This here is my special list. Now—"

For the next fifteen minutes the room echoed to the sound of dropping names. Then he said:

"There'll be a buffet and liquor?"

"There'll be something. But I do not wish anybody to become, uh, overexcited, neither do I wish to use up all the prof—uh, surplus."

"So charge them a hundred, a hundred twenty-five tax-deductible dollars a couple and give them a good sendoff. Put them in the right mood to enjoy the movie. Hey, I got a great recipe for lobster-and-pineapple salad I'll give you."

I felt he was rather exceeding his instructions, but he evidently meant well. A thought, however, occurred to me. I said:

"By the way, I don't know any of these people. I suppose you will come along and prompt me?"

"Well, I don't usually need to. Still, since it's for charity I'll look in just at the reception line for another six hundred. Nah, make it five, because you're a nice gentleman."

Frankly, by this time I was rather torn between pleasure at the success of my mission and annoyance at his gross overfamiliarity. However, to show willing, as the saying goes, I said:

"There will be imported champagne and caviar for a selected few in a side room. I shall save a special bottle for you."

He held up a hand.

"Please, for me Perrier Water. I got terrible liver trouble."

46

I DO not know whether there are in my family tree any Scottish people from whom I may have inherited the occult faculty known as second sight, or whether there is any other explanation for the sense of foreboding which was now haunting me with ever-growing strength. I managed to shake it off while I was working, and indeed at that time I was as busy as a whole hive of bees, for The Dickstachel Research Institute was fairly humming, heh-heh, with activity.

Apart from the varied activities I have already described, we had recently received two new, important and potentially remunerative assignments. One of these, entitled "Investigation into the Id-Activation of Non-Constructive Impulses by Newly Enfranchised Voters in a Compassionate Society," I am happy to say was financed from Washington. It had to do with the tendency of certain middle-class teenagers to drive their expensive automobiles at high speed through streets which might or might not be deserted, firing hunting rifles at store windows.

This of course was a highly complex psychological study which would need to, or at any rate could be made to, extend over at least two years. Using my casting vote, I took it entirely out of Darrell's hands after he had suggested a three-line solution identifying the phenomenon as a retarded/affluent version of small boys with rubber-band catapults.

The other project, "Comparative Chromatic Recognition in Underprivileged Societal Groups," had to do with beercans.

In addition to all this I was employed in setting up a series of panels to re-evaluate the evaluations of our divers Administrative Committees with, of course, a master panel to pass judgment on the decisions arrived at or vice versa. I felt—I still feel—that one cannot do better than imitate the system of checks and balances which the founding fathers set up.

I therefore experienced more than my usual feeling of hostility and apprehension when Darrell entered my office and, without preliminary greeting, said:

"Among all the other things of mine you've never read, I wouldn't doubt you've never read that material I gave you before I left for Ventrivia?"

I passed a weary hand over my weary brow. I recalled the document perfectly. I also recalled the raspberry in a plastic box which had accompanied it.

"Oh, that," I said. "What of it?"

"Oh, that," he mimicked. "What of it? *What of it?* My God."

He began to stride about, seriously flattening the deep pile of my carpet.

"I come to you, Tillevant," he resumed, "I come to you with an idea which may hold out more hope for the future of mankind than anything since Louis Pasteur lived and breathed, and all you can say is 'What of it?' Through all the centuries, Tillevant, great minds such as mine have had to grapple with the forces of stupidity, obscurity, slothfulness and ignorance. But I doubt whether Galileo, Fleming, Spinoza and—and—I doubt whether any of these towering intellects was ever faced with such complete, dyed-in-the-yarn, impenetrable lack of understanding, vision, foresight, as I am at this moment."

"Do sit down, Darrell. You are making me giddy."

"I can't sit down, my ass hurts. I fell off a horse this morning."

But he flung himself into my multi-thousand-dollar Chippendale chair with a fury which made its joints—and mine—creak. I instructed my secretary to bring me the relevant papers.

"This seems," I said, after perusing the half-page Summary, "this seems to have something to do with antimatter. What is antimatter?"

"Fully explained in the body of my memorandum."

"That may be," I said, riffling the many pages of single-spaced typescript, charts, tables and diagrams. "However, would you be good enough to answer my question?"

He took a deep breath, and rapidly uttered:

"Antimatter is matter composed of particles which are analogous to but have charges opposite to those of common particles of matter, for example positrons which are analogous to electrons but are positively charged. Is that clear?"

"No."

"I hardly thought it would be. Let's try again. You know what a black-and-white photographic negative looks like?"

"Certainly."

"Antimatter is to ordinary matter what the photographic negative is to the print. The particles of matter and antimatter exist as nearly as possible in the same space, revolving around each other but never touching. If they ever did touch—"

"Well?"

"Blooie. They would destroy each other and, so far as is known, start an irreversible chain reaction. Everything would vanish. That desk. You. Me. The earth. The solar system. The galaxies. The universe."

"To what conclusion do you lead me?"

"I'm glad you asked me that. Now even your skimble-skamble mind will easily realize that this involves a hell of a lot of energy. An unimaginable amount of energy. If you look at the rows of zeros on pages 42 and 43—"

"I'll take your word for it."

"They're merely a graphic representation of 10^{-16}. But my idea is that if we could shift the particles of matter and antimatter just a wee, wee bit nearer to each other, we could tap the tiniest trickle of the energy involved and bleed off enough light, heat and power to supply the whole world for ever and ever, amen."

I had never heard Darrell in this vein before. He sounded like a combination of a biblical prophet and an old-time TV pitchman.

"It sounds as controversial as nuclear power," I said. "And at least as dangerous."

"What isn't dangerous? The point of a pin is dangerous. A grain of earth is dangerous. Taking a shower or heating a can of soup—dangerous activities, my timid Tilly."

"And extremely costly. I—we—should have to put up an extremely convincing case and be prepared to argue it not persuasively only, but long. In view of our manifold activities at the present time—"

"Don't worry about dollars. I already have enough backing for a pilot project."

"Oh? Where from?"

"Ms. Kalman."

Damn the man. There was no knowing where to have him.

"The question of working space—"

"There's all the space I need in one corner of the new building."

"The Tillevant Building?"

"The Tillevant Building, that conspicuous example of institutional erectophilia. Think of all the fame and glory that will be associated with your name."

There was that, of course, if the experiment was successful, and Darrell had not failed in anything yet. But there was always a first time.

"The Trustees—"

"I'll handle the Trustees, if you'll back me up."

But some voice within me urged me not to give way. Perhaps it was my Monarch of the Glen ancestor.

"No," I said finally. "I am sorry, Darrell, but there is something about this whole idea which strangely disturbs me. You can talk to the Trustees, of course, but I cannot see my way to supporting your argument."

He looked tired and disgusted.

"I suppose that puts paid to it. The tale of woe you'd put up, you'd scare the pants off them."

"Thank you, Darrell. I am glad you admit that my opinion carries some weight in the right quarters."

"Oh, dammit, Tillevant. You make me lead as much of a whore's life as a restaurant fork. Seeing the amount of shit you offload on me, you might give me my head on something real—and something as big as this, when I ask you. Christ, if it comes off—when it comes off—we'll never again have our asses kicked by the stinking OPEC countries. Boanerges told me—"

"What did Boanerges tell you?"

"Forget it."

"What did Boanerges tell you?"

"He said all the time he knew you, you were a weak, opinionated bastard, but lovable at bottom, and he supposed you hadn't changed."

"And what did you say to that?"

"I told him the only respect in which you'd changed was the last one."

There was a pause. I said:

"People don't change, Darrell. Not in any respect. What else did he tell you?"

He looked at me innocently. Too innocently?

"Nothing."

"Nothing?"

"Nothing. We went on to talk about women. He didn't seem to like them very much."

I still could not decide whether he was speaking the truth. I had just averred that people did not change. If that was true I could still rely on my old friend's discretion. Yet if, perhaps in a drunken moment—and if Darrell, with his impish sense of humor—humor? —was reserving that weapon to some last, crucial moment to bare it to the world, or at any rate to the Trustees, I was in more danger to my career than even the failure of his incomprehensible experiment could cause me. Or so, at the time, I thought. I could not take the risk.

"Very well," I said. "You can count on my support."

My acceptance seemed to deflate him even more than my refusal had done, but he recovered quickly, held out his hand and said awkwardly:

"Thank you."

"You won't neglect the Cosamo?"

"Oh, the Cosamo, the Cosamo. Poor Harry. No, don't worry, I'll keep after it."

At the door he said:

"This means a lot to me."

"It means a lot to me too," I said; but of course we were not talking about the same thing.

After he had gone I closed my door and unlocked one of the cupboards at the bottom of my Duncan Phyfe bookcase, where I kept a file of *Science for Everyman*. It is only a pulp magazine, though such is the effect of inflation that it sells for a dollar-fifty a copy; but I had frequently found it helpful in grappling with the, uh, technical issues with which I was daily confronted. When I had found the issue I wanted, I sat on the floor and read. By the time I had finished, my head was awhirl not only with positive and negative charges of oddly named particles but with such phrases as "escape velocity greater than that of light," "Black Hole," "X-ray emission," "emerging in a different universe," "Inside a Black Hole all the ordinary laws of science break down," "a thimbleful of matter tons in weight."

Possibly I was confusing two of the articles in the magazine. It made very little difference to the chance outcome. As I locked the cupboard again I prayed that on this occasion too it would prove that Darrell knew what he was doing.

47

To CHEER myself up I decided to recap the list of guests whom Mr. Willem van der Lust, under penalty of sacrificing a percentage of his fee for each no-show, had promised would attend the premiere of *Discovery*. As I took out the neatly typed sheets—Mr. van der Lust used paper of a weight and quality rare these days—I wondered whether refunds would be the same for each guest or whether they would be graded in order of importance. It was a point which perhaps I should have cleared up at the time, but I felt that I had hardly been in charge of that interview.

Taking the most distinguished names in alphabetical order, and recalling the brief biographies of each with which Mr. van der Lust had provided me, I found:

Jerry (Attrick) Attenborough, the aging rare-earth heir and still at the age of seventy noted playboy. Jerry's father had been a simple farmer until prospecting geologists had discovered almost the world's entire supply of bratium in the north forty. Bratium is essential as the activating ingredient in military anti-anti-water-poisoning devices and is eagerly sought by the armed forces of all nations, especially those who have signed the various agreements on humanizing warfare.

When Jerry inherited he set out to have a good time. He used up two or three wives a year. Someone once pointed out to him that it was cheaper to rent, but he said he had been raised a strict Baptist.

Mr. van der Lust had also promised to get me the last three of Jerry's ex-wives.

"Hardly used," he said. "And are they hooked on social betterment. You'll see."

"What unusual names," I said, peering at the sheet. "Stheno? Euryale? Medusa?"

"You pronounce 'em good. Ah, don't you worry about that, they're just nicknames. Shows how popular they are."

Then there was Mr. Albert Bridges, perhaps this country's most famous corporate lawyer.

"But he's just narrowly escaped a jail sentence for falsifying evidence," I said.

"So he escaped it. Now he's countersuing the people who sued him. He'll get a billion in damages."

Next came Mrs. "Penta" Costa, widow of the famous religionist whose career in saving thousands of souls for Jesus and, after his conversion, for Mohammed, had been so abruptly terminated by an enraged parent's bullet. Mrs. Costa was now busily drinking herself to death while maintaining a stable of salaried studs. Her checks were still good, however.

Then, Miss Doris Dobermann, the partially deaf entertainer

whose affliction had boosted her to fame since in order to hear herself she was forced to sing loud enough to make sound equipment unnecessary.

And, of course, Sherman Kotz, the millionaire sports nobbler.

And Judge Knott, whose amenable decisions had secured for him a long career on the bench.

And Sexton "Sexy" Mbangi, the legally rehabilitated tennis champion.

The next name was Jonni Patewski.

"I don't think I—"

"She's the casket heiress. Must have a million or two deep-frozen in Switzerland. Dollars, not caskets. Works for no end of good causes. The Society for Abolishing the Speed Limit, stuff like that."

I read the next name with some surprise. Ulrica Paulette Francesca Marylou Ortes y Vega.

"Why, you know who *she* is? International dress designer from Bedford-Stuyvesant. She kept the Marylou out of sentiment."

"Oh," I said. "And who, pray, is Blick Yote?"

"You're not into Blick Yote? Why, he's this country's top porno film director. The first guy to win a Coppy—you know, a Coprolalia Award. He got high-class religion last week. Very tchick."

I was somewhat dubious about Mr. Yote at the time, and as I came to his name again my doubts revived. However, I was forced to assume that Mr. van der Lust knew his own job and had in fact provided me with a selection of names fully representative of our leaders of style, thought and mores as the twentieth *siècle* approaches its *fin*.

Mr. van der Lust had also promised to secure the attendance of Miss Dulcietta Sucrose, who does those delightfully bitchy social notices in the *New York Times*.

At this point my secretary interrupted me.

"Mr. Matthew Montgomery to see you."

"I know no one of that name. When my door is shut I am not to be disturbed. You know that."

"He's from Washington."

"Show him in at once."

I rose and hurried towards the door, preparing my welcoming

smile. When, however, Mr. Matthew Montgomery came into view I received rather a shock. He was a tall man, as pale as a plucked chicken and apparently suffering from facial paralysis. As he advanced towards me, head lowered, eyes fixed on me, he made me feel guilty, though I had no idea of what. He also gave me an extraordinary feeling of *déjà vu.*

"Most happy to meet you, Mr. Montgomery," I said. "From which department, uh—?"

To my horror he then performed the rite known as "flashing identification." Flashing is certainly the right word, as his card appeared and disappeared with the split-second effect of a recognition test; but the phenomenon of persistence of vision left floating in the air before my aghast eyes the dread words:

FEDERAL BUREAU OF INVESTIGATION

48

HAD BOANERGES divulged? Had the FBI impounded the mailing list of the Weird O Ranch?

I got back behind my reassuring desk and sat down as fast as I could.

"Yes, sir," I said. "What can I do for you?"

"Dr. Tillevant," he said, in a voice as colorless as his face, "you are harboring on these premises seven members of the Cosamo nation."

"I would not say harboring, and the Cosamo are a tribe rather than a nation; but yes, The Dickstachel Research Institute is engaged on a project in that connection."

He received this information with the same appearance of total disbelief with which he would doubtless have regarded the sunrise.

"What are the purposes of the project, Dr. Tillevant?"

I was able to answer this question with my accustomed fluency, though without evoking any apparent increment of credence in my visitor.

"What are the strategic purposes, Dr. Tillevant?"

"There are no strategic purposes."

"That is a positive statement?"

"Certainly."

I had sufficiently recovered to feel the first uprising of indignation. This cadaverous bloodhound was presumably following some definite trail, even if it was aniseed—a substance, I believe, occasionally used by foxhunters as a substitute for the live animal; but to be thus smeared in my own office—well, he had not done that yet, but I felt he would begin at any moment. However, Mr. Matthew Montgomery's next words threw me for a, putting it colloquially, loop.

"I have to inform you, Dr. Tillevant, that there are certain authorities which have a different opinion."

"What authorities?"

"I am not empowered to answer that question at this time. My instructions are to warn you that there is a possibility of a kidnap attempt or attempts against these aliens, or yourself, or Mr. Darrell, or any or all of you."

"Good God."

I had no objection to having the Cosamo taken off my hands. I should have been overjoyed to have Darrell kidnapped by anyone crafty and rugged enough to do it. But I should certainly register a vigorous protest if I were kidnapped myself. I had no illusions about my capacity to resist torture, and of course if my captors restricted their questions to the Cosamo project there was nothing of strategic significance that I could tell them, and they would not believe that, and—oh dear, oh dear, oh dear.

The pale voice of Mr. Montgomery was in my ears again.

"Starting immediately, a twenty-four-hour guard will be allotted for as long as may be thought desirable."

For any animation he displayed, he might as well have had a tape loop concealed in his chest. I protested:

"But this is ridiculous. There is absolutely nothing about the Cosamo project that is of any interest"— I was about to say, of any interest to anybody, which deep down I felt to be unfortunately true, but I managed to finish my sentence—"to any foreign power. I suppose it is a foreign power at the back of all this? Who is it? Russia? China? Botswana?"

"I have no detailed instructions as to that, Dr. Tillevant. You will not of course mention this matter even to your closest colleagues. Good day."

I needed oxygen after he had gone. What I think made the whole thing more frightening was that at no time thereafter could I detect anyone shadowing me, no one behaving as if they had any unusual interest in me, either offensive or defensive. I suppose I have read my share of spy thrillers, and it seemed to me that sooner or later anyone being tailed is bound to appreciate the fact. Surely I am not less perceptive than other people, yet, although I actually developed a rather telltale nervous habit of glancing quickly from side to side, and of turning around quickly to face in the opposite direction to that in which I had been walking, not once did I detect anyone ostentatiously reading a newspaper or looking into a store window.

I became expert at conjuring up possible friends or foes. My special waiter at Rinaldo's might be either. So might the driver of the next taxi I took. But no cars drew up beside me, their doors bursting open; no hands reached out at me in the crowd save those of well-fed young persons peremptorily demanding a donation of thirty-seven cents.

In short, I was left with an enhanced respect for the FBI's chameleon talents, coupled with an equal respect for the similar gifts with which the arcane foes of The Dickstachel Research Institute were endowed. The conclusion which was forced upon me was that our enemies were waiting until the end of the Cosamo project so that they could make their pounce when all the information, including the—purely illusory—strategic details had been gathered in. But I could not be certain of this, and it only partly relieved my present anxieties while giving me a more or less fixed date looming ever nearer.

49

MEANWHILE THE Cosamo themselves were occasioning me more and more worry, both through their own behavior and the popularity of various kinds which nevertheless poured in on them.

They would behave quite well for long periods. Then something would trigger their peculiar sense of humor and they would break out. Darrell had declared it an essential part of his researches that they should be shown as many as possible of what is left of our country's primeval beauties, although I strongly suspect that he simply wanted a chance to see them himself on expenses, frighteningly over budget though these were. The Cosamo flew to all these places, and thus arrived in the tranquil condition which the upper air always induced in them; but as soon as this and the first effects of natural loveliness had worn off, some small thing would set them going.

Niagara Falls kept them in thoughtful silence until they looked towards Windsor and Detroit. They drifted peaceably down the Grand Canyon until they noticed the graffiti on the Pre-Cambrian or Paleozoic rocks. They were entranced by Yellowstone National Park until the mounds of discarded socks, newspapers, combs, condoms and the hundred and one relics of nomadic barbarianism caught their eyes.

The only place which was an unqualified success was the Metropolitan Museum of Art. They were taken there after hours, and Darrell told me that they wandered through the deserted galleries as in a trance, sometimes freely shedding tears before the artistic nonpareil of this or that nation or age. They did not react in similar fashion to all countries and all periods, but by this time Darrell was so perfectly attuned to the Cosamo that he hurried them into another gallery and era before the mood was shattered.

They were invited to the White House. I was not actually included, but this was an evident oversight. For an occasion of such moment it went without saying that my presence was essential. At my urgent suggestion Darrell had more than once impressed on Harry, Chief of the Cosamo, that he was about to meet our own chief, whom we invariably treated with the awe and deference merited by his divinely inspired exercise of the lightning which our votes had placed in his right hand. Although I thought I detected a certain amount of skepticism on Harry's face, he was certainly aware of the courtesy due from one chief to another. I was sure from their reaction when he passed on Darrell's words to his own people that everything possible had been done to make this great occasion pass off worthily.

I was naturally in a state of considerable tension as we winged our way towards the nation's capital. This, added to my now fixed habit of looking this way and that in an endeavor to identify friends or enemies, quite possibly gave me the appearance of having succumbed to a nervous tic. Darrell, however, made no comment, and as he had removed one of my fears by donning an ultraconservative business suit with accessories to match, I was, temporarily at least, grateful to him.

We duly survived the security men at the official entrance, and were passed with notable rapidity into the actual Oval Office itself. I believe we even took precedence of the large number of variegated visitors in the waiting room. The President himself was not visible, and we had been lined up for some minutes before he arrived. He seemed to be in a bad mood, which might have been accounted for by the shrill female voice, making use of some rather uninhibited expressions, which we had unavoidably listened to while waiting. I was of course used to his Pan-Afro hairdo (which Jack Anderson later revealed to be a toupee). I could have forgiven his wearing jeans with "I Love America" iron-on patches. After all, he had an image to maintain. But I do think he might have shaved.

The President perfunctorily shook hands all around, picked up a sheet of paper and began to read from it. Darrell acted as simultaneous translator. I had been, to put it bluntly, sweating like a pig ever since the President entered the room. My worst fears were realized before he had mumbled more than two sentences in his North Dakota accent. Harry, despite heroic efforts, let go with a screech like a thousand macaws. His compatriots, who to their credit had been striving equally hard, naturally took this as a signal of release. In a few moments their combined efforts reached disco level, and they were rolling over the floor and bumping up against the furniture.

The President stopped, glanced around, dropped the paper and hurried out, muttering something which I sincerely hope was *not* "Damn the lot of you." The female voice took up its plaint again in a timbre which miraculously cut through the din in the Oval Room.

Notably unscandalized functionaries helped to restore order, very sensibly picking up those Cosamo who seemed to be choking to death and slapping them on the back until they began to breathe normally. The din slowly died away, though the off-stage voice kept unweariedly on. We left the White House even more rapidly than we had entered it. Once we were airborne, enchantment again crept into the Cosamo's faces as they stared out of the windows; but my head movements really did seem to resemble St. Vitus' Dance.

50

THE INCIDENT which I have just related was thoroughly covered in the media but I do not think it was the prime cause, though doubtless it contributed, when the President failed to secure renomination. The most pertinent comment, which was never traced to its source, was that if the guy couldn't even hold the respect of half a dozen pygmies it was time to find someone who could; but I cannot feel that this fully expressed what the anonymous speaker had in mind.

My fear of retaliatory action in the shape of canceled Government contracts was well founded. Several attempts were made; but as a considerable amount of work had been done on all those we held, and the General Accounting Office was at the time on one of its periodical warpaths, we escaped unscathed for the time being. However, the notable lack of new contracts would have created an ugly gap if—but I am anticipating again.

I endeavored to build up my nervous system by consuming even more hearty breakfasts than usual. I doubled my intake of bee pollen and manganese, but I am afraid without sufficient effect.

To add to my difficulties, the scaly tongue of commercialism was licking out towards the Cosamo. I could not make up my mind whether this manifestation of soulless greed should be sternly repressed or whether, in view of the considerable amounts of money which were involved—indeed I may say very considerable—indeed I may say in some cases enormous—where was I? Oh yes. I was strongly tempted to exploit—no, that is an ugly word—to explore, that is what I really meant, to explore—as many opportunities as possible with a view to enabling the Cosamo to return to their homeland, as so many other nationalities had done before them, sufficiently endowed not only to end their days in more comfort than they could previously have envisaged in their wildest dreams, but also to provide for their kinsmen, even having enough left over to capitalize the beginnings of intensive agriculture and thoroughgoing industrialization—observing of course all possible concern for the environment—for the institution of trade unions, pension plans, health care, compulsory education, professional sports . . . the list is really endless. To summarize, I could see at my fingertips the means of helping the Cosamo to move onward and upward through the various grades of consumerism and thus fulfill their proud destiny as members of the human race.

In view of the vast amount of work which the necessary negotiations would entail—for the Cosamo could hardly be exposed unaided to the rapacity of the commercial world—it would be only reasonable that The Dickstachel Research Institute should be allowed to retain some modest percentage, say twenty. Or thirty. To start with. I was indifferent to any benefit that might accrue to me personally, although I felt sure that the Trustees, who had always taken a very generous view towards me, would remember that oft-quoted part of Luke 10:7, which reminds us that the laborer is worthy of his hire. On further consideration I determined that there was no need to worry the Trustees with it at all.

I had little time to waste. Mr. van der Lust had evidently been correct in his statement that the Cosamo were becoming tchick. Only the day before I had noticed an impulse display at the supermarket checkout, a razor prominently bearing the brand COSAMO, so here already was one opportunity missed. If I did not jump quickly into the breach it would be too late to establish the rights of The Dickstachel Research Institute to that brand name for all kinds of mass products from fast food to contraceptives. And, of course, Whammo, although there Mr. Haversham had pulled rank on me.

Mr. Haversham had honored his undertaking to talk privately to Darrell about his offbeat reports from the rain forest. When they emerged from what must have been a mutually painful session, they both looked somewhat chastened. Mr. Haversham was saying in a low voice:

"I'm not saying you're wrong, Darrell, I'm simply saying it was foolish to put it in writing."

I happened to be standing outside the conference room at the time. In view of the massive nature of the doors they can hardly have suspected me of deliberate eavesdropping—indeed, I had been unable to hear one word of what went on inside—but when they caught sight of me they began to talk of other things. It was sadly apparent to me that Darrell's period of disgrace had been minimal, and that a working relationship, however uneasy, had been re-established.

Now I recalled a conversation between Mr. Haversham and Darrell while the three of us were temporarily imprisoned in a broken-down elevator.

"This Whammo stuff, my lad. What's it taste like?"

"Barley water."

"Barley water? Never heard of the stuff."

"A refreshing summer drink, also used in the treatment of diarrhea in infants."

"Never come across the stuff in my whole life."

"Perhaps you never suffered from diarrhea as an infant."

"No, no, can't say I did," Mr. Haversham replied. This suggested a remarkable degree of total recall upon which I prayed that Darrell would find it unnecessary to comment. At the same time I was happy to note that Mr. Haversham appeared to take in good part this offhand discussion of his entrails which, infantile though they had been at the time, were destined to play an important role in the economic history of our country.

"Well, but come along, my lad, what's the stuff made of?"

"It is brewed by primitive methods from the foliage of a variety of *Araucaria imbricata* found only in the Ventrivian rain forest," replied Darrell, whose objection to being called "my lad" was so extreme that his voice was shaking with ill-suppressed rage.

"A variety of *what?*"

"Monkey puzzle," Darrell hissed.

At this point the elevator dropped with great speed for a floor and a half and stopped abruptly. I fell to the bottom of the cage and Mr. Haversham fell on top of me, thus affording me the honor of saving him from injury, although since he is rather a heavy man I suffered pain in one ankle and the opposite elbow. As one would have expected of him, Darrell remained upright and made no attempt to assist either of us to rise. He had, however, derived audible amusement from our plight, and this improved his temper for a while.

"It's quite a—quite a—it works like rhinoceros horn, doesn't it?" Mr. Haversham, who as I have indicated is of fairly advanced years, inquired with ill-assumed carelessness as he dusted himself off.

"I've no idea, *sir.* I've never used rhinoceros horn."

"It makes you high, though?"

"Yes."

"What about those prairie oysters the Reverend mentioned?"

"They," said Darrell with contempt "are for children."

"No legal drinking age in the rain forest, huh? Pity. I was thinking we could form a separate corporation to sell the antidote. Still, must talk to Krebs about this. You could get us some of the—what is it? Foliage? Foliage?"

"*Leaves.*" Darrell's good humor had vanished again. "Yes, I could obtain some specimens for you, although there are not enough trees to warrant commercial development."

"Doesn't have to be the exact same tree, does it? We can find a substitute right here at home. Or we could what do you call it, synthesize whatever's in the leaves. *There's* a project for you, Darrell, my lad."

At that moment, perhaps fortunately, the elevator moved smoothly to the next floor, and the conference, if such it may be termed, ended. But enough had been said to make it clear to me that I—or rather The Dickstachel Research Institute—no, that I was as much out of the running with Whammo as I was with razors.

I had already received several telephone calls concerning other ways in which the Cosamo's special aptitudes could be turned to account. One of these was from one of those determinedly optimistic organizations which devote their energies to dissuading persons who wish to commit suicide. The idea was to record the laughter of the Cosamo and make it available to anyone who dialed a certain number. I pointed out that the quality of Cosamo laughter was not appropriate to the purpose. In any case, the organization had made no mention of a fee.

The other callers, male and female, exhibited what at first appeared to be a fine example of that spirit of generous hospitality towards the strangers within our gates which has from the earliest times been such a marked characteristic of our great country. Increasing numbers of dinner invitations for members of the visiting group poured in. Two things interested me about these calls. One was that the men at the other end of the line all appeared, from the quality of their voices, to be of an advanced age, while the women, on the same evidence, appeared to be of a somewhat hysterical tendency. Usually, though by no means invariably, the men were interested in making the acquaintance of female Cosamo, and vice versa. Some described themselves as amateur anthropologists, some did not. The other point was that the invitation was invariably enlarged by the suggestion of an overnight stay, "so we can get to know each other better."

Inasmuch as the implementation of these invitations would require Darrell's cooperation, I took these persons' telephone numbers and promised to call them back. It occurred to me that, just as with products, a considerable amount of administrative work would be involved, and there could be no reason why the cost of this should not be passed on to the hosts and hostesses.

I endeavored to put this whole matter to Darrell with all the not inconsiderable amount of persuasive reasoning at my disposal. Before I had finished more than two of my most mellifluous sentences, however, he burst out:

"Goddamn and blast it, man, what do you think we are—a self-employed masseuse joint? Are you trying to run this place into the ground, or what?"

As it eventuated, I was not the person who would nearly achieve that feat—but again I anticipate. However, the reply which I had with some difficulty brought to the tip of my tongue was forestalled by the unannounced arrival in my office of Miss Greta Love. I had instructed my secretary to admit her freely at all times, since I had found that her mere advent had the most emollient effect on any person with whom I might be having a somewhat acrimonious discussion. Needless to say, this was the case with Darrell, although equally needless to say I should have preferred to use any other means under the sun of pacifying him.

As the two of them stood mooning at each other I could almost hear the erectile tissue arising. My suite is not the proper place for two or indeed any number of persons to give visible evidence of being in rut. I broke up the mutual admiration society with a loud cough. Miss Love turned to me and said:

"Doktuh Till'vant, Ah just looked in tuh make suah y'all were ready for shootin' in heah this aft'noon."

"This afternoon? I thought it was scheduled for Thursday."

"This *is* Thu'sday, Doktuh Till'vant."

"Oh. Well, you leave me no alternative. You see how it is, Darrell. We shall have to continue this discussion at some other time."

Instead of accepting this sufficiently blunt dismissal, Darrell merely nodded absently and continued to examine Miss Love from a variety of angles. Since there seemed to be no way of getting him out of my office other than summoning a pair of goons, I continued:

"I think I had better fortify myself with lunch. Miss Love, you may wish to give me some last-minute coaching. Will you join me?"

Before she could accept or refuse, Darrell most ill-manneredly anticipated her:

"Good idea. I'll come too."

Without actually saying anything, Miss Love contrived to indicate that in those circumstances she would not be averse to accompanying us. If that was her reason, it was not particularly pleasing to me. I was in an ill humor as we left my office, and I took the opportunity of saying to my secretary:

"Why did you not remind me of this afternoon's shooting session?"

Without raising her eyes she replied:

"I did. Twice."

"Toh," I said, and swept on.

After the food had been ordered I was hardly able to get a word in edgeways, and was forced to listen to a dialog between Darrell and Miss Love of the following moronic order:

"Greta, can you cook?"

"Yuh should taste mah spaghetti."

"I don't want to taste your spaghetti. I loathe spaghetti, and anyway I wouldn't use that corny approach. I have a problem with eggs. Fried eggs. Poached eggs. I can cook them all right but I can't get them out of the pan. Either they break right in there when I dig at them with the spatula, or they fall off it onto the floor."

"Why don't yuh try ice tongs?"

"What the hell good would that be? Then they'd *all* break in the pan."

"Not if yuh cooked them till they were hard."

"You're not taking this thing seriously. I have no one else to ask except my sister, and she lives in Wyoming and eats nothing but raw cabbage."

"Aw, poo' poo'."

Dear Dr. Ampiofratello, imagine listening to that all through lunch. It ended with her promising to come up to his apartment that night and help him get his eggs out of the pan. Now there was a double entendre if ever I heard one. And corny or not, I once asked a girl if she could cook and she simply said "No," and I was no further forward.

My hands were quite shaking when we got back to my office. There were technicians and equipment all over the place, and some fool nearly let a great ugly spotlight fall through the glass of my Duncan Phyfe bookcase. Then we had to have a level test, and first I was too loud and then I was too soft. And then George Langston started to tell me what to do. I knew perfectly well what to do, but I made a pretense of listening to him. Then we had trouble with the teleprompter, and when I read from it he told me to look at the camera, and when I looked at the camera I forgot what came next; so he told me to read from a typescript on my desk, and for some reason or other that was a not very good carbon on yellow paper quite hard to read, and when I turned the pages they made a scratchy noise in the microphone, and—oh dear, oh dear, oh dear.

All this was only rehearsal, and at one point George Langston went to the other end of my office and said something to one of his people which sounded to me like "None of these fucking amateurs can take direction."

"What?" I said very sharply. He jumped and said: "Nothing, I was just getting the lights fixed."

That was the second time I had thought I heard someone say something he should not—the first time it was the President—and on top of everything else I was wondering whether my nerves were in such a state that I really was imagining things; and of course that hardly helped.

We got through my introductory address within two minutes of going into overtime, but I insisted on carrying on full speed ahead and damn the accountants. I felt if we stopped then I should never be able to start again. This was the voice-over part. I don't know how familiar you are with these things, dear Dr. Ampiofratello, but a voice over is where there is a picture of something or somebody and there is somebody quite different talking. I mean you are seeing one thing and listening to another. I mean what you are listening to is not what you are seeing. Well no, of course it isn't. I mean the sound coming out of the loudspeakers bears no relation to—yes it does, though. Perhaps I can explain it better next time you drop in for a chat.

Anyway, what I had to say had to take exactly as long as that part of the picture lasted. If the picture ran for ten seconds, my goodness the fuss there was if I took nine or eleven. George Langston explained to me that if that happened often enough by the time the picture was over it could be as much as a minute out of what he called sync. I said surely things would average out, but he started beating his head against the wall again.

By that time I was wet all over and I didn't care any more. I just went on saying the words again and again till they meant absolutely nothing to me, and sometimes the time was right and sometimes it was wrong, and I think they were running short of tape, and I had an impression that Darrell and Miss Love were tittering together in a corner, though he had no business on the set, which is the term that, oh, who cares.

When it was finally over it was quite dark outside, and Miss Love had disappeared long ago, I suppose to help Darrell with his fried eggs. I sat there until the equipment had been taken away. I was drained, drained. Then the cleaners wanted to come in, but I told them I had some important work to do and they would have to come back in the morning, even if that counted as overtime too.

I closed and locked the door and had two slugs of neat Chivas Regal from my butcherblock bar. I poured myself a third slug to drink, with a little ginger ale in it, while I was doing some light reading. I unlocked the Navy cabinet and reached inside for the Weird O literature, which was not there.

51

I WILL not describe, dear Dr. Ampiofratello, the effect which this dread discovery had on me. My heart became like a lump of ice inside my chest, my knees buckled to such an extent that I was fain to lean on the open drawer of the Navy cabinet, and thereby nearly bring it over on top of me, and my scalp prickled so intensely that every hair upon it would have stood erect had there been any.

Feverishly I rummaged among the other contents of the drawer —the issues of *Stag, Buck, Doe* and other instructive periodicals. The only result was that a full-color centerfold fluttered to the carpet, where in my agitation I placed upon the simulacrum of silicone-augmented mammary glands a heavy heel. Now in the other drawers I groped, but among all my souvenirs I found not that for which I sought. I examined the lock for signs of tampering, but desisted, as wise as when I started.

From the Navy cabinet I hastened to my desk, and thence to my Duncan Phyfe bookcase, and thence to the recesses of my butcher-block bar—my alligator-skin attaché case from Algernon Asprey of Bruton Street, London—a gift from a person to whom I had been able to render some small service—in short to every likely and unlikely storage place in my office where temporary blackout caused by nervous stress might have led me to place the stimulating but, in the wrong hands, accusatory documents for which I sought.

At last, pale and distraught, I made everything tidy and reluctantly wended homewards. Who had done this fell deed? Or had my suppositional blackout been so persistent that I had actually run the fearful risk of taking The Papers to my apartment? Supposing my wife . . . Faint though I now was for lack of food, I shunned the temptations of the refrigerator and with febrile excitement searched every nook and cranny of my study. But to no avail. When my wife came in from her art class she commented in her usual acid fashion on my disheveled appearance—her actual words were, "Are you on the sauce again?"—and when I coldly attributed my evident fatigue to the rigors of filming, made a brief but evidently ironic reference to some person named Mastroianni, poured herself a glass of milk and went to bed. I myself passed but a poor night on the convertible in the living room.

However, I chanced to awaken during the ten minutes when the sun streams in through the eastern window. There is a matter of fact no other window in the living room, but I am enamored of this poetic manner of referring to the single rather inadequate aperture which the builders saw fit to provide. During the rest of the day the living room is dark and cold, but for this brief spell Old Sol's golden light cheered and strengthened me. Although with returning consciousness my many cares rushed again upon me, I felt sufficiently renewed that, head up and fists clenched, I could with God's help vanquish them.

Moreover, this was the day of The Official Opening of The Tillevant Building. I have recounted something of the early stages of this undertaking, but I have not detailed the infinite lengths to which I went in order that the suggestion for thus perpetuating the name of Tillevant should come not from me—which would have seemed grossly immodest—but from some other person. I even nursed little Donzel for a solid forty-five minutes, during which time he peed on my pants twice before I could persuade Mrs. Stahl that she had thought of the idea herself and that therefore she was the obvious person to propound it to the other Trustees, who otherwise I verily believe would have been content to name this architectural masterpiece Building B.

Merely pausing to swallow a few tablets selected almost at random, I hied forth. On arriving at the ceremonial scene I noted with pleasure that the drapery which hid the pregnant words was in place, ready to be drawn aside by a simple pull on a silken—actually nylon —cord. The ribbon which symbolically barred the portals was already performing its function, and the golden shears which would sever it lay, watched over by our head Sanctuary Warden, on a table covered with costly fabric whose verdant hue admirably enhanced the pure gleam of their metal. Well, they were plated really, but the effect was the same.

" 'Institutional erectophilia,' " I said to myself, echoing Darrell's scoffing words. "Toh."

So uplifted was I that I made my way to my office with none of those sideways glances or almost involuntary pirouettes which had for some time past characterized my perambulations. My spirits were only slightly dampened when I found on my desk a hand-drawn and lettered greeting card with the message:

"Hope you'll be happy in your new home. Paul Darrell."

The sentiment was unexceptionable, but the effect was marred by the accompanying illustration of one of those shedlike constructions, with a crescent-shaped opening in the door, to which our forefathers were wont to retire when nature would not be denied.

Some fifteen minutes before the appointed hour—for I wished to display the punctuality which the occasion merited, while avoiding any appearance of overeagerness—I left my office, pausing only to invite my secretary to witness the ceremony, having no doubt that she would choose some suitably modest location in the rear from which to do so. I would have thought she would have taken this democratic gesture as some concrete appreciation of her admittedly efficient services, but she merely replied:

"I have to cover the phones."

"Toh," I said. "Surely you can get someone to do that for a few minutes."

"I'll see if I can get Marge," she said, making no move to do so. She did not in fact attend the ceremony, and I made a mental note of this.

I had decided to make the rite a simple affair, keeping it in the, as it were, family, in dramatic contrast to the gala style which I planned for the forthcoming premiere of *Discovery*. Only the Trustees were present. Mr. Haversham made a brief speech in the following terms:

"Our dear friend Rameses P. Tillevant, if he will allow me to call him so, has been Administrator of The Dickstachel Research Institute almost since its inception. Under his wise and fearless guidance it has steadily expanded the scope of its services, looking towards broader and more distant horizons and solving an ever increasing number of ever more diversified problems for an ever longer roster of distinguished patrons. But Ram Tillevant has not been content merely to accept the assignments which happened to come our way, or to go forth into the highways and byways to capture projects which a less tireless Administrator might have been willing to see allotted to other similar—I will not say less worthy—institutions. From his fertile brain, as a product of his own scholarly research, sprang the concept of one of the most meaningful, if not *the* most meaningful, scientific enterprises of the decade. I refer of course to the Cosamo project, which this magnificent new building houses. It is a fitting tribute that the name of Rameses P. Tillevant should be emblazoned over its threshold, and I now ask Mrs. Clara Stahl if she will be gracious enough to unveil this magnanimous inscription."

Incidentally, this had been the little quid pro quo which had finally decided Mrs. Stahl to suggest my name appearing on the new building. Tears stood in my eyes as Mr. Haversham concluded what I still feel to be the most sincere, the most moving, the most eloquent oration which I have ever written.

Mrs. Stahl moved forward in her usual fluttering manner to perform the unveiling. Little Donzel was clasped under one arm and, as she took the cord in her other hand, reared up and began to worry it. The confusion which this caused, added to the uncertain way in which Mrs. Stahl tugged—rather as if she expected an explosion to follow—although in these days . . . but somehow everything got tangled up and the drapery remained immovably in place. Mr. Krebs's gallant endeavor to assist merely tore the cord loose, and it fell in snakelike confusion to the ground without having performed its allotted function.

I had not thought it necessary to invite any of the, uh, scientific staff, partly because I had heard through the grapevine various hostile comments relative to the alleged greater need for toys such as electron microscopes and what they were pleased to term an adequate number of petri dishes, and partly because I could think of no way of admitting them while excluding Darrell. I should have realized that short of major violence there was *no* way of excluding Darrell. At this moment he provided the explanation of some shadowy movement which I had observed in the reception foyer.

He sprang forth like a greyhound out of its trap and with a balletic leap seized a corner of the fabric and brought it fluttering to the ground. By prearrangement—and that was the sole part of what in retrospect I realize to have been a ceremony not only doomed but foredoomed—two powerful spotlights sprang to life, their beams focused on the gilded letters of that inspiring phrase of which I had for so long dreamed so fondly—THE TILLEVANT BUILDING.

But at that moment, when all eyes should have been turned towards that noble sight, Darrell snatched up a fragment of cloth which had torn away from the main drapery and performed with it an impromptu scarf dance at the end of which he sank gracefully to one knee and acknowledged imaginary plaudits. My grand effect was ruined, and although the Trustees most courteously refrained from any visible or audible manifestations of amusement, if such they felt, for what person of any refinement could have found diversion in such a peasant pasquinade—there was a suspicious tremolo in Mr. Haversham's voice as he delivered his final sentence.

"And so, with the cutting of this symbolic ribbon, I declare The Tillevant Building open to the pursuit of knowledge for the good of all mankind."

He then seized the golden shears and attempted to wield them; but, as I subsequently discovered, not only was their rivet loose but the cutting edges of the blades would have been of little assistance to a person wishing to separate from the main body a portion of butter. The amazement, frustration and rage depicted in his face as he sawed away were pitiable to watch, but not a thread of the ribbon was severed. Here too Darrell provided his own solution to the problem. He snatched from his pocket a pair of battery-operated scissors and in a trice had cut the ribbon in twain, the whine of the electric mechanism providing a mocking obbligato. With a graceful bow he presented this beastly but effective apparatus to Mr. Haversham, and disappeared into the building in a final series of faunlike leaps.

Somewhat belatedly, in an endeavor to simulate taking all this ribaldry in good part while at the same time pricking his armor in at least one place, I called after him in imitation of Mr. Haversham, "Well done, my lad," but my throat was tight and bitter and I doubt if he even heard me.

I must say I had hoped that in return for my support of his antimatter project, or whatever it was, Darrell would, to put it bluntly, lay off me. The fact that he had not done so revealed not only a schism which it now seemed could never be bridged, but a marked streak of sadism which chilled my blood.

Later that afternoon, my morale partially restored by the complimentary lunch which Darrell did not bother to gatecrash, I returned to my office, closed the door and sought further consolation from the Navy file, wherein the first thing to catch my eye was the literature of the Weird O Ranch.

52

From this point on, dear Dr. Ampiofratello, my troubles now came upon me in, so to speak, duplicate. What rankles so much is that Darrell, in spite of the humiliation and disgrace that he heaped upon me and upon The Dickstachel Research Institute, has emerged, after a spell of well-deserved opprobrium, as some kind of messiah, while I lie here shunning the light like a cockroach.

Oh, at that time I hardly knew whether some of my experiences were illusionary or not. I would have sworn, or affirmed, or anything you like, that when I thought that Weird O literature had vanished —well, it had vanished. Yet here it was again, like a bad conjuring trick, or one of those devices that banks have where your specimen signature shows up only under black light, or whatever they call the wretched stuff.

I fear that I proceeded with the rest of my afternoon's work in mechanical fashion. I was still recovering from the shocks of the morning, and musing over the irony that I, Administrator of The Dickstachel Research Institute, with my recognized genius for fine detail, should have overlooked the necessity for checking that the cord would pull and the scissors cut. When I was a boy, if you bought a pair of scissors you took it for granted that they would cut. I suppose Darrell was at the bottom of it, as usual, so that even if I had checked he would have been up to his tricks as soon as my back was turned, although then what was the use of having the Chief Sanctuary Warden there? I decided to have that man rechecked very carefully by an outside agency if I could find one I could trust.

I could sit at my desk no longer. My tic had returned, and I was looking spasmodically from side to side as if I expected to see foreign agents scowling at me from behind the glass of my Duncan Phyfe bookcase, or lurking in the recesses of my butcherblock bar. I decided to go on a tour of inspection, although I found it necessary to refresh myself from the aforesaid bar, in which of course no one was lurking, and to smarten myself up and even to practice before my Louis Quinze mirror that warm smile which for so long had been instinctive with me as I passed among the administrative employees of The Dickstachel Research Institute, encouraging them in their labors by my very passage.

I went on my way at my normal pace, magisterial but not loitering. When I had concluded my rounds it occurred to me that my spirit might be refreshed if I visited The Tillevant Building, where I could check the progress being made on the interior decoration of my penthouse suite. I was having the walls of my new office finished with paneling from an old mansion in Virginia that was being torn down to allow houses on half acre lots to be built. I hoped thereby to preserve in a worthy setting some evidence of the historic past of our great country.

There would eventually be—alas, there would eventually have been—a connecting passage, or corridor, or cloister, that is the word I really have in mind as expressing the almost sacred nature of the regard in which I held the two edifices. However, this was not yet completed, and I was therefore compelled to make the transition by passing into the common street, where I risked being trampled to death by wild joggers.

Here a very odd thing happened. A man came walking towards me and seemed to be about to turn into The Tillevant Building. With a distinct shock I recognized Mr. Matthew Montgomery, the agent of the Federal Bureau of Investigation. He evidently recognized me at the same moment; but instead of saluting me, even in his expressionless manner, he turned right around and walked away from me, at such a pace that I had no hope of overtaking him without running, which apart from its undignified nature would have placed a severe strain on my heart. I therefore contented myself by calling out:

"Mr. Montgomery, did you wish to speak to me?" although it was evident that this was very far from his desire. It occurred to me, somewhat belatedly, that he might not want to be thus publicly identified. Indeed, I was not sure that I had not committed some breach of protocol in so doing. Nevertheless his conduct seemed very mysterious, although I supposed one must expect that from the Federal Bureau of Investigation. The incident was not good for my tic, and indeed I was almost afraid to ride up alone in my private elevator. Summoning up all my courage, however, I refrained from asking the Sanctuary Warden to accompany me, and found myself calmed by the smooth, quiet operation of the elevator and the absolute silence with which its doors opened and closed.

When I stepped out on the penthouse level, however, I was aghast to hear voices. I was about to step back into the elevator to summon the Sanctuary Warden when a burst of laughter caught my ear, followed by these words in a woman's voice:

"Paul, I think you're being very unkind to the poor little man. I think he's rather sweet, really, and anyway that evening was the funniest I ever spent in my whole life.

It was Miss Love—by some instinct I was sure of it—but where was her Southern accent? Instead I heard the crisper timbre of, I thought, Arizona. Darrell answered:

"You've got an odd sense of fun, baby, but tell me more."

"Later. We've got work to do."

"No. Now. Our Tilly will be the last thing I'll want to talk about later."

"I wish we could sit down. My feet are killing me."

"Look, here's a clean plastic dropsheet. We'll sit on that, back to back, like so. Mm. You have a very sensual back."

"Yours is too bony. Shift over a little. That's better. Well, before lunch he made a side trip to the bar. He hadn't done that before. I was wondering whether he planned to slip me a Mickey Finn and drag me off to a deserted mansion in Oyster Bay so he could have his wicked way with me."

"That's quite an extrapolation from two drinks at a bar."

"Well, he had this funny look on his face."

"He always does."

"Yes, but this was different. It lasted all through lunch, and he kept trying to invent plausible leads and play kneesies and falling off his seat and getting ice cream and cigarette ash all over himself. No, the cigarette ash came later."

Darrell sounded as if he had whooping cough.

"Then he announced that he was going to play hookey and practically com*man*ded me to share his infantile peccadilloes—"

"His what?"

"You heard me—and really I was beginning to be *fas*cinated by the spectacle of an Administrator at play. He took me to a nice respectable little place that I should think might have been mildly raffish forty years ago. And there we drank and drank and drank—"

"Very bad for your liver."

"Never *mind* about my liver."

"But I do mind about your liver. If it's as beautiful as the rest of you—"

"Do you want to hear this or don't you?"

"I wouldn't miss it for a first edition Scott Fitzgerald."

"Suddenly he leaped off his stool and scuttered out of the bar, muttering to himself. I had to see what came next. When I caught up—"

I think at this point I must have swooned. At all events, the next thing I consciously heard was:

"So I gave him his miserable bag of pom-e-gran-ates and called a friend of mine to come around and fix me up."

Through his laughter Darrell said:

"I always suspected he was AC/DC."

"No, I think he's AC all right. He's just inadequately wired."

I stole into the elevator and started it down. I cannot remember very much for a while after that—until three in the morning, when I awoke as suddenly as if someone had fired a gun in my bedroom. I wondered how I could ever look Darrell or Greta Love in the face again.

Oh, the joys of three in the morning, when every error you ever made, every humiliation you ever suffered, come vividly back as, turning your head on the pillow, you unknowingly press this spot or that which triggers the snickering memory. The joys of three in the morning, when the red flashers on the radio transmission masts blink on and off, on and off, and a man comes out of the side street and stands on the corner looking from side to side, and then goes aimlessly back again. He is a mugger looking for someone to mug; or he is another lost and sleepless soul like you, inviting death to come to him on the open street at three in the morning, because he does not have the courage to turn on the gas or open the vein. The joys of three in the morning, when every tiny problem becomes a crouching monster and terror lurks in the closet; and at last you realize that you are beaten again, that in an hour or so you will awake agonizingly from the depths of your delayed sleep and go forth to endure for another twenty-four hours.

For of course that is what I did. It was not the first time nor the hundredth that I faced a day in which my most important task would be to brazen things out. As I drove to work I reminded myself that men in my high position must expect to have base canards bowled at them to trip them, although, as I listened on the car radio to the partially intelligible advice of the traffic adviser whose helicopter I could see blattering its way up the Hudson River, I realized that I had put my metaphor through a Waring blender. The mark of greatness is survival. He laughs best who laughs last—no, that reminded me of the Cosamo. In war there is no substitute for victory. Very well then, alone; and I secretly shook my fist at the sky and hastily replaced it on the steering wheel, for that was where, as a safety-conscious driver, both my hands belonged.

But even as I strode, positively strode into my office, happy in the knowledge that my adrenal glands were by no means exhausted, two questions clanged like great bells inside my skull. What was this "work" that Darrell and Miss Love were engaged upon? There was nothing in the script of *Discovery* that called for such joint endeavor; and anyway, why the hell was he not getting on with his beloved project, into which he had dashed with such enthusiasm the moment the Trustees had approved it? Surely to heaven "work" was not merely a flippant reference to their intention to copulate in my unfinished office. On a plastic dropsheet?

And secondly, what was Mr. Matthew Montgomery up to? I had had enough of intangible kidnappers and invisible bodyguards and men with paralyzed faces hastening away from me into the approaching twilight. I closed my door, picked up my personal outgoing telephone, and dialed 202-324-3000. Some time later I dialed 535-7700. Some time later yet I put back the handset in a state of complete mystification. The Federal Bureau of Investigation denied all knowledge of any agent named Matthew Montgomery. Now that could only mean that the person so describing himself had employed a pseudonym; and if I was not to know the real name of the man who somewhere in the outer world was mysteriously protecting me, then the plot of which he had in veiled terms apprised me was of a magnitude and sinisterness at which I could only attempt to guess.

My tic manifested itself with redoubled vigor, and it was hardly placated by the thought which almost simultaneously occurred to me, that the whole devilish affair was a hoax. A cruel hoax. Perhaps one of the cruelest hoaxes ever perpetrated, because it had been aimed against me. But surely even Darrell would not be so irresponsible as to lay himself open to the heavy penalties for impersonating, or inciting someone else to impersonate, an agent of the Federal Bureau of Investigation? Unless he had taken leave of his senses.

It was a question I had often rhetorically put to him. His behavior had always had its eccentric aspects, but of late surely his actions had become increasingly unbalanced? That scarf dance, for example. Was that the act of a wholly responsible person? Tragic though it would be to see that finely poised brain topple into the abyss, if Darrell was going, to put it bluntly, nuts, I should have only one real problem left in the world.

How to get it, again putting it bluntly, up.

Masterly inactivity. That, surely, was my key to final victory. It could not be long now before Darrell's progress down the slippery slope would so accelerate itself that everyone would agree on the need for his receiving humane but firm treatment of the most advanced yet sympathetic nature. Personality-changing drugs. Electroshock therapy. Even, perhaps, minor surgery. Whatever the details, with any kind of luck he would be in for a good long stretch in the booby hatch.

Yet it was odd that no one else had noticed this progressive deterioration. What, for example, of Miss Love? She seemed to think him quite normal. But then perhaps that showed that she too. . . .

I wondered how they behaved when they made love.

Did he throw her down and leap upon her, quenching their mutual heat with great stabs of his godlike yard, the plentiful tool of youth? Was the room loud with moaning and grunting and the twang of snapped mattress springs? Were their open-mouthed kisses, their intertwinings of saliva-wet tongues, so urgent yet so unending because impossible of climax—were they so clamant as almost to distract attention from the impending, inevitable explosion from the mighty terse sliding with such tigerish familiarity inside the palpitating vagina? Like a thunderstorm in a hill-bounded valley, did the echoes of their coupling menacingly persist in a sullen diminuendo until the returning storm grew louder and nearer and burst upon them again and again.

There was a young lady of Spain
Who liked to get stuffed in a train.
Jolts over switches
Reheated her britches
Again and again and again.

There was a young lady of France
Who led all her lovers a dance
By squealing "Encore,
"Plait-il, do heem some more,
"You mak' lof weeth such exuberance."

A certain young lady of Venice
To her boyfriends became quite a menace.
She cried "Fifteen-a love,
Thirty, forty-a love—
Oh! I thought-a the game-a was tennis."

There was a young lady of Norway
Who liked to get laid in a doorway—

Thank heaven that is all I can remember of that one. Perhaps I should have my brain washed out with soap.

But probably Darrell did not, uh, plunge into the, uh, heart of the matter with so little finesse. At all events, not every time. One must remember his preoccupation with research, his fund of scholarly knowledge.

"Paul, I never met anyone who kissed the way you do. It's different, and it keeps on being different."

"All according to the book."

"Mm. Who wrote the book? I believe *you* wrote the book."

"Thank you, but it was written in the sixteenth century by a guy called Johannes Secundus."

"Mm. Oo. Must have been quite a—"

"He lists two hundred kinds of kisses."

"Well bless him. Are you counting?"

"We have one hundred eighty-four"—interval—"well, one hundred eighty-three now, to go."

"Great. Don't use them up too fast, will you, Paul. I mean, we haven't exhausted the possibilities of the first—sixteen, is it?"

"Seventeen."

"I specially like number three. Could we have that one again? Mm. Ahh. Put your hand here, darling. And the other one *there*, and just—ssss. You're so good to me, Paul."

"Thank you, madam. I endeavor to give satisfaction."

"Me too, honeybunch. Let me stroke your spine with my long, long nails."

"God*dam*mit. Watch it, everyone, I'm coming in."

"AHHHhhhh."

Was I having my own erotic fantasy or some other person's? Two other persons'? A special kind of voyeurism? I know I promised not to indulge in self-diagnosis, dear Dr. Ampiofratello, but I wish you would discuss it with me next time you come in, because it might help if we could put a clinical name to the special kind of anguish I suffered when I imagined those two people together, writhing, twisting, BUCKING at the height of their perfectly coincident orgasms. Jealousy is far too weak a word. No man before me ever suffered, should have to suffer, as I did, as I am suffering now. Where is my handkerchief? Lost, lost. I will use my pajama sleeve, I cannot let that damned nurse see me like this.

Because of course I knew, as vividly as I knew how they made love, that in the recurring moments of calm they would, every now and then, ridicule me. If I were a dictator I would have them shot. Just like that. No preliminary torture. I am a merciful man. I would not wish to pass on to them any of my own agony. A word, a fusillade, and—curtain.

It did not help that the next time I saw Miss Love two of her long, long fingernails were broken, just as I had imagined them breaking when she dug them into Paul Darrell's pleasurably tensed back.

53

You may have noticed, dear Dr. Ampiofratello, that I have a certain propensity for quoting Kipling. I am aware that the work of Rudyard Kipling is at the present time unfashionable and that the electoral returns from here, there and there too continue to indicate that there is little likelihood of their returning to popular favor. I am also fully conscious of the mockery which has been directed at his poem entitled "If—."

Every person is entitled to his own opinion, provided he employs due discretion in expressing it. I will merely state that I have found this poem a very present help in time of trouble, and if the point which I had then reached was not a time of trouble then I do not know what a time of trouble is. The fact that very shortly things were going to get a billion times worse, and that a situation was about to arise which even the most potent words could not conquer, was mercifully hidden from my ken.

My habit was to carry a copy of this poem, laminated in plastic, in one of the compartments of the lid of my alligator-skin attaché case. It was thus sufficiently hidden from prying eyes yet readily available when my spirit needed fortifying by means other than those afforded by the Navy cabinet or my butcherblock bar. Such was its need when, a day or two before the world premiere of *Discovery*, I began my morning's labors at The Dickstachel Research Institute.

I searched the poem—which of course I knew by heart—for the couplet which I felt most closely met my present need:

> If you can meet with Triumph and Disaster
> And treat those two impostors just the same. . . .

I studied those lines for the hundredth, the thousandth time, and once more they lit in my breast a candle such as I was well aware could easily be put out but for the time being shone brightly. I went boldly forth to perform the most courageous act of my career, namely to beard, so to speak, Darrell in his, so to speak, den.

The forebodings which had originally assailed me in relation to Darrell's own project of drawing unlimited energy from the air, or whatever it was, had recently returned to me redoubled. I had been overpersuaded—I may say, blackmailed—into supporting the project with the Trustees. Now I felt so much in need of reassurance that I had determined to visit the, uh, laboratory in order to try to get into my head just what the, uh, hell it was all about.

In my capacity as Administrator of The Dickstachel Research Institute at that moment I was prepared to tolerate almost any amount of sarcasm and downright insult so long as Darrell could be induced to explain his theory anew in the actual presence of the mass of, uh, electrical and electronic gear the exotic names of which I had uncomprehendingly read when I countersigned the requisitions.

There was another reason why I approached Darrell's precinct with such reluctance. Immediately on entering, one's gaze was irresistibly drawn to a sign:

FROWN. GOD HATES YOU

and on his desk was yet another placard:

I HAVE DETERMINED THAT THE SURGEON GENERAL
IS DANGEROUS TO MY HEALTH

Comment seems superfluous, but I must confess that, high as my resolution had been when I left my office, it was already dwindling when I reached The Tillevant Building. It was merely a delaying subterfuge which caused me to halt my private elevator on the floor where the Cosamo were housed, although I told myself that it was my duty to check that our guests were in good health and, so far as their peculiar makeup allowed, enjoying life.

It seemed to be my fate, however, that the information which I gathered within the precincts of The Tillevant Building was neither that for which I had come nor of a nature which I should wish to receive. The Cosamo appeared to be in a good, or at least a quiescent mood, since no sound of laughter came cackling down the corridor; but upon my astonished ears came the almost equally discordant voice of Ms. Kalman:

"Lor' luv yer, myte, in a serciety like yours people like me'd be aht of business in two shakes of a duck's bottom. But what abaht women's lib, eh?"

Harry's voice replied:

"What about it? Our setup is our setup, and it works at least as well as yours."

I am not an eavesdropper—at least, not habitually—but I was intrigued by Ms. Kalman's reference to "people like me." I had always regarded her as something of a mystery figure. This might be an excellent opportunity for filling in the gaps in my knowledge. I therefore arrested my progress, which my rubber heels had rendered inaudible.

"Werl, I mean ter say. Look at the way you allercate the poor gals every night. It ain't like it was wiv me, where they was 'ired for the purpose. Don't they get no freedom of cherce? S'pose they ain't in the mood?"

"We don't allocate them, except to visitors. We draw lots. Makes it exciting for both sides. And Bessie, you live out there a while, you'll be in the mood the whole time. Like I told Paul, in our hometown life comes right down to drink and fuck, fuck and drink."

"Sounds proper boring ter me. Couldn't you go into politics, or play football or golf or somethin'?"

"Politics? Bessie, don't make me laugh—and I do mean that. Football? Look, you start with the ball in the middle and it goes down to one end and it comes back to the middle and it goes down to the other end—what the hell? Golf? You sweat to get the ball in the hole, then you pick it out and start over. So?"

"I s'pose that's one way of looking at it, but I do like to watch a good punchup on TV, wiv p'raps the ref gittin' one in the eye, and that."

"Cosamo don't want to punch anyone in the eye. And lookit, Bessie, I don't think so muchamuch of the way you people are willing to pay for it. We got all we want for free."

"An' roll around in the mud while yer doin' it. Let me tell you, I 'ad one of the 'ighest class establishments in the West End of London. A real first-run place, none of yer re-releases. All the nobs come ter me. 'Let's go on to Bessie's,' they'd say when they wanted ter finish the hevening. I 'ad a butler wot 'ad been wiv the Earl of Dorset before 'is lordship got jugged fer buggery. I 'ad a French chef—'e'd done time for forgery, but 'is pheasant under glass was super. That'll give yer an idea of the staff. Nah then—"

"Bessie, what's buggery?"

"Eh? Don't yer know what buggery is? Werl, it's not very nice really. Get Paul to explain it to yer some time. But as I was sayin', I 'ad carpets almost up to yer ankles, and reel crystal chandeliers, an' Vi-Spring mattresses an' silk sheets, an' a gadget that sprayed scent when yer pushed a button—reel refined it was. But that there 'Itler spoilt it."

"Wha hoppen?"

"Got bombed aht in World War Two, ducks. It was daytime an' nearly orl of us was in the shelters, so no one got 'urt, but I didn't 'arf cry when we come up agen. Funny 'ow that there bomb blast works, though. It 'ad wrecked the 'ole place except the back wall an' just one room on the second floor. The front was orf so yer could see in, but the furniture was untouched, not an 'air aht of plyce as yer might sye. An' there in the bed was an American three-star general wiv 'is girl, screwin' away as if nothin' 'ad 'appened. Werl, I 'ad ter larf even though I was cryin' at the sime time."

"How did they get down?"

"That's wot the Civil Defense people was for. It gave them a bit of a giggle too, specially when the general told 'em ter wyte till 'e'd finished."

Harry chuckled.

"I did fink of reopenin' when peace broke aht, but what wiv taxes an' all this socialism it didn't seem 'ardly wurf it. So I married a gentleman 'oo was over there wiv the Quartermaster Corps, an' 'e brought me back ter the Stites. One of them there war brides I was. I'd managed to sive a bit and 'e'd bin doin' a spot of black market on the side—in France, that was—so we was comfortable. 'E went into business fer 'isself, mykin' religious hobjects. Did very nicely at it, but then 'e fahnd 'e could myke more money wiv pornographic hobjects. I couldn't bear ter fink I was bein' supported like that, so I divorced 'im. Wouldn't tike no alimony neither. But bless yer, I fahnd I 'ad a 'ead fer the stock market, so that was orl right. Sold aht in 1973—that was when the Dow-Jones topped a fahsand—good old Nixon—put it in tax-free municipals, an' 'ere I am, fat, dumb an' 'appy, as they useter siy over 'ere."

"Good for you, baby."

"Course, nuffin's like it was. I 'ad a strictly private connection. You 'ad ter be hinterduced by someone I knew, or give two hunquestionable references. Nahadays it's just massage parlors hadvertisin' in the Yeller Pages—'otel, 'ome or hoffice—and all machines and 'ot baths. Un'ealthy, I call it. An' anyone can git in. I s'pose it's all this 'ere democracy. Any'ow, I'm as old as God, really. I couldn't start orl over agin."

She sighed enormously, and went on:

" 'Ere, 'Arry, yer won't tell on me, will yer? Paul knows, but 'e's a gentleman. An' there's one uvver bloke what's one of me ex-patrons, but 'e'll keep 'is marf shut fer 'is own sike. But if that little runt Tillevant got ter 'ear abaht it—"

"Trust me, Bessie."

"That's orl right, then. 'Ere, wot's that?"

I suppose I must have made some faint noise, because I could hear her pounding her way to the door. I just had time to get into motion before she reached it.

"Good morning, Ms. Kalman," I said, and continued to walk into the room as if I had just arrived. "I just looked in to have a word with Harry. How are you today, Harry?"

"Oh goddamn, I slap-up."

"Good, good. Are they giving you everything you need?"

"Oh yah-yah. Plenty big boobery."

"Mr. Tillevant, did you just get here?"

"Why yes."

"Are yew sure?"

"Certainly I am. Is something wrong?"

"Nah. It don't signify."

"Well, I must be getting along."

265

I slipped a few of Harry's cigars into my vest pockets, gave both of them my warm smile and went back to the elevator. Behind me rose the sound of Harry's discordant laughter. I moved quickly into the car and pressed the button. However, I had abandoned the idea of visiting Darrell. I wanted to get back to my office to consider this new disaster. Imagine. A Trustee of The Dickstachel Research Institute was, by her own confession, nothing more nor less than an ex-brothel keeper. Suppose that intelligence reached ears other than mine and Harry's. Suppose the Foundation's heard about it? Suppose—my God—suppose Washington heard about it?

And if the Trustees voted her off the Board, ought we to give back her money?

54

PONDERING THESE questions, I was passing through the reception foyer en route for a solitary lunch when I was, shall we say, intrigued to observe Darrell in evident altercation with none other than the *soi-disant* Mr. Matthew Montgomery. As I approached the pair in such a manner as to escape attracting their notice Darrell was saying, in a voice of such repressed anger that even though it was not addressed to me I shuddered:

"You fornicating, hopped-up son of an Easter Island statue, I told you never to come near this place. Get out before I put your ass through a meat grinder."

He then threw Mr. Matthew Montgomery away in the direction of the revolving door. In my most commanding manner I called out:

"Stop that man."

The security g—uh, Sanctuary Warden neatly applied what I believe is known as a half-nelson to the fugitive and stood awaiting further orders. Darrell had whipped around and was looking at me with, I was gratified to see, a certain degree of apprehension.

I flatter myself that I had exactly the right degree of weary disgust in my voice as I said:

"I think we had better discuss this matter in my office. I presume your friend will accompany us without the need for an escort?"

"Come on, you," he said to Mr. Montgomery. I nodded at the Warden, who released the fellow. Arriving in my office I indicated the two ordinary chairs and said:

"Please sit down, gentlemen."

I then installed myself in leisurely style behind my desk, put my elbows on its top, brought the fingers of my two hands together and remained for some moments looking silently at Darrell, bringing my juxtaposed forefingers slowly to my lips and slowly taking them away again. This device had proven effective with many kinds of person, but it was a mark of the unusual nature of Darrell's nervous tension that in short order he snapped:

"For godsake, man, let's get on with it."

"By all means," I said, now placing my forearms flat on my desk and leaning forward a little. "I fear that your little, uh, practical joke has boomeranged."

He tightened his lips and said nothing. I continued:

"Perhaps you will be good enough to introduce me to your friend, whose name, I take it, is *not* Matthew Montgomery."

"He's Alan Jackson. Calls himself an actor."

This gave me pause, for now I recollected where I had seen Mr. Montgomery/Jackson before, though only for a few moments. He had been the immobile-faced participant in that boring dialog on the TV set in my San Francisco hotel bedroom. If I had chanced to watch the program a little longer I might have identified him when he first came to my office, and saved myself weeks of fear, suspense and physical degeneration.

I removed my spectacles, held them to the light to check their cleanliness and replaced them, using both hands throughout. When performed with due deliberation, the use of both hands adds a certain air of menace to this ordinary procedure. Confessedly, I was what is known as hamming it up, but I felt I deserved it.

"I congratulate Mr. Jackson on his thespian ability. However, I presume you are both aware of the penalties for impersonating an agent of the Federal Bureau of Investigation. And for inciting, aiding and abetting such impersonation?"

Mr. Jackson muttered:

"I haven't worked in nine months."

Darrell said:

"This is what I've always dreamed about when I was having bad dreams. Come on, Tillevant, what are you going to do about it?"

"I have not quite decided. The childish mind which is capable of conceiving and perpetrating such a prank is *not* capable of conceiving the amount of mental torture thereby inflicted. I wonder, Darrell, how *you* would like to spend several weeks under a kidnapping threat, bogus or not?"

Darrell in turn muttered: "It seemed funny at the time."

Then, of all things, he chuckled and said: "It *was* funny, too. You've no idea how hilarious you looked, poking into this corner and that in quite a different way than you usually poke into corners."

Frankly, I was shaken by this confirmation of a streak of real sadism in Darrell's character.

"Darrell, you and I have had many fights in the past, but I always felt that there was an underlying stratum of good humor. Why did you do it?"

Until then I had never heard anyone literally speak through clenched teeth:

"Because. I. Hate. Your. *Guts.*"

When I had recovered from that, I said:

"I suppose that is just something I have to live with. You have asked me what I intend to do. I do not wish to appear to be seeking a personal revenge in this matter, but neither do I wish to be guilty of condoning an offense, whatever the legal term for it may be. I have also to consider the matter from the point of view of The Dickstachel Research Institute. You are, after all, the Scientific Director, and as such are assumed to be a responsible person. Therefore—"

"Get on with it, man."

"Therefore, as I was about to say, I must give mature consideration to the question. In the meanwhile perhaps Mr. Jackson will be good enough to furnish me with his address."

Mr. Jackson did so, and added:

"It's my sister's apartment."

"And her name is—?"
"Sybil."
"Thank you."
I verified this in the telephone book.
"Well, gentlemen, I think that is all for now. Mr. Jackson, if you should move from that address it will be as well for you to let me know."
I let the implied threat hang.
"Good morning, gentlemen. Darrell, you know your way out."
When they had gone I closed my office door and—yes, I must confess that I performed a little dance. I felt that I could not have handled the situation better. Heaven had indeed delivered mine enemy into mine hands and if, under pretense of lengthy consideration, I could make Darrell suffer one-tenth, one-twentieth the suffering he had caused me, I should be well rewarded.
I slept that night like a tired child.

55

However, the night actually before the premiere of *Discovery* I hardly slept a wink. There were so many things that might go wrong. There might be a waiters' strike, or some human rights group might decide to bomb the Grand Ballroom. The canapés might give everyone food poisoning. In spite of the threat hanging over his head, Darrell might decide to turn up in riding breeches and leather leggings, with a peaked cap worn backwards.
Not even an extra portion of ginseng at breakfast restored me to my normal urbane energy. When I reached my office, therefore, I instructed my secretary that I was not to be disturbed and would take no telephone calls. I closed my door and—yes, I must confess it—stretched out on an untrodden portion of the carpet and napped for the rest of the morning. Somehow, even in times of stress, my office always seemed much more homelike than my home. I awoke around noon and had a modest lunch at Rinaldo's.

At four o'clock I left for the day, warning my secretary to be in attendance at the Louis Vingtième in good time. There had been quite some unpleasantness over whether she would or would not be present. Disregarding for the time being her failure to attend The Official Opening of The Tillevant Building, I had in the first place actually given her one of the embossed and gilded cards which gave the entree to *Discovery*. The card of course cost me nothing, but other people were paying a hundred dollars or so for similar cards, and it seemed to me that this gesture would conceal the fact that I required her to be there to perform any small ancillary services which might be needed.

However, she merely stated that on the night in question she would be attending a rehearsal for her choral society. When I made it clear that she would in any case have to forego this frivolous activity, she reminded me of the amount of unpaid overtime she had put in during the past six months and that it was some two years since her last raise. I compromised by agreeing that without creating a precedent on this occasion she should be paid at a flat hourly rate, and retrieved the card. I made a mental note, however, that inconvenient as it always is breaking in a new girl, the time for a change was fast approaching. I then went home to dress.

I had chosen my dinner jacket specially for this occasion—it was custom made, naturally. I was delighted with the fit which the tailor had achieved, but at the last moment, keyed up as I was, I could not help wondering whether I had been right in choosing a blue-and-white check. It had seemed to me at the time that since I was, as you might say, now connected, so to speak, with, heh-heh, showbiz, I might for the nonce abandon the austere garb which in my view befitted the Administrator of The Dickstachel Research Institute. When I reflected, however, on the dress likely to be worn by the audience, it occurred to me that I might be merely blending into the scenery.

I descended to street level and got into the rented Rolls-Royce which I felt, in spite of everything, I might justifiably charge to the funds of The Dickstachel Research Institute. On arriving at the Louis Vingtième I was somewhat distressed to find that my car was immediately behind another Rolls-Royce which was in process of discharging several individuals whose appearance suggested that they had journeyed from some desert commune. The effect which I had counted on producing was of course gravely nullified. However, I hid my mortification as well as I could, and waited until the other car had driven off before alighting from my own. This, in spite of the raucous hornblowing in which the driver of a battered taxi behind my Rolls-Royce was, without cessation, indulging.

I had arrived early in order that I might supervise the final arrangements. Except that the name of the film had been spelled *Disc Ovary* on the bulletin board of the night's events, thereby imparting a quite erroneous impression, everything appeared to be in order. The error was corrected with, for these days, a minimum of delay and recrimination between the banqueting manager and the somewhat withdrawn individual whose duty—at one time I should have said simple duty—it was to insert the proper letters, figures and punctuation in their proper slots. The banqueting manager's distress was so evident—he was of an earlier generation—that I forbore to do more than comment lightly on the increasing prevalence of pseudo-dyslexia among a population which at one time was claimed to be the best-educated that our great country had ever produced.

I then proceeded to the projection booth, as the place where a cinematograph film is actually passed through the projector is termed. When I opened the door I disturbed Darrell and Miss Greta Love in the advanced stages of foreplay. They had the decency to desist as I entered, but in view of the necessity for their appearing among the guests later on both of them had cause to be grateful to the inventors of wrinkle-resistant fabrics.

Darrell, I was surprised and annoyed to find, was attired in an extremely conservative black dinner jacket which made my tartan affair, however beautifully made, look like a refugee from turn-of-the-century vaudeville. Greta—ah, Greta. Divinely tall, and clad in a long, flowing dress of some transparent material patterned with huge flowers. As I gazed at her—oh, so humbly, yet so desiringly—I could see her engorged breasts dwindle to half the size. It was Darrell, curse him, who had raised them up. It was I, unhappy that I am, who had caused them to fall like a soufflé in a carelessly opened oven.

I affected to have noticed nothing, although it was rather like affecting not to notice the climactic scene of *Götterdämmerung.* After we had greeted each other I inquired:

"Where is the film?"

Nowhere could I see the precious aluminum receptacle which contained my first venture into the realms of pure creativity.

"The projectionist's bringing it," Miss Love said. She seemed quite unconcerned.

"Oh. But isn't it time he was here? I mean, surely the machine should be tested, and—and so on."

"Ever'thing will be fahn. Jes' fahn."

By now I had sufficiently recovered from my first sight of her to remember her traitorous, scoffing rendition of the events of a certain fatal evening. Had not at least superficial harmony been desirable on this occasion I should have begged her coldly not to trouble any longer with the spurious Southern accent which had obfuscated me, and doubtless many other clients of Zeeta Productions. But at that moment the projectionist, chewing gum in a singularly distinct manner, arrived.

"You have brought the film?" I said. I could see the case under his arm, but such was my nervous condition that I was unable to refrain from this blinding glimpse of the obvious. He, however, merely said:

"Yeah, I brought the film," in a rather tired way, put the case on a table, whipped the reel out of it and began to thread the machine with an offhand speed that might have been professional but struck me as bordering on the careless. He did not even check the machine first. I could not help saying:

"I trust that everything is in order?"

He glanced at me—he had a very cynical face—and said:

"Yeah, everything's in order."

Then he glanced rather oddly at Miss Love and Darrell, and they glanced rather oddly at each other. It was very brief, and indeed I did not recognize the significance of it until too late. But how could I have guessed? Still, I felt quite out of it. Darrell ended the awkward moment by saying:

"It's almost eight. Shouldn't we get down to the receiving line?"

I agreed to this, and we left the booth, Miss Love of course first and Darrell, confound him, next. They went downstairs so quickly that I was left to follow at a considerable distance. Really, one would have thought that instead of being the evening's principal figure I was a mere appendage. However, they were not so far ahead but that I could hear Miss Love say, in what by now I assumed to be her natural voice, though in an undertone which only the peculiar acoustics of the staircase brought to me:

"You won't change your mind?"

Darrell answered:

"Hell, no."

"We could still switch."

"You switch and I'll—"

As luck would have it I stumbled slightly at that point. They both looked around and Darrell did not finish his sentence. I had no idea what they were talking about, and in any case I was too disgusted really to care what perverted assignation they were discussing. Later, of course—but at that moment I was determined to enjoy my great moment as fully as might be. I drew myself up, assumed my most genial and confident mien, and re-entered the Grand Ballroom.

56

THE TRUSTEES were already formed up. Mrs. Stahl looked quite alarming in arsenic green, but thank heaven she had not brought little Donzel. She called out:

"Mr. Darrell, Mr. Darrell, do come and stand next to me."

But Darrell got out of that by saying:

"Strict order of rank, Mrs. Stahl, darling. I'm only a working boy," and he marched firmly to the end of the line.

I was amused to see Mrs. Stahl's wrinkled coquetry when he called her darling, and the look of jealousy as arsenic as her dress when she saw Miss Love lightly touch his arm.

I paid the penalty for the slight delay which my sly observation caused me when I found that Darrell had established himself with Miss Love between him and the most junior Trustee, whose composure she was visibly wrecking. To avoid creating a disturbance I had to stand next to Darrell. But for that fatal pause I might have stood next to Greta. I could have accidentally touched her dress. And her dress would have been touching Her. Ah me.

As we waited for the first arrival, Darrell turned to me and said casually:

"Alan Jackson killed himself last night."

"Who?"

"Alan Jackson—Matthew Montgomery to you."

It seemed to me that Jackson/Montgomery's death came at a very convenient moment for Darrell. I wondered what part he had played in it, and whether he might not have rendered himself liable for indictment at least for destroying evidence. I had barely had a moment to consider the new turn which this development gave to our mutual relations, when with a spinning head I found myself bowing to and shaking hands with the first of the utterly repulsive people who had nevertheless paid their money. At my left hand Mr. van der Lust performed nobly in identifying his menagerie, but during a lull Darrell muttered:

"Where in hell's name did you dig up this bunch?"

"They're famous," I said indignantly.

"Famous? For what?"

For all I know it is normal for such affairs to resemble the inside of the cage of a circus troop of jungle cats when their trainer is having an off day. It was certainly that night that way. That way that night. Oh dear, the mere thought of it destroys my powers of concentration.

By an unfortunate coincidence, the three ex-wives of Jerry Attrick Attenborough whom I had been promised arrived at the same moment. According to Dulcietta Sucrose's writeup in the *Times*, which I read several weeks after the event, the one who was into pollution came in her own custom-built carriage drawn by four matched palominos, although I should have thought that horses were scarcely. . . . The refugee one was in a 14-karat gold-plated rickshaw drawn by a rather hungry-looking Vietnamese. The energy-saving one was on a solid mahogany skateboard hand-carved in the Elector of Brandenburg style which is so fashionable just now for bathroom use.

All these means of transport arrived simultaneously outside the hotel, creating such a plethora of calculated eccentricity that no one of them drew the attention of the jaded passers-by to the extent it perhaps deserved. This by no means reduced the hostility which Stheno, Euryale and Medusa felt towards each other, and they entered the Grand Ballroom showing their huge teeth, of which they seemed to possess far more than the usual number, in a way which suggested that it would be necessary to intervene with whips and blank-firing pistols if the feed boy did not promptly show up with the lumps of raw meat.

They intimidated the entire receiving line except Darrell, who kissed each of them on the cheek with that effusive insincerity which tides over so many awkward moments, and Miss Love, whom they greeted with marked respect. They then separated as widely as possible after falling on the lobster-and-pineapple salad with loud cries about calorie-guilt.

Two of them were escorted by a stockbroker each, the third by a Deputy Mayor who had sprained an ankle on his skateboard and seemed to be finding the pace too hot for him in other ways. The SEC got after the stockbrokers a few weeks later, about the same time that the Deputy Mayor was indicted for embezzlement.

We were also honored by the presence of Judge Knott, who greeted us all very affably. It may have been only my imagination that he seemed to be calculating the chances of renewing our acquaintanceship on some professional occasion. As it happened, he was removed from the bench shortly afterwards on a doubtless trumped-up charge of taking kickbacks from an international adoption ring headquartered in Lebanon.

All my feelings of excitement at being connected with showbiz were revived on shaking hands with Blick Yote, the famous pornographic film director. Unfortunately, Blick, as he insisted on my calling him, was arrested and imprisoned next day when through an error in navigation his private plane landed in one of the Bible Belt states.

After a while I almost ceased to distinguish individual faces. From the stream of blurred carbon copies, however, emerged the distinctive features of Ulrica Paulette Francesca Marylou Ortes y Vega, clad in one of her own handwoven floursack creations on which her trademark "Clabber Girl" stood boldly out. She died a couple of days afterwards when her automobile, as they say, "went out of control" on the Pennsylvania Pike after a party.

And of course there was no mistaking the enormous eyes and still more enormous voice of Doris Dobermann, who was soon to burst a blood vessel singing without a microphone in the Houston Astrodome; or the thin-lipped, snarling face of Sexton "Sexy" Mbangi, legalized tennis champion, who was fatally shot a month later by an enraged opponent; or the suffused features of Mrs. "Penta" Costa, fated to die from an overdose of sleeping pills after reading in The Revelation late one night.

Nearly the last arrival was Jerry (Attrick) Attenborough, the aging rare-earth heir, himself. By the way he made his entrance it seemed probable that he would soon become earth, though not particularly rare, himself. As a matter of fact, around 2 A.M. two policemen about to visit a Park Avenue massage parlor, not necessarily on duty, found a bouncer neatly depositing poor Jerry's naked corpse in the plaza of the International Universal Building next door. One of the cops identified him by the name engraved on his solid silver walker and instituted some routine inquiries. The therapist stated:

"I knew he was coming, then I saw his eyes turn up and I knew he was going."

This is just one more example of the way in which moral standards have degenerated. Why would Jerry depart from the strict religious principles in which he had been raised, except that he had been led astray by the pernicious example of the younger generation?

The reception line broke up a minute or two later, and I was able to take a look at the party in perspective. I must confess to a feeling of disappointment. The affair had split into two natural factions—the Trustees and the van der Lusts—which, except for occasional glances of mutual incomprehension and dislike, ignored each other. The women were all wide-open mouths which needed to be huge to show all those lupine grins and let all those saw-edged voices come out. The men were just as bad, smiling tight-lipped in a temporary truce from their daily battles in the law courts and the government offices and the executive suites and the proper lunchtime restaurants.

Striking an average, it seemed to me that we had reached the moment when the audience might be considered sufficiently mellowed, without being actually unconscious. I asked Willem van der Lust to undertake the chore of moving them in to their seats. He accomplished this very neatly, despite a tendency to burp caused by too generous potations of Perrier Water, by addressing them as "Ladies and gentlemen" over the loudspeakers. I think this is an excellent way of beginning one's remarks to any coeducational gathering of more than three. Unless they are irreclaimable hooligans, it does tend to encourage them actually to behave as such.

The heterogenous collection of kooks began to drift into the position known in heraldry as sejant-gardant. There was some lip-licking over the prospective shots of the Cosamo. At last we were all ready. I instructed my secretary, who had been laying into the buffet as if she had paid her share, to run up to the projection booth and give the signal to begin. I took my own place in the front row, next my reluctantly present wife.

The high spot of my career had arrived.

57

THE FIRST, inspiring notes of the trumpet fanfare sounded with the considerable degree of quasi-realism which our present, uh, technology has reached. The violins took up the theme. Though wiry-sounding, they swept to the uppermost limits of their range in a most exciting series of glissandi. The full orchestra gave out with all its strength the final chords, and the whole terminated with a most satisfactory wallop—it is a vulgar word, but somehow there is no better—*wallop* on the bass drum. There was an instant's pause, and then the first fade-in, that is the term, fade-in on myself seated at my desk. It was a medium shot which gave a fairly adequate idea of the grandeur and dignity of my private office. I, or rather my simulacrum, began to speak.

I, *in propria persona,* settled back to enjoy the rounded cadences, the subtle inflections with which I enriched the important message that it was my mission to deliver. I will not quote this in full, although it well deserves it. I am, however, dear Dr. Ampiofratello, sending you the full text for you to study and appreciate at your leisure. To you it will come in all its majesty, unsullied by the painful associations which, for me, it has since acquired. I cannot, however, refrain from repeating some of its more memorable phrases.

"You are about to see and hear the saga of a noble endeavor—to participate in the throbbing life of one of the greatest forces for the betterment of humanity that the world has ever known—The Dickstachel Research Institute. Modest in size though The Dickstachel Research Institute may be, nay, modest in size though it is—and I will not conceal from you that the purpose of this cinematic presentation is to plead with you for the wherewithal to enlarge, to widen, to multiply the services which The Dickstachel Research Institute offers the world—the rollcall of The Dickstachel Research Institute's achievements already re-echoes proudly upon the pages of history, illumined by the sweat of the most gifted scientists of our time, not only from this great country of ours, whose vitality may be temporarily dimmed by doubters and flouters but will ever arise phoenix-like from the mud—not only from our beloved America but from the resurgent countries of the Old World, whence came Mediterranean Civilization, and from the ancient continent of Asia, whose age-old wisdom is turned in these later days towards the unraveling of Old Mother Nature's secrets, yet not forgetting the heroic escapees from the frostbound slavewastes of Russia or the newly burgeoning genius of the Third World."

Conning these reverberant words again, there is not one that I would change, except perhaps "sweat." I was doubtful about this from the first. I felt that "perspiration" would have been far less crude. Yet Sir Winston Churchill did not hesitate to say "sweat," and what was good enough for Churchill is good enough for me.

I had not neglected the more human aspect of the manifold activities of The Dickstachel Research Institute. For example, there was a shot of a quite toothsome laboratory assistant operating some piece of electronic apparatus. I said:

"And here we have pretty Maryann Beidebecker adding graceful charm to the task of—" whatever it was, I really forget. "Maryann is engaged to Frank Winch, who efficiently leads our Microfilm Section."

Or again:

"We pause for a brief look at cheerful Stanley Anakaios, who with his staff of willing helpers keeps atop our heating and air-conditioning systems, and all the diversified services which are so essential to the full and proper functioning of the equally diversified activities of The Dickstachel Research Institute. Stanley is the proud father of two growing sons and a daughter, and recently welcomed a new baby girl to the Anakaios home."

You see? It is simple, cost-free gestures such as these which help to unite our band of workers into one family, and to make them realize that they are by no means regarded as cogs in a machine, but that they are looked upon as persons, as individuals, as *people*. I cannot imagine why two years ago they all went on strike.

I am bound to say, however, with an indignation which revives itself within me whenever I think of it, that the first public showing of this meaningful documentary could not have been made before a more ill-mannered audience. The coughing began almost at once. At first the coughers made some attempt to suppress their ill-timed outbursts, but as the story unfolded the hacking and barking grew until I was fain to instruct my secretary to run up to the projection booth and tell the operator to turn the sound up. One would think that people who had paid around a hundred dollars for their seats would have paid also attention to the instructive and inspiring spectacle on the silver screen. It was, I suppose, simply above their heads. The message, that is, not the screen, which was giving me a crick in the neck. I endeavored to console myself with the reflection that the path of the true artist is all too often a wilderness trail rather than a signposted highway; but nevertheless my tension mounted until I was all but at the point of making an eloquent plea for silence.

Before I was driven to such an extreme, however, something happened which at first I attributed to a hallucination produced by my overwrought condition. A sudden though momentary hush among the audience suggested that they were collectively suffering from the same hallucination. For a few frames, as they are called, the nature of the picture changed radically. The interruption lasted only for a couple of seconds and the effect was almost subliminal; but for that fleeting instant I was convinced that I was watching a simulacrum of myself, not in the fitting surroundings of my stately office, but in the most unfitting—for public exhibition—surroundings of the Weird O Ranch.

There had been no disruption of the sound track, and immediately afterwards *Discovery* continued to unfold as before. For several moments the coughing was replaced by an excited murmuring, but this soon died down, and the bronchial manifestations again broke forth. Some five minutes later, however, in the midst of an extremely important and dignified sequence depicting the president of one of our foremost soap manufacturers reading a report from The Dickstachel Research Institute proving conclusively that the ingestion in drinking water of large quantities of used detergent was not only beneficial to the digestive and, uh, excretory systems of the human body but led to a marked heightening of sexual desire in both men and women—where was I?

Well, anyway, that was when it happened again. This time it went on for, I should think, half a minute; long enough for everyone, myself included, to be absolutely certain that it was no hallucination. Laughter arose around and behind me; cruel, mocking laughter, charged too with gloating enjoyment, as if these people, these warped, degenerate representatives of our half-baked upper crust, were not only jibing at the central figure of the interpolated scene but were vicariously sharing in his enjoyments. Outraged, bemused, paralyzed though I was, I could not help thinking that if they were obtaining this kind of gratification from the spectacle they were also getting quite extraordinary value for their paltry hundred dollars. I repeat that even the Commuter Special at the Weird O Ranch cost four hundred.

Dear Dr. Ampiofratello, there is little I can tell you about the Weird O Ranch that you do not already know. You have seen its sixteen-page brochure, lavishly illustrated in full color on glossy paper. You have read of the esoteric delights promised in the text, ranging from fetishism and algolagnia to frottage and eonism, gerontophilia and necrophilia. You have read too the hints of distinguished, even illustrious patronage, not only by eminent legislators, wealthy philanthropists, leaders of thought, industrialists, financiers and the clergy of all denominations, but by highly placed European refugees fleeing the predations of the secret tax police.

Nevertheless, some strange force impels me to recount every detail of the crowning humiliation to which I was subjected on that dreadful night. In longer and longer installments came those libelous interpolations displayed for all the world, or at least the four or five hundred people who were present, to see, to wallow in, to fleer at. The color was vivid, although the photography left something to be desired, at times emphasizing the weaknesses of the hand-held camera. Even so the detail was all too clear, particularly of the central figure. Me.

At last the spasmodic insertions became continuous. Accompanied by the most nauseating kind of rock music, a main title appeared on the screen:

WHAT I DID IN MY HOLIDAYS

This, if you please, was followed by a repetition of the actual opening shot from *Discovery*—none other than I in my splendid office, while from the loudspeakers came the following shameful words in a voice which I would almost have sworn an affidavit was my own:

"Well folks, I expect you've all had enough of that crap. I get pretty pissed off with it myself, and I'm going to let you in on a little secret. I know you're all good sports and I shan't have to spell out things for you too much. But for those of you who haven't yet visited the good ol' Weird O Ranch—and to revive happy memories for those of you who have—you are about to see and hear . . . well, wait till I tell you.

"Now this is Ruby. What a sweet little thing she was. A Rhode Island Red. I could have grown quite fond of her, only unfortunately she died next day.

"And Florabelle. What fun I'm having lashing her with my rawhide whip after they've tied her so securely that she can neither kick nor run away. She was in season at the time. I wonder whether there are masochists among animals as well as humans. It would be fascinating to take a valid statistical sample some time.

"Then of course Fido, the two-hundred-pound Newfoundland. Such a dear, and so good-tempered. He seems to be enjoying himself too. I wonder if he's gay. The Victorians used to talk about gay dogs, but peculiar as some of the Victorians were that can hardly be what they meant. I wonder if that little adventure makes me trisexual? Anyway, I offered to buy Fido, but it was like trying to buy a sultan's favorite. They said he was far too popular with their regular patrons.

"And now we come to the Ms. Mazeppa sequence. This girl wasn't very attractive, and she was quite a bit retarded, but she served the purpose. Watch them tie her naked to the back of a white stallion that gallops in a circle while I shoot flaming arrows—"

"And get a load of dear old Grandma Perkins in her bathchair. Sporty old gal, isn't she—?"

My office had been replaced on the screen by the most explicit portrayal of the corrupt, degraded, aberrant debauchery specified on the soundtrack. And I appeared in every shot—I, who was as innocent of these practices as—as—who was innocent of these practices. How the illusion was wrought I cannot tell. Whether the figure on the screen was a professional actor whose chance resemblance to myself had been heightened by makeup, and whose imitations of my conscious and unconscious mannerisms had been achieved by skillful coaching—or whether the sinister light of perverted science had torn my simulacrum from its decent, its proper place and transferred it to this shameful ambience, even using film from the cutting room floor, or shots secretly made as I proceeded on my lawful occasions through the august precincts of The Dickstachel Research Institute, whose name in such a context verily sticks in my throat—Or how? I did not know. I could not tell.

And my voice. Was that the work of an exceptionally gifted mimic, or was it in truth my own, snipped with infinite patience from a copy of the tape that I had made for the genuine commentary and reassembled into this false and lying replica? I had read of such things, but what knew I? Nor indeed did it matter *how* the mischief was wrought. Suffice it that the dastards who had perpetrated this feat of aural and visual legerdemain—and I knew who they were—oh yes, I knew who they were, suffice it that they had succeeded. The audience, hitherto so cynically inattentive, now alternated periods of wide-eyed concentration with outbursts of cacophonous laughter which they could hardly have surpassed if every last one of them had been Cosamo.

I say again, as I have repeated so many dozens and hundreds of times, that I was never in reality at the Weird O Ranch in my life, and that the whole of that interpolated film was a base, heartless canard. Yet not one of the people to whom I have made that claim has even pretended to believe me, or if they have that pretense has been a mere thin mask for underlying disbelief. But *you* will believe me, will you not, dear Dr. Ampiofratello? You will believe that I could never, never. . . .

At last I managed to cast aside the paralysis which had benumbed my every faculty—it was during the sequence under water, just as the camel, which of course was equipped with an aqualung—where was I? Oh yes. I rose from my seat, and at a pace of which I should never have deemed myself capable ducked past the serried ranks of guffawing imbeciles and up to the projection booth, where by some miracle I found and flipped a switch which darkened the screen and brought the soundtrack to a growling halt.

58

THE PROJECTIONIST, who had been reading a publication which I subconsciously identified as the *Wall Street Journal,* now raised his head, and saying, "Hey*hey*hey,*"* attempted to turn the machine on again. But I, standing in front of it with my arms spread wide—rather, I imagine, like a mother defending her child in an old, old-time melodrama—prevented this. A moment later he recognized me and stood uncertain until I said:

"Were you aware of the scatological contents of this travesty?"

"Huh?"

"Did you know it was a dirty movie?"

"Look, dad, I just thread 'em up and keep 'em rolling. All the same to me if they're dirty or Disney. But they ain't," he added, apparently reverting to my first question, "they ain't no transvestites in it, far zino."

"I forbid you to show another foot of it," I said. "You will rewind the film, place it in its container and hand it to me forthwith."

He shrugged and began to do as I had ordered. Before the rewinding was complete, however, my secretary appeared at the door of the booth.

"They're going crazy down there," she said. "You'd better try to calm them down or they'll wreck the joint."

I was torn between my desire to get the incriminating evidence into my hands and an uneasy apprehension of the possible bill for damages with which, if her gloomy forecast was correct, The Dickstachel Research Institute might well be faced. Loyal to the last, my fears took precedence.

"Wait here and pick up the film and give it to me," I said to my secretary, and hurried back to the Grand Ballroom. My secretary had summed up the situation with her usual accuracy, confound her. Gusts of laughter were still coming from here and there, and the entire audience was clapping in ominous rhythm—clap, clap, clap-clap-clap, with a counterpoint shouting of:

"Show-us-the-rest, show-us-the-rest."

With what dignity I could still assume—and that, as I tasted wormwood, was little enough—I made my way to the front and climbed on to the platform above which, gaunt and glimmering, rose the empty screen. Now I knew the meaning of all that tittering and giggling between Darrell and Greta Love, and of their last cryptic utterances on the stairway that evening. Now I had solved the mystery of the documents stolen from the Navy cabinet. Almost certainly my career lay in ruins around my feet. But I would fight back. If I fell, I would drag down with me that guilty pair.

I would sue Zeeta Productions for triple damages. Paid or not, they would bring the company crashing to the ground, and surely the sadistic whore who had brought about this debacle would never be able to obtain other employment in her chosen field but would end her days begging her bread from welfare department to welfare department. And Darrell. With the weapon now in my hands he would soon discover that the time for clemency had long gone by. Treading the winepress of my wrath, I would pursue him from conference to seminar, from Trustees' meeting to the highest court in the land, until at last, utterly discredited and bearing the jail pallor upon him, he would be forced to eke out a miserable existence grading test papers for some fifth-rate correspondence school.

In the instant of my facing that howling mob, what analogies of martyrdom passed through my mind. Saint Sebastian, as full of arrows as a pioneer in Indian country. Sydney Carton, classic victim of mistaken identity. The director of any season's lowest-rated TV series. The mere thought of my reckless courage in being there at all enabled me to strike a heroic stance, head flung back, feet wide apart, arms eloquently raised to command silence. Thus I awaited the flinging of the first missile.

But it came not. Instead, a mighty roar of cheering, whistling, clapping, stamping fell upon my bewildered ears. Never before had I faced such a demonstration of popularity. Never before, indeed, had I faced any demonstration of popularity at all. How, in face of that tumultuous welcome, could I deny the authenticity of the shameful spectacle to which the crowd had just been witness? How could I apprise that happy, smiling, laughing throng that it had been subjected to a gross fraud? I could not do it. My attitude relaxed, I allowed my most gracious smile to overspread my face, I bowed right, left and center. Thus I stood for what seemed an endless, blissful time, until at last the plaudits subsided and again the chant arose:

"Show-us-the-rest. Show-us-the-rest."

Here indeed a problem loomed. Not only was I unsure whether there *was* any more of that shameful footage, but something—was it returning sanity?—told me that even at the risk of the unpredictable mood of the crowd changing from joy to rage, it would be most unwise to resume the showing in the full knowledge of what might be to come. I bowed again, I even kissed my hands, in the hollow of which for those fleeting moments I held the audience. Then I raised my arms again for silence and with my sweetest smile, in my most persuasive manner, I said:

"Dear friends, I thank you. I love you. But"—and I assumed an arch expression of regret—"that's all there is. There isn't any more."

For a moment it seemed that my fate hung in the balance. Then, with a groan of disappointment, the audience began to disperse, a few pausing for a final denudation of the already decimated bar. I remained on the platform, listening to the wane of their voices. The exaltation of the last few minutes was draining out of me. My great need was the recurrent need of the artist—to be able to relax, to unwind in solitude. But that I could not do. However difficult it might be, I had to begin my course of vengeance, and before that the process of justifying, nay, it might be of rehabilitating myself in the eyes of the world. I had the Trustees to face. I had my wife to face.

I became aware that I was facing my wife at that very moment. Of all the audience she alone remained, in the center of the front row. Her eyes were fixed upon me with an expression which would have been enigmatic if it had not been so clear. I assumed a nonchalance which I was very far from feeling, descended from the platform and approached her with what I felt to be the correct blend of professional abstraction and husbandly assiduity.

"I have several things to see to here before I can get away. Let me put you in a taxi."

Not a word said she, but hooding her gaze she turned from me and glided towards the exit. There was a certain dignity in her passing.

But I had no time to consider possible outcomes. The Press must be, as far as possible, dealt with. Muzzled was the word which actually went through my head, but of course ... The Trustees were standing in a kind of phalanx, hemmed in by reporters, the foremost being Dulcietta Sucrose. I do not know why they had not approached me first, as the central figure of the proceedings. Mr. Haversham was acting as spokesman, and appeared to be in the process of denying not only that there had been any untoward incident but any such film as *Discovery,* hence that there had been no premiere and indeed that everyone concerned had spent the evening in divers other places and was not standing at that moment in the Grand Ballroom of the Louis Vingtième. I have the greatest respect for Mr. Haversham, but I felt that he was not putting his case in the most convincing manner possible. By an adroit flanking movement I pushed through the Trustees from the rear and reached his side, where I interrupted him with an admitted lack of deference which was in the circumstances justified.

"Ladies and gentlemen of the press, I am sure you will realize that we have all been the victims of a heartless hoax. A search for the instigators will be commenced immediately and the sternest measures will be taken against them. Meanwhile The Dickstachel Research Institute is suing the producers for negligence and defamation. The matter is thus *sub judice,* and I know you will treat it as such."

My last sentence was of course sheer bluff, as it is practically impossible to persuade the American press to treat anything as *sub judice* even in the middle of a long court case, still less when proceedings have not actually been commenced—a point on which my antagonists were quick to seize. However, I got rid of them eventually, consoling myself with the thought that in view of the lateness of the hour their stories would probably not appear until two days had elapsed. By that time, who knew what additional weapons might have fallen into my hands?

Mr. Haversham now turned to me.

"You claim it's a hoax, do you, Tillevant? But it was you on the screen and your voice on the soundtrack. You can't deny that."

He leaned close to me and muttered in my ear:

"What's the address of that place?"

"I'll tell you later," I muttered back; and then aloud: "I can and do deny it. I cannot as yet specify how the deception was accomplished, but I know we must all regard it as yet another example of the terrors and dangers to which each one of us may be at any moment exposed. Each one of us, sir."

I uttered this last sentence in such an accusatory manner that Mr. Haversham actually recoiled. Whether he simply felt the force of my remark, or whether in his own closet—. Even with all my preoccupation it occurred to me that by accident I might "have something" on Mr. Haversham, if only I knew what it was.

"Who do you—" he began, but Mrs. Stahl interrupted him.

"What a dear doggie that was in the movie. You know, Dr. Tillevant, I've always thought you weren't so fond of dogs as you might be, but it did my heart good to see you romping with him like that—"

Mr. Krebs saved the situation by saying loudly:

"Mrs. Stahl, do you know what time it is? I expect you want to be getting on home. Let me see you to your car."

"That would be very kind of you. Unless of course dear Mr. Darrell—"

"Yes, where *is* Darrell?" Mr. Haversham said. "Darrell. *Darrell.*"

In a moment I myself saw Darrell, only a few feet away. He had been telephoning, and now dropped the receiver so carelessly that it fell from its hook and dangled loose, stretching its coiled cord ever straighter with each swing. I noticed that he was very pale and his eyes were fixed on some point a long way off. Instead of heeding Mr. Haversham's summons he rushed past us, hurled himself through the revolving door and vanished into the night.

59

HAUNTED BY demons though I was, I eventually slept deep that night, exhausted by the cataract of emotions which had engulfed me the previous evening. After turning off my clock radio on awakening I realized that from the kitchen was coming the sound of another set which my wife kept permanently tuned to an all-news station and often left running at full volume because she knew it annoyed me. I was about to turn this set off also when my sleep-dulled ears caught the sense of the words which were pouring from it in an almost unintelligible gabble:

". . . there's something darned odd happening, Jim, but the question is, what? It's a lovely bright morning, yet the building looks like it was shrouded in mist, though that's not right either, it's more as if the building itself was the mist, as if it was turning into mist, if that sounds crazy it's not half as crazy as it looks, the mist kinda comes and goes, just now it seemed to—to *reach out* towards the buildings on either side 'n then it drew back again, the cops aren't letting anyone through, in fact they're cordoning off the whole area for a block around, though they don't seem to know what it's all about either, hey have a heart will ya fella, it's no good, Jim, I'm gonna hafta move back but I'll be talking to you again soon's I get any hard facts; this is Bill Street for news radio 1570 from outside The Dickstachel Research Institute."

Imperfectly heard as they were, the last few words caught at my heart. The usual I-am-speaking-to-you-from-inside-a-soupcan quality of such broadcasts had been further confused by the sirens of emergency vehicles and the noise of an excited crowd, but I would have recognized that name under far worse conditions. I stood unbelievingly for a moment while a public-service commercial asked me if I was suffering from four loathsome diseases. Then the phone rang. I clicked off the radio, picked up the handset and was half-deafened by the voice of Mr. Haversham.

"Tillevant? What the hell's happening down there? Fool radio doesn't make sense. What's it all about?"

"I know no more than you do, Mr. Haversham, but I'll call and find out."

"I already tried that. They're not answering the phone. Get down there yourself and put a stop to the nonsense. I'm hog-tied with a meeting here in Connecticut. Call me back."

"Yes sir," I said automatically, and hung up. I had not called anyone "sir" since my Army days when, before I succeeded in being invalided out with a gasoline-induced allergy on the eve of being posted to Korea, I had a top sergeant with a voice very similar to the one Mr. Haversham was using that morning.

I performed no ablutions and flung on my clothes with results that were anything but dapper. I paused only to gulp down a strengthening glass of yogurt and two kelp tablets and set out on my journey with such haste that I scraped a front fender against the garage wall. The damage probably amounted to several hundred dollars, but in such a cause what cared I? My expense account. . . .

I arrived without further damage, however, but the official parking lot of The Dickstachel Research Institute was inside the cordoned-off area. Since in the circumstances I did not wish to spend half an hour seeking out a metered spot, I pulled in opposite the first available fire hydrant and finished my journey on foot. Very much in the forefront of my mind was Mr. Haversham's injunction to "stop the nonsense," but until I had a clearer idea of what the nonsense was I could hardly formulate any plans for stopping it.

The sight that met my eyes when I turned the last corner was so eerie that I could not avoid exclaiming aloud, "My God!" The man on the radio had in fact described it with extraordinary vividness, especially when he used the peculiar phrase "as if the building itself was the mist." How else can I put it? Well, the building—it was, in the nature of things, The Tillevant Building—seemed to flicker, like a neon sign that needs repair. For infinitesimal periods of time it actually seemed to disappear, and yet during those less-than-moments, when logically one would have seen other buildings behind it, and the sky and clouds, one—one didn't, you know, dear Dr. Ampiofratello.

I am afraid that sounds terribly nonspecific, but what I am trying to say is that the visual image of the building was replaced by a black rectangle—oh, fantastically black, I can think of no effective simile for—for its sheer *blackness*. It was as if everything within the framework had been annihilated, as if there was nothing, not even air, not even light, not even space itself. And I was terribly afraid.

I was afraid because of more than the terrifying phenomenon that I was watching. I remembered the look on Darrell's face when he ran out of the Louis Vingtième. He was afraid too; and if even he. . . .

Phrases from my too-hasty reading on antimatter came back to me with painful clarity:

> *All the ordinary laws of science break down.* . . . *If it were possible for an astronaut to penetrate the event horizon, he might emerge in a different universe.* . . . *If a particle of antimatter came*

in contact with a particle of matter, the two would destroy each other.

And then there was something about the development of unimaginably powerful forces of gravity which would draw into the disaster area innocent bystanders, so to speak, from vast distances away.

It was all too evident that Darrell had chosen this cosmic venture for the first fumble-footed step of his career. I of course could not even guess what had gone wrong. I presumed Darrell knew; I presumed he was at that moment inside the building trying to correct the error. If he managed to do so then naturally I would step in, exert my authority and with the full weight of the Trustees behind me, cancel the whole project. But if Darrell failed—then what?

At that moment the ultra-black space-annihilation effect repeated itself, and indeed seemed to reach out in a circle towards anything that stood in its path. At the rim of the circle everything grew fuzzy, and then cleared again as the wave of energy, or antienergy, or whatever it was, retreated. It seemed that this time the circle had extended further than before, since the police, looking very worried, to say the least, now came running to move barriers and onlookers farther back. The new boundary reached a shabby but still viable apartment block near where I was standing, and under police orders the tenants began to evacuate. Their high-pitched chattering did nothing to calm my nerves, but it made me realize that so far I had done nothing to achieve the purpose for which I had come. I recalled again Mr. Haversham's order to "stop the nonsense," and in spite of the fact that the world as I had known it seemed to be in suspense I could not refrain from a one-sided smile. I could not even get into the building, much less reach my office and from there, reinforced by the panoply of administrative procedures, issue trenchant directions. Even if I had been able to do so, something told me that here was a situation in which not even paperwork could avail. It was indeed a bitter moment.

It seemed that the only way of getting in touch with Darrell was by telephone, if he could be coerced by sheer persistent ringing to answer. Reluctant as I was to use one of today's pay stations, the appearance of which reminds me of those Parisian *pissoirs* which are, fortunately from the aesthetic, unfortunately from the physical point of view no longer existent, I was feeling for the necessary dime when my attention was distracted by a rather peculiar sight.

Along Broadway, with much noise of sirens, came a Con Edison truck bearing two of those huge drums on which electric cable is wound. One of the drums, nearly empty, was revolving slowly as it paid out its load along the surface of the street, which had been cleared of traffic and pedestrians. The truck drew up to the barrier and the driver engaged in an altercation with the policeman in charge. This ended after a few moments, when a very senior policeman, to judge from his gold braid, got out of a car and evidently instructed his subordinate to let the truck through. Here was an opportunity for me. I hastened to the barrier, identified myself and after some forceful persuasion obtained permission to ride the truck to its destination. This of course was hardly the method of transportation to which I was accustomed, but in such a time of crisis I was prepared to sacrifice something of the outward insignia of my station.

The driver, whom I judged to be near the age of retirement, was a mild-mannered-looking little man with a certain tenseness about him which was, in the circumstances, excusable. I said to him:

"Can you tell me what all this is about?"

"Not too much. It seems your folks are having some kind of a clambake in there, and they're running out of power. They called Head Office and asked them to hitch up a cable to the nearest substation and snake it into the Institute."

There was a shout from the men riding behind us, and he stopped the truck. They started the cable running from the second drum. Men jumped from a smaller truck following us and began to splice the two lengths. We went on. Frankly, I needed reassurance. I said:

"I suppose—I suppose there is an element of risk."

"We're all volunteers."

"Good for you," I said, although this did not cheer me.

The driver said, as if to the windshield:

"Always was a volunteering fool, even back in the Army."

"Oh. What—uh, what—uh—?"

"Paratrooper."

I had always assumed that paratroopers were husky fellows with deeply seamed faces and teeth permanently on edge from holding knives in them. I felt more out of place than ever until it occurred to me that there was no real need for me to be riding in that truck at all. In my own way I too was a volunteer.

A voice which with difficulty I identified as Darrell's came over the truck's radio. It hailed us by some sobriquet which the driver evidently recognized, although since I am not a Good Buddy myself it meant nothing to me, and went on:

"Stop right where you are. Now here's what I want you to do. Roll out enough cable to reach the front of the building, and another three hundred feet on top of that. Cut it off, and tell me when you're ready."

The driver acknowledged, and the men set about their work. They went at it willingly enough, but their movements were curiously slow. I myself felt a peculiar heaviness throughout my body which made it hard work to move my limbs. This feeling came and went, and at the same time my surroundings seemed to blur and sharpen again. It was almost as if I was part of some cinematograph film which was being put in and out of focus. The simile was unfortunate, since I had had enough of cinematograph films to last me for a very long time to come, if indeed there *was* a very long time to come.

When the men had finished laying and cutting the cable, Darrell told them:

"One of the side doors is fastened open. That gives you a target about three feet wide. When I give you the word, and not before, line up the end of the cable with the opening and run like hell. You'll have about five minutes altogether."

They took four minutes by my watch. Just as they got back to the truck, running in that curious slow-motion fashion, the end of the cable stiffened like a fire hose full of water and rushed into the building. The men, panting heavily, found enough breath to cheer. Unfortunately the cable did not stop its rush. Whatever force was acting on it continued to pull, and the cable—my driver told me there was about a mile of it—continued to vanish into the maw of the building until the far end came whipping up Broadway and snapped ridiculously and uselessly out of sight. The entire heroic venture had aborted.

The Con Ed men sighed but said nothing. After a few minutes the radio told them to go back to base. I noticed that the farther away we were from the building the lighter I felt, although when they dropped me at the barrier it was still a noticeable effort to move my arms and legs. In fact, the police were again moving the barriers back several blocks. It seemed that the swings of energy, or radiation, or gravity, or whatever it was, that the building—*my* Building—was putting out were growing stronger. I went to retrieve my car before the restricted area engulfed it. But it had already been stolen or towed. Life went on.

I could see no point in standing around feeling, and no doubt looking, more like a tramp every minute, and I certainly did not feel like going through the aggravating procedure of bailing my car out of the pound even if it was there. I took a taxi home.

After I had showered and shaved, put on a robe and poured myself some brandy, I found a note from my wife taped to the refrigerator.

60

WELL, MY friend, that does it. I've put up for long enough with your conceit and your alfalfa and your stump. Stump! What a stump!! A stump!!! If a man's going to bed with a woman, common decency demands that he produce something better than a *stump* like that.

Knowing about that, I've never worried about your mooning after anything with big tits.

But last night was the last straw. Fido. Grandma. My God. I'm divorcing you. Forward my mail to my sister's.

61

WELL, SOMETHING like that was bound to happen sooner or later. On the whole I was rather glad about it, in a way, although I do feel she could have put her point of view in a less offensive manner; but what was going on that morning made me wonder if there was enough time left for me to receive even a formal request for the name of my lawyers. I turned on the news radio again.

In spite of all that he had on his mind at the time, they had contrived to interview the President of Con Edison. He was articulate, courteous and extremely patient, even though the interviewer asked him the same questions three or four times over.

"The reason we have taken this unusual action is that Mr. Darrell called me and convinced me that it was essential to the success of an important experiment."

"What is the experiment?"

"Oh, you would have to ask Mr. Darrell that."

"But isn't this an extraordinary way to get service?"

"It is unusual, yes."

"Couldn't they have waited?"

"Apparently not."

"Suppose you had insisted on keeping to the book?"

"In that case I gather that there would have been a considerable extension of the abnormal conditions which, as you know, exist in the vicinity of the Institute."

"In other words the experiment is out of control?"

"I could not be a judge of that."

"How do you account for the disappearance of a mile of cable? About a mile of it, wasn't there?"

"About a mile, yes. As to why it vanished, there are evidently technical reasons of a highly specialized nature. It would be wrong for me to speculate. We are installing a replacement."

"Is there any point in doing that?"

"The second cable will be anchored every hundred feet. We are tying it down and securing the lashings to the buildings along the way."

"You think that will hold it?"

"I certainly hope so."

"Hasn't the Institute been pretty careless to allow a situation like this?"

"I could not comment on that at this stage."

After they had been several times around the circle the reporter said, actually with a certain respect in his voice:

"Would you be good enough to sum up just once more, so that our listeners can understand what is going on?"

There was the slightest pause before the other voice said:

"Well, O.K. Early this morning I had a call from Mr. Paul Darrell, Scientific Director of The Dickstachel Research Institute, asking for a surface installation of additional power supply urgently needed in their work. I was convinced that we should furnish that supply. Our first attempt was unsuccessful, but we hope the second try will meet with more luck. We shall of course revert to normal working as soon as possible."

Warned, perhaps, by the pause before that "Well, O.K.," the reporter did not press his luck further. Instead we were taken to the Office of the Mayor, who was threatening to set up commissions to investigate Con Edison, The Dickstachel Research Institute, the cable manufacturers and one or two other organizations which he would think of in due course. Asked what action he proposed to take to relieve the immediate emergency, he indulged in some rather coarse invective which led me to turn the set off. I sat thinking for a while.

It was pretty obvious to me at least that the President of Con Ed knew a great deal more than he had allowed to be dragged out of him. I thought he had done a magnificent job of stonewalling. The Mayor, on the other hand, obviously did not have the slightest understanding of the elemental forces which Darrell had impertinently stirred up, or of the vastness of the imminent cataclysm.

If my rather muddled memory of as much as I had understood of Darrell's original explanation, plus what I could recall of my own simplified reading—if these were correct, then if Darrell was unable to retrieve his error The Dickstachel Research Institute was in danger of turning into a Black Hole. That is to say that it would shrink in upon itself until it became the size of—I don't know—a baseball? —but a baseball so incredibly dense that it would weigh many hundreds, or thousands, of tons. Its gravitational pull would be so vast that no light could escape, and it would become to all intents invisible, except as a blackness, a kind of sable nothing, an interruption in space. But an interruption that I suppose you could stub your toe on if you were foolish enough to go near it.

I say foolish enough, because the enormous gravitational pull would irresistibly suck you in, you would be mashed down to the same density as the Black Hole, and you would become part of it. I had seen an illustration of that force, not yet, I imagined, nearly developed to the full, when it had reached out to other buildings with that strange flickering effect. Darrell's experiment was in what I supposed he would call an unstable condition, and when I left the scene it was evident that the instability was growing and reaching out farther. If something finally gave, if a Black Hole came into being, I could imagine it reaching out with all its force and seizing, first, the nearest buildings and so on out in an ever-widening circle until it had taken in all of New York City, drawing in and compressing buildings, people, everything in its mighty grasp. Even that would not satisfy it. The process would continue, over this continent and over the oceans until it reached the other continents and drew them crushingly in. It would be, in fact, the end of the world—a novel way to go for a human race which had just reached an uneasy coexistence with the possibility of atomic annihilation, but no more attractive for all that. I speculated for a moment on how far the devastation might ultimately reach. The moon, perhaps? One or two of the nearer planets? Not very interesting, really, since I should not be there to see.

The phone rang.

"Haversham here. Why are you there? I told you to get to Darrell and instruct him to stop this—this. . . . It's a damned poor best, then. Stop arguing with me, man."

I remembered the end of that cable flicking into the building like a strand of spaghetti being sucked into a greedy mouth. But what spaghetti, and what a mouth. The cable was getting on for two inches in diameter, and from what I learned during the next few days the mile-long strand weighed around fifteen tons. So really—really—

"I'm perfectly willing to try again, Mr. Haversham, but I think it will require more than single-handed authority. If you would care to join me?"

"I—I—I told you, I'm all tied up here. Can't possibly get away. Well—well—keep me informed."

I thought he would refuse that gambit, and I was glad when he did. What I needed just then was not Mr. Haversham but some more brandy.

62

A LITTLE later I did return to the scene of action. It took rather less courage than I expected. My immediate impulse was to get as far away as I could, to the other side of the world, so that I could gain a few more days before the end; but then I thought of the uneasiness of the waiting period and decided to stay where I was.

The barriers had been set even farther back, and I had considerable difficulty in arguing my way through; but I managed it for the second time just as the Con Ed truck arrived again. It had been considerably delayed by the need to lash down the new cable which stretched behind it, the fastenings reaching across the roadway to the buildings on each side like some insane kind of bunting ready to be hoisted in some lunatic celebration.

The Con Ed men were visibly tired and considerably more tense than before. They had to wait a good deal longer for a favorable moment to make their final rush, but they aimed well, although it seemed to me that the doorway was narrower and indeed that the whole building was smaller. It may have been my imagination, but it seemed to me that the nearest buildings groaned when the strain of the taut cable came on them. But the lashings held.

We waited in the safe zone for half an hour, watching the all-too-familiar fadings and blurrings and brightenings and sharpenings. Suddenly these ceased, and everything stood out clear and firm, although the rooftops were noticeably lower. The Tillevant Building seemed to have lost as much as forty feet in height.

The work crew made a kind of self-congratulatory noise—I think they were too exhausted to cheer—and scrambled back on the truck, slumping wherever they could find space.

Just as the truck was about to move off, the flickering started again.

63

DEAR DR. Ampiofratello, you lived through the ninety-six hours that followed, along with the rest of us. I need not remind you of the course of events.

Somehow or other an additional cable was run and linked to a different substation. Again the trouble was cleared up, but for a few minutes only; and a third cable, with the same result; and each time the danger zone grew larger, and Darrell's calls for more power increasingly demonic. Yet somehow these calls were met, for the whole story was abroad by now, and there was growing panic as people fled the city, going south and west. There was no electricity for ordinary uses in New York, for heavier and heavier lines were being run from the power stations themselves, diverting the entire output. Cable was flown in on cargo planes, direct from the factories and on loan from other utilities and other states; and relief crews too —hundreds of men, thousands for all I know. The streets were choked with mile upon mile of electric intestines piled on top of each other. I could no longer get anywhere near the building, but it must have been a nightmare sight with all those tentacles poking through doors and windows; and still the cry was "more."

There were of course no newspapers, radio or TV transmissions.

However absurd it may seem when one puts matters into relative proportion, I was thankful for this. It meant that the *Discovery* fiasco would not reach the outside world, and indeed would probably have been all but forgotten by the time, if that time ever came, that things got back to normal. There was practically no looting, not because basic honesty had returned but because panic had caused the city to evacuate itself. Nobody got too far by automobile, because after the first tankful or half tankful of gas it was impossible to refill since there was no power for the pumps. All kinds of problems arose, not only in finding food and shelter but in paying for it. Checks and even credit cards were unpopular with vendors. As town after town went dark and factory after factory and office after office stopped work, there were more and more people milling around, unable even to draw unemployment pay; and the children could not go to school, although in areas which had frequent teachers' strikes this made little noticeable difference. The whole miserable setup was like living inside a disaster movie.

Certain powerful battery radios, tuned to Canadian stations, picked up a story that the Russian city of Novosibirsk had disappeared. More accurately, the Russians were putting out a denial that it had disappeared because it had never existed, and of course a city that has never existed cannot disappear.

The blackout spread up into Connecticut and New England as Darrell, sleepless and full of unmuffled oaths, repeated his calls for more power. I heard him once, on a CB radio. It was amazing how little weariness or hysteria his voice revealed. He must have been very hungry and thirsty too, for the stocks in the cafeteria were not large and there were people working with him, and of course the hapless Cosamo, unless by then they had killed themselves laughing.

Almost the whole of the Northeastern grid had been thrown into the battle, and as the hours went by the West Coast was conscripted. I did hear the total figure that could have been drawn on, but it was meaningless to me. Around two hundred and fifty million watts, was it? I have a vague idea how much a domestic light bulb takes, but how can an ordinary human mind begin to imagine that larger figure? I only know that Darrell must have got precious near it; and of course the men, from New England and the West, the work they did, constantly at risk, in running in and linking up ever more and more cable, is beyond description. Another thing I simply could not understand was how all that power could be fed into just one building without bursting it; but it was.

At the last there can have been very little margin of extra power left to feed into the overloaded cables, which were running hot and hotter; and if Darrell drew on the last reserves and failed, or if the cables started to go. . . .

Indeed, two minutes after the last switch had been thrown, two of the heaviest cables went up in smoke. But they had held for that last surge of power, and this time Darrell's unstable mini-universe stabilized, and remained stable for five minutes, ten, thirty, an hour, two hours . . . At that point the man himself came on the radio. His announcement of victory was, I think, typical.

"O.K. You can turn it off now."

As soon as it was physically possible I made my way to whatever might remain of The Dickstachel Research Institute. I had to detour the streets where the piled cables were being severed and rolled back on their drums, but I observed that from Fifty-seventh Street to my destination, and I suppose for an equal radius in other directions, the New York skyline was noticeably lower. The effect was increasingly pronounced as I neared the storm center, until I stood in front of my personal memorial, The Tillevant Building, now no taller than a Depression-era taxpayer.

Tears came to my eyes. I was wiping them away, confident of being unobserved, when I heard a voice, too familiar yet subtly changed.

"Cheer up, Tilly my boy. Aren't you going to congratulate me?"

Considering everything, he looked remarkably chipper, although he also looked as if he might collapse at any moment. He held out a hand, and sad and wrathful though I was I reached down to shake it. This involuntary obeisance was necessary because Darrell was now only two feet high.

64

ONE CANNOT, I suppose, indict a scientist for making a mistake, although of course if the mistake is bad enough he will probably not have much future as a scientist. The shower of obloquy which poured on Darrell's head was, I should have thought, copious enough to drown his reputation for good and all; but his aplomb was so puncture-proof that he merely reacted with exasperated outbursts against the many official bodies and the enormous number of private individuals who at that time wanted, putting it bluntly, his balls on toast.

Darrell claimed that he had come within a micron of success—whatever a micron may be. He was perfectly clear as to where the trouble had arisen—he had simply brought his particles of matter and antimatter a shade too close to each other. He was confident that next time he would get it right and fulfill all the roseate promises he had made before starting. When it was made plain to him that there was not going to be a next time he became imaginatively abusive to an extent which even I was compelled to admit was magnificent, especially when one remembered that all this rodomontade was issuing from a manikin only twenty-four inches in stature.

His trump card—and while it did not turn out an ace, for a while it certainly looked like a king—was one simple question:

"What has happened to Novosibirsk?"

He said that he was a modest man (!) and he could not believe that his was the only brain to which had occurred the possibility of harnessing antimatter. The disappearance of the city of Novosibirsk provided a strong inference that the Russians were working along the same lines. Here he was supported by the tales brought back by package-tour visitors, the hints which despite heavy censorship remained in UPI cables and the leaks, intentional or not, from diplomatic dispatches. These told of massive blackouts, hasty cancellation of certain Intourist schedules, and train journeys during which all blinds were drawn down under the supervision of armed MVD guards. He claimed that the Russians had boobed badly, though not to the extent of final catastrophe, as evidenced by the fact that we were all still here. By comparison, the incidental inconveniences which a small percentage of Americans had suffered were trivial.

The Russians, Darrell asserted, would undoubtedly try again, and this time there was a fifty-fifty chance that they would get it right, thereby acquiring an enormous lead over everyone else. (He passed with appalling lightness over the fact that there was also a fifty-fifty chance that the Russians would get it wrong again, perhaps in their sinful pride irreversibly so.) Were we through sheer pusillanimity going to let the game, in which the stakes were so high, go by default? And he emitted a balance of equations to prove himself right. It was natural that I could not understand these, but I was disconcerted when it became apparent that despite their cautious statements the massed savants of two continents, hastily assembled in the Hawaiian island of Kahoolawe and occasioning by their presence a famine of suckling pigs and milk of magnesia, could not understand them either.

The fact that Darrell had at last cut himself down to size—in more ways than one—was of only peripheral consolation to me. I was fully occupied with the writs which came fluttering down in such numbers that if they had been put in one pile they would, I verily believe, have reached higher than the buildings of The Dickstachel Research Institute in their newly compressed state. The electricity bill alone, if I may thus flippantly denominate the charge for the colossal amounts of energy which Darrell's featherbrained escapade had consumed—the electricity bill alone would have purchased a fighter plane or two.

Landlords, operators of small businesses, operators of very large businesses indeed, municipalities, nonprofit organizations ranging from the Metropolitan Opera to the Orange County Oldsters Outings Club, which had been deprived of a projected visit to *Oh! Calcutta!*, several of its members dying before the rain date—the combined damages, not to mention the legal costs, would have swallowed up the total endowment of The Dickstachel Research Institute plus any conceivable total of grants, bequests and so on for a century to come.

And a century it might well take to settle that writhing mass of litigation, which included a class action by three Con Ed crewmen who had been sucked into The Tillevant Building and emerged in excellent health but reduced, give or take a few centimeters, to the same minute proportions as Darrell.

From the legal angle alone—not to mention the moral and ethical and psychological and transcendental and community-orientated and concerned-citizens-on-a-one-to-one basis—the fair reputation of The Dickstachel Research Institute was hopelessly besmirched. Its projects were summarily canceled and, almost the unkindest cut of all, the poor squat relic of what was once a proud and lofty pile was being picketed night and day by militant members of something calling itself, in the confused way that one so often comes across, the Anti-Energy Society.

But deep in my heart I could not believe that Darrell was finally and totally and irrevocably finished. For one thing, there was no slackening in the loyalty which he inspired in the people who had been working with him. All of them had been reduced to the same miniature proportions as Darrell himself, but they continued to proclaim loudly though squeakily their faith in him. I could not convince myself that it was beyond the bounds of possibility that, although all power to The Dickstachel Research Institute had been cut off, he and his myrmidons might not feloniously regain admission to The Tillevant Building and bring the experiment to a triumphant conclusion with the aid of nothing more than a hand-cranked generator from an 1880-model wall telephone.

For myself it was different. Shock upon shock had been hurled against me for lo, these many months, remorselessly stripping my nerve sheaths layer by layer like onions until I had no more resilience than a wet feather. Thus it was when, one morning, I found myself closeted with Mr. Haversham in the one small and ill-furnished room which, by the meager charity of our lawyers, rubbing their hands in anticipation of the generations of fees to come, formed but a poor substitute for the lavish splendors of my old office. Heavy was Mr. Haversham's brow, protuberant was his lower lip, as he thus addressed me:

"Y'know, Tillevant, I can't help feeling that you are partly responsible for this mess."

"*I*, Mr. Haversham?"

He shifted uncomfortably on the ill-stuffed cushion of his chair —I myself was sitting on bare wood, having yielded him the marginally softer seat because I knew he had piles—and, rocking from side to side, repeated:

"You, Tillevant. You can make mistakes like anyone else. You *have* made mistakes in the past, but in view of the generally high level of your work we have overlooked them."

It all flooded back on me from over the years. The Research Library which at its start had been lavishly equipped with audiovisual apparatus, microfilm indexes, tables, chairs, shelves—everything but books. The time when, owing to a malfunctioning computer programmer, two separate and distinct teams had, unknown to each other—or, for a while, to Darrell—been set up to work on the identical but differently named project, and had issued diametrically opposed reports. My recent doubts and fears about antimatter. My uncertainty about Boanerges. My gamble that once again Darrell's wayward, solitary genius would succeed. But Darrell had let me down. And now Mr. Haversham was seeking to make me the scapegoat, to cast me to the wolves, to—to—

"It's not fair," I sobbed. "I did my best. You always blamed me for not getting along with Darrell, and now just because I tried to please everybody you're blaming me just the same. It's not fair, it's not fair, it's not *fair*—"

I was standing up, stamping my feet like a naughty child, banging my fists on the stained, dented wood of the old-fashioned desk.

And that, dear Dr. Ampiofratello, is how I came to myself later that afternoon in this bed in the Vellutomano Center for the Nervously Exhausted.

65

THE HAPPIEST days of my life, dear Dr. Ampiofratello, were the first few I spent here. I do not mean that I am less happy now, but oh, the ineffable bliss of just letting go of the helm, of ceasing to fight, of not having to pretend to abilities that I knew I did not possess; of having really no obligation to society beyond the avoidance of messing my bed. A simple reversion to infantilism if you like, but if only my own infancy had been so idyllic, with yourself for a loving, all-knowing father and a succession of mothers in eight-hour shifts so that not one of them was around long enough to acquire any rights. . . .

Yes, I know I am fantasizing, and you have told me not to do that, and besides this particular fantasy involves all kinds of chronoclasms and cornplasters. I'm sorry, it was naughty of me and I will try not to do it again.

Of course when I had recovered a little from being so dreadfully tired the whole time and I began to take a renewed interest in what was happening in the outside world, it was not quite so happifying. I admit that it was with a great deal of malice that I learned about the antics of the miniaturized Darrell and his troop of performing midgets. For example, at the Congressional investigation Darrell, perched on a chair so he could reach the microphone, insisted that he had solved his problem. He nearly got himself committed for contempt when one of the Senators, the one they call Sideways Shirley because his left profile looks so good on TV, asked him how he made out that he could produce cheap energy when it took all there was around to avoid ruin, and anyway did he seriously think that the American people would submit to the risk of being cut down to two feet in height.

That was just before both houses of Congress sat up all night to rush through a bill forbidding Darrell or anyone else to meddle with antimatter. At dawn, the bill and four gross of Bic pens were rushed in an armored limousine to the discotheque where the President was relaxing, and a fine storm the First Lady raised when she found that the free pantyhose which went with a wholesale order for Bic pens had mysteriously disappeared.

But that remark about people not wanting to be two feet high put an end to Sideways Shirley's career. He had insulted the entire Cosamo nation, which had not only started off three feet high—near enough to the Senator's pejorative statistic—but were still three feet high when all the excitement was over. This led to some very arrogant claims by Harry about the superior physiological makeup of the Cosamo stock.

At the same time there came ominous protests from the Andaman Islands, Sri Lanka, Sumatra, Zaire, Cameroon, the Philippines and Australia. (I apologize if I have left anyone out.) The pygmy tribes living in each of these areas issued a joint proclamation declaring that they had been individually and collectively insulted, and they demanded not only an apology but, now that the means were readily available, that immediate corrective measures should be taken to end the intolerable stigma of inferiority.

From that moment on the word "pygmy" became tabu, and was replaced, after considerable debate by a hurriedly summoned conference of the World Council of Euphemists, by the term "Supermin." This appealed immensely to all the tribes, who unanimously elected Darrell Super Supermin, a distinction which did nothing to make him more bearable.

Only part of the Supermins' nonnegotiable demands had been met, however. A special delegation arrived at UN headquarters to press for an early start to the work of equalizing the height of everyone else. The leader of the delegation stated in his opening address that this was the age of minority rights, and that as he represented the world's smallest minority in both senses he had no doubt that his very reasonable request would be given top place on the agenda before Southeast Asia, the Middle East, and the application of the United Kingdom of Great Britain and Northern Ireland to file under Chapter XI of the Bankruptcy Act.

Then came the rebuttal. All those extremely warlike African tribes which regard six feet as the irreducible minimum for their adult males raised the shout heard around the world. They took hostage all the local wire services representatives and forced them to send cables demanding immediate abandonment of the two-foot standard, failing which each and every correspondent would be fatally pierced and their relevant components stewed and eaten in order to raise the local standard of literacy. One correspondent actually underwent this treatment, but proved so indigestible that the project was abandoned, without, however, relieving the new stress line in international relations.

At the moment it looks as though the six-footers are going to lose. The current global recession has brought to the world of business the revelation that if everyone is reduced to a standard height of two feet, or its metric equivalent, a vast new demand will be created for scaled-down products from buildings and airplanes to condoms and jockstraps, thereby abolishing unemployment and restoring profitability. As is usual with these Utopian exordiums, no one seems to have thought about what will happen when the new supply has caught up with the new demand. I suppose they will want to stretch everyone out again.

If the Little Party wins, the first thing that will have to be done is to cancel that panic legislation. The people concerned have certainly had plenty of practice in that sort of thing. Then they will have to try to make some sense out of the situation they have landed themselves in with Darrell. They will have to persuade or coerce him into perfecting his process but also to, as he would no doubt put it, bastardize it so that it is still capable of shrinking people. Unless they make up their minds pretty quickly he will have lost interest altogether and be deep in some new and entirely different freelance project. I wish them joy of it—and of him.

For myself, I really do not care which way it comes out.

Truth to tell, I have *always* felt two feet high.